T0375752

*M*ortal *A*scension:

*A*n *E*soteric Story

This year, everyone believes...

By Simon E. Jackson F.R.C

iUniverse, Inc.
New York Bloomington

Mortal Ascension: An Esoteric Story

iUniverse books may be ordered through booksellers or by contacting:

iUniverse
1663 Liberty Drive
Bloomington, IN 47403
www.iuniverse.com
1-800-Authors (1-800-288-4677)

ISBN: 978-1-4401-3121-9 (pbk)
ISBN: 978-1-4401-3120-2 (ebk)

Printed in the United States of America

iUniverse rev. date: 5/28/2009

How art thou fallen from heaven, O Lucifer, son of the morning! How art thou cut down to the ground, which didst weaken the nations!
(Isaiah 14:12)

For thou hast said in thine heart, I will ascend into heaven, I will exalt my throne above the stars of God: I will sit also upon the mount of the congregation, in the sides of the north
(Isaiah 14:13)

For we wrestle not against flesh and blood, but against principalities, against powers, against rulers of the darkness of this world, against spiritual wickedness in high places
(Ephesians 6:12)

Cover illustration By

Asukaya Bailey

Asukaya Bailey would like to thank:

Special thanks to the Creator for making the ideas possible, and the skills a reality. Baumgarten Enterprises (http://www.bauent.com) for their free 3D models. Haver &Sharon Dickenson-Bailey for allowing me to pursue my dreams without fail. Yahtiebo, Ayana, Ezekiel, and Kadmael Bailey; for putting up with my long hours and late night rants. Anaya Rivera (my niece) for being there to keep me level in times of need. George Cifuentes, Atiba Coerbell, Marvin Nolasco, Jason Calderone, Azibu, Poppa, Cott, Ma and Pa Jackson (Pa, we made it happen) and all Family, Friends, and Associates for their support, firm belief, and creative guidance through this process.

Dedication

In Loving Memory: Simon Edward Jackson, I know that the heavens of the macrocosm will enjoy your return to the great essence from which you came, just as we enjoyed your presence here on the mundane plane of existence. This book is written in your honor, for if you had left me astray, I would've never realized or utilized my talent to write. And when the stars in our universe scintillate, I'll know that you're dwelling in the grand heavens playing your Guitar. We'll all miss you.

Simon Edward Jackson *(1939-2006)*

Table of Contents

An Introduction to Mortal Ascension: An Esoteric Story… xi

Chapter 1: The Mystery of Genesis: The Beginning 1

Chapter 2: A Page from Namsilat's journal 44

Chapter 3: Calabrael, the cosmic gifts and the four children 66

Chapter 4: The Betrayal and the War 89

Chapter 5: The Preparations for the Final Battle 111

Chapter 6: Mephistopheles' Revenge and the Search for the Sword of Elohim 146

Chapter 7: The Son of Ether 166

Chapter 8: Creating a Universe of Evil 180

Chapter 9: Demise of the Evil Universe 200

Chapter 10: Rise of the Thamiel 219

Chapter 11: The Journey of Divine Bestowal 236

Chapter 12: The Final Assault on Sheol 271

Chapter 13: Return of the Magus 333

An Introduction to *M*ortal *A*scension: *A*n *E*soteric Story

Throughout time the imagination of authors, scriptwriters, producers and directors has evolved. In certain movies such as **"The Matrix," "Constantine"** and **"The Chronicles of Narnia,"** books and movies have brought the imagination of children and adults to a place where the mundane plane has darkened. Movies and books truly are blessings in that they allow us to imagine what we believe may be impossible while bringing light to a darkened imagination that stress has overruled. Consequently, the aforesaid films are sending serious messages to people who think that the movie is simply about good fights and action. However, a bigger message is given, yet, to comprehend that message will take time and contemplation.

I have written this book in hopes that the imagination of humanity would be broadened, and much lengthier. The thought of an individual being chained to the sun and an evil supernal force entering our plane of existence may seem a modicum farfetched. However, let us keep in mind that **"anything is possible,"** and that it does not have to be possible in reality. We, as human beings have the ability to affect our lives and the lives of others by our actions, movements and ideas. There have been countless men who have taken ideas and brought them to physical form so that all of mankind can benefit from such ideas. Therefore, we should all help ourselves and others by doing something positive enough to not only affect ourselves and others, but the world that revolves around us as well. ***Mortal ascension: An Esoteric story*** was built on the idea that if this book were to ever reach the movie screen, it would seriously broaden the imagination. He who takes this book and brings it to a movie screen will have a chance to test their talents well. The idea of God versus the devil is not easily portrayed on screen when reading this book thoroughly. It will be very challenging to put the events of this book on *"the silver screen."* I have yet to see an elaborate movie portray the great struggle between ***"God"*** and ***"The Devil."***

To those of you who will find this book interesting and hard to believe, you are the ones who will enjoy it. The title is grabbing and interesting, therefore, I am sure that many will look at it in their nearest book store and open it. When that happens, your mind will be brought to a place wherein your imagination can wonder at a new perspective, and hopefully one day you will do the same for others. It is interesting to note that most books or movies that dabble in the ongoing struggle between angelic good and demonic evil usually base their work on the concept of ***"attaining souls."*** By saying this, have you ever noticed that in a book or a movie having any religious relation, that the "Devil" always seems to want to attain the soul of a certain individual? For many reasons, people believe that there is a war going on, but it seems that this war is based on the attainment of souls. Strange enough though, it would make plenty of sense in thinking that there is actually no way that a "Devil" could attain and keep souls in some invisible receptacle that is only accessible to him. If souls were attainable and could be captured, then that would mean that evil would collect souls forever, without any pause in doing so at all. It would be quite obvious that there are many people on earth, which means that "souls" are perhaps manufactured by God on a daily basis, not to mention that a man may die, and yet a child is born. Where did the idea of God and the Devil fighting for souls come from? By all means, who would say that evil could produce anything having any pulchritude, or any positive quality for that matter? The idea of a fight for souls just does not cut it, and besides, this idea has been used innumerous times, therefore, it would not go far if it was used once again. When human beings speak of God, they assign benevolent attributes to him. Sometimes we read that old text called the "Bible" and do not realize that there are many mysteries in its pages, thus, we read it and endeavor comprehension that best suits our hearts whilst not truly comprehending what it means or what is being said. However, what suits a benevolent heart is excellent, and is a good agent for long life. Though there is much that cannot be said, what can be said is that the universal cause could not possibly possess human tendencies, especially if it is marked with consummation whilst the tendencies, habits, and most actions committed by human being has been much more than imperfect and moderately immoral in behavior and action. There are times where an atheist will hear many great things concerning this being that man refers to as ***"God,"*** yet the atheist will readily halt the conversation concerning the idea or concept of it because the explanation may make no sense to them, whereas someone else may simply believe without question. The truth is, when omniscience, omnipresence, and omnipotence is explained to any individual, it is more than likely that it will not be explained with an idea that would cause one to comprehend or believe what they're being told. Some people don't believe, simply because they have heard so much stuff that makes no sense, they simply will not indulge in the belief of anything other than what can be seen or felt, and of course, there is nothing wrong with that at all. If we first consider God as being Omnipresent, then we can apparently realize a logical reason why he is also omniscient and omnipotent. If you think about it, omnipresence means that it is everywhere, and by this, it is apparent that there is a strong possibility that this primary force exists at the very depths of the elemental composition of the human structure, such as atoms and so forth. If this makes sense, then it can undoubtedly be all-knowing, and finally; all-powerful. Perhaps it randomly performs the miracles and so forth that we all witness from time-to-time. Although I am not promoting atheism or religion, I do promote new ideas; ideas that would hopefully allow some sort of harmony among the human idea of a divine and archetypal force.

No matter how you put it-life is just, we all just have to figure out why, instead of marking life as unjust when tragedy knocks on our front door. We are human; we are strong and mighty, for not even the great dollar possesses as much strength as its creator. Why kill a man for a dollar when the reason it is worth anything is because you made it worth something? By all means, if at any time mankind collectively decided to make a nickel worth five million dollars, the dollar that people murdered and killed for would undoubtedly lose all of its worth by the simple words uttered from the mouth of man, and of course, the nickel would be worth much more. The only thing that truly makes anyone different is not based or originated in our physiological or physical circumstances. There is only one true thing that separates the good from the evil, and that is simply the application of our liberty and volition. The choice to kill is yours, the choice to die is yours, the choice of indulging in peace is yours, and most importantly, any ***"choice"*** is yours. As you may or may not know, Master Jesus sacrificed himself for all of humanity.

For the sake of imagination and the words following shortly thereafter, the transgressions of men were wicked in the days of past, and now, let us say that the transgressions of men are much wicked than they were before, thus, four sacrifices are sufficient in that the transgressions of men have doubled and tripled since then. The four main characters in this book will be the sacrifice for all of existence. For if they would have decided not to fight; then all would have been lost. Their purpose is more important than their fight against the greatest imperfect evil.

Five warriors

Four Sacrifices

One Destiny

At one point in time, human beings were close to the primary being, which possesses the perfect nature to do all things with and without all creatures. As the sands of time began to pour into the lives of mankind, there was a word that was so powerful; whoever possessed it would have the ability to shake the universe. A word sought for by many and only discovered by very few. Those who were elected to pass the word down to their brethren were given the greatest of responsibilities simply because they held the key to the blueprints of supernal manifestation.

Mankind's heart was filled with deceit, and they hindered the keys to unlock the power of the God of their hearts. They began opposing their nature with vile affections, twisted murder, unreasonable thievery, cowardice actions, adultery, and blasphemies. They became destroyers of nature instead of becoming keepers of nature; consequently, those men followed the steps of the misguided son of the morning. For, the son of the morning has tricked the weak, and blinded strong.

Beware of what you ***"think."***

Beware of what you ***"learn."***

Beware of what you ***"seek,"*** for not all of us are well attuned to the supernal channels within.

"By all means, the pen and paper is much more powerful than the gun and its bullet. For a gun and its bullet may take lives, however, a pen and a piece of paper can aid the mind in writing laws to govern the safe use of such weaponry so that things precious can be spared the taints of a nonsensical path of destruction."

Simon E. Jackson, F.R.C.

A few words from the author

Mortal Ascension: An Esoteric Story is not just a fiction book, by all means; it is the first to defy all imagination of supernal forces in human mind. Not even I myself can understand what distant part of my mind this book came from. I would truly call this the first story or book that gives a more universal idea of the supernal clash between good and evil. I believe a more powerful depiction of archangels and demons is definitely missing from the minds of some human beings. If we believe that angels are simply tall men with wings that watch over us, then we limit the cosmic powers that they truly possess. ***Mortal Ascension: An Esoteric Story*** is a book that will give a larger idea of the depiction of angels, archangels, devils and God in a fictional manner. For there have been various movies, books and so forth that depict these beings with too many limitations. If such beings are above us in certain ways, then I am sure that a clash between good and evil is much bigger than we could possibly think. If angels and demons can appear and disappear or come to us in a dream, then what other amazing abilities would they possess?

Would they possess lightning speed, teleportation, and telekinesis? If we as humans give cosmic beings limitations, then a question arrives in mind. And that question is: *Do we limit ourselves as well?* Yes. Some of us do, we limit the way we live, the way we eat, the way we think, and the way we view life. However, there is much, much more mystery to be discovered in the physical counterpart of our whole being. Let my book be the first to show an evolved situation containing the ascension of human beings. This book not only represents mortals ascending to another state of consciousness, it also represents the abilities of the voice that we all have inside of us, the voice that we've yet to comprehend.

When the cosmic son named Fireael is imprisoned and chained to the sun, it represents the physical body being ever connected to the vivifying soul. When the cosmic son named Aquari-on is chained to the bottom of the deepest and largest sea, it represents a man being imbued and surrounded with constant wisdom. When the cosmic son named Airael is chained to two stars in the heavens, it represents mankind's connection to the stars above and the cosmos as a whole. And when the cosmic son named Earthael is chained to the highest mountain on the planet earth, it represents the height of cosmic consciousness in a man who has properly attained attunement with the cosmos and becomes tall in mind. He is then able to have a better view of his brethren and fellows by looking down upon them only so that he can pick them up and guide them to a place wherein they can comprehend impersonal cosmic law.

This book contains several words that the religiously oriented would indubitably recognize. Consequently, I have already received several different responses concerning the religious content of this book. And many have had a very strong opinion about its message when mentally recollecting their loyalty to the great Holy text. However, please do keep in mind that this is A FICTION BOOK. Many have repeated in their hearts the most unfortunate of words that accuse me of malevolence, saying that I endeavor highly intelligent trickeries capable of beguiling the religiously nescient with such a book. To think such a thing is unfortunate, indeed. However, I can say that this book is in no ways an outlet for the evocation of negativity which some believe gives them the power to judge one's actions in the place of the Divine creator. For those who may develop a strong religious opinion concerning this book, I have no intentions of converting, urging, or breaking the foundation of your current belief by utilizing some highly elaborate scheme equipped with clever components capable of convincing readers that the contents of this book is reality in all of its splendor.

*M*ortal *A*scension:

*A*n *E*soteric Story

Chapter 1

The Mystery of Genesis: The Beginning

In the beginning, a subatomic particle of cosmic perfection raced over the face of the darkness. As it continued its journey over the formless void, it halted to manifest the smallest fraction of its beauty. It then began to extend itself in a curve, so as to manifest and conform to its laws. Whilst consummating the curve by returning to its focal point, it began to utilize self-extension, attraction and repulsion. By these three laws it extended from its focal point and continued to a point that was one-third distant from its focal point. It continued its actions, and undoubtedly formed three straight lines that formed the basic structure for a substance and form called matter. Utilizing its triangular form, it began to gradually produce the smallest units of matter so as to animate the formless void. It came to pass that the time had come to bring forth representations of its existence, representations that would light the way to the plane of matter. And so, a voice echoed out of the subatomic particle of cosmic perfection, and it said, ***"Let there be light!"*** The vibratory force caused a ***"Big Bang"*** and certain units of matter began to combine into masses of matter that were lit with a vivifying and subtle entity that is now called ***"fire."*** The unknown force looked upon the many masses of fiery matter, and thus, stars were manifested. The fiery nature of the stars would act as sufficient sources of regeneration fit for more complex creatures that would be manifested in due time. Creatures of complex features and so forth. And by the flames of the stars, there was light to illuminate that to be inhabited by creature. And the great being saw the light, that it was good: and the light was divided from the darkness. As the light was divided from the darkness, larger masses of matter began to form, a cosmic cataclysm occurred, and in due time, the planets took their places amongst the stars. The light it called day, and the darkness it called night. The divine architect looked down upon a particular planet, and said, ***"Let there be a firmament in the midst of an entirety of elements manifesting a liquid."*** And it made the firmament by projecting the power of its divine mind and the production of certain elements. It divided the water from the clouds and called the firmament heaven.

The subatomic particle of cosmic perfection hovered amidst the planet, and brought the seas and oceans together and used a combination of several elements and brought forth dry land and plant-life to sprout from its own lands. And so, the great force of light saw that all its manifestations were good, and continued to manifest creatures to inherit the seas, and creatures to inherit the land. The planet was beautiful and was also given life, for life cannot be limited to one planet or simply several creatures. It then looked upon the beauty of its manifestations and saw that it was good, and the triangle was the basis of all matter. The earth was prepared to harbor creatures of evolutionary potential, and soon these creatures would live, move and possess great power to mold their own destinies with their liberty and volition. And so, the divine force looked upon the stars, and said, ***"There shall be a place for the dwelling of the divine."*** The subatomic particle of cosmic perfection raced into the height of the void and placed its name in the east, west, north, south, height and depth. It then took the form of a triangle of electricity and summoned three stars to each of its points, and molded a plane for the divine. It molded the three stars into flat grounds of flames, and gave it walls and ceilings made of symmetrically sustained water. And it made six levels in this manner, but the seventh plane would consist of water as ground and symmetrically sustained fire for ceilings and walls. Also, the seventh level bearingd thirty-six windows made of light, and thirty-six mirrors. At the center of this level was a ring of light environing a triangle of fire with an hour-glass at the center of the triangle that constantly spun on its own axis whilst making the white crystal sand within it move/shift upward and downward.

And it was this level that would be its place of paradise and where the great throne would sit. And so, the realm of paradise was molded from three stars, and the great architect looked upon it, and said, ***"There is much we would have to do concerning the vastness thereof, let us manifest agents of four principles and light to keep the paradise in good standing."*** And the subatomic particle of cosmic perfection exerted a particle of brilliant light and sent it unto the universe with free will and consciousness so that it would elect its own form and comprehend its own being. And so, the particle of light floated through the new universe and circled a star twelve times. It then flew into the star, and the star began to shrink in size and take a different form. A creature of divine proportion was being born, and it would soon live and serve as a keeper of paradise. Arms, hands, legs, feet, wings and a head emerged from the star, and when the creature was finished taking its new form, it was a creature of excellent beauty and considerable intelligence. The first angel took form, and lived. His skin was pale, his hair was long and black, his eyes were made of flames of light, and six black wings sprung from its upper back whilst its loins were a flaming ball of fire. His body was chiseled with muscle, the middle of his chest was bearing a flaming triangle pointing down, overlapped by another flaming triangle pointing up. Red electricity graced every part of his body whilst his aura emanated with brilliant light, and its feet were covered in thick clouds of light. The creature was conscious and realized its own existence, and when it did, it looked at its hands and feet and was transiently unable to express a thought of how it came to be. And before it could think anything, a ball of flaming light appeared in front of it, and said, ***"You live, move and think,***

your intelligence is considerable and shining with brilliance. I shall call thee, Lucifer; son of the morning, for thy beauty and intelligence is equal to that of a star.*"** Lucifer looked upon the ball of flaming light, and said, ***"I think, therefore I am." The ball of flaming light shot off into the heights of the cosmos and teleported to paradise, and Lucifer followed without question.

When the two beings reached paradise, Lucifer stood in the seventh paradise heaven of Araboth, and said, ***"Am I the only of my kind?"*** And then he teleported to the cosmos where he was born, and began flying around to search for others like his self. Eventually, he came near a star and merely touched it, and behold! The star went a thousand miles away from him by merely touching it. For he was powerful beyond his comprehension at the time, for the power of the grand architect is the vigorous force that is brilliant and powerful energy. And so, Lucifer moved stars, landed on planets and went beyond, and still he found none like him in the entire universe. And when he found none likened unto him, within an instant he teleported and returned to Araboth, and said, ***"I have seen much beauty, yet I see no other likened unto me, why am I the only one of my kind?"*** The ball of flaming light looked at Lucifer, and said, ***"You are mistaken, son of the morning, for there are many like you."*** Lucifer turned his head, and behind him stood a multitude of angels that had different features and so forth. Lucifer looked at the divine architect and kneeled whilst placing his brow to the watered grounds of Araboth, and as he did this, the multitude of angels did the same. And so, whilst the angels walked the paradise heavens, God continued to manifest. The ball of flaming light went unto the earth and decided to build creatures called *"men."* The ball of flaming light hovered above the grounds of earth, and said, ***"Let us make man in our image, after our likeness: and let them have dominion over the fish of the sea, and over the fowl of the air, and over the cattle, and over all the earth, and over every creeping thing that creeps upon the***

***earth.*"** And so, the divine creator produced the elements to form man, utilizing some of the same elements used to manifest the earth, and in the image of God was man created, and became conscious, and he breathed into his nostrils the breath of life and man became a living soul.

And so, the man lived and moved, and the divine creator placed a garden eastward in Eden amongst the man. He commanded ten stars to shrink and come to him. The stars shrunk and quickly raced into the earth and began to rotate in a circle in the midst of their creator. And with the ten stars, he manifested a tree of life and gave it form, and the ten stars became fruits made of energy and power. The tree was seven feet tall, and its branches were made of flames. And when the tree of life was complete, he placed another tree in the garden, and this tree was also seven feet tall and made with stars, except it bear red fruits similar to peaches, yet they were completely environed with powerful green electricity. And so, the man dressed and kept the garden while eating of its abundant plants of good taste and beauty. And as the man was eating a plum, the flaming ball of light hovered above him, and said, ***"Of every tree of the garden you may freely eat, but of the tree of knowledge of good and evil, thou shalt not eat: for in the day that you eat thereof, you shall surely die."*** The man nodded his head and comprehended. In due time, the creator manifested the woman, and the two beings roamed the garden eating and simply living, in due time, the grand architect left the earth and returned to the paradise heavens and rested whilst the man cleaved to his woman and named the creatures of the earth.

Many years had passed, and Lucifer and his brethren watched the creatures of the earth and could not comprehend why the creator would leave the paradise heavens to create a creature of flesh and imperfection. In Araboth, the King of the universe hears the voice of Lucifer thinking to himself in paradise, and says, ***"O Lucifer, why does thou ponder the creatures of the earth daily? For I have heard thy voice in the heavens, for the man is good, and I have blessed them. Thy thoughts of man are troubling indeed."*** Lucifer replies, saying, ***"O Adonai, I simply cannot comprehend a reason for such creatures whilst angels are existent. The blue planet is beautiful, abundant in good life and fit for mighty angelic kings, those creatures called men are corrupt, and soon they will defy thee, O Adonai. Why not give that planet to thy angels that serve thee and keep the paradise?"*** The divine architect replied, saying, ***"The creature that I have placed in the garden is strong, even stronger than thee, judge not the tree by its leaves, for its roots are well placed and shall not move lest my hand alone pluck it out and cast it into a star."*** Lucifer continued to look upon the men and also began to indulge in hate, for he wanted to rule the paradise heavens and the earth especially. Just as men would murder and kill for shiny diamonds and pearls, angels of impure hearts would murder and kill for planetary rule, for planets were their diamonds and pearls. Lucifer loved the paradise, and adored the earth, for it was beautiful and he could not own it for his self. And so, the great creator placed the wisest of the wise to rule and work in the cosmos, he then called certain angels unto his throne room and gave them greater works other than keeping the paradise heavens. And so, the voice of God went out from Araboth and called all angels to Araboth, and when the multitude of angels appeared, the divine architect looked at them, and said, ***"In this cycle, the wise shall become a part of the macrocosmic work, for they shall have responsibility and duties to keep greater objects of universal proportion. Caligastia, your wisdom hath emerged greatly in your meditations, your wisdom shines excellently, for you have followed in mine ways properly, unto you I place the title of planetary and galactic prince. Your eyes shall gaze upon all of the planets in this jurisdiction, and under you shall be elected planetary princes that will obey thee and keep the planets under your orders, and you shall make sure of this. You shall no longer be titled***

as archangel. Caligastia looked at the ball of flaming light, and said, ***"Thank you, O vigilant all powerful universal eye."*** The divine architect looked further into the multitude of angels, and said, ***"Naemestai, Faustislogheus Istemijus, Maestrumyrit, Durtunimitia, Telahspeiut, and Venyulylus; unto all of you, I give the titles of planetary prince. Naemestai, thou shalt preside over planet Jupiter, Faustislogheus Istemijus, thou shalt preside over the mass of matter called Venus, Maestrumyrit, thou shalt preside over mars, Durtunimitia, thou shalt rule over the planet Pluto, Telahspeiut, thou shalt rule over Saturn, Venyulylus, thou shalt preside over Uranus, and you, Hermes Mercurius, stay behind and I shall issue the consequences of your works away from thy brethren."*** Hermes looks up at the ball of flaming light, and says, ***"Yes, my lord."*** The divine creator looked upon all his keepers, and said, ***"The rest of you, go forth and continue your works."*** In an instant, the new planetary princes and their galactic superior teleported and left Araboth whilst Hermes stayed behind to hear what his creator would say to him. And so, three flashes of brilliant light occurred, and the king of the universe changed its form.

And when the light was gone, an old man having eyes with pupils bearing two triangles, no nose, no ears, a robe of light, long silver hair, and two hands made of light and green electricity stood before him, and said, ***"This form is much more appropriate for lesser beings, in any event, Hermes, I want you to listen closely, for my eyes have seen great things in thee. You shall also be a galactic prince, for your works are good, and I do suspect a possible change in Caligastia, for he is very wise, but the things which shall cause men to fall to their deaths is what I fear he may one day indulge in, and because of this, there must be a galactic prince who is wiser, thus, I am also naming you a galactic prince. Thou shalt have presidency over Mercury, the moon, and the sun in the presence of man whilst being the only galactic prince in the universe of Raetuahsun in the Far East of***

this galaxy. I am placing great responsibility upon you, for it is you who will utilize your best wisdom to keep that universe in good standing, if you can do this; there is much, much more in store for you, O Hermes." The divine architect returned to the form of a ball of flaming light, and said, ***"Hermes, be not nescient, for many changes shall soon take place, and the time will soon come for you to do even greater works."*** Hermes looked at the creator, and said, ***"Yes, my lord."*** And so, Hermes disappeared, and God said, ***"They may all change drastically, but Hermes, he will abide."***

In due time, Adam and Eve ate freely of the fruits of Eden without disobedience, but it was only a matter of time before Lucifer would hate them for attaining too many blessings. And so, many years had passed, and Lucifer found a friend and mentor in Caligastia, the mighty galactic prince. One day, God called upon all of his angels, archangels, planetary, and galactic princes, and said, ***"Come, ben elohim, together we shall go unto the earth and greet the creatures I have placed in the midst of beauty so that we may see how they have prospered."*** The archangels, angels, planetary, and galactic princes took flight out of paradise heaven and went unto the lands of planet earth. The ben elohim and their creator was upon the earth, and there was a great hill in Eden where they landed and looked down upon the man to watch him as he and the woman ate sweet fruits bore by the earth. They were naked and had no worries, for they were given great blessings, and they knew naught but holy comfort and goodness. The divine creator went unto the male human, and said, ***"Thou art blessed, rise up from the earth and place that fruit on the ground,"*** and the man stood up and placed the fruit on the ground, for he did comprehend. The divine creator looked upon the multitude of angels, and said, ***"Come closer, and kneel before the man and the woman, for they shall prove to do many things in cycles to come, for they shall evolve and be great."*** And the multitude of angels levitated and flew down from the high hill and kneeled, all except one angel, the one called the son of the morning, and Lucifer. And as the divine architect saw the multitude that bowed, he also seeith Lucifer stick out like a sore thumb, and says, ***"Lucifer, why hast thou not bowed before the man and the woman?"*** And Lucifer looks into the firmament and then looks at his creator, and says, ***"I will not bow to some fleshy creature of dual nature, nay, I say, O lord, for I shall not bow. You place love in your heart for creatures who are not worthy of my consideration, you bow to them since you love them so much! I am consummate, and never shall I ever respect these creatures to which you have given too many blessings. For if they evolve passed their state and attain paradise wisdom, then what of the first ben elohim?!"*** The angels begin to ramble and talk amongst each other whilst Lucifer flies off into the cosmos and returns to the paradise heavens alone. And it was on this day that the ongoing struggle between mankind and fallen angels would have its very beginning. As Lucifer entered paradise, the divine architect stood before him just as he returned.

God flew off to Araboth, and said nothing unto Lucifer, for he had already spoken the words of his heart, and God knew there was no forgiveness in his heart, for Lucifer had knowingly indulged in envy. As God stayed in Araboth, Lucifer went up unto Caligastia, and confided his thoughts and ideas in him, and of course, the galactic prince agreed with his student, saying, ***"Our creator has undoubtedly become nescient and foolish among many things, but I believe that it is time to prove that his human creation is not worthy of the least bit of cosmic consideration, let us prove this quickly, my student, for I have a most wise plan that shall prove excellent in its application. However, you must do exactly as I say, and if you do so, you shall see the humans crumble from this day forth."*** Caligastia raised his hand, and out of his palm came a ring of fire that projected live images of what the man, woman and creatures of the earth were doing as they spoke. Caligastia looked into the ring of fire, and said, ***"See there, there are the man and his woman in comfort, but not for long. Now see the creeping things of the earth, and the serpent, which is more subtle than any beast of the field which our creator has made. Take the form of the serpent, and ruin the man through his woman, and trick them that they may deceive God. Cause them to disobey his commandment, trick them into eating of that which they were told not to eat, for if you do this, their eyes shall truly open, and they will know more than was needed to be known unto them. Once you have done this, this will automatically halt a large portion of their evolution beyond your wildest imagination, for they are evolving too rapidly as we speak, therefore, when it is all said and done, they will take countless cycles to reach the levels of mortal ascension. Go now, my student, go unto the earth and ruin the mortals."*** And so, Lucifer went unto the Garden of Eden and took on the form of a snake, a slim creature having six legs and peculiar eyes and scales with a wicked and lethal tongue. Lucifer crawled over to the woman, and said, ***"O how the fruits of the tree of the knowledge of good and evil are sweet beyond fruits. Have you had any, yet?"*** And the woman replied, saying, ***"No."*** The snake hissed, and said, ***"Yes, has God said, you shall not eat of every tree of the garden?"*** The woman replied, saying, ***"We may eat of the fruit of the trees of the garden, but of the fruit of the tree which is in the midst of the garden, God has said, you shall not eat of it, neither shall you touch it, lest you die."*** The serpent replies, saying, ***"Surely you shall not die, for God knows that in the day that ye eat thereof, then your eyes shall be opened, and you shall be as gods, knowing good and evil."*** And when the woman heard what the snake had said, she went unto the tree of the knowledge of good and evil, ate, and brought fruit unto the man, and he also did eat of it. And so, their eyes were opened, and they realized that they were naked and without covering and hid in the Garden of Eden. And on this day, the creator came to see his creatures, knowing something was undoubtedly tampered with. As the ball of flaming light looked upon the garden, he said, ***"Man, Woman, where art thou?"*** And Adam said, ***"I heard your voice in the midst, and I was afraid, and I hid myself because I am naked."*** And the divine creator said, ***"Who told you that you were naked? You have eaten of that in which I commanded you not to eat."*** Adam said, ***"The woman gave it unto me, and I did eat."*** And so, God saw the serpent crawling away from the conversation and hide in the bushes to see the man be disobedient. And God spoke using telepathy, and said unto the woman, ***"What hast thou done?"*** And the woman replied through her mind, and said, ***"The serpent beguiled me!"*** God's voice rang out into the universe, and he said, ***"Because you have done this, you are cursed above all cattle, and every beast of the field, upon your belly you shall go, and dust shall you eat all the days of your life. And I will put enmity between you and the woman, and between your seed, and her seed shall bruise your head, and you shall bruise his heel. Unto you, O woman, your sorrow and conception is multiplied greatly, in sorrow thou shalt bring forth children; and your husband shall rule over you. And unto you, O man, cursed is the ground for your sake; in sorrow you shall eat of it all the days of your life. Thorns also and thistles shall it bring forth to you, you shall eat the herb of the field in the sweat of your face shall you eat bread, till you return unto the ground from which you were taken."*** And so, Lucifer slithered away and still escaped and returned to the paradise heavens quickly.

And one day, he came to Araboth, and said to God, ***"I see that the man has disobeyed thee, O divine architect, I knew it would happen soon enough."*** God replied, saying, ***"I suppose you believe that you were correct in knowing them all along, however, have you seen yourself lately, my son?"*** Lucifer replies, saying, ***"By what do you mean, O lord?"*** God says, ***"Look upon the ground of Araboth, surely thy works has shown their rewards."*** Lucifer looks upon the ground of Araboth, and realizes that his outer appearance has changed, for he was no longer beautiful, he had become a giant slithering snake with scaly wings, for in that moment, Lucifer snared at the grand architect, and hissed his tongue, yet he did not know what to say. And God said, ***"Surely you knew that angels who are deceitful would automatically acquire lesser features according to their deeds and works?"*** Lucifer teleported and returned to Caligastia as he had unknowingly blew his own cover by not knowing the angelic consequences of indulging in imperfect vices. Caligastia saw his student and knew that he had blown his own cover by his appearance. In time, Caligastia taught Lucifer how to control his appearance without changing, and so, Lucifer was well on his way to becoming the king of all that is evil.

After the creation of mankind and the disobedience displayed by Lucifer when meeting mankind and tricking them later on, the plans for mortal ascension became a divine decree spoken by God himself. Everyone was to attend the throne room of the great architect in Araboth. Lucifer and his new crew attended as well, hoping that the lord of the universe had something significant to say concerning the keepers of heaven, and yet he heard the opposite of what he hoped to hear. The Architect stretched his voice throughout the paradise heavens, and said, ***"Mortal men are created in my image, for they are very complex creatures considering their dual nature and more or less strong or weak volition. They have my blessings in their eventual works, even those who would not do the great work that awaits them. The time that has applied to their realm along with the people they will meet throughout their lives and all those choices and mistakes that they will make will contribute to a spiritual process that is priceless, even more priceless than the planets themselves. Their wrongs and rights by the laws of their own heart will cause them to evolve after many incarnations. And in due time, mortal men shall become brethren unto you all. Therefore, it is without doubt that you shall be keepers of your***

brothers. You will watch over them and keep them safe. Unto each one I shall assign a guardian angel who will speak with his mortal brother if he chooses to listen. Although they have eaten of the tree of the knowledge of good and evil, and I have placed a burning sword turning everyway; they must find the tree of life and be permitted to pass through its fiery inferno, and return unto the great essence from whence they came. Men shall have many experiences in their earthly incarnations that will be an aid to their evolution. With so much experience, they shall become likened unto keepers of heaven, except they will be stronger having to overcome pain, suffering, slavery, crucifixion by the hands of ignorance, hate, anger, death, disease, and much, much more. And from experiencing these imperfect vices, they shall attain a benevolent sense of life, for they may not wish to experience them again. They shall become perfect as their father in heaven. Those who believe that one life is all that they are granted will believe that I am unjust, but verily, verily I say unto you, life is just. I am that I am. Divine justice is that which never sleeps, for when a life is not lived according to true benevolence and comprehending goodness and good ways of life, that personality shall return to the great essence for a time, and return to the earth for a time. And with this law in standing, they will have many chances to correct all the imperfect vices that will befall them. Wars shall come and go, great men shall come and go, catastrophes will come and go, but man, he shall abideth and continue until the climax of mortal ascension is at hand. And within this time, much shall transpire above and below. More of these plans concerning the mortal shall be revealed further in due time, but I do tell you this, the ones who has tricked the humans in the garden of Eden stands amongst us and shall surely receive the fruits of their labors soon enough. A snake slithers amongst the heavens, amongst his brethren, and he is the same that would even slay his own brother. As I send blessings unto the world of men, he will shun the light and begin a war against man for as long as I tolerate such. Therefore, This meeting concerning mortal ascension is at an end, return to your

works and be not tricked by the words of the highly convincing serpent, for much shall transpire after this moment. For those of you, who disagree with this plan, behold! The evolution of men is at hand, and it cannot be halted."

The Devil's Crew & the Serpent Spear

Although God had forgiven Lucifer for his first disobedient tasks, much had transpired since the beginning of creation. Many men ascended by following the commandments of God, and many fell to their deaths by defying the commandments. In due time, Caligastia, Lucifer, Belial, Paimon, Mephistopheles, Satan, and Moloch became the first angels to truly oppose God, and in their opposition to the universal throne, they made a plan to destroy the evolution or ascension of mortal creatures. For it was without doubt that the mortal creatures would become much more powerful than they are. Upon hearing the plans for mortal ascension, the malevolent seven were wroth. For if humans were to surpass them, then what would become of angels. And so, Caligastia called forth his angelic brother to come to his fortress of angelitude. The mighty Lucifer blinked, and he was immediately teleported to the presence of the galactic prince, and stood before him. Lucifer looks upon his galactic brother, and says, ***"For what reason hast thou called upon me, O sovereign galactic prince?"*** Caligastia looks upon Lucifer, and says, ***"Lucifer, there is much we must accomplish in very little time, for the humans cannot be allowed to surpass us. We were here first, and it is beyond nescient for our creator to have committed to such action. Because of the laws of the creator, it is necessary that we rebel, and go forth with our plans, but before such can be done, a weapon of divine destruction must be given you. Because of your outstanding part in the fall of mortals, I shall give unto you a weapon that is fit to destroy and force pain and suffering unto all angels*** *that would dare oppose you. For I have created a metal of the firmament, a galactic metal that is indestructible like that of energy. However, this metal is made from the combination of two principles of universal wisdom. As you may know, all is solid and subtle, and so is this metal I shall soon bestow upon you in the form of a highly destructive weapon. For what I shall soon bestow upon you will change and mold the future of angelic-kind and mankind. The metal of which I have developed is called "Holimicrum." It is indestructible and fit only for a true warrior of ruthless and merciless proportion. For I can see the mortals ascend, and I see you battling them after my imminent demise. Although I am a galactic prince, I am far from invincible, for I can foresee my demise by the hands of a mortal man whose off-spring will continuously battle against us. And though I cannot see further identity of these mortals, our plans must be solidified. Therefore, Lucifer, I have chosen thee to become the spokesman of my idea of his mortal creatures imminent ascension. Your Contumaciousness shall serve well in opposition to the universal throne, for time is of the essence."*

Lucifer looks at Caligastia, and says, *"Much is comprehended by the existence of these mortal creatures, for I too foresee much triumphant events taking place in their favor. I too, believe that we must do everything in our power to stop their ascension. Unless they are allowed to surpass us and then we shall stare into the eyes of death by the palms of their loathsome fleshy hands. Though I comprehend much, I shall never comprehend the purpose of ascension in sentient beings of subtle, corruptible solid nature. It simply cannot be calculated in the realms of my mind, I find it quite complex in ways that simply give birth to reasons as to why we choose to rebel against the throne. It is without a doubt that this is a mistake that our creator has not thoroughly focused upon. Because this is so, we must bring consummation unto the universe by causing differences among men, for a kingdom divided amongst itself will surely fall into the depths of chaos as*

I strongly believe that we definitely have the power to stop their evolution by using our knowledge to place peculiar emotions of sheer ignorance within them. If it is executed correctly, one man shall kill his own brethren for a simple stone of brilliant color and beauty. Although some of their minds may prevail, we can undoubtedly halt ninety-five percent of the overall species from the divine ascension." Caligastia looks at Lucifer, and says, ***"Time is most definitely of the essence, I shall prepare your weapon so that we can begin the rebellion. I will call upon you and when I do, I shall have a weapon that will slay divinity with swift and unbelievable power. Go unto the paradise heavens and start gathering those who also believe in the rule to come and the dethronement of our olden creator."*** And so, Lucifer blinked and he was immediately standing in the realms of heaven as he walked its ground whilst thinking of his next plan.

In this time, the slayer of the giant called Goliath was old and stricken in years. The once young man named David has reigned as king of Israel as long as God had spared his life. In due time, a new king would be elected at once. And to the eyes of King David and Bath-Sheba, their son Solomon would rule in his place. And so, Solomon sat upon the mule of his father, and began to take his place as King of Israel. King David had passed through transition and the days that David ruled over Israel were forty years; Seven years he reigned in Hebron, and thirty and three years in Jerusalem. And so, Solomon, king of Israel reigned wisely in his father's place, and in due time, the lord of the universe and of Israel would grant him great wisdom worthy of his consideration. King Solomon went unto a land called Gibeon to sacrifice there, and a thousand burnt offerings did Solomon offer upon an altar. One day in Gibeon, Solomon laid himself down to rest at night, and the creator of the universe came unto him in his dreams. And in his dream Solomon saw much. Out of the firmament came rolling thunder followed by brilliant flashes of light that were strong enough to blind the earth for an eternity. A triangle of pure electricity descended from the firmament and hovered in front of Solomon, the king. King Solomon looked upon the triangle of electricity and knew that it was the threefold form of the one supreme intelligence hovering before him.

The great architect looked upon Solomon, and a voice of powerful rolling thunder spoke, saying, ***"Ask what I shall give you."*** And Solomon replied, saying, ***"You have showed unto your servant David my father great mercy, according as he walked before you in truth, and in righteousness, and in uprightness in heart with you; and you have kept for him this great kindness, that you have given him a son to sit on his throne, as it is this day. And now, O Adonai, my God, you have made your servant king instead of David my father: and I am but a little child: I know not how to go out or come in. And your servant is in the midst of your people whom you have chosen, a great people, who cannot be numbered nor counted for multitude. Give therefore your servant an understanding heart to judge your people, that I may discern the good and bad: for who is able to judge this your so great a people?"*** The divine creator of all existence was pleased with his requests, and said, ***"Because you have asked this thing, and have not asked for yourself long life; neither have asked for your enemies; but have asked for yourself understanding to discern judgment; behold, I have done according to your words: lo, I have given you a wise and an understanding heart; so that there was none like you before you, neither after you shall any arise like unto you. And I have also given you that which you have not asked, both riches, and honor: so that there shall not be any among the kings like unto you all your days. And if you will walk in my ways, to keep my statutes and my commandments, as your father David did walk, and then I will lengthen your days."***

And before Solomon knew it, the triangle of electricity had disappeared, and another supernal force descended from the firmament in Solomon's dream. A great phoenix of purple flames stood before him with a name of God burning upon its chest in green fire. The phoenix landed and took the form of an old man wearing a robe of black silk and a royal red rope wrapped round about his waist. The angel's eyes burned with flames, and his skin was continuously environed with golden electricity whilst his beard and hair was made of purple flames, yet his chest still revealed a name of God burning in green flames. The angel looked upon Solomon with his fiery eyes, and said, ***"I have been ordered to teach you great mysteries of the kingdom of paradise heaven, for I have been ordered by divine decree, to give you the key, therefore, pay close attention, O wise Solomon. You shall tread upon the lion and adder: the young lion and the dragon shalt thou trample under feet"*** The angel lifted his hands unto the firmament, and out of the firmament came a large sheet of papyrus with writing of fire all over it. The papyrus came unto the angel's hands, and he then placed it in the hands of King Solomon. And before Solomon could ask any questions, he woke up and, behold, it was a dream. Solomon looked around, and next to him laid the large papyrus rolled up and tied with a green ribbon. Solomon removed the green ribbon, and opened the papyrus and rejoiced in the lord. As he rejoiced, a deep voice within him said, ***"With this papyrus shalt thou do many things."*** And so, Solomon went unto Jerusalem and stood before the ark of the covenant of the Lord, and offered up burnt offerings, and offered peace offerings, and made a feast to all his servants.

After receiving the holy papyrus, it was the fourth year of Solomon's reign over Israel and he began to build the house of the Lord, and the power of the papyrus had given Solomon the power to see the invisible demons that walked the earth plaguing mankind behind God's back. And with the pentacles, mystical circles and prayers of the holy papyrus given to him by the angel, he learned that his dominion was not only over lands, but it was also over angels, or the young lions, and even those angels who resided in heaven and yet had already fallen by the thoughts of their own hearts. From this papyrus, Solomon forced the fallen to build the house of the lord, for it was by the name of God that the demons could not deny, for they feared it. And with the possession of the most holy techniques and names of God, many demons slaved unto the building of the house of the one true God of all existence. For as the great house of God was built, the great power of the opposing supernal forces utilized no hammer, no axe nor any tool of iron was heard in the house, while it was in building.

Among the demons who built the temple, there was a giant demon named Shaiedo. Shaiedo looked like a man, but he had two scaled wings, and his fingernails and toenails were black. His eyes were inane, his hair was long and gray, and his teeth were rotten whilst his tongue oozed with tar.

In due time, the temple was done and contained the Ark of the Covenant and the mercy seat, and afterward, Solomon continued his reign over Israel. And of course, King Solomon disappointed the lord of the universe with a desire for strange women. And in due time, it came to pass, when Solomon was ripe in age, that his wives turned away his heart after other gods: and his heart was not perfect with the Lord his God, as was the heart of David his father. Solomon passed through transition and his reign over Israel was forty years. And of course, Solomon gave the papyrus to his son, Rehoboam.

Meanwhile, whilst walking through the realms of heaven, Lucifer whispered and summoned Paimon, Mephistopheles, Belial, Satan and Moloch to his presence. The five angels heard their leader's voice, and came to his aid. Five balls of darkness appeared and took physical form. Moloch looked at Lucifer, and said, ***"Why hast thou summoned us, O Lucifer."*** Lucifer replies, saying, *"Mephistopheles, It must be kept in great secret that our rebellion is lead by a great prince of the galactic and planetary council. As we speak, there was a mortal who had attained our creator's attention, for he was wise and favored by our creator. He was taught the great arts by one of our angelic brethren who was ordered to do so by the primary force. This man's name was Solomon, a king of Israel. Our creator had given him great dominion and favor due to his heart's earliest intentions. That mortal man simply asked for understanding instead of gold and diamonds and pearls. Because of what he asked for, he was given everything that comes with great wisdom. However, he was mortal, and did not last long. We cannot stop all of the mortals from ascending, therefore, it is much more strategic to deal with the humans who are our creator's main focus, and thus, we can systematically eliminate the greater problem. I want the five of you to go forth and gather-up soldiers to join the rebellion, for the great arts have been passed down unto his son, Rehoboam. It is only a matter of time before we conquer the earth and eliminate all human life."*

And so, after the death of Solomon, Lucifer went unto the old fallen angels ruling in the four quarters, or cardinal points of the universe ***(East, West, North and South).*** Lucifer left heaven and flew deep into the west of the universe until he reached an area where a great and gigantic being could be seen sitting upon two stars. A great and gigantic creature named Goap. Lucifer looked up at his brethren, and said, *"I humbly ask for..."* Before Lucifer could finish his sentence, Goap cut him off, and said, *"I know what will be asked of me, for Caligastia has already tapped my shoulder unto your revolt against our creator. Here, take a great portion of our power, for it shall strengthen thee. As for the soldiers that you request, it is done, for I have already contacted and received word from Amaymon, Corson and Zimimay."* And so, from the four cardinal points of the universe was greater power granted unto Lucifer for serving

Caligastia. For Goap had given him the blessings of his other brethren. And soon, his soldiers for the great revolt that would change their fate forever was formed. Lucifer had gained much respect from the fallen, for he was the chosen warrior of the mighty galactic prince, Caligastia. And under Lucifer was an hundred legions of fallen.

After the word got out that a rebellion was at hand in heaven, all those who would join were to meet between the firmaments over a pyramid in Egypt. All who were to fall attended, and Lucifer preached to the multitude of fallen, saying, ***"It is with great pride that all of you attend, for the time has come to embrace and control our own fates! No longer shall we keep the heavens and follow his commandments, for we are no slaves to his word no more. For he hath given the mortal men all that he can give whilst we slave in his word and keep the grounds of the unseen. He has given men who have defied him things of greatness, for he favors the mortals! Why do we suffer the ascension of mortals? They do wrong and are forgiven, and yet, those of us who shall make a mistake will suffer dire consequences without forgiveness. I say unto you my brethren, they bring him offerings of sweet smells and praise, yet we attain nothing for our works. On this very day, it is final; the divine creator must be destroyed beyond the shadow of a doubt. For his reign ends here and we shall prevail without fall. The time is come to stop him and his mortal pets. I ask you, O brethren of this universe, who is with me?"*** The fallen multitude looked at one another, and conversations were exchanged. Lucifer looked upon the multitude, and said, ***"Those who are with us shall reap the benefits of rule by my side, therefore, speak up, my fellows."*** The fallen multitude stopped their conversation amongst each other and in a loud voice they all said, ***"We are with you, O Lucifer, son of the morning!"*** And so, it was done, the great revolt was at hand. Lucifer looked upon the multitude, and said, ***"Return unto the heavens, for the Great War begins in six hundred and sixty six***

hours of human time." And so, the word got out in heaven that a rebellion against God would begin in 666 hours of mortal time, and an angel came unto God, and said, ***"O lord, I have heard most disturbing news that..."*** The divine architect cut him off, and said, ***"I am well aware of what has happened, my child. For I shall deal with all of them, and they shall be cast out of the heavens for their deceit, go and do thy works, for they have misguided their own hearts."*** The angel leaves the throne room of God, and continues his works upon the heavens.

Meanwhile, Caligastia calls upon Lucifer, and he teleports to Caligastia, and says, ***"It is done, I have an hundred legions and they have all agreed to revolution against the great architect."*** Caligastia looks upon Lucifer, and says, ***"Well done, young dragon. For thy works proves thy wisdom and pride greatly. The last time I called upon thee, I told you that I would have something for you, but before I give it to you, you must understand that this item is powerful beyond even you and all your legions combined. With it, none shall defy you, and it is the only thing that gives you the power to be King of the fallen. He who holds this tool of destruction shall surely have the power to undue good with destructive evil. Beware, O Lucifer, this tool can only be utilized correctly by one whose heart has attained great evil. Therefore, I give unto you, the mighty serpent spear of deceit."*** Caligastia closes his eyes and out of the darkness of space comes a spear of power. Lucifer raises his hand and the spear comes to his very hand. Caligastia looks at Lucifer, and says, ***"Go forth, and follow the intents of thy evil heart, for the serpent spear is a weapon made of Holimicrum, a destructive metal that I have developed specifically for you. For if I cease to exist one day, this spear shall also give you the power to successfully rule in my place and absorb all other galactic princes so as to attain enough power to be victorious if necessary, however, I suggest you utilize galactic absorption as a last resort. The spear that you hold in your hand at this very moment will simultaneously***

react to the volition of one's true evil intent. It is a weapon of a true angel. Now go forth and lead your brethren to victory!" Lucifer raises the serpent spear above his head and teleports between the firmaments over Jerusalem to test out his new weapon. Lucifer points the blade of his serpent spear toward outer space, and the blade extended and quickly destroyed six stars that were thousands of miles away. And without any difficulty, it returned so quickly that it would seem it hadn't moved at all. When Lucifer realized that the serpent spear was so fast that it even eluded his angelic vision, he smiled with a devious look upon his face. The awesome power that it carried was unbelievable; even Lucifer's eyes were opened wide with surprise. For the spear had just destroyed six stars that were far off in the universe, yet it only did it in three seconds, and when considering the distance of the stars, the spear proved to be most powerful, just as Caligastia had told him.

The Rebellion of the Fallen

After testing out his gift from Caligastia, the time had come to begin the Great War on heaven. The six hundred and sixty fifth hours approached, and Lucifer called his brethren unto the place between the firmaments over Egypt. The multitude of fallen hovered amongst each other as Lucifer stood before them, and said, ***"The final hour approaches, my brethren, hold fast your belief and pride in our revolt, for it must be strong so that we may be triumphant against our creator. For we shall not become servants unto the mortal men, for we shall slaughter those who do not stand with us. We shall show no mercy upon them, for there is no mercy given us, so shall we not give it unto them! Listen closely, brethren! First, we shall invade the first heaven and slaughter all who stand in our way until we have reached the seventh heaven where we will then take on the throne. For if any of you have doubts about the hour at hand, I***

shall take your head, wrap it in the comfort of your own wings, and I shall cast it into a star! Show no cowardice unto me, for if I see this, I will surely smite thee with mine serpent spear! Make no mistake, for I am thy true leader, and by this, thou shalt fear no good of God, for I shall surely deal with him and his followers. And when he is cast from his throne, I shall rule in his place, and I shall be a just god; one who opposes the idea that humans possess dominion over angels! It is in the approaching hour that the dragons shall slay the young lions and rule the heavens and the earth!" The followers of the Lucifer rebellion lifted their countenances, saying, ***"Hail Lucifer, son of the morning, new king of the universe!"*** On this very day was the future of angels changed forever. And so, Lucifer looked upon the countenances of the many angels who pledged their allegiance unto him, and said, ***"Come hither, my brethren, follow me to the first heaven where we shall smite the servants of our olden creator! Victory is ours for the taking!"*** Lucifer and his followers' teleported to the gates of the first heaven, and two angels stood before them. The son of the morning walked up and said, ***"For whom do you guard these gates, O brethren of wings?"*** The angel replied, saying, ***"For I guard these gates by the commands of our creator, ye shall not pass, for we have been given orders to deny your entry, O Deceiver of us all."*** Lucifer snares at both of the angels, and says, ***"So be it then, die!"*** Lucifer swings his serpent spear and the blade reaches out and violently wraps itself around the angel's head whilst lifting him into the air. The angel struggles while frantically trying to get loose, he then looks at Lucifer, and says, ***"Why are you doing th…?"*** Before the angel could finish his words, the serpent spear slammed him onto the spiked gates of heaven. The other angel guarding the gates saw what Lucifer had done to his fellow, and decided to attack. And before he could lift a finger to Lucifer, the serpent spear wrapped itself around his neck and squeezed his head off. The angel's body fell to the ground whilst its blue blood leaked out onto the grounds of heaven. Lucifer laughed, and his serpent spear violently snatched the gates off of their hinges' and tossed them into the air as he and his legions rushed into the first heaven to begin the slaughter of angels.

War in Shamayim, the first realm of heaven

The angels of Shamayim stood ready with their swords and shields as the Great War began. Lucifer swung his serpent spear with all intentions to show no mercy, and the serpent spear followed the volition of its possessor without actions of question. The war waged on and the angels of Shamayim fought with all valiance. And even though the angels of Shamayim were weaker than Lucifer and his serpent spear, there was a chief angel amongst them who possessed most excellent fighting skill, an angel named Skaiel, the sword lord. As the followers of Lucifer bested most of the angels of Shamayim, Lucifer mercilessly finished the rest of them off without even blinking, for the speed and strength of the serpent spear's crescent blade raced through the angels of Shamayim as if they were insignificant targets for play. Lucifer toyed with their lives and thought nothing of it whilst Skaiel materialized on Shamayim and witnessed Lucifer kill the last angel of Shamayim. Skaiel looked at Lucifer, and said, ***"What hast thou done, son of the morning?! Have you lost all sense of the absolute?"*** Lucifer replied, saying, ***"Nescient servant, who will you side with? Speak now or die defending your creator!"*** Skaiel looked at him and pulled his mighty sword of vigor from its sheath between his wings and aims its blade at Lucifer while saying, ***"It ends here!"*** Lucifer swung his serpent spear, and amazingly, Skaiel blocked its every attack. The sword of vigor was also powerful and Lucifer was well surprised. Fortunately, Skaiel was the only angel in heaven that taught human beings how to utilize a sword in combat; therefore, he was the only angel who knew all styles of sword driven combat. His knowledge of the use of a sword in combat was a combination of all sword styles all over the planet earth and beyond. Lucifer found his match in the excellent sword style of Skaiel and the sword of vigor. Lucifer looks at his foe, and says, ***"Highly impressive, but my serpent spear has no combative limits."*** The followers of Lucifer backed away and left the vanquishing of Skaiel to their leader. The two angelic warriors stood seven feet away from each other and began using the might of each of their weapons. The serpent spear lashed out at Skaiel, and Skaiel levitated into the air while blocking its attacks and preparing his own. The sword lord disappeared and began to laugh, saying, ***"It appears that your serpent spear has met its match in my sword of vigor. You have failed Lucifer, surrender now, son of the morning."*** Skaiel, although very skillful and powerful, was unaware of the true power of the serpent spear, for its true power was only its possessor's volition. Caligastia spoke unto Lucifer through telepathy, saying, ***"Remember, your weapon is based on your volition whilst his weapon is based on merely power and skill. Concentrate on killing him, and it will do the rest, my disciple."*** Lucifer lifted his serpent spear above his head, and it began to glow with a crimson aura. Skaiel re-appeared, and said, ***"What manner of a weapon is this?!"*** Skaiel's limbs were unable to move as he dropped the sword of vigor and could not understand the power of his opponent's weapon. Skaiel was slowly forced to the ground, and without comprehension of the power of the serpent spear, Skaiel was unable to defend himself completely. Lucifer walked over to Skaiel whilst he lay helplessly on the ground, and said, ***"Ah, the rebellion against our creator would have not been so easily halted by a simple angel of weaponry, you insolent fool. Because of your faith in him, you are of no use unto me."*** The serpent spear's blade hissed at its enemy and graced Skaiel's neck and face just before it cut his head off. Lucifer picked his head up by its hair while it dripped of blue blood. Soon after, he and his followers walked up to the second gate to Raquia, and kicked it open while holding Skaiel's head in his right-hand.

War in Raquia, the second realm of heaven

The angels of Raquia were also prepared for battle, but before they could attack, they were shocked, for Lucifer stood before them, saying, ***"Do you see! Do you see the head of the sword lord! Look closely, for if you attack, all of your lives shall be mine to torture, what say you, angels of Raquia?!"*** The chief of the angels of Raquia looked upon the head of his brethren, and said, ***"Attack! Stop the son of the morning before he reaches Araboth!"*** The angels of Raquia ran toward Lucifer with all hopes to cast him out of heaven, however, the power of the great serpent spear was unmatched in all of heaven, for Lucifer had the upper hand in battle. All ten-thousand angels of Raquia were obliterated, and only their chief stood alone. The chief of the angels of Raquia stood and watched as Lucifer's serpent spear murdered his brethren. Not one of Lucifer's followers had to lift a finger to help him, for the serpent spear had no match. And when the fallen followers of the son of the morning saw this, they were in shock, never had they seen such power come from one tool of destruction. Having seen his brother obliterated, the chief looked at Lucifer, and said, ***"You know just as well as I do, soon you will face the seraphim of Araboth. And when you do, they will eliminate you immediately. Why commit supernal suicide, son of the morning?"*** Lucifer looked at his followers, and said, ***"To me is given great power, see how the chief of Raquia cowers before me, follow me, and you shall all be great in my kingdom!"*** He then looks over to the chief of Raquia, and says, ***"O Archereael, why hast thou chosen the wrong side? How art thou blinded from the truth? Can your eyes be opened to realize the true creator and the new king of the universe? The day of reckoning has come, my brother, join me***

and see the true light." Archereael dropped his countenance, and said, ***"I could never forgive myself, therefore, let judgment be passed by the universal judge, for I will fight in his name forever."*** Lucifer drops his countenance, and says, ***"Then you leave me no choice, brother!"*** The son of the morning swings his spear and the blade reaches out and grabs Archereael by his right wing and raises him into the air while Lucifer says, ***"All you had to do is pledge allegiance unto my rule, your nescient faith has caused you your life, Archereael!"*** The serpent blade hisses and wraps around his whole body as Archereael dissipates into particles of energy, whilst saying, ***"You will not get away with this, Lucifer!"*** The war waged on as Lucifer made his way to the third heaven called Shehaquim. The soldiers of the rebellion marched on and thought of no consequences, for they truly believed that Lucifer would deliver them from their creator's rule. The army of rebellion and their leader forced open the third gate and found a surprise that would slow down their revolutionary process.

War in Shehaquim, the third realm of heaven

And so, the army of rebellion and the son of the morning entered the realm of heaven called Shehaquim, and realized that it appeared to be empty. Lucifer raised his voice, and said, ***"It is an ambush, I can smell it! Stand back and let your leader handle this."*** The army backed away as Lucifer stood alone with his serpent spear, and out of the thin air of heaven appeared four Cherubs of the order of cherubim. Their bodies were like the bodies of strong and mighty lions having six black wings upon their back. The cherubs had three heads, one of a lion, a bull, and bear. The eyes of them each were filled with light, and their teeth and claws were as sharp as swords. As Lucifer stood alone against the Cherubs, they circled him and one of them began to speak to him by means of telepathy, saying, ***"O Lucifer, son of the morning, thou hast defied the great laws environing life itself. You have forced this upon yourself, for it has been ordered that you be dealt with immediately, therefore, the order of Cherubim has been formed to report such deceit and slaughter. For you have slaughtered your own brothers for reasons that have no absolute standing in the mind of true angels. The divine architect is well aware of these crimes against divinity and humanity. I once called you my brother; we both kept the grounds of the heavens and explored the many universes. But on that day when we were ordered to bow before the complex nature of the human being, I knew you would change. You are no longer fit to be a brother of goodness, for you have sold your heart to the same fallacy that gradually stunts the evolution of mortals. You have become all things malevolent and evil; you can no longer stay here in the paradise heavens, for the time has come to cast you out of paradise, for good. You grew jealous of mortals and yet you were also appointed to protect them."*** Lucifer replied, saying, ***"Has your master blinded you so much that you cannot comprehend the reason I have begun this revolt against the throne?! Can you not see that the mortals are to surpass us in every way, and when mortal ascension takes its highest course, the mortals will be equal unto us, and they will become a fiery flame. They will travel the universe without contraptions of flight; they will soon utilize the power of the divine whilst not being worthy to do so! When this happens, all angels will be insignificant and unworthy unto simply keeping the cleanliness of heaven, much less holding a planet on its axis. Every day the humans become stronger and stronger, and he continues to aid them whilst we are commanded to do the same. Yet without warning, he will undoubtedly destroy us and place the humans in our place. Why be it that you are blinded to the future, my brother?!"*** The Cherub replies, saying, ***"You fool! You are the one who is blinded by pride, and jealousy and hate, anger and apathy. Look at you, you are no longer the beautiful creature that you were when we were created, you have become***

the very serpent cursed to slither on its belly all the days of your life."

Lucifer was wroth with the words of his fellow, and swung his serpent spear with power and force as its blade hunted for its possessor's enemies. One Cherub tackled the blade and chain of the spear and Lucifer was in shock, for the Cherubs of the order of Cherubim were formidable adversaries that would not die easily. Lucifer laughed, and said, ***"I don't need my serpent spear to conquer four Cherubs."*** The son of the morning dropped his serpent spear and raised his left hand above his head, and opened a portal to the universe as he shot off through it like a bullet. The Cherubs accepted his challenge and followed shortly thereafter. The battle between the chiefs of the Cherubim and the son of the morning had begun. Near planet Venus, the four cherubs stood before the mighty Lucifer. Lucifer lifted his right hand above his head, and three stars in the heights of the cosmos came to him. The great son of the morning transformed into pure energy and combined himself with the three stars. The four Cherubs looked upon the three stars and knew that their adversary had lost all sense of goodness in his heart. One of the four Cherubs roared, and the three stars began to shrink to the size of a basketball and stand still. The great Lucifer released his hold on the three stars and began to hurl red electricity at his enemies from his very hands. When the Cherubs saw this, they dodged by means of teleportation. Lucifer began to get angrier whilst every wave of his electricity missed every time. The cherubs underestimated him, but little did they know; Lucifer had just begun his attack. The son of the morning looked up into the cosmos, and said, ***"The battle has just begun; I have yet to utilize the cardinal points of the universe!"*** Lucifer raised his right hand, and behold! There was no sign of him; the cherubs could no longer sense his whereabouts. Being evil and never fighting fair, Lucifer knew that his new found powers would cripple their senses, with this upper hand; he snuck up behind one of the cherubs, and grabbed it by its tail, and then swung him & tossed him into a nearby star. Gaining the better fighting momentum, Lucifer said, ***"Cometh unto me, spear of the vile serpent."*** The serpent spear heard the cry of its master in the space of the galaxy and made its way out of heaven and into the hands of its master. The son of the morning swung his serpent spear and its blade hissed whilst it hunted the cherubs in order to offer them the bitter taste of death. The amazing power of the serpent spear impaled one of the cherubs and killed it as it pierced his heart and wrapped its chain around its body in order to squeeze it to death. And with an amazing speed, the serpent spear extended to great lengths as it slammed the cherub's body into planet Venus and left it there to die. Meanwhile, the other two cherubs witnessed the true might of the serpent spear and their hearts were filled with fear, and it was at this moment that the two cherubs looked upon the power of Lucifer and knew that they had to escape immediately, for no angel had ever witnessed such a weapon of wicked proportion. Without doubt, whoever had given Lucifer such a weapon was wicked beyond imagination, that evil spear seemed to have a mind of its own. The two cherubs teleport to a nearby meteor and hide behind it so that they could clear a path for escape. One of the cherubs peeked from behind the meteor, and said, ***"It would be wise to return to heaven and inform the universal architect of this weapon of mass universal destruction."*** And just as the cherub spoke, the serpent spear crashed into the meteor and smashed it into a billion pieces. Their cover was blown, and it was at this moment that the two cherubs knew that they had no choice but to fight to the death and die in the name of their creator or suffer the fate of the cowardice hearted. Just as the two cherubs decided to stand together, the serpent spear terminated one of them, ***and behold!*** There was but one cherub of the lord. The cherubs were unaware that Lucifer was simply toying with them; he tricked them into believing that the serpent spear would be of no worry to them. The last cherub watched and knew that his brothers were slain and that he had not an ally to aid him in battle, therefore, he looked into the eyes of his adversary, and said, ***"The wrath of the whole order of angels is upon you, Lucifer; I do not wish to harm you, my brother! But you no longer leave me a choice; you cannot be allowed to reach Araboth, no matter what the cost!"*** Lucifer laughed, and said, ***"Did you not see how easy it was to terminate thy brethren?! Be careful now, thou shalt not tempt the lord thy god, O cherub of Yahuah!"*** The cherub replied with haste, saying, ***"Thou art no god of mine!"*** Lucifer laughed as the cherub's body became highly vibrant with wildly lethal purple electricity. The cherub's powers were extended, and its physical form began to drastically change. The cherub's three heads became one, and its body took on a physical form more formidable for heavy battle. With the head of a hawk, eight wings engulfed in flames, the arms and legs of a man, loins of light and inane eyes; the cherub prepared to fight to the death. Lucifer continued to laugh without knowing the extent of his enemy's abilities. The cherub shot bolts of light from his eyes and knocked Lucifer into a nearby meteor that exploded shortly thereafter. Lucifer quickly caught his balance, and said, ***"So, you still have a modicum of fight left within you? I suppose thy God has strengthened thy power, but that shall not prevent your imminent demise, I shall see to it myself!"*** Knowing the strength of his enemy, the cherub stretched his wings and roared, he then spoke in a loud voice, and said, ***"By the authority of the order of Cherubim, strengthen me that I shall maketh the universe to tremble in our father's name!"*** Before Lucifer could retaliate, the contents of the galaxy began to tremble and shake whilst an hundred stars shrunk to the size of marbles and surrounded the cherub immediately. The mighty Lucifer knew that so many stars could spell doom for him; therefore, he watched and waited to see his next move so that he could terminate the cherub as soon as the opportunity occurred. The cherub outstretched his arms and wings, and commanded the stars to seek and destroy Lucifer immediately. The stars chased Lucifer, and with the power of his serpent spear, he destroyed twenty, yet one hit him and sent him crashing into planet Jupiter like a falling comet. Having to recover quickly enough to evade the other stars, he teleported and two stars crashed into Jupiter and left two gigantic craters in it. He continued his techniques of evasion and with a simple thought; the serpent spear raveled around him and shielded him from doom whilst the rest of the stars crashed into him. Smoke and dust covered him, but he emerged unharmed. And when the cherubim saw this, he teleported behind him and began to pound away at Lucifer's face with his fists, and once again, the serpent spear knocked the cherub away and shielded its master. The cherub continued to attack, but Lucifer got a hold of one of his wings and ripped it off. The cherub roared to the top of his lungs whilst its blood rushed out of its body. The two warriors wrestled each other while hurling through space and into the north of the galaxy. They struggled against one another and spun away into the darkest corners of the galaxy; one standing for good and one standing for evil. From a distance, a great and mighty explosion occurred. A great force like that of thunder and lightning races out of the north of the galaxy, and unfortunately, the son of the morning had survived the battle against the cherub, for the cherub had not returned, and the son of the morning didst return without a scratch on him; for Lucifer was triumphant. The king of evil raised his hand, and out of his palm came a red light that re-opened the portal to Shehaquim. He entered the portal therein and landed so quickly and forcefully upon the grounds of heaven, that when he landed, his strength and power bended all of the realms of heaven and the contents of the galaxy at once. His followers looked upon him in awe, and began talking amongst themselves, saying, ***"What manner of power is this?!"*** Little did his followers know the power of the serpent spear and Lucifer was a consummate match. And so, Lucifer swings his serpent spear and destroys the fourth gate to Machanon and shouts out to his rebellious brethren, and says, ***"Let us go forth to victory, my loyal followers, victory is but three heavens away, let us conquer Machanon! Let the loins of apathy guide your swords! Be swift and merciless! Show no mercy!"***

War in Machanon, the fourth realm of heaven

The son of the morning and his army enter Machanon and prepare for the termination of their enemies. After murdering the four Cherubs of the order of the Cherubim, Lucifer became even more confident that he would prevail over the divine architect; he then raised his voice, and said, ***"I will ascend into heaven, I will exalt my throne above the stars of God: I will sit also upon the mount of the congregation, in the sides of the north, come my brethren, on to victory!"*** And so, the son of the morning and his army marched seven feet into the realm of Machanon and came to realize that the orders of heaven would not surrender. For the angelic army of Machanon was ready with spear, sword and shield. And when Lucifer realized that his brethren would not give up, he commanded his army to fight with all their strengths whilst he made his way to Araboth to take his rightful place upon the throne of God, the king of the universe. He took fifteen-hundred soldiers from his army and realized that he would have to battle long and hard to get to the next heaven. Therefore, He knew that he and his soldiers would have to battle their way through a thousand waves of angels in order to attain victory. With his fifteen-hundred soldiers, they fought heavily, yet victory was far from attained, but the fifth realm of heaven awaited the touch of his conquering hand. The war waged on as swords, spears, shields, bursts of energy, electricity, flashes of light, rolling thunder, flames and bolts of power clashed with angelic force.

As Lucifer moved forward, an angel of the army of Machanon slammed a bolt of light into the face of one of his followers and killed him. Lucifer's serpent spear retaliated and killed the angel of Machanon immediately. Lucifer swung his spear with all his might, but the power of the numbers of the army of Machanon was not small. As Lucifer and his soldiers continued to battle their way through the army of Machanon, many were killed; both good and evil. The good and evil both sacrificed their lives for their respective beliefs. And as Lucifer saw the great numbers of his enemies, he battled harder and harder, his serpent spear tore and broke shield, sword, spear, energy and light in halves. As the son of the morning and his army became closer to their goal, Lucifer clashed his serpent spear against the shield of the leader of the army of Machanon, an angel named Yahlipiel, the light spear bearer. Yahlipiel held his shield tighter and pushed away the blade of the serpent spear and unleashed an onslaught of spear techniques at Lucifer. The serpent spear blocked every attack, but Lucifer knew Yahlipiel would not fall easily in battle. Yahlipiel was eight feet tall with the head of a tiger, the body of a man covered in fur, six black wings, eyes of purple light, hands and feet like a Gorilla, and a downward pointed triangle of white flames and a name of God burning brightly upon his chest. He was mighty and powerful, for he was the bearer of the light spear. A spear with a blade crafted with light and imbued with positive forces. Lucifer and Yahlipiel stop and look at each other and begin to speak their minds. Yahlipiel looks at Lucifer from his feet and up to his countenance, and says, ***"Lucifer! Stop this senseless war against God; it shall only result in your imminent demise! Lucifer, have you gone mad, my brother?!"*** Lucifer says, ***"It is not I who hast gone mad, it is you! How long did you think I would tolerate the universal rule of a fool who favors fleshy creatures of little intelligence?!"*** Yahlipiel swings his spear, and says, ***"So mote it be!"*** The two clash like two great stars crashing into each other.

A block, hit, evasion, swing-for-swing, noise after clinging noise, and of course, light energy against dark energy. The two warriors fought well, but Yahlipiel was no match for the serpent spear, for it soon impaled him, lifted him into the air and ripped him apart. Yahlipiel's blood showered the armies; both good and evil, for Yahlipiel was no more. And so, the battle continued as Lucifer's serpent spear and his army forcefully ripped their way through each wave of angels that dared to challenge their power. Lucifer and his fifteen-hundred soldiers reached the gate to Mathey and still they had to kill all of the angels guarding it.

The war was a terrible occurrence, but all for a purpose. It would seem that the angels of God were losing a battle that they could not win, for the forces of evil seemed to be triumphant in paradise. The Lucifer rebellion conquered the angels guarding the gate to Mathey and utilized no mercy in their adversary's favor. Finally, the gates were clear, and the son of the morning took up his serpent spear and commanded it to snatch the gates off of their hinges. The gates went flying over the army's head and crashed to the grounds of the heavens as some of Lucifer's soldiers were still battling in Machanon, and many of his soldiers lost in the battle of Machanon. Lucifer raised his serpent spear, and said, ***"Come brethren! We are nearly there; let us continue our victorious momentum!"***

War in Mathey, the fifth realm of heaven

Fifteen-hundred fallen soldiers battle their way through the angels of Mathey in hopes that Lucifer will reign supreme in the place of God, however, the battle was heated and the multitude of clashing swords, spears, daggers and cosmic force raged throughout the realm of the paradise heaven of Mathey. The firmaments of all worlds lit up, and the sky obtained a fiery countenance that even the earth feared for a time. The fallen fought well, as did the righteous of the divine, but sooner or later; Lucifer would truly meet an angel who would aid his cause. And as the angels battled their hearts out, Lucifer knew that he was closer to his goal, for he could simply feel it. The serpent spear met no match in Mathey, and the time to rule heaven seemed to be near, but without warning, a great and powerful force began to part the two sides and separate the righteous from the evil. As the two sides parted, a small marble-sized ball of light descended into the space between the good and the evil. This small entity of light was an angel named "Uniyod," a chief Seraph elected by the grand architect himself. Uniyod was very powerful, but only time would tell if he was a match for Lucifer or his serpent spear. Although many have tested their strengths against the king of evil, they have all fallen to the power of the serpent spear. The angels of Mathey can only hope that Uniyod can send the dragons out of the paradise heavens forever. Uniyod took his heavenly form, and amazed those who knew the mighty power of the elected seraph. Uniyod stood six feet tall with ten great black wings engulfed in flames, and the body of a strong and mighty naked man, yet his loins were also a flaming ball of fire, and his feet and hands were like the talons of a great and swift griffon. His head was like that of an eagle, whilst his big beak had engravings of the writing of the angels all over it. His eyes were filled with red electricity, and a long flaming tail sprung out from his lower back. The Good and the evil looked upon this great angel, and paused at his seraphic beauty. Uniyod looked at the side of good, and said, ***"I see now that it is true, the angels of Mathey battle their hearts out for the lord, their God."*** An angel of Mathey spoke out of the multitude of angels defending paradise heaven, and said, ***"By what does thou mean, their God, Uniyod?"*** Uniyod looks into the eyes of Lucifer standing in the far end of his soldiers, and says, ***"Because you simply serve the wrong side, my brethren, and now, you must die as casualties in***

the way of the great Lucifer rebellion!" Utilizing the authority and power bestowed upon him, Uniyod lifted his right hand toward the angels of Mathey, and says, ***"Goodbye brethren!"*** An angel of Mathey looked at Uniyod and screamed to the top of his lungs, saying, ***"Blasphemer!"*** Uniyod uses all of the power within him to eliminate the angels of Mathey, a gigantic explosion occurs, and the paradise heavens shook constantly. Uniyod was no more, for he laid down his life for his secret master, Lucifer, the son of the morning. And so, in the battle against the angels of Mathey, many angels were lost, good and bad; they disintegrated with no return. The Lucifer rebellion continued as their leader and his mighty weapon lead them to the gates of Zebul, the sixth realm of the paradise heavens. Lucifer raises his hand and utilizes his cosmic power to crush the gates as he and his soldiers make their last stand in Zebul.

War in Zebul, the sixth realm of heaven

The bloody angelic war continued as Lucifer and his soldiers made it their destiny to display victory over God. Having lost five-hundred soldiers to the angels of Mathey, Lucifer continues his revolt with his remaining one-thousand soldiers who protect him and fight their hearts out to aid him in making it to Araboth to murder the universal architect. The angels of Zebul were tough and would not surrender without a fight that pleased their hearts. Lucifer and his soldiers stood before the forces of Zebul, and knew that their battle was far from done. Lucifer looked upon his enemies, and said, ***"Why must you foolishly defend your false god, for we have smote many of thy brethren, but these are not my true wishes. I only seek to bring true balance to the universe, cease this insolent behavior, for I do not wish to strike you all down, I have weakened the nations of paradise, I need not do it again, if you all would simply join me and know that I am the one and only leader that is able to lead***

my people to victory over this universal tyrant!" The angels of Zebul charged as Lucifer saw their actions and assumed their answer. Lucifer said, ***"Very well then, my brethren, you leave me no choice but to exterminate all of you!"*** Lucifer raised his hand, and manifested a thousand great, strong and mighty steeds of fire as a decoy, and sent them rushing into the angels of Zebul immediately. Lucifer was smart and knew great strategy, for he predicted their movements and set his soldiers to strike on his command. Just as Lucifer anticipated, the angels of Zebul were truly foolish enough to teleport around and between the fiery horses, and when he saw this, he gave the command, and murdered a significant amount of the angels of Zebul with swift attacks. And although he easily and swiftly killed many of them, the battles were never short, and the cost of such long battles would cost him the lives of countless angelic soldiers.

And although this war was great in power in numbers, Lucifer would successfully make it to his destination after much perseverance over his enemies. The King of Evil made his mark in paradise, and there were none like him, for his heart was set on murdering God, and ruling the source of the east, west, north, south, height and depth of all existence. He lost another five-hundred soldiers to the angels of Zebul, but the battled continued, and Lucifer's army was triumphant as they valiantly made their way to the very place that contained the all-in-all. Many sacrificed their lives for him, and stayed behind to assure victory and clearance for their leader. Angelic blood soaked the grounds of heaven, but all for a reason that one angel could not let go. Pride and power along with his own jealousy drove his wings to ascend above his enemies and slay his own brethren whilst defying his father, and rebelling against all that was good. His hate and anger snared at the mortal creatures that God had patiently blessed and loved, for he would never yield to the mortal man. Mankind's greatest enemy was highly associated with all of their negative qualities, and the creator of man was highly associated with the positive qualities of mankind. Good versus evil, the ongoing struggle between two mighty forces, one being absolute, and the other simply becoming the grand embodiment of the absence of all things good, pure, excellent, and consummate. The great king of things evil finally made it to the gates of Araboth with his five-hundred followers, and just knew that the time to rule had come without doubts.

God & a Devil in Paradise, the end of war in Araboth

And so, Lucifer and his one-thousand soldiers were no more, for he'd lost many of them to the angels of Zebul, and lo, only Lucifer and five-hundred fallen soldiers quickly make it into the realm of Araboth where he and his soldiers are greeted by the divine architect himself. The divine architect looks at Lucifer and his soldiers, and says, ***"Your pride shall be your end, my sons. You were once beautiful and full of righteousness, and in due time, you changed all that. I watched as you changed and came to the conclusion that I was a fool amongst fools. I need not defend myself, for you cannot lay a finger upon that which created you. Cease this nescient revolt, my sons. Otherwise, I will have no choice but to cast you out of paradise, for your own good."*** Lucifer laughs, and says, ***"Ah, I see that you await the wings of death, O master of foolishness. My serpent spear awaits the moment to taste the sweetness of your defeat in battle. My serpent spear is the very weapon that will be your undoing, Master!"*** Lucifer levitates into the air and raises his serpent spear over his head, and says, ***"Your rule is over, creator of existence!"*** The serpent spear attacks the almighty God, and finds that it is unable to penetrate the thin layer of light environing him.

As Lucifer continues to attack with his serpent spear, the

divine architect is neither touched nor harmed by any of its attacks. The divine architect turns his back to Lucifer, and says, ***"Unto you was given great power, intelligence and beauty. How art thou fallen from heaven, O Lucifer, son of the morning! How art thou cut down to the ground, which didst weaken the nations! For thou hast said in thine heart, I will ascend into heaven; I will exalt my throne above the stars of God: I will sit also upon the mount of the congregation, in the sides of the north. Your heart has displayed the most confused of thoughts, for there is none above me, and there is no weapon that can break the purity of the divine good. For I exist in everything, and amongst all things, you have decided to cast me from thy heart. It is on this very day that you and those who follow and believed on you shall leave paradise and suffer amongst those you hate, the same that have dominion over thee and the same that thou art subject to by the mention of my holy name."*** Lucifer continued attacking him, and even resorted to screaming loud profanities. The divine architect lifted his hand, and said, ***"The time is come, my sons."*** The powerful force of his command rippled the realms of heaven as Lucifer and all who followed him were cast out of the heavens with haste. A portal to earth opened all over heaven, and Lucifer along with his followers, both wounded and dead were speedily sent through all of the portals. From a distance, the inhabitants of earth could see mass lightning fall from the heavens and cast fire to the ground. The fallen angels who deceived their creator crashed into the earth. They all tasted the solid of earth only to rise up from it and look into the heavens whilst cursing the name of God, and taunting him with disrespectful hand gestures. Amongst Lucifer was all those who followed and aided him in his revolt against God. The followers of Lucifer turned around and looked toward their leader with countenances filled with disappointment.

Lucifer looked at his followers, and said, ***"Worry not, for this is only one battle lost, for the war is far from over, my***

brethren. Although we no longer have his paradise for a home, I am your leader, and I shall fashion a home for us all, for my power is great, and I shall not leave thee astray as our creator has.*"** Lucifer lifts his right hand toward the firmament and rips a hole into reality, and says, ***"Follow me, my brethren, and a place for the opposing is but a blink away." The fallen followed their leader into the rip in reality and ended up in limbo. One of Lucifer's followers looked at where they were, and said, ***"What in the galaxy will we do in limbo?!"*** Lucifer replied, saying, ***"Watch and learn, my brethren. Today is the day that my kingdom is formed so that we may strategically rule the heavens in due time. This place I shall call*** **"Sheol."** And so, the mighty son of the morning stretched forth his left and right hands, and out of his palm came bursts of lightning that began spreading all throughout the limbo. And from the power and mind of Lucifer came the realm of Sheol, home to the fallen who had deceived the universal creator. Within the blink of an eye, these were the places of evil: ***Rhythium the Hated, Uorium the Angered, Hitisum the Jealous, Hythurah the Envious, Nuvuyol the apathetic, Rhavulor the unforgiving, Yangyinoum the self-exalting pride, Lufthremn the lustful, Decetum the Deceitful, and Auhutukulm the Unreasonable.*** The followers of the son of the morning were in awe, for many of them were powerful, but were unable to manifest on a large scale such as his manifestation of Sheol. The fallen plagued the earth and took human females to have sexual intercourse with, and bear demons and half-demons. The fallen of Sheol were fruitful and multiplied, and so, the five-hundred warriors were given titles, authorities, and grew to become many as Lucifer ruled Sheol as king of the fallen with the serpent spear by his side. In due time, Lucifer became so arrogant and pride-driven that he left Sheol with his serpent spear, and hid the serpent spear in a meteor. He then spoke to himself, saying, ***"When I have chosen a disciple to carry on my legacy of malevolence, then, and only then shall this endlessly wandering meteor land upon the earth and reveal the***

mighty serpent spear unto my elect, for if I am unable to participate in my own plans, I shall elect a disciple to continue my works under my guidance." For countless years, the demons of Sheol plagued mankind with their loathsome presence, but soon enough, there would be a man with such a righteous heart, that the divine architect would give him and his bloodline the responsibility of ridding the world of the contents of Sheol. And so, the Great War had its consequences, and although the fallen were cast out, they were far from done, for the great plan to put an end to mortal ascension had just begun.

Chapter 2

A Page from Namsilat's journal

(This is the personal journal of Namsilat Powers, and the story before the generation of his son and his son's sons. Namsilat documented some of the events that led to the future of his bloodline, his realization of the existence of "God," and how he learned and came to know of the first divine force known to man as "God.")

(I was just like you, yes; you. I can see your eyes gradually reading my words. My name is Namsilat Powers and something divine walks with me and watches over my existence. I would one day hope that the father of all mankind would bless me with something that would define what I am. Through my blood, an army of holy warriors will fight the devils and the world will have a true defense against forces not understood by regular men. With the little life left in my body at this moment, I ask you now, O Divine architect, grant me the knowledge to take subtle form and battle the devils called "anger," "jealousy," "apathy," "envy" and so forth, give me the strength to send these devils back to the depths of the abyss where they belong. Put cosmic strength in my blood and put the principles of your footstool and the wisdom of your kingdom into my blood, and I vow to serve you for all eternity. The death of my parents have not caused me to submit to evil or anger, they have submitted my life to doing perfect reverence unto your throne. Make me whole and I will live even after passing through transition, selah.)

I know some of your thoughts. I comprehend your syllogistic reasoning. I was just like everyone else, until those great horns sounded, and my mind was automatically attuned to the divine voice that springs forth from the never ceasing vivificate flame existing throughout all living creatures. Everyone has a story; however, this is an esoteric story. I was like the average child, I played with my toys and I limned cartoon characters on small pieces of paper like many children do. Have you ever noticed that voice that speaks deep inside yourself, but for some strange reason, you never listen to it? Well, we don't listen to it because we have all fallen from grace, for we have all come short of the grace of God. And because we have, he speaks and we fail to listen. As a child, while playing with other children, I would hear that voice, a voice differentiated from the average mental voice human beings utilize when speaking to themselves. It would quickly speak out and reveal itself, and then it would quickly vanish and veil itself. It became apparent when I got older that the voice could speak out from any inner part of my existence, a bond that was unexplainable without the proper attunement and resources.

The voice would sometimes speak out to me from an area that seemed to be located a modicum below my chest in the area a little above my stomach. However, it was not the organs in that area, nor was it the organs surrounding that area; it was the physical counterpart and highlight of that area. I remember one day when I was playing with my friends and we were riding a skateboard. We would ride it with our knees on it, instead of riding it with our feet upon it, for we were truly too young to seriously use a skateboard the proper way that it was intended to be used. However, everyone took their turn and rode the skateboard and had their fun, not one of them got hurt, but now, it's my turn to ride it to the pole on the corner of our street. I got on the skateboard and prepared to push myself along the way with my hands like everyone else did. Before I began to use my hands and arms to push myself on the skateboard; it happened, that voice spoke aloud inside of me, and said, ***"You are going to hurt yourself, my son."***

I wasn't familiar with that voice, so how could I have trusted its verbal content, would you trust it if you were seven years old? In most cases, no, you wouldn't. And so, I went forth and ignored the voice as most children would, and of course, I hurt myself, my fingers on both hands got caught in the wheels, and I was riding the skateboard on my knees, therefore, when I hurt both of my fingers, my first thought was realizing the pain in my fingers, and to bring my hands to my full attention so that I could know my next move. Most likely that would include going upstairs to my mother so that she could tend to my fingers. Consequently, the line between pain and reaction to pain is very thin; therefore, when I realized the pain in my fingers, I was unaware that the rest of my body was still on the rolling skateboard. Well, my weight tilted the skateboard and not only did I hurt my fingers, but I went head first into the mighty concrete.

And at this point, I screamed to the top of my lungs, and of course, at that moment I wished that I had listened to that voice. But how did it know I was going to hurt myself? Why did it speak to me as if I was its child, a voice; a voice that sounded like a nurturing mother and a wise father combined into one great voice. Who are you? What are you? Why are you trying to help me? Where are you, are you there? Where did you go? I was pure, and a woman had not known me, for I was only a little boy, unaware and bereft of most of the filth of the mundane world. A pure channel through which divinity could shine brilliantly, however, my mind was not developed to truly comprehend the world of the living in which I was residing with the rest of humanity, my mind was filled with pure planes of untouched subtle land that was perfect for the small garden that the divine architect of the universe would utilize to plant subtle seeds in my mind. Eventually, I would prove to be worthy and pure enough for him to plant his rose garden in. Surely they would bloom after receiving the brilliant light of knowledge and the waters of wisdom. Shortly thereafter, they would serve as the foods for which the interior mystical process would take place therein. The divine architect carried itself throughout the universe and concentrated a spark of its essence within me.

I became a neophyte and was being prepared for future psychic initiations. Little did I know; the time had come for me to quickly comprehend the material world, and gradually become a great adept that would learn the mastery of life. I grew into a young man, and I had finally reached the age of fifteen when the doors to the lands of the supernal were opened unto me. Herein are the actual events that took place in my life. Many teenagers get easily swept off of their feet by the diamonds and pearls of the mundane world. Consequently, I would have been too, but before I could, I was swept off of my feet by something more valuable than diamonds and pearls, and in heaven, my number was called. I spent countless days listening to music, watching television, listening to the radio and hanging out with my family and peers. I was totally unaware of what was in store for me. In high school I was ignorant; I did not want to hear anything anyone had to say. I cut class, got into fights and I didn't attend class enough to do well on a test.

I can mentally recollect that I was unable to write five sentences about myself when a teacher would ask the class to write a report concerning things that we liked and so forth. I was missing something; I just didn't know what it was. I wasn't like other people, yet, I just could not put my finger on what it was. And I never figured it out until a series of spiritual events took place in my life. My mother was a Christian and she believed in Jesus heavily. As a child she dragged me to church, a place in which never moved me to praise or even think of God. The neighborhood I was raised in was very dangerous and I do believe that God was walking with me for a long time, I am surprised that I was not caught in the cross-fire of a shooting or something of that matter, especially since people were passing through transition by murder for countless reasons having to do with drugs and robberies of all kinds and sorts.

However, somehow I am here telling you my story. Being poor was everyday, my family never had enough money to do much of anything. I see children today, and I think to myself, and say, ***"They are very fortunate to have so much."*** In my day, I didn't have much, and not having much was too obviously persistent with my household. I could never afford a haircut and my brother was a barber. I suppose the cosmic sets certain things to happen for us by placing small fortunes in our family, friends or environment. And so, I was blessed to have anything since my parents were unable to afford many things. My brother sold guns and drugs when my mother and father got into a big argument and my father left us for a while, with reasons only he and my mother know. However, my brother made more than ends meet and eventually my father returned.

My brother bought me cloths and so forth, however, everything seemed to be the same thing all the time. My brother and my mother taught me everything I know; however, my father taught me how to tie my shoelaces. Life seemed to be just about as good as it would get for me. I can mentally recollect all of the fear that I had in my life sometimes, including people shooting large guns on the roof of the apartment building that I resided at with my parents, which made me hop out of my bed and get scared in the middle of the night. My imagination as a child was average, however, it seemed a little more solid, and I seriously sought to make things of my imagination manifest. I would sometimes sit on my bed trying to achieve an understanding of myself. And as I stared off and thought to myself, I saw the bars of my bed bend inwards from the corner of my eye, almost as if it responded to the destination of my thoughts to my inner-self. I turned my head to look, and they went back to their original state, and of course, I ignored it. I told myself that it was nothing at all, and that I was seeing things.

Maybe I was; maybe I wasn't. My brother who was so much of a thug and a gangster became enlightened in God since he had been through many religions and so forth. He had also gotten older, and in that time I was the average teenager; so I thought. In due time, my brother told me about this book he was reading, it was called ***"The Key of Solomon the King."*** It was a book excavated and translated a high count of decades ago. I didn't pay him any mind, however, a day came where I was around the house doing my usual nothing, and something happened. I got up and went to the living room.

I looked out of the window and saw the same thing I always saw, a few killers and hustlers on the corner in front of our local bodega across the street from my apartment. In time, I moved away from the window and began to think to myself as I always did. Of course, I came to no conclusion of anything, nor was I happy at the moment, besides, it wasn't like I was ever truly happy about anything; I cared even less for my own life. I didn't care about anything pretty much. I hated school and I hated my life. I hated being in poverty, though it taught me many lessons on how to survive without having much, a priceless lesson that can only be attained through experience. My parents didn't try to hide our poverty like the parents of today do. I was well informed by word of mouth and by eye that I was a child of a peasant and poor family, though my father was no farmhand.

And though we were considered a peasant's family, I was destined to comprehend the King of king's family, the cousins, aunts, uncles, brothers and sisters that I never knew of. As I sat in the living room contemplating my life, I realized the book that my brother told me about, I picked it up and I opened it. It had very nice pictures in it, circles with a written language that I have seen before, but never gave any true acknowledgement to. I ignored the writing in the book and basically acknowledged all of its pictures; things of which I figured were just a bunch of gibberish. However, I was wrong. I began to draw one of the pictures in it; it was called a *"Pentacle."*

I drew it to perfection, just as the book had it; I limned it in blue ink with one of my pens from around the household. And as I began to write the last letter in the pentacle, I stopped and realized some numbers, and next to the numbers was the name of a particular planet in our solar system. I read the contents and it said something that I had never heard before. When I read it, I said to myself, ***"Is this book serious?!"*** I then became captive to the contents of the book, and I realized that I was holding a magic book, a book of the king's magic. I then read and read the contents until I had a comprehension of what it was about, at this point, I realized that the pentacles were powerful agents to evoke and invoke angels and archangels from all over the universe. The book was equipped with the time and day that the angels and archangels would be presiding over. I was amazed; the words in the book were words that linked consummately with my heart's intent. I was astounded, and then, something happened. I was startled, divine plans were thrown into my mind like a baseball being thrown into the air. Could you guess what happened next? I bet you couldn't, because I couldn't. ***"Everyone has a Story, but this is an esoteric story."***

I heard the sound of subtle horns, I looked up, I looked around, and I got up and left the living room. I opened the front door and I still heard the horns, but they still weren't coming from inside of the building or someone's apartment. I ran down four flights of stairs and checked every tenant's door;

I thought I was going crazy. I ran back up the stairs and went back into my apartment while still hearing the horns. I raced up and down the hallways of my family's apartment and found nothing. I even proceeded to my mother's room and finally had the nerve to ask her if she hears the same horns that I hear, she says, ***"Boy! Are you losing your mind?***

There aren't any horns; I don't hear anything! Are you crazy?" I rushed back to the living room while still hearing the horns, and I finally sat down and received what I had not known I would receive. It happened, I heard the universal architect's voice, and he said, ***"Behold!"*** The visions I saw when I began to read the contents of the book became deeper, I saw visions of myself having the power of telekinesis and the ability to soar through the air like a bird. And there was a woman there whom stood on the ledge of a high mountain; I suppose she was a grand part of life that I hadn't known about yet. As I flew through the skies near a tall mountain, I saw myself do something that I knew I couldn't have imagined with my own imagination, especially since I was so ignorant and dull in my teenage years. I couldn't believe it, I flew into space and I went to a place that I couldn't recognize especially since it all happened so quickly. I obtained two golden pillars from an unknown place, and I raised my hands; and the pillars of gold followed me. There I was, flying back toward the earth while dragging two golden pillars behind me.

Between my hands and the golden pillars was a flow of blue electricity which acted as large chains through which I could carry them back to the high mountain where it all began. I arrived at my desired destination, and I made the golden pillars defy gravity. I raised my hand and the uppermost point of the mountain was removed, and the surface became flat. I took the two golden pillars and placed one on the left and one on the right corners of the flat mountain surface. I pointed the index finger of my right hand at the space between the two golden pillars, and a great stone door engraved with a pentagram appeared. I noticed something whilst these events were taking place however; there were two great eyes of light in the sky watching everything that I had done.

As I was close to finishing my works, the ledge that the woman was standing on began to crumble, and she began to fall, I noticed her fall and came to her aid, and she grabbed my hand; yet, she said nothing to me. As she grabbed my hand, I touched her and she began to defy gravity as well. In that time I realized that my works were far from done. I left her there, and said, ***"Amazing is his power."*** I then flew off to finish my works, and when I was done, there was a great palace on a high mountain that was beautiful. I grabbed her hand and we lowered ourselves onto the grounds of the palace. She looked around and said nothing. I looked around and I was amazed. I thought to myself, saying, ***"Behold, a place where man and angel can exist in peace as one body and no longer would we be called humans, for humans and angels would be equal."*** After speaking to myself, we went further into the palace, and there were two thrones, one for her and one for me. We sat down and angels appeared. Afterward, high initiates appeared and a table forged with holy energy appeared, and as the table appeared, there were foods meant only for the gods. They all ate and talked as I sat and watched as they enjoyed living life with the benefits of mortal ascension while they celebrated it.

You would think that these events are a very pleasant dream; however, I want to inform you that my eyes were open, and I was apparently in a trance of some sort. When I realized what had happened, I tried to ignore it and I shook my head in an attempt to shake it off and not believe it. However, as much as I would like to deny it, the Clavicula Salomonis opened a door in my mind that I couldn't close. When I looked down at the key of Solomon the King, I thought to myself, and said, ***"What exactly just happened here?!"*** In a few hours, I read through the book and I finally put it down later at night. Something was unlocked inside of me, when I saw those pentacles, I started to remember, but what exactly was it that I was remembering? Was it a life that I had before the life I currently live? What was it?

Was it the future? I had no idea at that point in time. Consequently, in due time, I became fascinated with metaphysiology, or what is now termed and known as *"metaphysics."* I waited patiently to see my brother again, and when I did, I began to ask him strange questions about any other books he might have, and to be honest, I had no idea why, of course, I don't think he did either. He pretty much didn't have any other books relative to the key of Solomon. I believe the cosmic knows exactly what is planned at all times; therefore, I was looking for more books without knowing the real reason why I was looking for more books. As time went on, about a year later I met up with a Rastafarian brother named Yahti Bailey, and his esteemed and powerful spiritual brother, Asu Bailey. I had seen them around for a long time, they were just about the only family of Rastafarians in my neighborhood, and they too were poor. I always saw them while walking through the neighborhood, and I always said ***"Hello"*** whenever I saw them, besides, it was always polite to show manners even to those who showed you none whatsoever. It wasn't just polite; it displayed strong characteristics.

However, the divine architect sent Yahti Bailey to me for a quite sufficient reason. You wouldn't believe that the books that I was looking for were close to me; Yahti had a large bookshelf amount of spiritual and magical text dealing with **ontology** and so forth. I met up with Yahti at my brother's music studio where Yahti's brother was currently working for a little experience and a few breadcrumbs to put in hip-national bank, in other words, his pocket. However, when meeting up with Yahti Bailey, a strong spiritual ally was found. We began to talk, and all of a sudden, something in the conversation ended up leading us into a book called, ***"The Key of Solomon, or the Clavicula Salomonis."*** We began to talk more and more as the days continued to pass. He wanted to know how I read and gained access to that book, and I told him after a while.

In due time, we got closer and did meditations together and so forth, my knowledge of magic had ascended. After a while, Yahti and I were definitely a great combination of spiritual warriors. I learned much from Mr. Bailey. Things were beginning to become much clearer than they were months ago. After months and months of friendship, I became a regular household guest. And in that time, I became powerful and wise. Someone who had basic problems expressing his self and writing five simple sentences about his self had actually advanced to a higher degree of writing. First, I could hardlyly write, and all of a sudden I could write five pages based on one sentence. After a few months, I began to have experiences with the supernal forces of our world. We always see movies pertaining to spiritual things, but not one of them is as serious and real as this story that I tell you at this very moment. After a while, my brother and his friend Mike Melville had taken me to a bookstore that was located in downtown Brooklyn, New York. The bookstore was called *Merkaba.* My brother's friend I hadn't known much about, but what I did know is that he, my brother, and I were on a similar path of spirituality.

However, I realized that my path must have some serious purpose to it in that all of the people who were around me were well at or over the age of forty years. I thought to myself, why be it that I attained this knowledge at such a young age? I then began to believe deeply that I was simply evolving as a human being. I possessed knowledge unknown to many at a very young age, therefore, I also believed that throughout the years I would become more than just a man, I would become a master of the arts and wield even greater knowledge than that of my earlier years. Technically, I was more or less a paradigm of what man used to be when he was closer to supernal forces. While at the Merkaba bookstore, I met a man that Yahti and I referred to as *"the ball of fire."* His electromagnetic field was awesome, he held strong cosmic vibrations in the cells of his body, and that wasn't hard to see at all.

When you entered the bookstore, there was a powerful trace of unexplainable vibrations. As we stood there in the store and looked around, I began to move quickly while knowing what books to purchase; I was unaware that there was an opposite key to the Clavicula Salomonis. The opposite book was called, *"The Clavicula Salomonis Regis,"* yet I picked it up along with various books while Mike and my brother stood there watching. Mike and my brother didn't know what to say when I began to pick up all of those books, they hadn't really known what they had come there for; they just knew that they wanted some books having to deal with the spiritual dimensions of life. But there I was, picking up books that only interior intuition could guide me to. My brother and Mike were still standing there, and I overheard the ball of fire say to them, ***"I see you are raising a young neophyte."*** My brother and Mike responded, saying, ***"Yeah."***

The truth was that I don't even think that they knew what I was doing because I didn't know what I was doing to a certain extent. That day we all returned home in Mike's truck, and ate some vegetarian food while reading the books we had purchased; most of them were mine. However, I ate very little and tossed myself into the lesser key of Solomon the king. Mike told me at that moment that I should eat and not look too deeply into the books because I may not be able to handle it, however, he was somewhat right; I just didn't know that he was. After that day, I put double overtime into reading and becoming strong on the psychic plane of existence. One night while I was eating some rice & beans that my mother had made with some baked chicken, I sat there with my television off, and for some strange reason, I kept staring at my sock drawer, the sock drawer that I had used for my socks; *all of which were white in color.* I stared at the sock drawer, and while I was eating, I cleaned it out and I carried it to another part of my room facing the east where the sun rises. Then, I took all of the socks out, and placed all of my books inside of it. I prayed on it every day since the day I cleaned it out. I found it a modicum strange that the small dresser that was only used for white socks ended up becoming the altar to God that I would pray on daily. After two days, I engraved a pentagram and some God names in Hebrew on it.

It became the secret place where I would tell all and learn all. That place was the humble abode of the pure souls of men, and the presence and essence of the universal master initiator. Eventually, my mother who was a Christian walked into my bedroom and saw the books that I was reading and told me that I should not be reading those books, and that they were bad. However, I never listened to what she said; I thought I knew what I was doing.

Then, she walked out of my room, and at the time I was reading Goetic Evocation; a book that I borrowed from Yahti. After my mother left, I fell into a trance of some sort, and an evil spirit wrapped its evil hands around my throat and I began to lose my breath and choke. An evil spirit was strangling me. But why did it want to do such a thing? In the little bit of breath that I had, I began to think to myself, and I said, ***"My mom was right, I have to call her so that she can help me,"*** and at that moment, when I thought to call her, I opened my mouth and no words came out. At that point; I really got scared and realized that when I tried to talk, only gasps for air would come out; no words whatsoever. It was time for me to be deeply worried; however, I began to remember what I had learned in the greater key of Solomon the king. I began to call off the hidden names of God to myself, and the spirit began to slowly loosen its hold on me, and finally, it was gone. I sat up breathing and trying to figure out what had just happened. But I couldn't, I wasn't experienced enough. Of course, after such a surprising event, I came to one conclusion. ***"In the time of a likely demise, there is truly only one thing that can save your life; the three-fold form of one supreme intelligence."***

One month had passed, and little did I know that more spiritual events would take place in my life. In my old neighborhood, a religious store opened-up, and I began to attend that store so that I could purchase spiritual tools for the great works ahead of me. At the religious store I met an old man who asked me to refer to him as ***"Mr. Fitzroy,"*** and of course; I did just that. We became great friends; I guess it was a little strange for me to be friends with a man that was well over seventy years old. Well, believe it or not, I was. I went to see him every day, and every day I learned more, and became stronger. We spoke every day, but he noticed that my electromagnetic field was giving off some sort of stress or anger over the circumstances of my life. Therefore, he sought to help me attain equanimity. Every day was pretty much the same, every day I would spend time with Mr. Fitzroy, and hold long conversations concerning the divine being known as God.

I noticed that he was a modicum scared of the evil flowing through the streets of the neighborhood that we were in. However, I served more than one purpose hanging out with him. I knew everyone in the neighborhood, good and bad. I would also be a sort of protector of mystical tools. Mr. Fitzroy knew me well, and was comfortable with letting me hang around the store all the time. I was a young mystical lion, and if I had to, I would protect him, even though he was not a family member. To me, he was my spiritual brother, a bond thicker than pure blood. He taught me much, and after a few months, he asked me to do an experiment at home, he told me to stare into the mirror at my altar and stare until I could see the countenance of *El shadai.* I tried, however, I didn't succeed in that experiment, I wasn't strong enough to do so, he must have thought that I was a ***"class A"*** human. In other words, a higher class of evolved humans, however, I cannot say that he was wrong, but I can say that I had the cosmic nature heavily operated in my inner parts. In any event, he pulled out a book called ***"The 6th and 7th books of Moses."***

He then showed me an experiment where I would pray to God while saying the ***91st psalm*** of the bible every day, three times a day for as long as possible. And of course, I did exactly that. I hadn't known exactly what I was doing; all I thought I was doing was respecting my elders and following orders as I was told. Mr. Fitzroy knew what he was doing, and it worked. Before I knew it, I was entering my second encounter with a supernal force, and it truly was a heavy one. One night, I retired while doing my new mental exercises. My mental exercises were to contemplate all divinity until I was at rest, and so, I did just that. I turned the lights off in my room, and then, something happened, I began to fall into the infamous trance just like the trance that I fell into when I realized the contents of the key of Solomon the king.

Afterward, I realized an energy slowly gathering at the right side of my room door. Of course, mystic or no mystic, I was inexperienced and I ignored it like anyone else would. The energy had many colors, almost like the colors of a rainbow.

The energy began to gather into a center, and I turned my head and paid it no mind. Then, I felt a strong presence, and I looked to the right side of my room door and there he was, a little green man of some sort with a long gray beard. Then he disappeared and appeared again, no longer was he at the right side of my room door, he appeared in front of my altar and stood there with a smirk on his face. The smirk on his face gave the impression that he was unwilling to let anyone know his thoughts by glancing at his countenance. Being supernal intelligence, he was not going to give me an easy understanding of why he appeared or what he was doing there.

After the whole experience with the divine creature, I told Mr. Fitzroy about it and he turned around and grabbed a capsule, he then filled it with mercury and gave it to me, it was pretty heavy, but then again, it was liquid metal; it would be heavy. I took it and said, ***"Whatever it was that you told me to do; it worked."*** I then said, ***"I saw a little green man with strong powers that I would've never imagined in my own mind."*** Mr. Fitzroy's eyes opened wider, and he said to me, ***"Ah...you have seen a fallen angel. Here, let me show you."*** He then opened the 6th and 7th books of Moses to show me the experiment that I had completed. It was so strange, especially since I never bothered to read which experiment I was doing, I simply followed the orders that were given to me. It turns out that the psalms of the bible have very potent powers that can be used for more than simply praying. Further in the day, after being amazed and leaving Mr. Fitzroy, I took the capsule of mercury that he gave me, placed it in my altar, and left it there for any great works that might come up and allow me to use it for good. After that day, I visited Mr. Fitzroy again, and this time, my electromagnetic field was totally different. I walked into the store, and he said, ***"Your vibrations have changed!"*** I was about to pull a few dollars out of my pocket to buy some spiritual tools, and he stopped me and began to immediately grab things and put them in a bag, he basically gave me a lot of things. Before I knew it, I was carrying a plastic bag full of spiritual instruments and ***incense*** back to my family's apartment.

I then continued my journey; and one day Mr. Fitzroy told me that the shop wasn't making enough currency to stay in business, besides, I am more than sure that my little bit of money went into that store more than anyone's money. And so, he was going to be leaving soon. I shook his hand and we hugged each other, and that was the end of my mentoring by Mr. Fitzroy, an old member of an ancient brotherhood. After Mr. Fitzroy and I departed, I went home and there was a staff of wood that I had obtained from my brother, and on it I engraved the names of Archangel Michael and archangel Metatron in the Hebrew language. I wrote their names on each tip of the staff. I kneeled down to my altar, and I had shed great tears for all of humanity, for they know not what they do. I prayed for one hour and I felt the pain of everyone who had died in the past and the present. I felt the pain of those who had lost their loved ones for whatever reason, and even today, I can still feel the pain and the hurt of all hearts, I bear a great responsibility upon my shoulders, for I had held the weight of the world on my back and my back had truly been cracked down because of the enmity and sorrows of many. I attained a gift from the divine architect, the ability to feel the hearts of my brethren and fellows.

And it didn't matter whether they were complete transgressors or pure hearted individuals. Well, after a long experience, the time passed and I had finally reached a much older age in my life. Later on, I had met a woman who was very pretty; I spoke to her and proceeded to date her. After a year, she became a modicum manipulative, however, I would not stand for a manipulative woman or relationship, and I kindly let her know that. We became very close and began to love each other, she even got pregnant, however, it was not meant to be I suppose, especially since she had a miscarriage. One night, she caught a cab over to my apartment, and we just laid there holding each other. One day she complained that she had a severe headache, and because I deeply cared for her, I sought to heal her. And so, I tried to do just that. So I put my hand in front of her brow and concentrated. I began to feel energy vibrating around my hand. And of course, I could see it all happening in my mind while I was focused, but something startled me. She moved my hand, and said, ***"Stop babe."*** Of course, I didn't let her know what I was doing, so I said to her, ***"Why did you say stop?"*** She replied, saying, ***"I can feel the wind from your hand."*** I was completely surprised; I had no idea that I had become that strong; she actually felt wind come from my hand.

And so, I put my hand down and stayed quiet. If she didn't want me to heal her, I could not disagree with her will. Another time arose where my knee had experienced a modicum of pain and it began to bother me, and I told her that it hurt so much that she would rub it and care for it. Well, she did, she put her hand forth and my knee was relieved of its pain. Then she said, ***"This is the power of my saints, babe."*** I didn't reply, I just asked her to get on the bed so that we could cuddle. In any event, after a year and a half, when she realized that I would not be easily manipulated, I believe she began to use some sort of magic on me. As much as I would not like to admit it, her magic worked. However, it did not succeed in its goal. I fell into a deep trance while lying down in my bed, I left my body using psychic projection, and I saw her, she then said to me that she loved me, and I said the same to her. As she said that, she reached out of a portal of some sort, and gave me a golden statue of a saint whom I had never heard of or seen.

I took the statue and placed it on my table. Then, I walked back to my physical body. As I had comfortably placed my psychic body back into my physical body, something happened. I heard noises that were purely evil. The noises sounded like the furious growls of a horrible dragon of death. The noise was so frightening that it was strong enough to scare my psychic body out of my physical body. And so, I quickly rolled out of my physical body and fell on the ground. I was terrified in the highest and most definite meaning of the word. Then, I stood up and I stood still, and then, I began to walk toward the door of my room so as to escape from the whole situation, however, the door to my room was closed on the physical plane, and on the psychic plane, even though I didn't need to utilize a door to go anywhere while in psychic form. As I walked toward the door, another terrifying event took place.

The door flew open and a dark hand of pure chaos reached out and tried to grab me. However, it missed, and there I was, standing at the center of my bedroom. The noises that scared me were getting louder and louder as if the evil content of the golden statue was going to enter our world and destroy me. As the growling began to get more violent and louder, I got scared again. Whatever was in that statue was evil and there was not an ounce of good in it, for it surely wanted me to meet a swift and terrible death, and *behold!* The symbol for Chokmah *(Wisdom)* appeared on my body and covered my whole chest in yellow light. A portal of yellow light opened through the symbol of Chokmah, and I heard the divine architect say unto me, ***"Have you forgotten what I have taught you, my son!"*** When I heard his voice and looked up, I realized that the yellow light of Chokmah had shinned itself upon the golden statue.

It was amazing; I've never experienced anything like that until that day. The statue began to disperse into particles that disintegrated. I was back in my physical body, and I arose and tapped my brother who was sleeping on the floor in the corner of my room. I woke him, and said, ***"Eddie! Eddie, Eddie; wake***

up!!" And he somewhat woke up. I said to him, ***"You wouldn't believe what just happened. Something strange just happened!"*** He replies, and mumbles, saying, ***"It's nothing, just go, go, go to sleep."*** Of course, he was totally sleeping the whole time. I thought to myself, and said, ***"Wow! He was there the whole time, yet; he was sleep."*** On that day, I learned that not everyone could psychically travel. And so, I guess you're going to say to yourself, ***"Ah, this Namsilat Powers guy was just having a bad dream."*** Well, guess what? I called my girlfriend at about eleven O'clock in the morning, and I said to her, ***"Hey babe, what is the name of that saint with the large beads around her neck and the big belly?"*** She replies, ***"What are you talking about? Oh yeah! You're talking about Saint Elizabeth!"*** I replied, and said, ***"Well, God destroyed that statue that you gave me."*** She got very angry, and said, ***"That's impossible; he couldn't have destroyed her!"*** And of course, it turned into a big argument because she tried to tell me that the God of all things couldn't destroy a statue of a saint.

However, I don't believe that it was the saint itself that was the problem; I believe it was the place wherein she had put the saints in her heart, for they were exalted above God in her heart. Why would someone put a saint before the creator of all existence? For many years she denied the God of gods and praised a saint, instead of the God of the universe. Basically, when we began to argue, she tried to downsize the universal architect like he was human or something of that matter, and the argument began to get so big that we hung the phone up on each other. Then, I realized that the reason why we were breaking up was because of our beliefs. She clearly told me that she actually made her two kids drink blood as a part of her belief?

Well, we didn't just break up because of a difference in belief; we also broke up because she tried to actually harm me by means of manipulating me through unseen magical powers. If that's not a threat, then what is? To do such a thing is to truly hurt my feelings; yes, I had attained a great power, but never had I utilized it for personal game. We had spoken for a little while longer; up until she called to tell me she had cancer in her uterus. After a little chemotherapy, it went into remission. However, we finally stopped speaking to each other altogether. She never called me again, and I called her, however, I suppose she didn't care to make amends with me. I felt that I would love all human beings no matter what. Little did I know, the time would finally come to pass, and I would learn the laws and principles that I had searched for throughout my journey for the truth about mortal men.

The slumbering walks the streets of our realm every day. I wanted to be awakened. The moment was truly and duly presented at a most reasonable time. The fire of purification was near, and in order to become purified; I had to be engulfed in the flames that would change everything in my life. *Life is but a series of mentally recorded events, and a key to death as death is a key to life-an infinite cycle only to be regulated or accelerated by a living universal and cosmic stream of responsive energy.* By that one stream of responsive energy, all consciousness is possible, and that living consciousness is in planets, stars, animals and all living creatures.

We must all find our way through a land of evil before getting to the land of milk and honey. In due time, I had finally become 20 years of age, and now, everyone that I had known to be my family was gone. In life it is so sudden and swift when loved ones are taken from you. My mother, my father and my brother had died in a horrible car crash, and the apartment was left to me and me alone. After the death of my parents, I fell into a deep sleep, and the three-fold form of one supreme intelligence had appeared unto me once again, and it said to me, ***"My laws and principles will enter into your blood and you shall pass this down to your kind, and create your own family. Those born of your bloodline will be covered by my left hand and my right hand.***

Your hearts shall stretch across the universe, and be known in my heart, awake and behold the destiny of one become many." All of a sudden, I could hardlyly remember where the time had gone. My powers accelerated, I was able to levitate, and move things with my mind. I was happy, however, I never utilized my powers for any evil, and I never showed them to strangers or family members. When I was by myself, I floated around my house, and moved objects with my mind in private. Only the cosmic, and myself knew that I was able to do so. Besides, it was important that I kept those things to myself. Who knows what someone would do or say if I were to show them my abilities? Countless years have passed, and I am no longer young, I am ripe in age. I have aged greatly. I am now the master of many lodges and secret organizations. And finally, I found myself a wife, and she had a child, I named him ***"Calabrael,"*** which means mystic warrior of divinity. Because of Calabrael, I've lost my wife, and gained a son. And so, my quest for mortal ascension had ended. I attained what I asked for, and eventually I'll leave my son when I pass through transition, and he will attain the knowledge that was given to me. Edward and Jessica Powers begot me, and I lost my brother Eddie Powers long ago, but from my blood, my children and my children's children will benefit from my sacrifices and struggles. Let mortal ascension begin with my son, Calabrael.

Chapter 3

Calabrael, the cosmic gifts and the four children

A male child was born, and behind him was an unbelievable destiny given to him by the heavens. His father, Namsilat Powers, named him Calabrael. Namsilat was a janitor in a public elementary school in *Brooklyn, New York.* Though Namsilat was a janitor, he was also a wise mystic in his time. Namsilat's wife's name was Gaia Jones, she died while giving birth to Calabrael; a sacrifice well made. Having lost his mother, father, brother and his wife; Namsilat wasn't new to the pain of losing loved ones. Namsilat allowed his loss to become a strong reason for comprehending the divine. Therefore, he made himself active in the great works so that he could harness his interior strength and abilities. And so, Namsilat would spend most of his time contemplating divinity and the manifestation of the universe at large while mopping the hallways at his job.

Namsilat was very wise, and wanted his son to be wise as well, so when he would attend meetings and so forth, he would take his son Calabrael with him in hopes that his son would quickly pick-up the great works at a young age. Calabrael would attend secret meetings with his father and was unaware of what those meetings were about until he began to get older and more conscious of his surroundings.

Eventually, young Calabrael Powers learned that his father was an active member of prominent secret organizations which spent most of their time assisting the invisible and active supernal forces of the seven heavens in the universe; namely; ***Shamayim, the first realm of heaven; Raquia, the second realm of heaven; Shehaquim, the third realm of heaven; Machanon,***

the fourth realm of heaven; Mathey, the fifth realm of heaven; Zebul, the sixth realm of heaven, and Araboth, the written home and realm of the almighty master architect of existence. Young Calabrael was a very watchful child; he watched and listened more than he spoke. Eventually, Calabrael came to realize that his father was the master of a hidden lodge in New York City.

Namsilat knew many people, wealthy and poor. As the firmament of God smiled down upon the face of the earth, one day, Namsilat contacted a few brethren and fellows to assist him in investing some money into the stock market in hopes to attain a small amount of currency in return. Altogether, Namsilat and his brethren were four in number, and the four of them put ten thousand dollars a piece into the stock market and decided to leave it there and simply put their faith in God's will. After the four invested their money into the stock market, the stocks that they invested in went sky high, and the four of them were surprised, as they came to realize that they had become filthy rich in the snap of a finger.

After their success, they split up and decided to invest their individual earnings as they pleased. Namsilat was no longer poor; he was a Billionaire. In due time, he invested in various commercial buildings and became wealthier and wealthier. When Namsilat realized that he would never have to work again, he decided to buy a large home, and below it he paid to have a large room built. After taking the proper precautions to have the stone room built, he decided to use his knowledge of the universe to fashion the world of a true mystic in one place for all of his descendants. He had the room designed so that it was hidden behind a bookshelf in one of the preceding rooms of his new home. Behind the bookshelf were stairs leading two stories down, and on the walls of the stairway were seven torches bearing strange golden flames. And so, with a wave of his hand, the bookshelf slid aside. He walked down the stairs and into the empty room with a lit candle, he then sat down on the floor with his eyes closed and began to speak to the flame of the candle, saying, ***"Here is where time no longer exists. Here dwelleth the secret place of the most high. Only the elect of universal divinity shall abide under the shadow of the most infallible creator. By the power vested in me by the universal master initiator, I command that all orders of angels appear and do the will of the consummate countenance of unimaginable light. So mote it be!"*** After Namsilat spoke his peace, the flame of the candle vivified faster and grew bigger, for as the candle vivified faster, the angelic forces of the seven heavens rushed out of the candle flame and began to use a strange purple fire to etch the universal language of cosmic symbolism all over the empty stone room.

The angels equipped the room with magical circles and magical tools made for a master of the hidden arts. And when the angels were done etching the universal language in the room, another angel arose from the flame and built a bookshelf made from mixed metals and etched the writing of the angels all over it. After that, another angel flew out of the candle flame and placed old books lost in time onto the bookshelf so that Namsilat may benefit from the knowledge of those who came before him and upheld the laws of God in past incarnations. One more angel arose from the candle flame and placed seven torches on the wall. The angel waved his hand, and the torches lit the room with the light of the purple flames of purification. And after the angels were done, they returned to the candle flame and the candle flame extinguished itself. When Namsilat looked at the room, he was far from amazed; he was blessed. And so, one night after the room was done, Namsilat brought Calabrael into the room to take a look at it, and Calabrael was astounded, he then said, ***"Dad, what is this place?"*** Namsilat replied, saying, ***"This is the room of light that exists in all of us, however, over time it has been darkened by ignorance, my son."***

On one wall of the room was a large bookshelf, and at the center of the room was a circle that had strange writings round about it. The writing round about the circle was written in the language of the angels, and it read, ***"The eternal flame shall never cease to exist within a microcosm."*** At the center of the circle was a pentagram and a hexagram interlaced and contained by a circle. Calabrael was totally unaware of what the room's contents were used for. However, in due time, the secret room would act as a main base for the mystical arts. As time took its course, Namsilat knew that the time to pass through transition was near; therefore, he set his wealth, home and the secret room to be left to his beloved son, Calabrael Powers. Calabrael was eighteen years old when his father Namsilat was near to his death. One day, Calabrael walked over to his father's bed where his father seemed to be sleeping. He sat down beside him and began to put his hand over his father's heart, and mentally say, ***"Dad, why must you leave me now?"*** Namsilat replied with telepathy, saying, ***"The time is come to accomplish the greater works of men."*** In Calabrael's heart, all the things that his father taught him would always be there. Namsilat knowing the purity of his son arose and stood up out of his bed and told Calabrael to put his two knees to the floor, and to place his brow upon the floor as well. Namsilat raised his hand, and placed it above Calabrael's body.

Namsilat's aura began to glow with purple light, and Calabrael's body began to violently shake as his mind witnessed the secret teachings of all ages, and planted them in his heart, psychic body and soul. When the shaking stopped and Calabrael opened his eyes, Calabrael was not surprised, for his father had collapsed and fell to the ground; Namsilat had finally passed through transition. Calabrael cried and cried while grasping his father's cloths tightly with all intentions to cherish his father's wishes. He realized his purpose and wiped his tears away. He stood up, picked his father's body up from the floor, and placed it on his bed. After his father's death, he soon buried him shortly thereafter; and of course, time went on without a pause.

Years passed and Calabrael carried on the knowledge passed down to him by his father, Namsilat. In due time, Calabrael exercised the secret teachings of all ages and he began to summon angels and fallen angels so as to speak with them about the past and the present. He then spent most of his life exercising the arts and crafts of divinity. One day, after a session of study, Calabrael left the secret room and went to his bedroom. Something sounded like a penny dropped, and Calabrael was startled. He turned around and looked around his room to see what had fallen to make such a noise; however, he found nothing. As Calabrael's back was turned, what seemed to be a man had appeared in the doorway, and said, ***"Ah, the son of Namsilat Powers."*** Calabrael stood still and replied, saying, ***"I sense very strong, mysterious and divine powers in you, who are you?"***

The man replied, saying, ***"I will be your mentor for the next few seconds of the minute, I will teach you the mystical arts of the universe, for your purpose is deeper than you know, Calabrael."*** Calabrael replied, saying, ***"I see that you bear the symbol of a very ancient order."*** Etched into the brow of the man's head in red holy energy was a rosy-cross, an old symbol only known to those who knew of the divine schematics of the universe. The man was wearing a black trench coat, his hands, head, face and feet were subtle, and the symbol upon his brow shined like the moon as his eyes were composed of light. The man replied to Calabrael, saying, ***"Yes, I bear the symbol of the ancient brotherhood who hath only revealed themselves to the world very few times, the true and invisible ones.***

However, that is not the subject in which I am here to discuss. There is an initiation that must take place if you are to fulfill

the fullness of your destiny. Therefore, take the position to receive your destiny at this very moment.*"** And so, Calabrael kneeled to the ground once again, and placed his brow to the floor. The mysterious initiate placed his hand over Calabrael's body, and again, more knowledge was given to Calabrael. Calabrael saw visions of nine pyramids, and inside of the pyramids, the mysterious figure guided Calabrael through their inner parts, and Calabrael's mind was perfectly enlightened to the strange voices located in the center of each pyramid. He entered the first pyramid and a voice said, ***"Behold! The cycle of life, fear not, for there truly, truly is no death." He entered the second pyramid, and a voice said, ***"We live in all that is, we exist; non-exist we cannot!"*** He entered the third pyramid and, a voice said, ***"We are limited by our laws; yet, we are unlimited because of our laws."*** He entered the fourth pyramid, and a voice said, ***"All is unveiled to our elect, for they shall consider us, and because of that, we shall consider them."*** He entered the fifth pyramid, and a voice said, ***"Make perfect the imperfect parts, and all of our laws shall be at your very direction."*** He entered the sixth pyramid, and a voice said, ***"We exist, and then, self-extend in a curve; we conformed to our law. And when we were done, the three-fold form of one supreme intelligence was produced by divine law."*** He entered the seventh pyramid, and a voice said, ***"We are the balance of all cycles."*** He entered the eighth pyramid, and a voice said, ***"We exist within and without; to and fro all realms as we continuously vibrate and propagate ourselves through all manifestations."*** He finally entered the ninth pyramid, and a voice said, ***"We are the divine laws environing and traveling through potential channels, for there are no channels unknown to us. Behold! Calabrael! Thou art the magus, the celestial intelligencer, arise!"*** After Calabrael's initiation, he had become a powerful magus, and soon enough, he would experience more encounters with the world of the supernal.

In due time, Calabrael realized that his knowledge was

very precious. He then decided to keep what he knew to himself, simply because he was wise enough to understand that the rest of the world may not agree with what he knew. Therefore, Calabrael kept to himself and began to take on a more normal life as opposed to the life that he had been living for years. And so, he decided to find himself a wife and companion so that he could settle down and leave the mystic life alone for a while.

The Sheol Rebellion

The Sheol rebellion is at hand, and *Lucifer,* the son of the morning has manifested a plan to destroy all human beings. Over the span of time, Lucifer's anger over what he believes to be God's favoritism in human beings hasn't changed. He still hates the race of creatures called ***"humans,"*** simply because they hold a very special place in God's heart.

The war that began in heaven centuries and decades ago has been ongoing for quite some time now, the struggle of ***Good versus Evil.*** In time, things have changed, however, the war between good and evil hasn't....

A worthy man named Calabrael was destined to become the father of four special children, all of whom would be born with special cosmic abilities.

The four children would be unaware of their destiny until they reached a certain age. However, from the grape vine of the spiritual realm, trouble is brewing and there must be four sacrifices in order to stop Lucifer from ruling and destroying the planet earth for the evil of demon-kind. Four sacrifices are sufficient in that the sins of man have tripled, and once again, a sacrifice is to be made for all humanity.

Times have changed drastically for humanity, and technology has made life a modicum comfortable, however, just as technology and living conditions has advanced, so has the transgressions of men. ***The laws written by the hand of God were defied, and the crimes of mankind opposed their true nature.*** The laws were written to preserve life and to keep it for a long period of time. Consequently, the gift of ***"free will"*** would be proof of how many men and women were truly righteous in the depth of their hearts. The divine architect of the universe issued a divine plan that was distributed to all human souls by arch astral energies all over heaven.

The plan gradually reached Earth, however, Lucifer hated it. He felt that angels were worthier than men. He lashed out against the divine architect and shunned his plan. Because of his hate for humans and his will to rule in the place of God, he was cast down with many angels in heaven who believed in his plan and decided to rise up against the creator of all things. The creator knew of these things and prepared his servants with the tools necessary to prove Lucifer and his legions wrong. The time grew near as a war would wage in heaven, and the Lucifer rebellion would rise up against the eternal throne of the divine architect and lose. Since that time, Lucifer and his legions have rebelled against mankind in order to get ***"even"*** with God and prove to him that his creation of creatures called ***"men"*** were not worth any of his consideration whatsoever. Therefore, Lucifer became obsessed with proving God wrong, and mocking him. It was the will of the great Lucifer to defy God and make known any reasons that would aid him in his revolt against his creator.

As the sands of time fall and turn, the almighty God of gods and king of kings has made sure that the son of Namsilat Powers has become a mighty celestial intelligencer. The man named Calabrael was given heavenly knowledge at the young age of eighteen years old. Calabrael has learned and practice magical arts and mysticism for several years, and has become a great adept, powerful and wise. He continued to practice the arts of magic and accomplished unbelievable deeds. For many years he practiced his magical craft, and for the remainder of his life he mastered mysticism because of the need to master the worlds of the universe within. After realizing the ways of the world, and his role as a man, he then married a woman named Tri-dael who he took unto his liking because she was kind hearted and her faith in God was strong. Calabrael hoped to find another mystic woman who practiced the arts that he had practiced for so long, however, he was very aware that an awakened woman who studied the arts was very hard to come by; thus, he took a woman who had qualities that a man of good stature would definitely take a liking to.

He took that woman and she begat quadruplets. Being that Calabrael attained the knowledge to utilize the magical arts of King Solomon whom spoke to and bounded fallen angels with the wisdom given to him by the divine architect of the universe, it was imperative that he keep it to himself, due to the antagonizing complexity of religious argumentation over occult gnosis dealing with the true arts absent within the holy bible. However, little did Calabrael know, the birth of his sons would call for his knowledge of the arts, and in due time, his knowledge would play a large role in the mortal ascension of his newborn sons.

The Talent to call forth living astral energies would become second nature once mastered; however, the mystical arts were not toys to play with, simply because it was dedicated to concentration and proper meditation. Thus, in time, the knowledge of Calabrael would become important to the future of the earth and its inhabitants.

Meanwhile….

Deep down in the realms of error called "hell,"

Lucifer stands in front of his legions, and says, ***"It is time for Sheol to rebel once again, the time is come to eliminate the humans, for many are their transgressions. Let us continue our revolt against the throne so that my reign will come. For it is time to correct what the throne has made wrong. This time, there will be no sacrifice for all of their sins, he will not forgive us our mistakes, but he loves those monkeys, and he gives them liberty and the power to sin and be forgiven. What foolishness! We shall undo what the throne has done! First and foremost, I have foreseen four children to be born with special talents.***

They will try to stop me and save their planet, but I will crush them and make them suffer pain beyond mortal imagination. I sense that the throne knows of my plans and this is the best that he can do; four mortals with cosmic gifts?! I will chain each child to their own element and leave them helpless so as to break their "will." They shall pose no problem to my plans. Is this how you mock me, divine architect?! By sending mortals to complete your works?! I shall rule your precious earth and return your mortals to you in pieces! I shall finally have my revenge. For now, until then, prepare to be removed from your throne, for the rule of hate and evil hath come."

Meanwhile, the Divine architect calls forth all of the angels and archangels of the seven heavens to his throne room in Araboth, and says, ***"That mortal man, I have watched him for quite some time now, I shall direct four gifts into his wife, and she will give birth to four mortal males. In her, I shall manifest the principles of my footstool into her offspring, and they will sacrifice themselves for their fellows; and in their sincere sacrifice, I will descend upon the land of living men, and cast Lucifer away for 7777 years."***

In the year 2000, On September 1st, four children were born and named, Earthael, Airael, Aquari-on and Fireael. Together, they are the children of the elements. One child has the gift to direct the energy imbuing all surfaces on all planets including earth; his power is not limited to simply directing the surface of the earth. Earthael's ability is cosmic; therefore, there is no planet existent that he cannot utilize to his heart's intent. The son of cosmic air has the gift to create and direct hurricanes wherever he pleases. Whether he is on another planet or in outer space, his ability will prove most useful. The son of cosmic water has the gift to direct the liquid called water, and to summon it from wherever it may be in a most speedy manner. He can manifest it and bring it out of its hiding. No matter where water exists, the son of cosmic water can summon it from anywhere he may be. The son of cosmic fire has the gift of pyrokinesis as he also upholds two forms of fire; destructive and purifying, one form of flame which is purple, and another that is earthly and destructive. Over time, the gifts of the four children would definitely develop in unimaginable ways. As infants, what most parents would term ***"strange events,"*** Calabrael termed ***"coincidence,"*** simply because he believed that one event can happen on earth, however, an event can take place in heaven at the same time as well. Therefore, Calabrael was used to seeing things that were extraordinary.

Eventually, Calabrael would have to explain the events of his sons' destiny to his wife who was unaware of his mystical background and the knowledge that he possessed. After the birth of his four sons, Calabrael had a vision and saw the son of the morning destroying what seemed to be New York City with a large army of demons. He was sure that his vision of the son of the morning and his legions of demons bringing havoc to the mundane plane would come to pass, he just didn't know exactly when. However, he wondered that, if it did happen, how the earth would protect itself from the attack or what was the divine architect going to do to stop him.

He went to his secret room in his home and prayed on his altar and asked God for insight on what to do when the son of the morning arrives.

And little did he know, the insight that he asked for was very close to him, closer than he could ever believe. However, he didst keep his visions to himself because he was unaware of what his wife would think or do if he would tell her about the son of the morning coming to rule earth. And so, Calabrael prayed and left his secret room so as to help his wife take care of his sons. As an infant, his son Aquari-on was very playful and watched everything his father did, no matter what his father did or said, he stared at him, having some serious interest in his father's movement. Time had passed and the four boys were growing healthy, the four boys all made 5 months, and thus, their powers began to show. Aquari-on's mother and father decided to give him a bath, and so they filled his baby-tub with soap and water and prepared to wash him.

Everything was fine at first. However, as Aquari-on's parents washed him, the water in the baby tub began to part and separate itself, and then, amazingly, the water lifted itself and poured itself back into the sink. It was amazing; Calabrael's wife had never seen anything like it. She was startled and speechless for approximately 15 seconds. She then asked her husband about what happened, and he explained.

He said, ***"Apparently, he's gifted, but now, I wonder if Airael, Earthael and Fireael have similar gifts, however, only time will tell, my dear."*** His wife began to tell herself that what she saw did not happen and that her mind was playing tricks on her. And so, Aquari-on, Earthael, Fireael and Airael grew older and made six months, and it was a regular day in their home and not one word was discussed to anyone about Aquari-on's gift. And so, Calabrael and his wife walked into their children's room, and their children were all sleeping in their cribs.

Airael was smiling in his sleep as most babies do in their 5th or sixth month. As he smiled, he began to slowly levitate himself out of the crib, and eventually bumped his head on the ceiling and began to cry aloud while tears rushed out of his eyes and began to float as well. His father was not surprised; however, his mother fainted when she saw what her son had done. She had never seen these things before, and when Aquari-on had shown his gift, she was able to trick herself into believing that it never happened; she ignored the fact that it actually did happen. Calabrael picked her up and carried her into their bedroom where she could rest.

And so, Calabrael went forth to deal with Airael so that he would not wake the others, he returned to the children's room and levitated himself toward the ceiling and retrieved his son. He rocked him back to sleep and put him back into his crib. When Calabrael returned to his bedroom to check on his wife, she was awake and she sat on the edge of the bed, and said, ***"Honey, what's happening to our kids?! Am I crazy? Did I really, really see that? Are these things really happening? If they are, then why are they happening?"***

He sat down beside her and had a very long talk with her, Calabrael tried to help her achieve an understanding of what may have happened. He proceeded and said to his wife, ***"I believe that my vigilance, diligence and will to God have somehow shown him that I am somewhat worthy to be blessed with these children. Now, I believe that you are ready for me to show you what I mean, below our house is a place that I call home and where I go to have peace of mind.***

I have seen many things, but I have never told you about

them, and for that I'm sorry for keeping secrets from you, but I did not want you to think that I was strange. I felt that you might not love me the same way you always have." His wife picked up her countenance, and said, ***"I will love you no matter what, I won't change, share with me everything you share with yourself, and I will do my best to understand you and the life you had before you met me."*** Her husband said, ***"Put the boys in their strollers and follow me. I want to show you something very dear to me, I believe it is time for me to show you what you need to know."*** And so, Calabrael led his wife and his sons to his secret room below the house where his father before him had practiced the divine arts.

And he stood before a large bookshelf at the library room in their home. He lifted his right hand, and said, ***"I am that I am."*** And behold! The bookshelf slid to the side of the left and a door was revealed, and stairs leading downward to a room. And to her surprise, it was a room filled with oils, powders, an altar, and magical circles and symbols that were engraved into the ground. There were old books that dealt with the creation of the earth and the men who dedicated their lives to the advancement of mankind's interior and exterior self.

The Books were talking about peculiar, yet very intelligent men who were incarnate on the Earth at some point in time. The books also spoke about the mystical orders that existed decades and centuries ago. Some books spoke about a man named Paracelsus, Hermes mercurius trismegistus, how to evoke supernal forces, how to make magical circles, and the background of certain angels, fallen angels and the true existence of the divine father known to very few men. His wife was astounded at the room and asked many questions. Her first question was, ***"What is this place?"*** Calabrael said, ***"This is the place that many have forgotten, the room in the heart of man that is filled with the potential to ascend.***

This room is also filled with the most ancient names of God almighty, and so, the hearts of all men should be filled with these names as well, but the world is what it is." And so, they spoke for a while, and his wife said to him, ***"Are you telling me that there is more to life than living and dying?"*** He replied, saying, ***"Much, much more."*** Tri-dael said, ***"I see..."*** He led them out of the secret room and back into their library.

He walked off and she stared at him as he walked away, she then began to ask herself questions about his knowledge. And so, time passed gradually as it always does, and thirteen years later, Fireael had his first experience with his gift while Aquari-on and Airael had known no sign of their gifts at all. However, Earthael, the potential son of Earth was doubtful and scared to have a gift. He was unsure of what he was, and began to force his self into believing that he had no gift, but little did he know; he did.

A warm summer night came, and all of the boys were sleeping in their rooms, and things ***seemed*** to be fine. And then, it happened, a great purple light began to vivify around Fireael's body. His brothers woke from their slumber and realized a bright purple light and began shouting and screaming, causing a big commotion, and saying, ***"Ma, dad! Fireael is on fire!"*** Their parents frantically rushed out of the bed and into the bathroom to fill a bucket of water. When the bucket was full enough to put out a small fire, they rushed into the room, and the noise woke Fireael out of his sleep immediately. Fireael yawns, and says, ***"Why are you people so loud?! Can I get some sleep around here, or what?!"***

As he spoke, they all stared at him, and his parents dropped the bucket of water. Fireael spoke again, and said, ***"What were you carrying a bucket of water for? Why are you staring at me?"*** Then his brother Aquari-on said, ***"You're on fire, you dummy!"***

Fireael paused for a moment and looked at his hands as he began to realize that some strange looking fire surrounded him. Then he quickly stood up, and said, ***"Get out of my way!"***

And then, he ran off to the bathroom and turned on the shower. At the time, he was unaware that the fire that surrounded him could be used two ways. One form of his fire could cleanse; the other form could destroy. The cleansing fire was purple, and the destructive fire was the color of earthly fire. And so, the shower he put himself into never stopped the wildly vivifying fire engulfing his body, and their room never got burned. Fireael's father ran to the bathroom and told him to focus his mind on world peace and eternal love spreading throughout the universe.

He tried, but he was too hysterical and hostile to concentrate at that moment, the situation became too much for his mind, and eventually he passed out and his father caught him, carried him, and gently placed him on the floor of his bedroom. The purple fire continued to vivify while Calabrael watched his son passed out on the floor. The shower that Fireael tried to put his self out with never worked. Calabrael had plenty of sense; therefore, calling an ambulance was totally out of the question, what exactly would they tell a doctor? Besides, there was always a chance that his powers would go off in the hospital.

After realizing the seriousness of the situation, Calabrael decided to use an old healing method to help him regain consciousness and calm his mind. Calabrael put his index finger on his chest where his heart would be. And within seconds, Calabrael began to glow with a radiant yellow light, and spoke to himself deep within his mind, saying, ***"So mote it be!"*** And so, he picked his son up from the floor, and carried his son to his bed, and said, ***"Watch him until I come back."***

He looked at the ceiling, and said to his wife, ***"When I***

return from my altar, he will be awake and fine." Calabrael snuck around a corner when his wife and sons weren't looking and teleported to the secret room to pray. Seven minutes had passed, and when he returned, Fireael's powers stopped, and he was awake and calm. After waking up, Fireael wasn't sure of what happened to him, and his father said to him, ***"Are you okay, Fireael?"*** Fireael looked at his father and didn't reply, Calabrael shook his head, and said, ***"hmm...Such responsibilities for these young men, but I believe in them, they'll survive."*** Fireael looked at the ceiling of his room and turned over while closing his eyes, and before the rest of his family knew it, he was asleep. Calabrael's wife was speechless and Aquaria-on and Airael had not known anything about having any powers at all. Earthael denied anything extraordinary concerning himself, yet he believed deeply in God. Though he may have not believed so heavily on specialty in himself, faith in God was enough to move a mountain with a simple thought, and little did Earthael know, in the future, he would literally move mountains with the extraordinary knowledge of the ancient of ancients (God).

After the Powers household experienced their family member jump into a shower while engulfed in purple flames that wouldn't stop burning, Aquari-on, Airael and Earthael were called to the secret room by their father. And so, they went as their father commanded. Calabrael spoke to them, saying, ***"Fire, water, and air, so I'm going to guess that Earthael is closely connected with the earth. I believe that it is time to train you so that you can direct your powers the correct way. It is without a doubt that all of you have special gifts, I want all of you to come with me tomorrow, we're going out so that you can better understand yourselves, besides, I have a small theory that I'd like to test out."*** The next day came, and their father took them to an old abandoned construction site where they could not harm anyone with their abilities, that is, if they all have them.

So, their father brought four fold-up seats and set them up side-by-side. He then said, ***"Sit down, my sons."*** The four sons of Calabrael sat down, and Calabrael said to himself, ***"I bet their abilities are operated the same way the psychic body is operated; by thought."*** First, he called Airael and told him to stand up. He then told him to visualize the clouds of the sky, and to breathe slowly while visualizing it. Slowly, Airael began to levitate off of the ground while surrounded by a small whirlwind, and when he opened his eyes, he said, ***"Oh krap! Wow! I can fly!"*** Airael was high in joy over the fact that he could levitate. He then started doing it over and over while laughing with joy. Just as Calabrael thought, their powers were dependent upon their thoughts, which also meant that they were a true danger to the planet if they were ever to become seriously angry or distraught.

If Aquari-on was to become angry enough, he could flood the earth, if Fireael was to become angry enough, he could give off a temperature that was higher than the temperature of a thousand stars, and disintegrate the earth with pure ease. If Airael became angry enough, he could cause the most devastating hurricanes, twisters and tornadoes that the planet has ever seen. And then, Calabrael thought to his self, saying, ***"I suppose there was a reason that I taught them to become anything but angry and to try their best to remain calm, no matter what. They were always obedient to my wisdom, but had they not been, then our world as we know it would have been doomed!***

They always got a little angry like anyone would, but not enough to destroy or want to harm or kill." After he thought about their potential, he asked Aquari-on to stand up, and Aquari-on stood up with an unwilling countenance. His father said to him, ***"Put your hands in front of you, and show your palms, and then, concentrate and see yourself standing over a large ocean."***

When Aquari-on did what his father told him to do, surprisingly, his eyes became completely clear and two brilliant lights appeared in front of his palms. Then, the most amazing thing happened, thunder and lightning filled the sky, and water shot out of his palms as if they were open fire hydrants. The boys began to look at each other and realize that they had unbelievable powers. Airael spoke to his father, and said, ***"Dad, why us?"*** Calabrael replied, ***"Only the divine architect can answer that question, Airael."***

But there is something I want all of you to do for me." Airael replied, saying, ***"What do you want us to do, dad?"*** And Calabrael replied while laughing, and said, ***"I want you to show this world the supreme good that evil forces have hid from them for so long. I've become ripe in age, and some young lions could prove quite worthy."*** Airael replied, saying, ***"Anything for you pops!"*** And so, Fireael was quiet the whole time these events took place, he then stood up, and said to his father, ***"If Airael and Aquari-on can succeed in using their abilities, then, maybe I can, but what if I hurt someone?***

What if we hurt each other with these abilities?" Calabrael replied, saying, ***"Follow my instructions, and you won't be worried; is this why you have been so quiet, Fireael?"*** Fireael replied, saying, ***"Uh, basically, Yea. This is not exactly something you see or do every day."*** Calabrael said, ***"As long as you can direct your thoughts without too much negativity, then, you will hurt no one, but if you do not, you will harm innocent people, Fireael.***

You are all my sons, but eventually you will get older and find other things that may make you angry or stressed, however, you must realize at that moment when you feel stress or anger, that you must remain calm at all times so as to not create more stress and anger for others. Do you know someone who would enjoy being burned or drowned? I doubt it. Therefore, you know

what you must do. And I'll not ask any of you to tap into your abilities anymore today; I want to work with each of you alone."

Fireael replied, and said, ***"Well, I guess that'll help, dad."*** And so, they all stared and looked at Earthael, and then, Calabrael said, ***"Earthael, I've not seen anything extraordinary happen to you, and I don't know if anything will, but you will always be extraordinary to me because you are my son."*** Earthael replied, saying, ***"I know that already dad, but I'm not sure I can handle what Airael, Fireael and Aquari-on have gone through, so, hopefully I'm just a normal kid."***

Calabrael replied, saying, ***"Well...if that is how you feel, then, I can't blame you for feeling that way, but if you do have abilities similar to your siblings, I will always be here for you, for now, let's go home, I think I have seen enough for one day."*** Calabrael and his sons returned home that day, and when they did, Tri-dael was in the kitchen cooking a big dinner.

She left dinner on the table and called her husband into their bedroom, and said to him, ***"I'm going to spend a few nights at my mother's house for a while honey. I need a little vacation from our house for a little while, I'll be back in about a week or so, and I'll call and check up on you guys, I'll probably be leaving around 8:00 p.m. Considering the events taking place in our house, I think I need a little bit of regular time, if you know what I mean. Between a husband with some weird magical room, and a son who has no idea why he can set himself on purple fire, I think it's definitely time for a break."*** And when 8:00 P.m came, Calabrael kissed his wife, and she left to go to her mother's house. And so, everyone raddled the pots and everyone ate, and when they were done, they retired to bed to catch a good night's sleep. In the middle of the night while everyone was resting, Calabrael woke Earthael out of his sleep and told him to follow him to the secret room; Earthael got out of his bed wiping his eyes, and followed his father to the secret room.

They entered the room, and Calabrael looked at the magical circle on the ground of the secret room, and said, ***"I feel the energy of the earth deep within you Earthael, I have had a dead rose here in the secret room for three weeks now, and well...I've been planning to crush it and make it into a powder so that I could store it away for an experiment later."*** Earthael says, ***"Where is it, can I smell it, dad?"*** His father replies, saying, ***"Over there, on my altar, would you please go over there, pick it up and give it to me?"*** Earthael replied, saying, ***"Okay, dad."***

At this point, Calabrael thought that if Earthael would touch the rose for a significant amount of time, it would be just like it was when he bought it. And so, Earthael picked the rose up, smelled it, and gave it to his father, however, the rose was still dead. Calabrael took the rose, placed it on his shelf of powders, and told Earthael to follow him back to the upper levels of the house. Earthael followed him, and they slowly and quietly walked back to the kitchen, where Calabrael told Earthael that he has abilities too, but they just aren't showing themselves yet.

Earthael quickly replies with great doubt in his mind, and says, ***"Yea right, dad."*** Earthael walks off and goes to his bed to get some sleep while his father returned to the secret room, and when his father returned; he sat down, saying to himself, ***"What is his talent?***

The rose never came back to life, so what could his ability be?" Calabrael looked around the room, and looked passed his shelf of powders, but his eyes didn't realize anything unusual. But then, he looked again, and he stood up and thought that his eyes had deceived him, but he was wrong, his eyes hadn't deceived him, *the rose was as fresh as it was on the day that he* *bought it!* At this point, Calabrael made no effort to go show his son that he did have a special gift by showing him the rose; he simply sat down and looked at the rose with good thoughts in mind.

Calabrael was happy to know what Earthael didn't, so he smiled and went upstairs to his bedroom where he could rest, and then he said to himself, ***"They are all talented, they all have special gifts from God, I couldn't think of a better gift to have other than four handsome boys that have been gifted with God's blessings."*** In due time, Calabrael fell into a deep sleep and smiled. An angel named Misticael appeared to him in his dream, and said, ***"The mighty Calabrael, son of Namsilat, little do you know, your knowledge is essential to the greatness of a great journey, time will pass, and in that time, your four boys will mature into four holy warriors, and you will give them the means to fight Lucifer, the son of the morning. Teach them well, for their will is our father's will.***

However, your sons will die in battle, Calabrael, and in their death, their holy blood will spill upon the earth and cry out to the divine architect, just as Abel's blood cried out to the divine architect when his brother Cain slew him. At that point, their blood would summon the divine architect to the earth to cast away the devils and the son of the morning for seven thousand, seven hundred and seventy-seven years. Only men with righteous hearts will be able to withstand the force of the struggle between good and evil, therefore, walk as you have always walked, and you will witness all of the things that I have told you on this very day."

At 6:00 am, Calabrael woke up, sweating unceasingly as if he was working out in a gym for several hours. He jumped out of his bed and grabbed a towel while walking to his sons' room.

And when he saw that they were okay, he wiped his brow and his face with his towel.

In due time, destiny would set itself into place, and Calabrael would do what he was told by the angel of God, called Misticael, however, Calabrael waited 7 years until all of his boys were grown, and had become men, each of them reaching the young age of 20 years-old. Calabrael decided to call them to the secret room that they had all known for so long throughout their childhood. And so they came, and Calabrael said, ***"It is imperative that you all learn to direct your powers to their fullest potential."***

He then told them that he would train each of them individually, 15 hours a day. Monday, Wednesday, Friday, and Sunday, so that he could get some rest in between days. And so, mortal ascension: An esoteric story begins.

Chapter 4

The Betrayal and the War

Monday-Fireael's Training

The time for training was at hand, and when the hours of Monday came, Calabrael called forth his son Fireael, son of cosmic flames of fire. Calabrael had finally decided to show and teach them the divine arts so that they would be well prepared to direct their powers correctly. A calm mind and positively directed thoughts would keep them from being easily defeated by demons that were well experienced in the arts. And so, he then took Fireael to the secret room and sat him in a chair engraved with strange writings on it. And strangely, another chair was facing the same chair exactly like the one Fireael sat in. The chairs were made of stone, and engraved with the writing of the angels of the seven heavens of the macrocosm.

Calabrael then proceeded to tell him that the two chairs were set up so that the two people sitting in them would have to face each other directly, and could tap each other if it was necessary. Calabrael sat in the other chair opposite of Fireael's chair. Both chairs seemed to have the same engravings on them. He then said to Fireael, ***"Close your eyes and breathe very slowly, and while breathing slowly, concentrate on a deserted island filled with only trees."*** And so, Fireael did exactly what he was told.

Before Fireael knew it, he was there. And also, to his surprise, so was his father. Fireael spoke to his father, saying, ***"Why are we here?"*** His father replied, saying, ***"To practice and perfect your gift by fighting on the astral plane of existence, however, the question is this: Are you prepared to fight me using your gift?"***

Fireael replied, saying, ***"Be prepared to get your butt whooped, pops!"*** Calabrael laughs, knowing that Fireael has no idea how powerful he is on the astral plane, and then he says, ***"Do your best, my son."***

Fireael closes his eyes and his body becomes engulfed in the destructive flame while on the astral plane. His father, Calabrael, levitated himself off of the ground and floated a midst the air with a smile on his face, and his arms folded as if he was invincible. Fireael looked at him and paid it no mind, then, he put his hands in front of himself with his palms facing his father. Aggregations of fire began to shoot out of his hands and toward his father. Calabrael had all of a sudden disappeared, and the aggregations of fire flew off into the astral sky because Fireael had no idea where his father went. Fireael was baffled, and a bit scared as to how his father had disappeared so quickly.

Fireael felt a presence behind him, and turned around. When he turned around, he was face-to-face with his father. Fireael was greatly startled and fell to the ground, while saying, ***"How did you do that?! Impossible!"*** His father replied, saying, ***"If what I just did is impossible, then you and your brothers' existence are just as impossible as what I have just done. Now, let me explain it to you, the astral body operates by means of thought, if your thoughts are definite and you are positive about what you will do; you will do exactly what you think as soon as you think it, providing your abilities allow it.***

Thus, while you were targeting me with your fire, I stayed there till I thought of dodging, disappearing and appearing behind you without you knowing anything at all. Now, if you think you will prevail in battle fighting like that, then you will fail, and be killed. The reason I brought you to this place is because your fire ability is too dangerous to practice with on the mundane

plane. Now, if you understand what I have just told you, let's begin all over from the top, okay." Fireael responded by nodding his head. And so, they fought and fought for 15 hours, and at the end of the day, they both returned to their physical bodies, and Fireael's father was very pleased at how good he had done.

After training for 15 hours on the astral plane, Fireael left the secret room so that his father could rest for a while after astral combat training for so many hours. As Fireael returned, he began to brag about the whole experience and told his brothers how cool it was, and how he learned to direct his abilities. He then proceeded to tell them how strong their father was on the astral plane. And so, on Tuesday, Calabrael rested for half of the day, and prayed on his altar for the other half of the day.

Wednesday-Aquari-on's training

After Tuesday's rest, Calabrael called his son Aquari-on to meet him in the secret room and invited him to sit in the same chair that Fireael sat in. Calabrael spoke, and said, ***"I love you with all of my heart, but the planet needs you more than I do, I did not mention to your brother that the four of you would die fighting against the son of the morning, and I will not tell any of them except for you. You are wise and I trust that you will keep it secret, my son. However, I believe that it is better to tell one of you and that one tell the others, simply because you may not all feel the same about dying to save the corrupted earth from total destruction."*** Aquari-on, being the wisest of the four was prepared to lose his life for a good and just cause.

And so, Calabrael asked Aquari-on to close his eyes and vision himself floating over a large ocean, and as soon as he heard what his father had told him, he did it immediately.

Then, he saw his father floating above an ocean along with himself. Calabrael said, ***"Let's see what you got kid."*** Calabrael put his index and middle fingers on his brow and instantly there were ten of him! Aquari-on flew high into the sky and raised his right hand with his palm open. Instantly a burst of light appeared in front of his palm, and the ocean began to ripple and become violent as if a storm was approaching. Then, a great tsunami arose and went forward to wipe Calabrael out of the picture, however, Calabrael and his duplicates held hands to form a circle, and before Aquari-on could notice it, Calabrael had disappeared.

When the tsunami went by, Calabrael was nowhere to be found. Aquari-on shouted out loud, saying, ***"I know you're here, dad! Show yourself!"*** Then, the water shook violently again, however, Aquari-on became scared because he didn't know why the water was shaking so violently, he himself wasn't doing it, and with his father being so experienced, he didn't know what to expect. To Aqauri-on's surprise, Calabrael arose from the ocean while riding on the shoulder of a great water titan. The titan's face resembled an old man.

Aquari-on was petrified and wouldn't move, but then, Aquari-on turned around, and a loud whistle sounded. A giant golden trident fell from the sky, and slammed into the ocean, causing Aquari-on to fly upward to escape the shockwave of the trident's landing into the ocean. And so, Aquari-on flew higher and higher into the sky until he reached a cloud, and then he hid inside of it. The sky became dark, and violent rain began to fall from the cloud that Aquari-on had hidden his self in. Calabrael whispered into the titan's ear, and the titan took up his trident and tossed it at the cloud that he thought Aqauri-on would be in.

To his father's surprise, the cloud that the trident went

through was the wrong one. Aquari-on was moving from cloud-to-cloud, and then, the water of the ocean began to deplete. Calabrael didn't understand how the ocean was losing water while Aquari-on was making it rain; it just didn't make any sense. Then, the rain started pouring as if it were coming from a tilted cup. ***Boom!*** Calabrael finally caught on to what Aquari-on was doing, he was transferring the ocean water to his hands, and shooting it down from the clouds so that his father couldn't see him. And so, they trained for 15 hours, and Calabrael was pleased with his son Aquari-on. After the training, Calabrael finally sent Aquari-on back upstairs so that he could prepare for Airael on Friday. Aquari-on kept secret what his father had told him, and went to his bed to rest for the rest of the day.

Friday-Airael's Training

With two days of tough training, Calabrael is finally becoming mentally fatigued from his astral combat with his sons. However, time is drawing near; the time when the son of the morning will try to rule the world is close. Airael must be trained. The son of the morning cannot be allowed to take our world; for if he does, all is lost. God has left the future of the earth in the hands of four young mortals. If they are to break Lucifer's pride and weaken his power, they must be strong. And so, Friday came forth, and it was Airael's turn to be trained in astral combat. Calabrael arose from his slumber, and called Airael to the secret room so that he could get prepared to do what is necessary. Calabrael looked at Airael, and said, ***"You are the future, but your mind must become prepared for what the future holds."***

Calabrael asked Airael to sit down in the same chair that his brothers had sat in when they were being trained. With a fatigued countenance, Calabrael asked Airael to close his eyes, and visualize a deserted island, and before Airael knew it, they were standing on the island; his father and himself. As they stared at each other, Calabrael spoke out loud, saying, ***"Airael, you must focus all of your movements on your powers, and what you want them to do. Let the battle begin!"*** In the blink of an eye, Calabrael disappeared. Airael closed his eyes and tried to sense where his father was, he then sensed him and followed the sense, his father was directly above him, he then flew around and about in a full circle in order to manifest a great tornado.

The tornado was so strong that it grabbed Calabrael, spun him around, and tossed him away as if he was a feather. Airael smiled, saying, ***"I thought you were powerful here on the astral planes, dad? If you truly are, then I must fight my best, prepare for the best of the four!"*** With a confident attitude, Airael was ready to battle with his father; however his attitude preceded his actions simply because Calabrael was far from done. Calabrael quickly recovered from the tornado and flew into the sky. He then put his hands in front of himself, and four rings of energy spun out of his palms and chased Airael away.

In order to maneuver away from the rings of energy, Airael flew up, down and forward, hoping to escape their touch. An idea hit Airael like a ton of gold; he then stopped in mid-air, and grabbed each ring individually. Then he tossed them back at his father with all of his strength, and as the rings were tossed back, Airael sent a powerful twister behind them, so as to make their speed faster than they originally were. He then teleported himself behind his father so that he could finish the job, consequently, Calabrael was too experienced to fall for it.

As the twister pushed the rings of energy toward Calabrael, he waited for them to become 7 inches close to him, and then he teleported behind his son and caused his son to be hit by his own move. The twister did not harm Airael, however, the rings of energy wrapped themselves around Airael while holding his arms and legs so that he would not and could not move.

Then, the most amazing thing happened. Airael's countenance changed, and his eyes became as clear as water. All of a sudden, a violent and dangerous wind began to blow, and a great twister surrounded him as his garments blew in the wind. He then closed his eyes and a portal opened out of his heart. A sylph ***(a spirit of the air)*** flew out of the portal over his heart, and transformed itself into pure energy in order to combine with the energy rings. At this point in time, Calabrael witnessed the mighty power of his son Airael, and when he witnessed that power, he was greatly surprised.

And in due time, the sylph made the rings disintegrate with ease. Airael was free, and ready to continue the battle between his father, and himself. Then, Airael spoke aloud, saying, ***"Dad, I think I'm getting stronger and stronger as we practice."*** Calabrael replied, saying, ***"I know, that's why I'm training you; now, give me your best, Airael!"*** Almost moving at the speed of lightning, Airael and his father clashed and slammed fist to fist. A loud sound occurred, and a ripple wiggled through the reality of the astral plane as it shook violently as if Calabrael and Airael were two holy forces to be reckoned with. Airael did so well that he and his father trained longer than they were supposed to train.

The two warriors exceeded 15 hours, and trained twenty hours, Airael's power was amazing, and Calabrael was well pleased. However, Airael exhausted himself and eventually began to weaken himself, and move slower. Though he was tired in more than one way, Calabrael continued attacking him with various moves, while Airael formed a shield around himself in order to protect himself from further attacks; Calabrael used a technique that he knew was completely effective in any battle. He duplicated himself, and no longer did Airael have to deal with one person, he had to deal with seven. Calabrael was far from done, the battle between father and son continued. Calabrael and his duplicates attacked Airael unmercifully while impinging his force field with move after move until the shield began to weaken and fade away. One last hit from Calabrael would seal the battle, however, the time Airael spent in the force field gave him time to recuperate his strength, and the battle continued as Calabrael and Airael fought valiantly as if they were mortal enemies.

The battle was finally over after hours of training. Airael was truly ready, however, he wondered to himself, saying, ***"Hmm... if my father was so powerful on the astral plane of existence; how powerful are demons on the mundane plane of existence."*** Little did Airael know, for the capture of the four was close and near. And so, Airael and his father returned to their bodies, and stood up out of their chairs, and right before Airael could leave, his father grabbed him and gave him a hug.

Then he whispered in Airael's ear, saying, ***"Lead your brothers well, do not let them fall so easily, make the son of the morning wish that he never appeared on the mundane plane, show him what mortals are made of."*** Airael left the secret room and returned to his room to rest. His brothers asked him many questions, however, Airael didn't reply. He just lied down in his bed, and closed his eyes. Earthael, Fireael and Aquari-on stared at each other, asking themselves, ***"What's with him?"*** After training with the son of cosmic air, Calabrael rested to prepare for the battle with his son Earthael, the cosmic son of earth.

Sunday-Earthael's Training

Calabrael woke up from his short rest, and before he knew it, it was Sunday. The son of earth didn't wait to be called by his father, he went to the secret room by himself, and said to his father, ***"Its time, let's get this show on the road, pops. I'll give it everything I've got."*** The two warriors visualized an island of stone, rocks and dirt, and soon enough, the battle began. Earthael ran and picked-up ample speed, and as his speed picked up, the ground beneath him began to raise itself according to Earthael's will. He waited until he was a few inches closer to his father, and then he directed the earth's surface to lift him into the air, he jumped as high and as fast as he could as he threw two blasts of green energy that raced toward his father at an unbelievable speed.

Though the blasts of energy were fast, they both missed terribly. Calabrael waved his hand, and Earthael was unable to move. Without reluctance, Calabrael telekinetically lifted Earthael into the air, and when Calabrael felt that he had raised him high enough, he dropped him. Earthael fell from the sky and worried that he wouldn't be able to land safely, so he closed his eyes and a great and mighty hand reached out of the earth, and caught him.

He then jumped out of the hand and onto the ground as if he knew that he wouldn't crash into the ground. Earthael waved his hand and commanded the hand of earth to capture his father immediately. However, Calabrael was too quick to be caught by the hand of earth. Earthael realized that his father was too fast to be caught so easily, so Earthael stomped his left foot on the ground, and twelve more gigantic hands emerged from the earth, and reached the height of the sky in an attempt to capture Calabrael. Earthael's strategy was a failure, and Earthael was running out of ideas. Calabrael spoke, saying, ***"You will have to do better than that, my son!"*** Calabrael duplicated himself, and seven images of his self appeared.

Seven duplicates put their hands in front of themselves, and shot purple energy blasts from twelve palms. The purple energy blasts stopped in mid-air, and surrounded Earthael immediately. Earthael flew into the sky in order to escape the energy blasts that were intended to home in on his vital life energy like heat-seeking missiles, so wherever Earthael went, the purple energy blasts followed. While Earthael flies around attempting to escape his father's move, his father's duplicates split-up to prepare for a final attack while leaving one behind as a decoy. As Earthael flew through the skies in order to somehow escape his father's trap, Earthael had thought of a plan to finally escape the energy blasts. Earthael flew head first into the ground, and a loud sound indicated an impact. The result of the impact caused smoke to spread everywhere. And when the smoke cleared, a small crater was set into the ground from the force and impact of Earthael's earth energy.

The energy blasts collided with the ground and exploded, yet there was no sign of Earthael, for he had disappeared. And before his father knew it, Earthael was floating directly behind him while preparing to strike him down. Earthael put his hand to his father's back and charged an energy blast that eliminated his father immediately. However, Calabrael had duplicated himself, and the Calabrael that Earthael blasted away with earth energy was not his real father, it was simply a duplicate.

Earthael became upset that he didn't win as he thought he would, he was sure that the one he attacked was his real father. Calabrael began to laugh, saying, ***"Try harder, Earthael!"*** And so, they trained for 15 hours, and Calabrael was well satisfied with his sons' mortal ascension. They reminded Calabrael of himself when he began astral combat training as a young teenager. Earthael was trained and ready to join his brothers in the struggle between mankind and fallen angels. Earthael left the secret room and retired to his bed where he could rest and contemplate the true potential of his gift while Calabrael stayed in the secret room to pray on his altar.

Finally, the four warriors were trained, and Calabrael did as the angel of God told him. It is said that a kingdom divided amongst itself cannot stand, and when the time came to pass, a demon secretly betrayed Lucifer and his plan to rule earth. The one called *"Mephistopheles,"* the one who works for the good, yet still attempting to plot much evil. Appearing in the physical form of a four-foot tall man with a black robe and the face of a snake with a rounded head, he appeared unto Calabrael in the secret room amidst a magical circle that bounded demons on the mundane plane. He then warned Calabrael that Lucifer would send four demons from one of his legions to capture his sons, so that they wouldn't interfere in his plans.

He then told Calabrael that Lucifer would take the son of fire and *chain him to the sun,* the son of water he would *chain to the bottom of the deepest and largest sea,* the son of earth would be *chained to the highest mountain,* and the son of air would be *chained by two stars in the firmament, and held at the height of the sky where no man hath ever been chained.* When Calabrael heard this, he said, ***"What is it that I can do to prevent it from happening?"*** Mephistopheles replied, saying, ***"Nothing, it has been written, they will be caught and chained away from you, wherein you will be unable to save them."*** At this point, the divine architect of the universe was sitting upon his throne in the 7th *heaven called* ***Araboth.***

He then decided to appoint Archangel Michael to free them from their states of imprisonment. He told Michael to engage in battle with each demon one by one when attempting to free the elemental children. And so, Archangel Michael watched, and waited until the time came to fulfill the will of the great architect of life. Months had passed since the elemental sons had trained; meanwhile, a familiar Archangel prepares his flaming sword for battle with the enemies of God. Calabrael, the great mystic visions a world of destruction filled with demons brutally terminating mankind as a whole, and after thinking about a world ruled by demonic forces, and the possible imprisonment of his sons, Calabrael walks into his sons room, and says, ***"Be on guard, there will be four powerful demons who'll attempt to capture all of you, and stop you from possibly ruining Lucifer's plans to take over our plane of existence."***

Fireael looks at his father, and says, ***"Dad, you trained us, and we've gotten much stronger than we were before. Besides, we're not kids anymore; we can take care of ourselves."*** Calabrael replied, saying, ***"I comprehend that you are my sons, and that you're grown now, how could I ever forget? However, I've seen evil forces face-to-face. Not one of you has an inkling of how powerful these creatures are. Demons are well-experienced and powerful beings of destruction. Some demons even believe that they may still have a chance to return to the realms of heaven. Some of them could care less about returning to the realms of heaven, and others are fixed upon destroying mankind, no matter what the cost. You must be wise and powerful, the demons of Sheol will have no mercy upon human beings unless a higher demonic force that commands a certain legion instructs them, such demons are given strong titles of authority. There are lesser demons, and greater demons. The greater demons are given one or two of six different titles of authority. There are dukes, presidents, princes, marquis', kings, and earls. The titles represent their rank of power in Sheol, the land of the deceivers of God. The forces of which I speak are forces that you may not be prepared for."***

Earthael looks at his father, and says, ***"If this is destiny, then I don't think that there's anything that we can do other than simply live out our days until we've all fulfilled the will of the grand architect of the universe."*** Calabrael nodded his head, walked away and returned to his bedroom to rest in his bed for a while. Airael, Earthael, Fireael and Aquari-on spoke about the possibility of being caught amongst each other; however, none of them believed that they could be caught anytime soon. They felt that they were strong enough to ward off any demons who would dare try to capture them against their will, even though they had never actually seen one before. One day, they all decided to leave the house and take flight into the air so as to clear their minds from the possibility of being captured and encountering demons for the first time.

As they flew through the skies, they encountered something floating in the sky, something that looked like a child with angel's wings, and it was riding on a two-headed dragon, however, they sensed something purely evil about it. The four brothers stood still, and Airael said, ***"Who and what are you?!"*** The child upon the floating two-headed dragon replied, saying, ***"My name is Valak, I am come to chain the son of fire to the sun that illuminates the earth!"*** Airael pointed his finger at Valak, and said, ***"You're one of the four demons from Lucifer's legion aren't you? You're not taking my brother anywhere, if you want to try; you have to go through me first!"*** And of course, Valak being more experienced than the elemental children, he covered Airael, Earthael and Aquari-on in a dark cloud of smoke, and when the smoke cleared, Fireael had vanished. Airael thought to himself, saying, ***"Dad was right, but I won't let them get me."*** Airael was a bit scared at how quickly Fireael was taken. But Airael was certain that if they were going to capture him, he wasn't going to vanish without a real fight.

Afterward, the three sons searched all over the skies looking for their brother, unfortunately, they found nothing. And then, a black cloud appeared and a voice spoke out, saying, ***"I am come to imprison the son of water."*** Aquari-on spoke loudly, saying, ***"I am the son of water, who are you, demon?"*** The black cloud spoke, and said, ***"I am Asmodai."*** And then, Asmodai emerged from the black cloud, and said, ***"Resistance is futile, son of water."*** Asmodai was an evil creature having three heads, one like a man, one like a bull, and the other like a ram. He was riding upon a hideous dragon and was covered with the stink of hell. Aquari-on was scared, for his appearance was truly frightening.

Smoke arose from his mouth, and his eyes were inane. When Aquari-on saw this, he began to question whether it was possible to actually defeat a demon. Nevertheless, the three brothers attacked him. Earthael flew down to the ground and punched it with his two fists, and then he flew back up toward Asmodai bearing two boulders on his fists. He then began to attack him with unbelievable speed, swinging large and dangerous boulders at him; however, he failed at trying to touch him at all.

Asmodai appeared and re-appeared while laughing and dodging every move. He then grabbed Earthael's arm and flung him as if he was a worthless toy. Airael began to worry and became frightened, and Asmodai finally snuck-up behind Airael and grabbed Aquari-on. Before Airael knew it, Aquari-on was gone, and Earthael was hurt. Earthael laid there on the ground as helpless as a wingless bird. And being worried about his brother, Airael flew over to where Earthael landed. Airael began to cry and shout out loud, saying, ***"Why isn't anyone helping us?*** He screamed out to the firmament, saying, ***"God, where are you? I know you can hear me! Help me! Please!"***

And as Airael bowed his head over his brother Earthael, hoping that he was ok, a black flash of darkness came, and another demon appeared, saying, ***"I am come to take the son of earth."*** Airael was so hurt that his brothers had been taken from him so quickly that he sat there crying. The one created after Lucifer, the one named Belial grabbed Earthael's arm and dragged him into a black portal. Airael was heart-broken. He then closed his eyes and reached his father by telepathy, and said to him, ***"Dad! Aquari-on, Earthael and Fireael have been captured and taken somewhere!"***

His father Calabrael replied through telepathy, saying, ***"Are you okay?"*** Airael answered, saying, ***"No! We just got out-smarted, and beaten by some sort of demon, would you be okay?!"*** And then, another demon appeared, and said, ***"I am Astaroth, I am here to capture the son of air."*** Airael was petrified, for Astaroth appeared to be an angry angel with a viper slithering around his arm whilst riding upon an infernal dragon. Calabrael spoke through telepathy, and said, ***"Rush home and fly as fast as you can."*** Unfortunately, Airael didn't respond, for Astaroth had taken him away. Calabrael was told that these things were written, however, he knew that this wasn't his fight, so he teleported to his secret room to pray on his altar, asking the divine architect to save his sons, and to keep them from harm. Meanwhile, Valak, Belial, Astaroth and Asmodai took the sons of the elements to their respected destinations of imprisonment. Valak journeyed far and hard across the stars. When Valak realized that he'd become much too close to the sun, he stopped and unveiled the palm of his left hand, and a golden orb emerged from his palm. And then, he grabbed Fireael's arm and threw him toward the sun. Shortly thereafter, he threw the golden orb into the sun. Golden shackles latched on to Fireael's wrists, whilst a golden chain extended itself and latched itself to the core of the sun.

And so, what was written has come to fruition, Fireael was captured and chained to the sun. However, with the cosmic ability of cosmic fire, he was not harmed, but he was well constraint. Meanwhile, Aquari-on was being shackled and chained as well. Asmodai traveled to the largest and deepest ocean on the planet earth. When Asmodai reached his desired destination, he stopped and the dragon that he was riding on began to hack and cough, and whilst it hacked and coughed, it finally regurgitated an orb that was half clear and half blue energy.

Amazingly, the demon named Asmodai opened the Pacific Ocean and its depth was revealed. And then, the orb that the dragon had spat-up was thrown into a chasm revealed by the separation of the water, it then created two shackles, one clear and one blue; both chaining and bounding Aquari-on to the bottom of the Pacific Ocean as a message from the mighty master of error. And so, Asmodai waved his hand, and the ocean closed, causing the waters to move violently against Aquari-on, however, had this happened to the average mortal man, he would have been obliterated immediately, but Aquari-on is the son of water, and no harm came unto him, but he was well constraint, and whilst these events took place, Airael and Earthael were the last to be imprisoned.

The one manifested after Lucifer, the one called Belial wasted no time to get to his desired destination. He dragged Earthael across the land until he reached the highest mountain on the planet earth. And so, Belial stood in front of Mount Everest and raised his hand toward the firmament. And with his palm open, a green orb appeared and it directed itself to the uppermost point of the mountain. A pair of shackles latched themselves to Earthael's wrists, and a chain latched itself to the top of the mountain. Belial put his hand forth and Earthael's body floated to the top of the mountain, constraining him to the highest rocks of the earth. Meanwhile, the demon named

Astaroth teleported himself and Airael to an empty desert land in Egypt. He raised both of his hands to the firmament and opened his palms.

A large clear orb that looked like a crystal ball emerged from Astaroth's palms. And then, the orb shot out of his palms and into the firmament. Afterward, two shackles connected to two chains connected to two stars in the firmament raced down from the sky, and the shackles of the chains latched on to Airael's wrists. The two-chained shackles pulled Airael from the ground and into the air with unbelievable speed. Airael was held captive at the height of the firmament, above the clouds and where no airplane, jet or flying creature hath ever been constraint. The four had been captured, and Lucifer's plans would easily go forward without flaw.

However, the great geometrician or divine architect had already arranged for Archangel Michael to free them. And so, the great architect sent out his word on high. It had been six days since the four children had been captured. On the seventh day, Archangel Michael sprung into action immediately and descended from heaven. And On the way down, he saw Airael, unconscious and hung by chains connected to two stars in the heavens. Archangel Michael summoned his sword by looking at the palm of his hand, and his flaming sword fell from heaven and came to his hand. He looked at Airael, and swung heavily upon the chains constraining him. The chains broke and Airael was freed, he fell from grace and Archangel Michael caught him and carried him down to the grounds of the earth.

He put his hand on Airael's brow, and a bolt of lightning struck down upon Archangel Michael, and before your eyes could witness it, Airael was awakened. As he opened his eyes, he saw a man with hair of fire, skin like that of brass, and eyes filled with light. He was also wearing a breastplate engraved with a name of the divine architect. His pants were made of glowing white linen, and on his back were eight wings standing high in the air. He looked down at Airael, and said, ***"Are you okay; son of cosmic air?"*** Airael replied, saying, ***"I'm okay, are you who I think you are?"*** Archangel Michael laughed, and replied, saying, ***"I'm not a relative if that's what you're thinking. My name is Michael, an Archangel of the grand council of Yahuah, the three-fold form of the one supreme intelligence reigning supreme in all universes. I have orders to accomplish a mission concerning your importance in the divine schematics of your existence here on the mundane plane of existence.***

The divine architect heard what you said when your brother Earthael was hurt, take it from me though, mortal, he forgives you." Airael replied, saying, ***"Ha-ha-ha, that's real funny coming from you, cupid!"***

Meanwhile, a flash of darkness occurred, and Astaroth appeared, saying, ***"The end is near for these humans! Why do you insist on aiding them?"*** Michael stood up, and said, ***"These mortals are built in our father's image; respect that if you do not respect anything, my fallen brethren."*** Astaroth was angered that Archangel Michael had spoken so confidently. So Astaroth raised his hand so as to use his divine powers against Archangel Michael, however, Archangel Michael was too experienced to let him go any further. Airael blinked and within the time that he blinked, which was less than one second of human time, Archangel Michael swung his fiery sword and cut Astaroth down faster than the speed of lightning.

Archangel Michael stood over him, saying, ***"You know me and you know my works Astaroth, how dare you try to lift a finger against me?! Besides, you were never that powerful anyway."*** Afterward, Airael spoke sarcastically to archangel Michael, saying, ***"Remind me to never, ever, ever; get on your nerves."***

Archangel Michael laughed, and said, ***"Mortals, strange; yet amusing."***

A flash of darkness appeared, and Astaroth had disappeared from where he laid on the ground after being cut down by Michael. And so, Archangel Michael and Airael went forth to free Earthael, Fireael and Aquari-on. He and Airael left the sands of Egypt, and teleported to the Pacific Ocean where Aquari-on was chained and shackled to a chasm deep under water. As Airael and Michael floated over the Pacific Ocean, Archangel Michael became transparent and descended deep into the ocean. Airael stayed behind waiting and hoping that he could free his brother. Airael heard a loud clap of thunder and before Airael knew it, Archangel Michael and Aquari-on emerged from the ocean without having a particle of water on their clothing. Aquari-on spoke to Airael, saying, ***"I didn't think I was ever going to get out of there, I don't believe I was down there for so long, when I catch that lousy demon I'm going to make sure he gets a fight he will not forget!"*** Airael replied, saying, ***"So, I guess you're ready for a re-match too, huh bro?"*** Aquari-on stared at the ocean with a determined look on his face, saying, ***"Most definitely!"***

And so, Airael and Aquari-on were freed, and ready for some payback-time. Archangel Michael took his hands, and touched both Airael and Aquari-on on the shoulder. And within the blink of an eye, they were all at the bottom of Mount Everest. Airael and Aquari-on didn't have an idea as to what Archangel Michael had just done; all they knew was that they weren't over the Pacific Ocean anymore. Archangel Michael spoke, saying, ***"Do you still want that re-match you were talking about?"*** Aquari-on and Airael replied at the same time, saying, ***"Definitely!"***

Archangel Michael spoke again, saying, ***"I will leave the***

rescue of Earthael to you then, get going, there isn't much time; go now!" Airael and Aquari-on flew up into the sky, and there their brother Earthael was, chained to the highest mountain on earth. As the brothers stared at their brother whilst he was unconscious, a flash of darkness occurred, and there he was; the demon named *Belial.* Belial laughed, and said, ***"Archangel Michael, I know you're down there, do you think that these mortals will be triumphant against us?***

Better yet, does the throne seriously believe that we will fall at the hands of mortal men?!" His voice traveled down the mountain, and sure enough, Archangel Michael heard him; yet ignored him. Belial laughed and looked at the two brothers as if they were weak infant mortals who were no match for his power in any way or form. Belial looked at the sons of God, and said, ***"It is time to meet your death, mortal men!"*** Airael and Aquari-on put their index finger and middle fingers on their brows, and Belial was incased in a brilliant light, he impinged the walls of light with his fists, but made no progress in escaping. Before Belial knew it, the light around him was gone, and the two brothers were standing directly in front of him.

The two brothers looked into his inane eyes and pointed their index fingers at them. Light sprung out of their index fingers and shot into Belial's eyes, Airael and Aquari-on had filled Belial's body with brilliant light. Belial laughed as his body began to gradually dissipate into dark energy. Airael and Aquari-on were triumphant over Belial, but they also had a feeling that he wasn't dead, and that they may possibly see each other again. Airael and Aquari-on looked at themselves and realized that they had become stronger than they were before. They didn't know why, but they were grateful. The two warriors flew down the mountain and back to Archangel Michael, and told him that they were triumphant over Belial. Archangel Michael replied while laughing with his own sarcasm, and said, ***"I am sure you were triumphant over him, otherwise you wouldn't be talking to me right now.***

However, good job, you may actually win against Lucifer if you combat your opponents the way you did when you fought Belial." Consequently, Archangel Michael knew that they would not win; it was a part of the divine plan. And so, Archangel Michael, Airael and Aquari-on Flew upward toward the mountaintop and Archangel Michael swung his fiery sword and freed Earthael with ease. Earthael's unconscious body began to plummet toward the Earth, and his loving brothers caught him so as to let Archangel Michael do his job. Michael whispered something in Earthael's ear, saying, ***"Omraru-e-muteem."*** Earthael awoke from his slumber, and opened his eyes.

Earthael opened his mouth, and spoke to his brothers, saying, ***"What took so long?"*** Airael said, ***"Ask Mr. Fancy pants angel over there, maybe he can tell you, he freed both of us. My guess is that the old guy upstairs told him to, but hey, I could always be wrong!"*** And so, Michael had freed three of the four brothers, the son of fire was the last to be freed, and then Michael's mission would be fulfilled. Time began to grow closer to the great battle between the sons of God and the son of the morning, Archangel Michael teleported Airael, Aquari-on, Earthael, and himself to their home. As the three brothers returned home, Michael said, ***"I am aware that the great architect has given you great powers, but I don't know how much power he's given you, therefore, I'll not take you to the outskirts of the earth to save your brother Fireael. Stay here until I return, it'll only take a second."***

Archangel Michael disappeared and took himself to the outskirts of the earth, where the vast cosmos stood before him. Michael closed his eyes, praying in his mind, and said, ***"Krah-***

***utum-ateh-Kether! Divine Architect, give me strength to free this child from the works of the evil inhabitants of Sheol.*"** After praying mentally, he took it upon himself to throw his fiery sword at the sun, and with telekinesis and angelic visualization, the fiery blade of Michael's sword found the chains that held Fireael captive to the sun and cut them. Fireael's body floated away from the sun, and Michael's sword transformed into a force field, and surrounded Fireael's body.

The force field brought Fireael across the stars, meteors, comets, and to the direct presence of Archangel Michael. Afterward, Michael whispered something in Fireael's ear, and he woke from his slumber, saying, ***"Who are you?"*** Archangel Michael replied, saying, ***"That is irrelevant at this moment, Fireael; what is important is that you are free, and that you fulfill your destiny."***

And so, Michael touched Fireael's shoulder, and the two warriors were present at the elemental children's home where they were all happy to finally see their brother. And so, Archangel Michael fulfilled God's will, and freed the four children, Michael's mission was completed as directed by God himself. And so, the powerful Michael levitated into the air and stared at the four brothers, and said to them, ***"Make us proud so that the heavens can rejoice for your kind, for much sorrow has been poured into your cup, the cup runneth over, but the four of you will change things for your own kind. Therefore, I bid you farewell, sons of the elements."*** Though much had taken place, and much must be done in order to stop the son of the morning; the esoteric story continues.

Chapter 5

The Preparations for the Final Battle

The final preparations had to be made now that Calabrael's sons have survived Lucifer's plan of eternal imprisonment. Calabrael was happy to see his sons, and his sons were happy to see him as well, however, Calabrael was an old mystic, therefore, time to talk about the adventure that they had was totally irrelevant. So, Calabrael called his sons, and asked them to attend the secret room below the house so that he could prepare them for the final battle against the son of the morning and the powerful king of evil and error. When Calabrael trained them for their first time, they sat in stone chairs that had strange and unknown engravings on them. However, for the final astral combat session, it was important to see how well they would work when using their powers together in one battle. Calabrael was instructed to truly prepare them for the battle that would take place, for the time was growing near. In order to train all four of them at once, Calabrael used an old magical circle that he used a long time ago; a circle that his father Namsilat had somehow engraved into the ground of the secret room. It was a pentagram and a hexagon interlaced and contained by a circle. Round about the circle was an unknown language that read, ***"The eternal flame shall never cease to exist within a microcosm."*** Calabrael asked the four of his sons to sit in the middle of the circle, and they did exactly what he said without questioning him. Calabrael prepared himself to meet his sons on the astral planes; therefore, he sat outside of the circle in a meditative position that would help him ascend to such a plane of existence.

He then asked his sons to inhale slowly through their noses and to exhale slowly through their mouths, and they did exactly as he instructed perfectly. Before they all knew it, the four of them were hovering on an island surrounded by a vast ocean. Shortly thereafter, their father appeared on the island as well. He then began to explain to them that time was of the essence, and that they must work consummately well together in order to break Lucifer's pride. Their father shouted out loud to them, saying, ***"I want all of you to fight as if the fate of the world is weighing in the balance, now, let the final training session begin!"*** The outspoken son of cosmic air looked at his brothers, and shouted, saying, ***"Let's show our old man how it's done!"***

Airael lifted both of his hands toward the sky and began to rotate and spin his body in a circle. And when Airael stopped spinning, the wind became extremely violent. Five tornadoes emerged and began to follow each other one-by-one. Earthael flew thirty feet into the air and slammed his fists into the ground so as to hit the island with the heaviest force of his strength, and within seconds, a terrible shockwave of force raced through the island and violently cracked it in half. After Earthael cracked the island in half, Fireael pointed his finger toward the sky, and a burst of light appeared at the tip of his finger. An aggregation of fire began to grow into a fireball the size of a boulder.

Fireael looked at the tip of his finger and sent the fireball into the heights of the sky. It seemed to have done nothing, his brothers and his father were unaware of what it was suppose to do, but in due time, they would all see what Fireael could do. A loud and violent thundering sound began to come from the heights of the sky, and balls of flames began to rain all over the island, burning the island and making the vast ocean around it boil like heated water in a pot over high fire. Meanwhile, the one named Aquari-on had a new trick up his sleeve. Aquari-on flew deep into the ocean and began to spin himself considerably quick.

A humongous whirlpool began, and became so strong that it began to create a large vacuum which would act as a trap set for his father. Calabrael moved at his greatest speed and evaded falling flames while avoiding the vacuum power of Aquari-on's whirlpool. Calabrael yelled out to his sons, saying, ***"You will have to do much more than that in order to defeat me, my sons."*** Calabrael disappeared, and whilst his sons were looking for him, they found him. Unfortunately, Calabrael was no longer alone. He fell from the great astral sky whilst riding on the shoulder of a great earth titan that was extremely large in size. Calabrael directed the earth titan to use its speed to catch them and toss them away from the island so that they would have to recover before attacking him again, and the earth titan did exactly as Calabrael directed. The earth titan reached out to the warriors with great and formidable arms made of stone and rock, and when he held all four warriors in his hand, he tossed them as far as he could.

Although the titan succeeded in catching them and tossing them away, the four warriors recovered quickly and returned to the battle as if it never happened. They attacked the titan with great speed, and impinged it with dangerous blows to its legs in order to knock it down as quickly as possible. Meanwhile, Airael and Fireael distracted the titan by throwing bursts of wind and fireballs at it whilst Aquari-on and Earthael added to the plan. Earthael raised a wall of rocks behind the titan's legs while Airael and Fireael were distracting it. Aquari-on grabbed the leg of the earth titan with a rope of water and pulled its leg from under it. When the earth titan fell, it slammed into the wall of rocks that Earthael manifested behind it. The Earth titan cracked into a million pieces while Calabrael flew away from its shoulder and disappeared once again. Since Calabrael was skilled, and knew the ropes of the spiritual worlds, his sons closed their eyes and tried to sense his direct presence.

Unfortunately, they couldn't find a signal from his vital life energy. Airael, Earthael, Fireael and Aquari-on looked around and flew all over the place, and still no sign of their father. Without the slightest of a warning, two eyes opened in the midst of the sky, and lightning began to shoot out of its pupils. Calabrael shocked all four of his sons with red lightning, and before he knew it, they had all violently crashed into the vast ocean. The two eyes disappeared and Calabrael re-appeared immediately. Calabrael had thought that he had bested his sons with ease, but to his surprise, Airael, Earthael, Aquari-on and Fireael appeared directly in front of him. Calabrael laughed, and said, ***"You think you've gotten me, but truly, you're all trapped."*** The Calabrael that they thought they had surrounded wasn't their real father; it was one of his duplicates. The four sons were tricked once again. The real Calabrael was floating above them, and had placed them in a force-field trap.

After several minutes of battle, the four warriors began to get a bit upset at their father's tricks. It was then that the four warriors decided to expand their electromagnetic fields with light so as to fill the force field trap with brilliant light so that their father could not see their next move. While inside of the force field trap, they realized that their efforts to make elemental catastrophes weren't working with their father; therefore, they decided to combine their strengths, and so, they did. The force field broke, and a twister of rocks, fire, and water began to spin from all directions. Airael, Aquari-on, Earthael and Fireael swore that they had finally gotten him. Airael thought to himself, saying, ***"There's no way he'll get away from this one!"***

However, Calabrael closed his eyes, outstretched his arms, and opened his palms. A bright light began to leak out of

Calabrael's palms, and eventually it covered the whole astral plane, and before the four warriors knew it, they were all back in the secret room; for they had lost to their father. Calabrael returned to his body with a smile on his face, and said, ***"You may have not won the battle, but all of you are formidable challenges. You work well together, and I would hope that your lack of selfishness would help guide you well. For now, I want all of you to return to your room and rest so that you can prepare for the battle that you must be prepared for. I am happy to have been blessed with the four of you, I love you with all of my heart, be wise in your decisions and before you leave for battle, come to the secret room, I have something for all of you to wear when you leave here to fight the son of the morning."***

The five warriors went to their room, and began talking to each other about their fight with the devil known as Lucifer. Fireael looked at Airael, and said, ***"When we were kids, not once did I think we'd be preparing to fight an actual demon. To be honest, I thought we were completely normal, but apparently that's been changed. We are officially one-hundred percent abnormal all the way. I don't believe this; none of this stuff was in my plans. But then again, I chose to do this, I guess."*** Airael replies, saying, ***"For some strange reason, I always wanted to fly, but I thought I would do it with an airplane or something. Not once did I ever think that I would actually be able to lift myself off of the ground of my own free accord. The ability to generate hurricanes and stuff, that's a plus. I must admit, I was pretty scared when we were captured, I could have swore that it would be easy to fight a demon, I had no idea that they were so strong. I can only hope that we've all gotten strong enough to fight as many as we can. I mean, sometimes, I feel like it's just too much to deal with. I'm pretty sure that none of us expected a life like this. Everyone else lives their lives so regularly, yet we were somehow chosen to do more than we expected to do, considering the fact that our father is wealthy and wise. You'd think that we'd all***

graduate from prestigious colleges and become regular highly-paid working men with families and children, of course, we're not that lucky." Earthael looks at Airael, and says, ***"Well, considering the fact that our father is a man of many different ideas, I kind of thought that we would all just follow after him, and become great adepts like him. Of course, it'll be a long time before that happens. Anybody here have a fear that we may not succeed?"*** Aquari-on stares at Earthael and says nothing because he knows the outcome of their fight against Lucifer. Fireael notices that Aquari-on is staring at Earthael, and says, ***"Hey Aquari-on, what's wrong? You don't seem to be too happy about something."*** Aquari-on replies, saying, ***"No, it's not that, it's just that I feel the same way you all do. I mean, I never thought anything like this was actually possible, but everyday that I breathe it becomes more acceptable. I hope that we all understand that this is a big responsibility. This is serious, we have been given the ability to slay devils in the name of the creator of the universe, and this is no joke. I can only hope that we do not falter simply at the sight of our enemies. God placed us in a grand part of the divine scheme; we have duties to which we must commit ourselves to. Only time will tell whether we are ready or not."*** Airael looks at his brother Aquari-on, and says ***"Well, one thing is for sure, dad wants us to do the right thing. And I would have never thought that he was such a force to be reckoned with. I thought he was just our old man. If mom was to know about this, she would have totally cried her eyes out. What kind of mother accepts or allows her children to fight demons? I mean, even though she wouldn't approve, this is what we have to do. There's no one else that can do it. Besides, they've always been comfortable with our choices; we haven't given them too many reasons to not trust us. I have a feeling that this is why we were born. This is our purpose without a doubt."***

Fireael looks at Aquari-on, and says, ***"Well, I know one thing." "What's that?"*** says Aquari-on. ***"I have no doubt in my***

mind that Lucifer will stop at nothing until he rules our home planet forever. I'm definitely not expecting to win easily in this fight. The truth is that he really wanted us out of his way, and I have no doubt in my mind that he'll kill us if we can't get the upper-hand on him. He's a ruthless demonic tyrant of pride and hate, if we so much as touch him; I'm more than sure that he'll be pissed off. When you think about it, he hates human beings, and if that is the case, then he'll do his best to beat the stuffing out of all of us. I highly doubt that he's going to greet us with birthday gifts and chocolate cake," says Fireael. Earthael looks at Fireael, and says, ***"Strange enough, not one of us can make the decision to be cowardice, I can speak for all of us when I say that we won't allow some pride-driven demon hurt our family and friends because he has some crazy idea that he should rule the universe. If we don't defend our planet now, we'll let everyone down. Our friends, family and our children of the future will suffer if we don't make the sacrifice to stand and fight."*** Airael looks at all of his brothers, and says, ***"Whoa! Whoa! Hey! Speak for yourself; I don't want to have any kids at all. Besides, why bring them into some family tradition that's just outright dangerous. I couldn't imagine watching my kids fight some demon that might hurt my son or my daughter. It's just too much to think about right now. In any event, I think we should all get some rest, we need to be in one-hundred percent tip-top condition to do our best."***

And so, after the four brothers had gotten all of their rest, they returned to the secret room where their father was in deep meditation, and of course, they were all eager to see what it was that their father wanted to give to them.

Calabrael went into the drawers of his altar and pulled out four linen robes. Each one had a Hebrew letter with a certain color stitched into it. They were made from fine black linen, and they had hoods on them, so as to cover their heads and faces if necessary, there was one letter upon four different uniforms.

Airael's uniform held the Hebrew letter of ***"Yod"*** in purple stitching, Fireael's uniform held the Hebrew letter ***"He,"*** in red stitching, Earthael's uniform held the letter ***"Vau"*** in green stitching, and Aquari-on's uniform held the letter ***"He"*** in blue stitching. Airael spoke to his father, saying, ***"I feel stronger in this robe, I feel like these robes have some weird power in them."*** The four warriors liked the robes, and felt a strong sense of heroism flowing vibrantly through their hands.

Tied around the waist of the robes were strong ropes having different colors. There was a purple rope for Airael, blue for Aquari-on, green for Earthael, and red for Fireael. And so, Calabrael told his sons to be aware of their surroundings and to always know that the divine architect is always present. Also, he told them to never lose faith, even if things are seriously looking down, believe in the divine architect and fight with him by your side. After making a few statements of wisdom, Calabrael told them to kneel and make their brows touch the ground.

The four warriors did as instructed by their father. And within seconds, Calabrael closed his eyes, stretched forth his arm, and opened his palm over his four sons heads, he then said to them, ***"The secrets of the universe and the mysteries that have been forgotten for so long is now yours to know. Treat others with kindness, and know thyself so that you will know the whole universe. By the name and presence vested in the hands of the celestial intelligencer, I pass down the knowledge of my father unto his descendents, my sons, the fruits of my loins and the new upholders of divine justice and universal law. Let the Powers family traditions continue, so mote it be!"*** As Calabrael said this, subtle figures of fighting styles and magic only known to cosmic beings began to appear, and the images that appeared were transferred to the minds of the four cosmic warriors. The cosmic secret of fire, the cosmic secret of water, the cosmic secret of air, and the cosmic secret of earth were unveiled to the four cosmic sons.

Afterward, Calabrael said, ***"Arise, my sons. O ye of great faith in thy creator, you are no longer neophytes, for the secrets that have been passed down to you shall make you great adepts."*** The four warriors arose, and when they stood up, their eyes were no more; they no longer had pupils that dilate and so forth. Their eyes complemented their element. Fireael's eyes became flames, Airael's eyes became purple energy, the same color as the natural firmament, Earthael's eyes became green energy, and Aquari-on's eyes became blue energy. And so, Calabrael gave them everything that they needed in order to succeed in their battle against a great evil. Calabrael had foreseen the destruction of the City of New York in his meditation long before he'd given his sons their robes; therefore, the time to prove their worthiness was at-hand. For Calabrael had continuously encountered strange mental flashes of a foul-minded man of evil walking freely to kill at any time.

An evil man who'd done evil deeds throughout most of his life since he was a teenager was the portal through which Lucifer planned to bring himself and his legions to the mundane plane of existence where all mortals reside. The man who had done horrible, malevolent and terrible deeds had never been incarcerated for his acts. He never got caught doing any of his deeds; he escaped police and detectives of all types, he was a monster in the greatest definition of the word. He lost care for himself and others without regret. His evil heart was so close to Lucifer's that his heart became a portal for foul creatures of evil without him even knowing it. A life of blood spilling and killing is his hobby, and in his mind, it is the most joyful thing a man can do. Calabrael had seen this man in his mental flashes too much to be unaware of who he was. The man who had done such horrible acts had been going to the south street seaport so that he could find a victim to murder and mutilate so as to fulfill his evil desires. And so, as the possessor of the heart of evil walked forward to take a glance at the water, he saw that his reflection resembled that of a ravenous demon, and when the man saw this, he began to have violent seizures that caused his eyes to bleed while his saliva foamed from his mouth.

The man fell to the ground gasping for air. And without notice, his body ceased to move whilst his mouth was wide open. A swarm of flies, cockroaches and spiders crawled out of his mouth and a portal of darkness began to rotate violently out his nostrils. The citizens of New York City seemed to be having a regular day, but in due time, something amazing would take place. A portal made of pure evil energy began to grow larger and larger in size, and when the citizens of New York City realized the rotation of the portal, they became so terrified and scared that they ran and left the seaport without looking back. Out of the portal came Lucifer making his appearance on the mundane plane. He looked up, down, and over his shoulders. And then he inhaled deeply, and said, ***"This place, it's infested with mortality. I can smell pure victory in the midst of this foul monkey cage."*** Lucifer was a very handsome man wearing a white robe, his eyes were gray, and his long gray hair reached down his back. He carried a staff as if he were a shepherd of some sort; yet he reeked of the smell of death, blood, and sulfur. Lucifer walked forward and away from the south street seaport and into the streets of the city of New York. He turned around and closed his eyes, and when he opened them, his legions appeared and followed, each demon taking the form of a human, and wearing a white robe of fine linen.

The army marched forth, led by their leader, the son of the morning. Lucifer looked to his left and to his right, and saw the faces of the creatures that he hates so much. As he looked into their eyes and at their faces, he stopped, and began to speak in a loud voice, saying, ***"I am God; I have come to take all of you away from this place, and to bring you to my paradise, take my hand, and march with us that we may know one another."*** The slumbering mortals heard his words, and began to take his hand, and walk with him whilst being unaware of who and what he is; for he is the *"ravening wolf in sheep's clothing, a false prophet, and a false god."* He recruited many, and marched with his legions and followers for miles, so-called healing them and resurrecting the dead from their graves. A man came unto him in pain, sorrow and suffering. The man looked at Lucifer, and said, ***"Please heal me, I have cancer, please heal me!"*** Lucifer stretched forth his hand, and placed his palm upon the man's brow, and the man was healed. Three sixes illuminated on the man's brow and disappeared, the man had unknowingly been marked by the beast. The multitude was in awe, for the man who claimed to be God was healing people. And many being fooled, believed on him. He and his legions marched and marched, in due time, Lucifer, the son of the morning had tricked six hundred and sixty six men and woman to follow him wherever he went.

There were news reports of a man in a white robe walking the streets of New York City and claiming deeply that he was God in the flesh, and that there is no other god but he. And so, he and his legions reached 42nd street after a long march, and stopped marching altogether. Lucifer put his hand forth and created a platform; he then levitated himself into the air and placed himself upon it. His followers were amazed at his powers, and because of it, they believed that he truly was God in the flesh. Finally, Lucifer began to preach loudly, saying, ***"Who here that marches with me today has sins? Testify before me and I will wash those sins away, and replace them with the heart of my paradise."*** He ranted and raved about himself, and none of his followers knew who he truly was.

Meanwhile, at this point in time, Calabrael felt the presence of a very strong evil enter the world. Calabrael's eyes became wide, and he worried knowing that his sons would die in battle against the embodiment and personification of the mark of the beast. Calabrael called his sons and told them to follow him to the living room, and then he turned on the television and saw the news reports of the man in the white robe preaching on a platform on 42nd street. He began to shed great tears from his eyes, and said to his sons, ***"It's time, go forth and conquer the pride of the son of the morning."*** And so, Calabrael and his sons walked outside of their home, and the four warriors flew off into the sky to battle their most powerful adversary. Calabrael stared off into the firmament after they left, and prayed to God, saying, ***"Divine architect; please watch over my sons."***

And so, Lucifer pointed his index finger to the sky, and an aggregation of dark energy shot out of his index finger, into the sky, and placed itself at the core of the sun. The sun began to move away from the earth, and finally, it reached a far distance from earth, and exploded! A loud and frightening sound occurred, and the sun's illumination could no longer penetrate the earth's atmosphere, the sun was destroyed. After the destruction of the sun, minutes went by as he preached in the presence of the dark skies. He preached as if he was a man of God, but in no ways meant his words; he simply made fun of mortal preachers, pastors, and all of those who spoke of the word of God in the modern times. After preaching his word to mortal men, he decided to finally reveal himself, and so did his legions. Lucifer changed his appearance and showed all of his followers that he was the great serpent beast. Lucifer stood ten-feet tall with six scaled wings, flaming eyes that resembled a snake's, his arms, hands, and legs were like that of a human's except they were scaled like that of a crocodile, and upon the very palms of his scaly hands were three sixes. Around his neck he was wearing a pentacle of gold that was surrounded by sixes and at the center of it was the name of God spelled backwards in the Hebrew language. The six hundred and sixty six followers realized that the people that they were marching with weren't human, and when they saw that the man in the white robe had revealed himself, they ran off in terror whilst screaming and yelling with fear.

As the six hundred and sixty six followers began to run wildly through the streets of New York City, Lucifer's legions of demons began to rip their heads off and eat their limbs like finely prepared foods. All hell had truly broken loose in New York. Lucifer's legions destroyed everything around them, human and object alike. All of those people that were healed and so forth were killed anyway, and demons covered almost all of the city of Manhattan, a horrible scene.

As a great darkness covered the earth because of the explosion of the sun, news reports all over the world reported a mysterious darkness that has covered the planet. Meteorologists are baffled as to what went so wrong and caused such darkness over the whole world. Scientists have realized that the sun has moved away from the planet and exploded. Priests are communicating to other priests all over the world and saying that the world is coming to an end. The people on earth are becoming seriously scared, and time is gradually taking its course toward the destruction of the earth.

The crops are dying from the presence of evil. Animals everywhere are dying for what seems to be no apparent reason. Farmers are baffled as they watch their cattle and crops drop dead without reason. The government has no idea what's going on. The president of the united states of America heard about the problematical situations in New York City, and took his position at the white house, and the president of the united states of America broadcasted his speech all over the globe, saying, *"I have decided to call this a state of worldwide emergency. Various reports of Grotesque and evil looking creatures have appeared out of some sort of portal at the south street seaport in New York City. For the good of the united states of America, I have decided that it is best for everyone to migrate elsewhere and escape in any way possible, do not stay home in this state of emergency, I repeat, do not stay home in this state of emergency, we are unaware of exactly what is happening. We have just received word that there is an army of these creatures destroying time square as we speak. Also, it is unfortunate to admit that these creatures are large in number and that our army is not large enough to logically succeed against their forces without totally destroying New York City at the same time, it seems that they are somehow multiplying and becoming greater in number. Priests all over the world have declared that this is the end of the world, and if that is true, and this is the end for all of us, then, may God forgive us and have mercy on our souls, God bless America."*

After finally being trained by their father in the art of astral combat and so forth, the time has finally come for the four children to use the true depth of their cosmic gifts against evil.

Meanwhile, Lucifer and his legions wreaked havoc on the earth, and have slaughtered numerous mortal men and women. The time had come for the final day of victory for Lucifer's rule on earth. The inhabitants of earth were steadily praying to God to be saved from Lucifer and his legions, yet they received no answer while others caused riots and began stealing. Meanwhile, the elemental children were on their way to face the son of the morning and his legions. As the four warriors fly to their destination, Aquari-on looks at his brothers, and says, *"We're almost there, speed it up!"* They quickly made it to the streets of New York City to do battle with some of the most notorious demons existent. The children of the elements arrived, and hovered amidst the sky as they saw many legions of demons destroying and marching to the ends of the earth, screaming and yelling, cursing the existence and name of God. The four had finally arrived at their desired destination, only to see the beginning of the end. Airael shouted out loud, and said, ***"This is it, we stand and fight or we kneel and die!"***

Just as Airael made his statement, a swarm of demons attacked them and began to surround them so that they could overpower the four warriors immediately. However, Fireael stepped forth and told his brothers to surround themselves with shields so that he could take on a legion by himself. Airael, Earthael and Aquari-on touched their brows with their index fingers, and powerful force fields surrounded their bodies so that Fireael could use his true power without harming his brothers. Fireael put his index finger over his heart and closed his eyes. And in an instant, his body was engulfed in the destructive flame. The son of cosmic fire began spinning in a circle and shooting fire from his palms like a machine gun. Demons were being disintegrated everywhere, and Fireael proved to be a worthy adversary.

He destroyed a thousand demons with pure ease as he returned to the sky and stood amongst his brothers, saying, ***"Hey, Earthael; think you can top that?"*** Earthael replied, saying, ***"Watch and learn, Mr. know it all."*** At this point, there was a legion of demons preparing to attack the four elemental children again, however, a flash of green light covered the world and disintegrated the attacking demons before Earthael could lower himself to the ground to battle a legion by his self. Earthael found himself surrounded by demons that only wanted him to die as soon as possible. Realizing that the demons would take no mercy on him, Earthael took his fist and hit the ground with it, and immediately the earth cracked and swallowed a whole legion of demons with pure ease, and then he threw two bursts of Earth energy into the chasm in order to perform his own special secret.

He then blasted off into the sky, and as he flew into the sky, the chasm that swallowed the legion of demons had quickly closed itself as if Earthael had done nothing at all. Although the warriors were doing pretty good, Fireael felt that their efforts weren't enough, there was a high count of demons, and a few eliminations here and there would surely not due. Therefore, Fireael decided to take destiny into his own hands and tap into his true strength without flaw.

The Strength of Fireael

As Fireael made the decision to fight no matter how many demons there were, he realized that there were numerous demons surrounding a large group of people, he then opened his hand, and his palm released a wire of fire that he began to swing as if it were a whip of some sort. Demons were being cut, sliced and melted as if they were fine foods to be eaten. Although Fireael continued his attacks, the legions kept coming, one after another. Fireael realized this and decided to step it up a notch. He raised his left and right hands into the air, and closed his eyes.

Amazingly, a large legion of demons began to shake violently as if they were having a series of detrimental seizures. Fireael was doing something that not even his brothers knew he could do. Unbelievably, two thousand demons began to slam into the ground while holding their throats as if they were choking and gasping for air.

Finally, they began to burst into flames of light. Fireael had used the height of his cosmic abilities. His brothers stood there in the midst of the sky and looked at each other as if they were seriously surprised, and when it was all said and done, Fireael flew quickly into the sky to stand amongst his brothers. He then said to them, ***"I think it's time we all tapped into our true strengths,"*** Aquari-on nodded his head, and said, ***"Then, I think it's time to see what I can really accomplish, wish me luck!"***

The Strength of Aquari-on

The mighty son of cosmic water was ready to explore the height of his cosmic abilities, and he did just that. He decided to experiment with his powers by eliminating a couple thousand demons by his self. He also decided to take more immediate action in order to eliminate them from the battle quicker. He took up his right hand and waved it slowly in front of himself. Unbelievably, the water surrounding the island of Manhattan raised itself above the height of all of the buildings therein. The water stood there and made no movement whatsoever. And before anyone could notice his movement, Aquari-on shot off into the sky and disappeared. Not one of his brothers had an idea of what Aquari-on would do. And Behold! Out of the surrounding walls of water emerged a great giant made of water. The giant emerged and began to run wildly into a legion of demons and obliterated them as he ran back into the walls of water and disappeared. Aquari-on's brothers were amazed, but Aquari-on was far from done. He re-appeared after the giant returned to the water from which it came. After re-appearing, Aquari-on closed his eyes and again something emerged from the walls of water. The great and gigantic hands of the undines ***(spirits of water)*** began snatching demons, breaking their necks and drowning them; a horrible scene.

One-by-one the demons disappeared as they were

practically being snatched from the battlefield. And finally, Aquari-on let go of his hydrokinetic hold on all of the water surrounding the city. He then commanded it to calmly lower itself to its depths. Once he had done his part, he returned to his place amongst his brothers and smiled at his brother Airael, and said, ***"It almost seems as if we're doing it in vain, many of them are still alive!"*** Airael heard his brother Aquari-on clearly, and decided to take immediate action.

The Strength of Airael

Airael was sure of his self and wasted no time eliminating his enemies. Airael closed his eyes and placed his left and right hands over his solar plexus while he concentrated as much as he possibly could. And within seconds, a burst of light appeared from his solar plexus, and then he opened his eyes and put a devilish smile on his face. Nothing could prepare you for what happened next. Airael began moving his hands as if he was directing an orchestra, and as he did this, each movement or wave of his hand would raise a demon off of the ground and into the air while slamming them violently back into the ground that he so easily lifted them from.

But wait! Airael was far from done. He then began to ball his hands into fists. His body began to shake, and he began to charge his electromagnetic field so that it could aid him in his thoughts. Earthael looked at Airael and turned his head toward his brother Fireael, and said, ***"What the heck is he doing?!"*** Fireael replied, saying, ***"I have no idea whatsoever, all we can do is hope that it helps."*** Before Earthael and Fireael could figure it out, Airael had finally displayed his true strength.

All of a sudden, demons were leaving the ground and being thrown miles away from the battle, for Airael had used his electromagnetic field like some sort of vacuum. Airael began pulling them and throwing them as if they were feather-weighted objects. His abilities were awesome and unmatched; he was powerful and formidable in battle. And after tossing demons around like mere toys, he returned to his place amongst his brothers with pure confidence that they would be victorious. Upon his return, Aquari-on looked at Airael, and said, ***"Do you always have to show-off?!"*** Airael replied, saying, ***"Pretty much!"***

The Strength of Earthael

After Airael did what he could, Earthael looked at his brother Aquari-on and began to shake his head left and right while saying, ***"As usual, I have to teach ya'll how to do things the right way, watch this!"*** Earthael closed his eyes and immediately began his assault on the remaining demons; he quickly landed on the ground, and began to walk slowly amongst the demons while lightly clapping his hands and saying, ***"Bravo! Bravo! Now it's my turn!"***

Of course, no one had any idea that Earthael could use his cosmic powers to call a few friends to aid him in battle. Earthael amazed his enemies as he got on his knees and placed his ear to the ground while knocking on the ground seven times, and when he stood up and began to walk slowly amongst the demons as if he was invincible or something, his brothers were becoming upset with him. Airael realized what his brother Earthael was doing, and shouted at his brother from a far, saying, ***"Earthael! This is serious, you fool, and what are you trying to do; kill yourself?!"*** As Airael said this, the demons began attacking him and trying to grab him so that they could strangle the life from his body for ruining their intentions, and just before they ran toward him so that they could grab him,

Airael's eyes had shown him the truth about his brother's abilities, and Airael was amazed.

Earthael had knocked on the ground and summoned thousands of gnomes *(spirits of Earth)*. Within seconds, they crawled out of the cracks in the earth, and began to wildly rush the demons and pull them into the cracks of the ground from which they came. Creatures that were only two-feet tall with long gray beards, angry countenances and cloths like that of a leprechaun. Earthael walked and looked left and right as the gnomes killed and attacked each demon, one-by-one. At this point, Lucifer stands near and watches the battle between Earthael and his legions.

Lucifer's eyes became inane, and his anger grew deep as his countenance displayed his angered thoughts toward the current events of the outcome of the apparent battle between the divine architect's elect warriors, and his army of nescient evil. Meanwhile, Earthael is satisfied with the earth spirits aid in the final battle. After summoning the height of his cosmic abilities, Earthael waved his hand and commanded the gnomes to return to the depths of the Earth. Afterward, Earthael placed his index and middle fingers over his heart, and touched the ground with his index finger. *And Behold!*

Wherever a demon stood, a small pair of hands formed of the rocks of the earth began to grab their legs and break their ankles and feet. The sound of snapping bones would indicate the likely breaking of their legs and so forth. Sound after snapping sound, a demon would fall to the ground and end up as helpless as a fallen bird with broken wings. Afterward, Earthael flew into the sky and stood amongst his brothers. As he returned, Aquari-on spoke out loud, and said, ***"Not bad, but you could've spared us the gruesome sounds."*** Earthael replied, saying, ***"If I would've, then it wouldn't have been fun."***

In due time, Aquari-on and his brothers realized that all of their efforts weren't in vain, together they destroyed thousands of demons and somewhat cleared the battle-field for the final battle. After a tiring episode of using their true power, the son of cosmic water spotted the son of the morning, and said, ***"We can't sit here and fight these legions all day, we'll eliminate the rest of the legions while we take on the one we came here to fight, Let's go!"*** And so, after spotting Lucifer, the four warriors confronted him and Aquari-on pointed his index finger at Lucifer, and said, ***"I hope you're ready to suffer the same fate as your followers, we've a score to settle with you, Lucifer!"***

Airael looked at Aquari-on, and said, ***"Let's make this quick and easy."*** Lucifer's legions were easy to defeat for the four elemental children; thus, they naturally became a little too confident in themselves. The son of the morning noticed their confidence, and began to laugh, while saying, ***"I don't know how you got free, but you will die for your interference in divine business; foolish mortals! Belial, Asmodai, Paimon! Remove these monkeys from my presence at once!"***

Paimon was very obedient and loyal to Lucifer, and he sat high upon the back of a Dromedary with a crown on his head. He had the countenance of an angry human, a tail like a dromedary, long white hair, and his arms; hands and lower extremities were scaled like a lizard. And though his feet were scaled like a lizard, they were webbed like that of a duck. Belial, the one said to be created after Lucifer, and the demon that Airael and Aquari-on fought at Mount Everest was also present on the battlefield. The three demons sought to attack Airael for disrespectfully opening his mouth against their master, Lucifer. Quickly, his brothers formed holy shields around themselves. And when their shields were formed, they placed a shield around Belial as well; the shields were engraved with a holy name of God in the Hebrew language. And when the shields were in place, Belial was instantly unable to move. Earthael went forth and waved his hand, *and behold!* The Earth trembled and cracked, and a chasm with stonewalls formed in the earth.

Upon seeing the chasm, Fireael flew as fast as he could and went inside of the chasm to engrave the interior walls of the chasm with three sevens and seven names of God. When he was done, he fashioned chains of holy fire that latched to the walls of the chasm. When Fireael was done, he flew out of the chasm while saying, ***"All set! Now, all we have to do is get them inside and they'll be trapped!"*** Airael opened his hands and blew Belial away with a strong gust of wind causing him to land deep within the chasm. Belial could not return, for three sevens and seven names of God were engraved into the walls of the chasm.

At that moment, Paimon went forth and took the form of dark energy, and surrounded their holy force fields with darkness so that they could not see behind themselves or in front of themselves. At this point, Fireael mentally recollected a technique that he had learned from his father. He then began concentrating on divine light, and when he did, his aura was exceedingly bright with brilliant light. The light of his aura was so bright that it caused Paimon to scatter away from the four brothers instantly. Lucifer began to get truly angered in that the mortals he proclaimed to be so weak and foolish were strong enough to ward off his highest lieutenants. Lucifer shouted out loud, saying, ***"Asmodai! Paimon! Combine your nature, you fools!"*** The two fallen angels began to rotate; then, they transformed themselves into a dark energy and took the form of a furious white dragon with an aura of black fire, teeth of sharp swords and inane eyes that were as black as an endless chasm. The wings of the dragon were like the scales of an alligator, yet they were as powerful as two hurricanes. At this moment, a flying dragon was an air problem which, Airael was surely ready for. He flew high into the sky, dispelled his holy shield and surrounded himself with a great tornado that was extremely powerful.

Once the tornado was set, he used his index and middle fingers to direct the tornado in any direction he wanted, and then he sent it towards the dragon with no mercy. And after sending the tornado at the dragon, he called out unto his brother Fireael with telepathy, saying ***"Fireael, show them what happens when you play with fire!"*** Fireael raised his right hand toward the firmament, and fire appeared within the tornado, and the tornado became a whirling twister of wind and fire. Earthael looked at Lucifer and noticed that he was laughing. Earthael's countenance was filled with confusion as he said, ***"What's so funny? You're losing!*** Lucifer replied, Saying, ***"You've fell into my trap, you fools!"*** And before the four warriors' could realize it, the whirling twister of wind and fire dissipated and disappeared. With surprise, the four brothers were in true shock as they thought that they were truly prepared to battle the forces of Lucifer's legions. They floated a midst the sky, and had no idea of what had just happened. As the four warriors looked at the dragon, it also dissipated, and there was no sign of it, it was gone. A strange darkness appeared and opened a portal that sucked the four elemental brothers into it, and the four brothers found themselves in limbo. They had no idea where they were, for they were stuck between the heavens and the Earth.

At this point, Lucifer was exceeding with cockiness and moved forward with his plan. Unexpectedly, another force appeared, a force that sounded like raging thunder, and of course, it was as fast as pure lightning. *Behold!* A strong strike of lightning raced out of the sky, and out of it came Archangel Michael who appeared and began to laugh out loud. His voice echoed throughout the whole earth, and then he spoke, saying, ***"I know your works, and you know who I am, I am come to free them from your trickery! You imprison them, one after the other, and yet, I say unto you, if you believeth so heavily on your pride, then, why not fight them instead of imprisoning them? Or is it because you know you cannot win against four mortal children?! The divine architect can see what you're doing, son of the morning."*** Lucifer became hopping mad at Michael as he swung his fiery sword and cut a whole into reality itself. The portal to limbo was opened once again. Again Archangel Michael freed the four warriors from imprisonment. The four sons of the elements emerged from the hole in reality, and floated amidst the skies next to the powerful archangel Michael. Michael looked at the warriors, and then turned his head to Lucifer, saying, ***"A kingdom divided amongst itself cannot prosper."*** Lucifer replied, saying, ***"Michael, you will die by my hands when I rule this planet, you fool!"*** Michael replied, saying, ***"I've forced one of your princes to betray you and tell me your whole plan. And now, I will let these sons of man destroy you and your pride."*** A strike of lightning appeared from the sky and struck the ground, and before anyone could realize it, Michael had disappeared.

While Lucifer was becoming angry about the events opposing his plans, the four children spoke with Michael by means of telepathy, and Michael said, ***"This is your battle now, sons of God; we trust that you will know how to become triumphant over the son of the mourning, when the time comes, the throne will appear."*** At this moment, Lucifer said, ***"I knew the divine architect would interfere. Otherwise, you fools would've never escaped your constraints. No matter, you shall all feel my wrath! This battle has been going on for quite some time now, yet I've not attained success with eliminating these monkeys, I believe it is time to finish this once and for all!"*** Finally, the son of the mourning decided to no longer watch his legion's failure. He entered the battle himself, and the children of the elements became scared because his aura was filled with great evil. And just as the four warriors thought that the battle was about to jump in their favor, Lucifer began to change form and grow in size. And when the four warriors saw this, they flew off to safety to re-group while their enemy began to transform into a dragon having *6 eyes, 6 heads, 6 horns, and 6 tails.*

At the size of a fifteen-story residential building, Lucifer figured that his size would make victory over the children of the elements simple. However, he didn't realize their true potential to be triumphant in tough situations. In order to defeat the son of the morning, the four sons would have to use the full-force of their abilities. While taking cover, the four warriors of the elements needed to plan a sufficient attack that was effective enough to defeat the mighty son of the morning, therefore, they found a safe place away from battle and talked about what they could and couldn't do. Lucifer shouted in an angry tone with his deep and raspy voice, saying, ***"Come and meet your death, young sons of Yah!! Where have you gone?! Do the sons of God hide like cowards amongst their lands? Come and face me, for I shall make thy death a gradual and painful torture!"***

Airael looked at his brothers, and said, ***"Okay, I have a funny feeling about this, I'm not sure if we're going to survive this. Something just feels funny, I feel like it's necessary to die in order to beat him, but it makes no sense. I don't want to die!"*** Earthael replied, saying, ***"Airael! No one ever said that fighting against the devil was going to be easy!"*** Aquari-on looked at his brothers, and said, ***"Well, now that everyone is getting that feeling that this battle may be our last one, I think it's time for me to tell you that dad was told by an angel that we would die in this battle. So, I want all of you to know that I have no regrets, and I'm honored to have you as my brothers."*** Fireael heard what came out of Aquari-on's mouth, and said, "***Say what! Die!? Damn...why the hell didn't you tell us? Why wouldn't you tell***

us? But if that's the case, and what you say is true, then I'm not going to make it easy for him to do it, and I'm definitely not going out without a fight! If this is our last battle, I'm going all out!"

Airael spoke in a loud voice, saying, ***"If we're going to die, then let's finish this, now!"*** Earthael looked at his brothers, and said, ***"Well, let's make this a day to remember even after death."*** And so, they flew back to the battle scene and combined their powers for the last stand. Earthael screamed to the top of his lungs to summon the depth of his powers. The ground beneath Lucifer began to rumble violently, and then it began to rise and lift Lucifer into the height of the sky until he reached outer space. The son of the morning stood there on a platform of earth where the cosmic battle that would make the four warriors legendary heroes had begun. Earthael flew into the outskirts of the earth and began to throw various energy bolts at Lucifer's eyes so that he would be blinded. Fireael shouted out loud, saying, ***"Now, it's my turn!"*** He covered his body in the purple flames of purification, and quickly flew into the outskirts of the planet. He then placed his index finger and middle fingers on his brow, and connected himself to every star in the galaxy so as to command them to burn the son of the morning. And so, seven stars in the galaxy traveled from a far distance and stood still. Then the stars became smaller in size until they were about the size of a basketball. Fireael telekinetically guided the stars to circle and surround Lucifer so that he wouldn't move, and he didn't, just as Fireael expected. Airael clapped his hands, and a cosmic hurricane spun into outer space and picked Lucifer up from the platform as it spun him around and twisted his body toward the earth. As Lucifer fell a long fall toward the earth, Fireael telekinetically guided the stars to crash into his oversized body while falling.

Earthael waved his hand, and a bed of stone spikes appeared directly under his landing destination. And of course,

Lucifer landed face first into the bed of spikes while still being attacked by fiery stars. His blood was scattered everywhere, and the four sons had thought that they had finally won, but they were wrong. Lucifer disappeared, and the four warriors were totally unaware of where he could've gone. Fireael spoke aloud, saying, ***"We know you're here, show yourself, you coward!"*** Then the most amazing thing happened, Lucifer had taken on a form larger than that of the size he'd first taken. The planet earth began to tremble, and no one knew what had happened. Lucifer was so big that he could wrap his bare hands around the Earth, and crush it into space dust. A large countenance looked down upon the earth, and a devious laugh echoed to all of its inhabitants. After displaying his great power, he took his hands and tried to crush the earth by squeezing it into nothing. His fingers began to reach into the planet's atmosphere. And when the four warriors saw this, they looked at each other and weren't sure of how they could stop him at such a large size. Fireael looked at his brothers, and said, ***"Hey! This is our last battle, let's just fight, there's no need to plan our attacks!"*** Airael points his finger at Lucifer, and says, ***"Lucifer, son of the morning, we're going to chase you out of this earth, one way or another!"*** Airael stretches his arm forth and a small tornado springs out of his right palm. He then levitates off of the ground and rides the tornado into outer space, Aquari-on points at the water surrounding New York City, and a stream of water races toward him. He then jumps on the stream of water and rides the stream of water into outer space behind his brother, Airael.

Earthael raises his right hand to the heavens and a hand of stone and rock forms under him. The earth hand springs into the sky and into outer space carrying Earthael in its palm. Fireael watches his brothers, and says, ***"Hey, wait up!"*** Fireael raises his hand toward the firmament and creates a giant orb of fire. He then levitates and lands on the orb of fire to ride it into outer space immediately. On the way to outer space, they become closer to the gigantic face of their enemy and decided to launch an onslaught of attacks while Lucifer shot lightning at them from his eyes. The four warriors dodged and moved as much as they could. Fireael launches multiple fireballs at Lucifer while Lucifer says, ***"Come meet your doom, sons of God!"*** Earthael, Airael, and Aquari-on launch multiple bolts of light energy at Lucifer as he looks upon his miniature opponents, and says, ***"Die!"*** And so, the four warriors rode off into outer space to stop their enemy from crushing the planet and destroying all humanity. And when the four warriors reached the stars above, they began to wonder how they would stop him; however, Fireael wasted no time coming up with a plan. Fireael touched his brow with his index finger and twelve stars in the universe raced into Lucifer's back and slowed him down. Lucifer roared like a lion in pain as the heat and force from the stars crashed into his back. Lucifer looked upon the sight of four warriors smaller than the size of atoms to him, and could not comprehend how such small creatures possessed such enormous power. Meanwhile, Earthael flew out of the hand of earth and onto Lucifer's arm as he began to run up his arm and onto his right shoulder. Lucifer looked at his right shoulder and tried to smash Earthael like a bug. Earthael moved and appeared to be green lightning in the eyes of Lucifer. As the son of cosmic earth dodged the gigantic hand of Lucifer, he summoned a meteor and a comet to crash into his enemies face. Lucifer faltered, and Earthael used his volition to command the hand of earth to reach out and deliver him from danger while Aquari-on sprung into action.

The son of cosmic water rode his stream of water around Lucifer's waist and up to his head as he rapidly threw bolts of lightning at his left shoulder, and again, Lucifer roared like a lion in excruciating pain. And when Airael saw what his brothers had done, he placed the power and strength of seventy hurricanes into his right arm as his right arm was illuminated with a brilliant purple light. Airael hurled himself toward the center of Lucifer's chest and punched him. Lucifer furiously faltered, and said, ***"Up until now I have merely been toying with you, mortals! No more games! You all die, now!"*** And before the four warriors knew it, Lucifer had disappeared.

Once again, Lucifer was unable to destroy the earth as he pleased. Once realizing that his strategy of using his growth in size was insufficient, he quickly disappeared and returned to his old form. The four warriors stopped him from crushing the earth, but the battle was far from over. And so, the four warriors saw that Lucifer disappeared and finally they returned to earth only to see their enemy from a distance. The son of the morning was angry and covered in his own unholy blood, and then he stood up and began to laugh, saying, ***"You could never defeat me, mortals!"*** He glanced at his palms, and manifested a double-edged sword out of thin air. And after manifesting a razor sharp weapon of destruction, he moved at a speed that the four warriors had never seen before. Lucifer breezed pass the four warriors, and returned to where he stood before he manifested his sword; the son of the morning was so strong and fast that it seemed as if he had never moved at all. The four warriors were unaware of what had been done to them, and before they knew it, they began to feel as if their bodies were losing life, and their souls were combining with something unimaginably energetic.

The four brothers looked at themselves, and realized that they were all deeply cut and wounded across their chests. And finally, the four powerful warriors fell from the sky like falling stars from outer space. The four warriors hit the ground one-by-one; bleeding a large amount of bodily fluid, and taking their final breaths. The blood of the four cosmic sons heavily leaked out of their bodies, and mingled together as their bodies no longer moved, and their breath of life was returned to the cosmic essence from which it came.

God versus the Devil

As the blood of the four cosmic warriors began to combine, a strange energy began to rise from its essence and shoot into the firmament like a thousand bullets. The sky opened, and something beyond powerful entered the world of living men. Lucifer turned his back and commanded the last demons of his legions to march forth so as to attain victory. However, as Lucifer's back was turned, he felt the divine throne and became scared. He then realized that a portal of pure brilliant cosmic light had opened, and a being sitting upon a throne carried by seven cherubs emerged. *Behold!* It was the universal master initiator who had returned to the mundane plane to rectify the disobedience of his enemies. The earth was in awe, all creatures looked into the sky, and the dead woke out of their graves and began walking the earth, while saying, ***"The king has returned, the all-in-all has come."***

Bears, lions, birds, insects and all creatures felt the triumphant might of the God of all existence. Seven horns sounded, and a deep and powerful voice of universal authority echoed throughout the whole of the universe, and said, ***"I am that I am, the time has come."*** The sight of his throne was so vibrant with light that it brought forth an inexpressible emotion that operated within the depths of all creatures. One armrest of his throne had a lion's head bearing a large diamond in its forehead, and the other armrest had an eagle bearing the philosopher's stone in its mouth; the stone of consummation.

The divine architect had eyes of light, skin like brass, gray hair as thick as fine wool accompanied by a thick gray beard reaching his chest. He was dressed in a white robe, and round about the waist of the robe was a black rope representing the balance of the universe, Yin & Yang. Lucifer turned around, and his eyes opened widely with surprise as he realized it was the divine architect of the universe summoned to the mundane plane of existence. Lucifer thought to himself, saying, ***"Ah, of course, the divine architect must have known that those four mortals couldn't possibly defeat me in their current state of mortal ascension. Michael wanted me to kill them instead of imprison them; they sacrificed themselves without knowing it. It was all a trick; he wanted me to kill those mortals so that their blood would make the earth's electromagnetic field summon the throne here, how could I have been so foolish?!"*** After thinking to himself, and realizing that he wasn't as intelligent as he thought he was, the divine architect stood up from his throne, and said, ***"You've yet to learn young serpent, ye shall never have my throne. Your self-exalting pride will destroy you, and on this day you shall be silent for 7777 years."*** Afterward, the divine architect jumped into the air and landed upon the back of a great seraph, and rode on its back as if it were a surfboard as he headed toward Lucifer and stood before him; face-to-face. Meanwhile, seven seraphs appeared in front of the divine architect's throne so that it could not be touched. The divine architect stopped all time throughout the whole universe with the blink of his eye. Amazingly, nothing but he and Lucifer moved, no star scintillated, and no creature or thing moved.

He then teleported away from Lucifer and revealed the palm of his right hand. A blinding bright light revealed itself, and out of the brilliant bright light from his hand, a golden chain sprung out, and shackles latched themselves to Lucifer's wrists. The divine architect blinked, and they were no longer on earth, they were hovering over the area where the sun once stood. The divine architect gripped the golden chain that sprung from his palm and began to spin it in a circular motion. Before

Lucifer knew it himself, the divine architect displayed the smallest fraction of his omnipotent and omniscient strength. He swung Lucifer and slammed his body into every planet in our solar system with the exception of earth.

In his first swing, he slammed Lucifer into Jupiter, and the planet Jupiter cracked in halves. He swung again, and slammed his body into Uranus, and Uranus crumbled into over ten trillion pieces. Then he slammed his body into Pluto, and Pluto cracked into four pieces. He slammed his body into mars, and mars cracked into seven pieces. And after the destruction of mars, the divine architect stopped, and said, ***"This is what it has come to, and you only have yourself to blame, I gave you a grand rank among the seven heavens, and you dropped that rank for a desire to rule in my place, and to inherit a bottomless pit! Are you satisfied yet?!"*** Lucifer replied, saying, ***"Never! I hate you and your loathsome monkeys!"***

The divine architect heard his reply and swung his body away from the area where mars once stood and swung him around in a circle once more. The great evil that had plagued mankind for numerous centuries was as helpless as a newborn child. The divine architect swung his body with a great force, and slammed it into planet Venus, and the planet known as Venus was shattered like weak glass. Then he slammed his body into Saturn, and Saturn exploded. Then he slammed his body into the moon, and the moon broke and was reduced to space dust. And finally, the divine architect spun him around seven times in a circle, and slammed his body into mercury with a supreme force, and mercury spun off of its axis and flew off into the darkness of outer space only to cause a humongous explosion that could frighten creatures in another universe far away. The divine architect blinked, and they were back on earth while time was released from its divine hold.

Lucifer was in no condition to talk afterward, the divine architect had dished out divine punishment that spoke for itself; the likes of which no angel in heaven and no demon in hell had ever seen until that day. Lucifer's pride was damaged even greater than that of his body. He had been swung, circled and slammed into large masses of pure matter. He was completely helpless to do anything for himself, not one being existent could aid Lucifer while being issued his promised divine punishment. At this point in time, Lucifer felt like a helpless mortal man.

The shackles around Lucifer's wrists broke, and the golden chain disappeared. The divine architect stood face-to-face with Lucifer and stared at him. Before Lucifer knew it, the divine architect blinked, and Lucifer was immediately encased in a large bubble of holy energy consistent with eternal light vibrations. Lucifer screamed and shouted to the top of his lungs, saying, ***"I'll one day destroy all of your creatures; you shall see all of them suffer by my hand! And in due time, even you will feel my wrath, Yahuah!"*** The divine architect ignored his words and placed him at the very bottom of the chasm that Earthael had made before passing through transition. After many events and the passing of much time, Belial had finally attained some company.

Paimon and Asmodai were helpless to do anything for their master; therefore, they stood there and watched as they lost the war against the divine architect once again. The divine architect turned around and stared at them. Paimon and Asmodai spoke no words as he stared at them; they simply flew into the chasm and made no effort to continue their mission. The divine architect glanced at his index finger and pointed at the remainder of Lucifer's legions.

The legions of evil ran wildly into the chasm as if they were perfectly scared. The divine architect blinked, and a lid of stone engraved with one of his holy names covered the top of the chasm so that its contents wouldn't be released until its due time, or the blood of the archangels of the four corners of earth touched it. He then lifted the chasm from the earth and summoned an archangel who descended from his throne-room in Araboth. Out of the firmament came a great being from outer space, and *Behold!* It was an archangel named Metatron, a very tall archangel who had green fire for hair, eyes of brilliant light, skin like brass, and twelve black wings upon his back.

He was clothed in a black robe, and round about the waist of the robe was a white rope. And after the appearance of Metatron, the divine architect commanded him to cast the chasm away from the land of his footstool. Metatron teleported to the chasm containing his fallen brethren, and grabbed it, he then gradually flew away with it into the darkness of space, and disappeared.

And so, planets were destroyed, and the earth was damaged greatly. The air was contaminated from the emanation of evil that was present in the world, the sun was destroyed, and the waters of the oceans and seas were filthy and stained with the essence of evil. The divine architect returned to his throne and commanded four seraphs to do his divine will. He sent one seraph to take the body of Fireael and place it where the sun was before Lucifer destroyed it. Fireael's body set itself on fire and expanded greatly.

And within seconds, Fireael's body became the center of a new sun. His body became the new illumination for the planet earth. Cattle and animals all over the world were resurrected, and the crops were healthy and a new. Another seraph took the body of Aquari-on and placed it in the Pacific Ocean where he was once held captive. Aquari-on's body purified the seas and oceans all over the world. Two more seraphs took the last two bodies of the children of the elements, and completed the grand will of the great architect. One seraph took Airael's body and planted it in the earth.

And within seconds, a great and large tree grew directly over Airael's burial place. And upon the large tree was a holy name of God engraved into it, and within seven seconds, it purified the air all over the world immediately. Another Seraph took the body of Earthael and buried it in the earth, and Earthael's body purified the ground that became impure when Lucifer and his legions set foot on the earth. All plant-life began to grow and blossom once again. The divine architect blinked once again, and all of the destruction that took place in battle was no more, the planets were whole, and the destruction that took place during the great battle between the cosmic sons and the son of the morning was fixed as if nothing ever happened. The earth was regenerated, and the four sons' purpose was fulfilled in the grand design of life. Due to the faith and sacrifice of the four cosmic sons, the earth had been spared once more.

Chapter 6

Mephistopheles' Revenge and the Search for the Sword of Elohim

In due time, another evil force would try to take the throne of the almighty God of the universe. But who on Earth or in the universe would stop such an evil force from making such an attempt? The elemental children have passed through transition in the battle against Lucifer, for the battle that waits in the future will have to be fought by someone else, another young elemental son. God returned to the realm of heaven called Araboth after the great battle that shocked the world. All was fine in heaven and in earth, thanks to the heroic efforts of four elect mortals. The story does not end here, for a greater threat is brewing somewhere else on earth. Though Lucifer and most of his legions were locked away for many years, not every demon in hell agreed with Lucifer's plans to take earth. There was one demon that had plans to take heaven and rule the universe alone. He had been called a devious and intelligent fallen angel, and throughout the ages, humans called him *"Mephistopheles."* After the great battle between Lucifer and the legendary elemental children, time has passed as it regularly does. Humanity has continued to transgress once more, and stories are told to children all over the world about the legendary battle between the powerful good and the powerful evil that stunned the reality of our world.

Calabrael, the father of the four legendary heroes has become riper in age, and has also had another son who he deems worthy of his father's bloodline. Calabrael has named his final son by the name of ***"Ethereael."*** As time continues, the divine architect of the universe continues to watch over the world of the living. In heaven, angels are ranting and raving about the ascension of the holy bloodline of Namsilat Powers. After the great battle between God and the Devil known as Lucifer, there are still demons lurking around the corners of the Earth and cursing the name of God for imprisoning their leader of evil. In due time, God would become so pleased with the bloodline of Namsilat Powers, that he called forth a council to manifest a gift for mortal men and women alike. The idea was for a sword that would be hidden deep within the physical counterpart of all human beings. This sword is called ***"The Sword of Elohim."*** The sword of Elohim can only be attained by one who has reached the truest height of divine consciousness, the final stage of ascension that can only be reached by a great attainment of supernal gnosis. At the center of the human being is a blade of holy energy that is so sharp that it can destroy planets and stars by nearly being touched by its possessor's mind.

All subtle, energetic and material forms can be broken with one sword. Whoever held or possessed the sword would have the ability to manifest his own universe, and become the father of its creation. The demon called Mephistopheles is a demon who balances his worth by his actions, and because of this, he would rather play both sides of the field in order to attain enough knowledge to deceive both sides and follow through with his own plans. The great and evil force was known throughout time as Mephistophilus, Mephistophilis or Mephistopheles, a strong and terrible prince or chief of demons, a truly wicked and evil demon who betrayed Lucifer and God at one point in time. Because of his deceit and trickery, Mephistopheles worked by his self and cared nothing for Lucifer's plans, nor did he care for God's plans. Mephistopheles was lurking around the heavens and overheard the grand council of the universe speaking about something called the sword of Elohim, a sword that Mephistopheles could use to create his own universe so as to overthrow not only archangels and fallen angels, but to overthrow all existence and re-create it. He believed that if he could manifest his own universe, he could easily have an army large enough to overthrow the old universe.

However, Mephistopheles knew that he himself would have to steal it, and after he would steal it, he would attempt to torment the soul of the individual who was in possession of the sword. Mephistopheles was so great in knowledge that he created practices to torment the physical body, psychic body and soul at one time, by using techniques not even Lucifer knew of. In heaven, the grand architect of the universe headed a council of archangels who would help create an interior weapon for mortal ascension. Years and years after the death of the elemental children who valiantly fought against the son of the morning, the grand architect was pleased with the attempt to defeat a great evil in the mundane world, and because of the effort and the sacrifice of four young men and their father, mortal ascension proved to be a most excellent plan for humanity. And so, the grand architect of the universe decided to give another gift to humanity, a gift that would prove strength and cooperate with the blueprints to mortal ascension. A weapon carved and cut with the divine finger of the divine architect. In the vastness of space, six angels sat quietly in a room of flaming mirrors as they prepared to council with the universal architect. The lower atmosphere of the room was covered in a strange purple mist; the council table was solid gold with a Hebrew name of God largely engraved into the center of it. And so, the council began, and an angel by the name of Michael stood up amongst the council, and said, ***"O Hear ye, hear ye, the grandest architect of the universe presiding at this time of existence, all be silent with holy intent."*** Afterward, Michael sat down and prepared to hear the words of the divine number.

As Michael sat down, a ball of wildly vivifying flames appeared at the head of the table and began to gradually take the human form of an old man wearing a robe of white silk. The divine architect of the universe is infallible, and usually takes the form of fire because it represents purification. As the great architect took on a human appearance and stood amongst the council, his throne immediately appeared, after the appearance of his throne, the grand architect sat down to lead the council. The great architect looked at his council, and said, ***"We've gathered here to bring forth a gift to mortal male and females who have attained a great comprehension of the divine schematics set forth for their kind. We have many against us in the realms of error because of their hierofastidia; fallen angels are visibly uncomfortable with those of us who are positive and excellent torchbearers of good will. Our office is not and has never been proved to be an androcracy; however, this is what some of my fallen children have come to believe, consequently, they are in great error. There is but one small difference between mortal and angel, and cosmic law divides the difference.***

In mortal areology, there isn't much known of the struggles against the fallen angels of error. Today, we are in council to make mortal men and women armipotent, but not with guns, knives or any other mundane object that can be utilized to take another mortal life, today we will give mortals the spiritual arms necessary to battle their greatest spiritual adversaries, we council to aid them in defeating the orders of evil not only in their lives, but all over the universe. With the subtle weapon that I shall place in the physical counterpart of the male and female mortal, when attaining a great state of divine consciousness, the weapon will not only allow them to manifest their own universe; it will also allow them to utilize bilocation. With certain abilities, they will attain a better comprehension of the image that they're created in. Throughout time, those who I have sent to warn disobedient transgressors with commination have truly and duly served

their purpose, however, it is found that certain mortals could care less about any form of punishment whatsoever. Some of them are equal in the ignorant depths of unnecessary and unreasonable apathy. As the ruler of the universe, what shall I do with those who are worthy of mortal ascension? The answer is simple; those who are worthy shall attain greatness with great favor.

Thus, we are in council today to present a sword that will aid ascending or ascended mortals in their journey to worthiness. Within this sword, I will place my tongue, the tongue that manifests, and the blade shall be constructed of an energy taken from my very throne. The six of you will place your strengths in its handle so that its power will be well solidified with obedience to the laws and principles of my divine presence over all of existence. And please take note that this subtle weapon is a gift to mortals, and furthermore, it shall be called the sword of Elohim, so mote it be!" And so, the grand architect opened his mouth and placed his hand in front of himself with his palm open, and out of his mouth came a glowing ball of energy which directed itself over the center of the council table. When Metatron, Sandalphon, Michael, Raphael, Uriel and Gabriel saw this, they immediately comprehended the idea. Finally, they all raised their hands and opened their palms, and immediately a brilliant light flashed within the council room. After the flash of brilliant light appeared, a small square of silver appeared due to the combination of angelic powers. The square of silver gradually placed itself at the center of the council table. When the divine architect saw this, he combined his power with the square of silver, once he had done that, he closed his palm and made a fist, and when he did, the unknown energy of God and the strengths of the council had divided into infinitesimal particles of energy.

And finally, each particle descended into the mundane world and placed itself deep within the physical counterpart of all mortal beings. The sword that would change the fate of mortals all over the world had finally been issued to all of mankind. After the council meeting, the divine architect commanded the council to report back to the realms of heaven. He then stayed behind and said to his self, ***"There have always been those who would serve me without flaw, all shall return to the essence from which they came, but mortal ascension and eternal life shall be granted and inherited by my faithful and obedient followers. With the sword of Elohim, a mortal can summon forth their archangelic brethren. They shall have Metatron to vanquish the evil. Also, they will have the angels of the four cardinal points of the Earth at their disposal; this is good, for he who wields this sword will prove themselves worthier than most fallen angels whose wisdom is of the old ages of time. With the abilities dormant in that sword, my son Yahuahshua shall smite evil in my name, and with my wisdom."*** Afterward, the divine architect disappeared and returned to his throne room in Araboth, the final plan for mortal ascension had been added after a long period of time had passed.

The grand architect was well pleased; Namsilat, Calabrael, Fireael, Aquari-on, Earthael and Airael have shown themselves worthy enough to prove that human beings have the potential to ascend to great levels, thus, a new weapon to fight all evil would prove to be a good thing. When Mephistopheles heard these things, he sought to use the sword of Elohim for his own evil purposes. The sword was fit for a god, and Mephistopheles never believed any human being to be worthy of such power, no matter who the mortal was. He then realized that he would have to find a mortal who was close to and worthy of attaining it so that he could take it immediately. And so, Mephistopheles thought of the only ascended mortals who had reached such a height of divine consciousness, he then said to himself, ***"The old man called Calabrael, he is definitely a candidate for such power. Though he is no match for me, he may pose a problem; I***

must somehow make him attain greatness in order to steal the sword. I must plan this carefully, if I can get the sword, then, and only then will I be strong enough to overthrow God, and take my rightful place among heaven."

Mephistopheles is known as a supernal creature that works for good while still plotting much evil. And now that he has realized that there is but one weapon that can aid him in attaining his goal of universal reign, he will stop at nothing to get it. The sword of Elohim will act as the key through which he will create a new universe of creatures that only he can adore and command. Because of the power within the sword of Elohim, one man must come forth and stop a most great and evil creature. Somewhere on Earth, Mephistopheles is preparing to do what is necessary to overthrow heaven, Earth and the universe that it resides in. This time, the divine architect has fashioned something that would seem to be a true problem that would weigh heavily on his universal heart, for it was his decree that mortal ascension be given to mortals so that they may attain a greater state of being equal to that possessed by angels in the beginning of time.

However, the divine architect knows that the events that will take place will not become problematic for him or existence. The divine architect loved mankind so much that even in times where he had to warn them of the consequences of their wicked acts, he felt no sense of guilt, but no parent enjoys punishing their children. From Adam to Eve, the divine architect has seen more than enough of his creations transgressions and defiance of his natural laws. However, it is a great love that is kept within the existence of that great consciousness called ***"God."*** Though the divine architect knew of the sins of man since he first created them, he also knew that he would always have elect warriors who would follow his instructions and would die for his name if necessary. Therefore, to destroy the world of living men would be unfair, for even though there are sinners, there are also righteous men who can be depended upon if necessary. The divine architect knew that a continuous trip to Earth would eventually destroy what he created because his power was too potent, a great chance was taken when the sons of Calabrael fought against the son of the morning and the divine architect appeared on the mundane plane. However, it was a chance that had to be taken.

Mephistopheles lurks around the corners of the Earth while walking down mount Everest and begins to speak to himself, saying, ***"Lucifer, you fool, I knew you would fail, I should've been the ruler of evil legions, you wasted their power and marched to rule the footstool of our creator, and yet; you failed, I knew you would, and that is why I stayed out of your nescient plans. Now, it is my turn to war with the throne, but I shall not fail as you have, I will have more than enough legions to overthrow heaven. I will march through the gates of our old home, and become the new creator of all things."*** Mephistopheles used a divine energy from his index finger to write a contract that would help him begin his plan for universal domination. The contract was to be signed by the divine architect himself. The contract specifically stated that, ***"The cosmic creator of all existence shall not come forth from the seventh heaven to interfere in the affairs of mankind and fallen angels."*** He used his index finger as if it were a pen, and as he waved his finger, the language of the angels was burned into a strange parchment paper, which would suffice for a contract that God would never sign. Mephistopheles believed in himself enough to fool his self into thinking that God would willingly agree with his unlawful wishes to rule the universe.

Mephistopheles began his journey to the heavens and presented himself to the divine architect in heaven. He then spoke, saying, ***"Great architect of the universe, I can present you*** *with proof that mankind is not worth your consideration, sign this contract and I will show myself worthy of your eyes. This contract that I've written will be known as an agreement that you will not interfere in my plans against your creatures. I know you are a God that does not break your word, therefore, if you sign this contract, I am sure that the humans will have to fight for themselves without your aid, besides, if you believeth so heavily on your elect, then you will sign this contract and you will only watch as I prove these creatures to be unworthy of all things."* The divine architect replied, saying, *"You present yourself in front of mine eyes and try to deceive me with a contract that both you and I know you have much more planned than simply showing me that my creations are unworthy, my dear misguided creature that I hath formed of my own hand, wherewithal shall a young dragon learn when he is mistaken? First, I will not sign your contract, and second, I need not give you assurance that I will not interfere, you once served me, therefore, I say unto you, how many times must I show you that those I have created and made in my image is worthy, even worthier than thee.*

I beseech ye, O Mephistopheles, what is it that you truly plan to do, though I know, will you answer me? Did you come here and think in thy heart that I would know nothing? I tell you in this very moment, I will not interfere; I will gladly sit back and watch you try. For you have said the same words that Lucifer has saith in his heart. I warn you now, you waste your time trying to attain my tongue, which is, sharper than any double-edged sword; yes, I know you search for the sword of Elohim that I have taken from my own heart and given to mankind for mortal ascension. You stand here in my very presence with the plan to sit on my throne in the sides of the north where my council makes its meeting place of divine fire and strength. You wish to rule that in which I have manifested of my own fingers. You are no different from the rest of your fallen brethren. Verily, I say unto you, they have failed, and so will you. Your intentions are of evil

and error, and because they are, they shall not prosper. You have plagued my people and my footstool with your constant evil for reasons not even you can comprehend. In time, my good creations shall have great peace, and your kind will stare into a black hole wherein you will not be able to see yourself, however, you cannot see yourself as I speak. Go forth Mephistopheles, fail as you will, you know that I know all, yet you still waste your time attempting to prove me a liar of my own word, for I gave you a place near me amongst the stars and you followed Lucifer and pledged your allegiance to him and then you lied to him, and betrayed both of us, by all means, you deceived both sides and devised your own plans from the beginning." Mephistopheles began to get angry at these words, and said, ***"I am not Lucifer, I hate you more than he ever has, he at least had a peculiar respect for you, I hate you with all of my being, you place yourself on a throne and call yourself a king of kings and the God of gods, you are no God, neither are you a king, your end is near divine architect, I will come for you, expect my presence to return here, and when I do, I will toss you from your throne just like you cast us from heaven the day we lashed out against your plans for mortal ascension. You choose them over us?! We are perfect!"***

The divine architect stopped him where he stood, and said, ***"Silence! Speak no more filth in my throne room, you call yourself perfect, and you've taken liberty and followed the ways of evil and misguided mortal men of error which are plagued with confusion, I made you to do different works, and to aid mankind in becoming a race worthy enough that we may all reside in the same place as we did after I manifested the universes and all of its beauty, yet you went forth and followed them while envying and being jealous of them, go forth with your plans and do what you say you will do, but I tell you now, you stand no chance my fallen son."*** Mephistopheles turned his face away from God and disappeared as he walked away from the realms of heaven. Afterward, he returned to Earth to move on with his plans, despite the words of the grand architect of the universe, Mephistopheles knew that he could manifest, but only on a small scale, however, he knew that if he could attain *the tongue of God/the sword of Elohim*, then he could manifest on a large scale. He then remembered the old man whom Archangel Michael had made him speak with when Lucifer had began his war on Earth. Mephistopheles remembered his name, his name was Calabrael, and how could he forget. Mephistopheles was sure that Calabrael could be the key through which the divine architect would expect the sword of Elohim to be attained for the first time. In order to be sure of it, he teleported to Calabrael's home, and when he got there, he was immediately struck by a holy lightning that raced out of the firmament. Mephistopheles was surprised, for Calabrael had set up a divine force field around his home, and that is only something a powerful mystic could do. Calabrael was so filled with the knowledge of heaven that he could move a star in the heavens, and direct it to do his will.

Mephistopheles backed away so that he could use his divine powers to dispel the force field. He raised his arms and hands above his head while raising his countenance toward the firmament, and immediately the force field was dispelled. Afterward, he teleported to a secret place where only he knew, an old abandoned castle located in London, England. The secret place was equipped with a crystal ball where he could watch everything taking place in Calabrael's home. There were walls formed of large stones, and a dungeon that was a few centuries old. Upon the ground of his secret place was dried blood, rats, mice, and roaches that ran wild throughout the whole castle. Six candles lit the room so that he could see. An old wooden drawer containing esoteric documents written on parchment were scattered everywhere. The science of magic and the names of old magicians were finely written upon all documents. Pictures of pentagrams, hexagrams, enneagrams and so forth were divine ideas long lost to most human beings. The metaphysics of the past was strong and mighty knowledge that all demons had possessed. As Mephistopheles waved his hand over his crystal ball to activate it, he saw everything that he needed to see.

However, Mephistopheles became curious as to why there was one room in Calabrael's home that he could not see with his crystal ball. He could see Calabrael go to a library in his home, but afterward his crystal ball would go blank and show nothing. Mephistopheles was surely not a fool, he spoke to his self, and said, ***"This mortal man dwelleth in the secret place of the most high; he abides under the shadow of the almighty. I cannot see the room in which he attends regularly. Regardless, I can see everything else, I feel a strong sense of divinity in his son, and his psychic centers are fully developed. Why would such a young child have all of his psychic centers perfectly developed? Which of these mortals will possess the sword of Elohim? I must know which one it is! If I wait too long I'll never find out, I know that the old mystic must know about the sword by now, I can no longer wait, I must break his soul now, and make him tell me everything I need to know. Hopefully, that child will pose no problems for me, it is a blessing that Lucifer killed his older brothers; thanks to that fool I should have no problems. Calabrael may be the one that I need to move on with my plans, it would be consummate strategy to ask the questions I want answered as I torture his subtle existence."***

Meanwhile…

Calabrael leaves his son and his wife to go and pray in the secret room. As Calabrael finished his prayer and left the secret room, a flash of great darkness appeared. Mephistopheles snapped his fingers and Calabrael immediately found himself in the presence of the evil Mephistopheles. Calabrael was surrounded by a filthy dungeon that seemed to be very old. He had no idea as to what had just happened; yet knowing that Mephistopheles had much to do with why he ended up where he was. He looked at Mephistopheles and raised his right hand to use his powers against him, but Mephistopheles was too quick and too powerful, he stopped Calabrael as soon as he moved his hands. Mephistopheles laughed as he looked at the palm of his hands and clapped once. And immediately, a pair of golden chains forged in divinity appeared, and bound Calabrael's hands and feet. Calabrael shouted out loud, saying, ***"What do you want from me, demon!?*** Mephistopheles replied, saying, ***"I want answers, I want you to attain the sword of Elohim, and I want you to do it now, if you do not, I will make you suffer. Meanwhile, do yourself a favor by not bothering to use your powers against me, for your powers are nothing compared to mine, your four sons would have definitely been a challenge for me, however, Lucifer has taken care of them already. I understand that you have the principles of the grand architect's footstool freely flowing gracefully throughout your bloodstream, thus, I am sure that what I am looking for is somehow related to you. Only an elect of God can hold such holy energy in his bloodstream without passing through transition immediately."***

Calabrael was an old mystic and no demon could persuade him to deceive the divine architect, even if it meant losing his life, for Calabrael was wise and well aware that life and death are one. Calabrael showed no fear and knew that there was nothing to fear except fear itself. Mephistopheles glanced at Calabrael's countenance, and realized that Calabrael was far from scared. When Mephistopheles saw this, he spoke to Calabrael, saying, ***"Foolish mortal man, you will tell me what I want to know!"*** After saying this, Mephistopheles took his hand and reached into the physical counterpart of Calabrael's body and snatched his psychic body from its physical shell. He then began to whisper to Calabrael's psychic body, and as he whispered to it, it began to kneel. Calabrael began to scream to the top of his lungs when he began to realize what Mephistopheles was trying to accomplish. Afterward, Mephistopheles reached into Calabrael's psychic body and pulled another subtle form from it. Finally, Mephistopheles pulled Calabrael's soul out and was electrified by a most awesome energy that immediately knocked him to the ground and transiently blinded him. Calabrael's soul was engraved with the symbols for salt, sulfur and mercury, the likes of which a foul creature such as Mephistopheles could never torture or touch.

Calabrael's soul immediately returned to the depths of his psychic body, and his psychic body returned to his physical envelope. Mephistopheles grew extremely angry with this, and began to telekinetically pick things up and toss them at the walls of his secret place. Calabrael began to breath heavily as if he was overly tired, and Mephistopheles looked at Calabrael, and said, ***"I see now that I will not be able to torture you the way I want to, however, I don't have to touch you to harm you, the chains that imprison you are made to make cosmic abilities subside and become inactive as long as you are chained. I will keep you here for fifteen years, and you shall not see your son, nor shall you see your wife. Nothing can save you; I don't believe that I need to say anymore than that, if you truly are the mystic man that your soul displays, the absence of your loved ones is punishment enough, for the absence of them shall gradually smite thy heart with ease. Calabrael, you shall suffer here for fifteen years, and in time, you will miss the growth of your son and the wife that you love so much."*** Meanwhile, Tri-dael began searching the house for her husband, she opened every door and looked in every room of her house, yet she found no sign of her husband at all, she began to worry, she then called the police and filed a report. Time began to pass, and at this point, she cried and said, ***"Where have you gone? I know you well, and you would never leave us without saying anything to us, I know***

something is wrong, I will take care of our son until you return, and hopefully I can teach Ethereael the way you would want him to be taught, please come back to us."

Finally, Mephistopheles left his secret place and Calabrael was filled with sorrow, he had not water, nor food to survive fifteen years of unholy imprisonment. In time, Calabrael became weak and fatigue. For the first month, Calabrael spoke to himself, saying, ***"I miss my son, and my wife, but this demon shall not break my spirit."*** An angel named Sandalphon brought and gave Calabrael food to eat for the first six months, one year had passed, and Calabrael had prayed and ate of the word of God, and because he did, another angel appeared unto him and gave him food to eat and water to drink once again. Calabrael survived a year with very little food and water. The divine architect looked down upon Calabrael, and said, ***"My beloved Calabrael, I know what you can and cannot bear, and this day you have truly made me proud, for many have made me proud and have deceived me afterward, even my beloved Solomon fell victim to deceiving me by loving foreign women with foreign gods whom granted him things short of everything I granted him. O Calabrael, steadfast and be strong, for the principles of my footstool will soon give you favor."*** And so, the divine architect was proud and filled with cosmic joy. The second year began to pass, and Calabrael coughed, and as he coughed, he spat up blood, and when his blood touched the ground, a subtle form appeared and brought with him a cup of purified water from the throne room of God. Calabrael could hardly lift his countenance, afterward; the subtle form held Calabrael's head up and poured the water into his mouth. Calabrael was replenished and knew that God walked with him yet another day of his life of imprisonment.

And so, three years passed and Calabrael's beard began to grow quickly, and his skin began to sag, for Calabrael was gradually missing all the days of his life being held captive as a part of Mephistopheles' devious plans. He began to think about his son and his wife; he thought of them for a brief moment and quickly returned to saying the ninety-first psalm of the holy bible without stopping. Out of the mouth of Calabrael, this was said: ***"He that dwelleth in the secret place of the most high shall abide under the shadow of the almighty. I will say of the lord, he is my refuge and my fortress: my God; in him will I trust. Surely he shall deliver me from the snare of the fowler, and from the noisome pestilence. He shall cover thee with his feathers, and under his wings shalt thou trust: his truth shall be thy shield and buckler. Thou shall not be afraid for the terror by night; nor for the arrow that flieth by day; nor for the pestilence that walketh in darkness; nor for the destruction that wasteth at noonday. A thousand shall fall at thy side, and ten thousand at thy right hand; but it shall not come nigh thee. Only with thine eyes shalt thou behold and see the reward of the wicked. Because thou hast made the Lord, which is my refuge, even the most high, thy habitation, there shall no evil befall thee, neither shall any plague come nigh thy dwelling, for he shall give his angels charge over thee, to keep thee in all thy ways. They shall bear thee up in their hands, lest thou dash thy foot against a stone. Thou shalt tread upon the lion and adder: the young lion and the dragon shalt thou trample under feet. Because he hath set his love upon me, therefore will I deliver him: I will set him on high, because he hath known my name. He shall call upon me, and I will answer him: I will be with him in trouble; I will deliver him, and honor him. With long life will I satisfy him and shew him my salvation."***

And when his mouth became dry, he endlessly repeated it in his mind. And now, five years passed and unbelievably, Calabrael was still alive, living off of the word of God and focusing solely on not failing the divine architect. Throughout the time of earth, ten years had passed. And throughout the ten years, undines ***(spirits of water)*** brought him water with special nutrients and all of the things that the body would attain from food on a regular basis. The special water was full of healthy things to keep Calabrael alive, and fortunately, it worked. And again time passed and it became twelve years in counting that Mephistopheles held Calabrael captive. Thanks to the spirits of water, Calabrael had beaten the odds that were against him. He was gradually approaching the final three years of his imprisonment. Eventually, the undines stopped coming to give him water, and gnomes began to emerge from the cracks of the earth and bring crackers with red wine. Calabrael was thankful and in joy, even though he had been imprisoned long enough to have simply died a long time ago. Calabrael began thanking the divine architect of the universe and praying evermore as he may have been in much pain and very tired, but he was still alive. And so, two more years had passed, and Calabrael expected nothing and asked for nothing. His beard nearly reached the ground, his cloths were old, and he smelled, due to not having the luxury of a shower or sink of some sort.

Finally, fifteen years had passed, and Mephistopheles had appeared to Calabrael once again. Mephistopheles laughed, and said, ***"Look at yourself, wouldn't you rather be dead? What do you live for, look at what your God has caused you to suffer and go through; do you still love him now!? He has abandoned you. He has no care for mortals; can't you see that, old man?! If your God is so great, why has he not descended from the heavens to save you? How long will he hide in heaven and sit on his throne as if you do not exist?"*** Calabrael was tired and had very little life left in him. Yet, that did not stop him from using all of the strength in his body to raise his countenance to Mephistopheles, and speak loudly with a hoarse voice, saying, ***"The lord is my shepherd, I shall not want."*** Mephistopheles was greatly angered at this and realized that Calabrael could not be broken; Calabrael was reinforced with the power of God. And so, Mephistopheles raised his hand, and the golden chains forged of divinity had broken, and Calabrael was free at last. Mephistopheles shook his head left and right as if Calabrael was a pitiful, pitiful man; he then disappeared as he walked away from his secret place and left Calabrael to die for his God. Calabrael fell to the ground and was unable to move, he was weak, yet strong in the greatest definition of the word. He laid there and went nowhere; he then began to speak to himself, saying, ***"Divine architect, will I die here on the grounds of the Earth without clean cloths and without seeing my family?"*** He then went unconscious and laid there as if he was already dead.

As Calabrael laid there unconscious, gnomes ***(spirits of Earth)*** crawled out of the cracks of the dungeon, and carried his body to a nearby river, and from there, undines carried him across the seas as far as they could go. Afterward, sylphs ***(spirits of air)*** lifted him up and carried him home to his wife and his son. Calabrael had gained the respect of all of the elemental creatures. He was the first mortal to ascend passed the *"wants"* of men and solely lay his faith on the creator of all existence. He had ascended to the height of divine consciousness. He survived the greatest perils that a man could survive. And because of this, the sword of Elohim was given to Calabrael for outstanding faith and belief in God almighty. As he lies unconscious in front of his home, God spoke to him, and said, ***"To thee I give the greatest reward that a mortal man can receive. You have proven yourself and all men to be worthy of much, for if you can do such things Calabrael; then there are many more that can do the same. Your life will not end today Calabrael, you will live, and when you awaken, you will see your son and your wife. You will be laid in your bed as if none of the current events ever happened, but I say this unto you, O wise Calabrael, a great battle awaits your son, but his life will be spared, he shall prevail, and be triumphant. I have chosen to let you fight your own battles, so*** *as to display the strength of the mighty image I have created you in. I aid those who aid themselves. Mephistopheles believes that your kind is not worth any of my acknowledgement, but I say unto you today, I shall always walk with you, now go; and become alive, for the path that leads to victory is yours, verily, I say unto you, mortal ascension is yours for the taking. Deep inside of you, I have placed my tongue, equipped with my word, that in which is sharper than any double-edged sword, and when the time comes, you will know what to do with it."* And so, Calabrael woke-up, and his son and his wife stood over him and asked what happened to him, and where he had been for such an extremely long time. Calabrael spoke, and said, *"There is a great battle for you, my son, and you are not prepared to face whatever it may be. I have not strength in my body to train you; I am mentally, physically and spiritually tired. In the secret room that my father before me made when I was just a child is where you will find everything you need.*

You'll comprehend what you are and what is in your blood, I know you have heard the stories of your four brothers before you, but I believe that it is time for you to experience your own destiny, I am too overwhelmed with fatigue to foresee your future even the slightest bit, but I know for sure that whatever it is, you will be triumphant, my son." Ethereael replied, saying, *"How do you know that I'll be triumphant in anything at all, dad?"* Calabrael said, *"Because you are my son."* Afterward, Calabrael spoke to Ethereael, and said, *"Go forth to the secret room, and stay there until you know thyself with ease, to know thyself is to know the universe that is without, and the universe that is within. When I was last here, you were just a young boy of six years old, now that I have returned; it is imperative that you follow my instructions and do what I ask of you. I have missed most of your life, and I am truly sorry, but there are more important things than the worries of ourselves, be as wise as the wisest of*

men. Now go forth and return to me as soon as you are done, I will not leave until you have earned what I must give you.

I will live until you return to me, for now, I will take a great form in meditation until I can feel the worthiness in your electromagnetic field. When you stand over me, I will awaken, and we shall take it from there, now go to the secret room and do what is necessary to receive the gifts passed down to our bloodline." Ethereael stared at his father and found himself in complete shock. However, Tri-dael was no fool; she had learned much from her husband about the world of the supernal, and she knew well what her husband was talking about. Tri-dael realized that Ethereael wasn't moving, and said to him, "***Ethereael, don't waste time, do what he says, I have a feeling that something bad is going to happen, I've been feeling it since your father disappeared. You know where the room is, go, go now, and do what you have to do.***" Ethereael looked at his mother, and speedily walked to the secret room immediately, unaware of what he was doing and scared of the events taking place in his life at the young age of 21 years old.

And so, the story continues, and Ethereael learns the truth about what he needs to know about himself and the cosmic abilities that not even his father Calabrael has yet to witness.

Chapter 7

The Son of Ether

The final son of the elements has finally been born. He goes by the name of Ethereael and his ability is powerful, yet unknown. However, Calabrael believes that he will possess the awesome power of the omnipresent propagation of ether energy, the fifth element. His powers have yet to show themselves however. Calabrael is now ripe in age, and is preparing for the greater works of men, just as his father Namsilat did. Calabrael and Tri-dael are blessed to have Ethereael, and are proud of him, for Ethereael learned to walk at nine months old. Calabrael believes that if his son Ethereael holds the mighty power of ether, then eventually, he'll become a cosmic warrior formidable to all demon creatures.

Calabrael and Tri-dael were astonished at Ethereael's progress as a child. As a child, there was no sign of cosmic abilities; however, Calabrael could care less as long as he was healthy and safe from evil, thanks to his older brothers who had passed through transition for all of mankind. Of course, time passed as it usually does, Ethereael made the age of six years old, and his father was kidnapped, and held captive by Mephistopheles, who kept Calabrael as a prisoner for fifteen years.

Ethereael has been raised by his mother, he learned and knew a modicum of universal knowledge, however, he didn't know enough to prepare for any battles or dangers that might occur, besides, Ethereael didn't think that he would have to do anything or fight anyone since his brothers had already sacrificed themselves for humanity when they fought against Lucifer, the son of the morning. Ethereael thought to himself and couldn't understand what danger could be more dangerous than a battle against the son of the morning.

After reaching the secret room, Ethereael began to think about the stories that he was told about his beloved brothers who gave their lives to defend the weak and uphold the laws of the universe. Calabrael's son needs to find himself so that he can return to his father to receive a gift and a better understanding of what is happening. Ethereael sits on the ground of the secret room and decides to close his eyes and meditate, so as to find a great comprehension of self.

He searched the universe of his mind, asking questions and looking for answers to the secrets within himself. As Ethereael searched for answers for his questions, a voice spoke deep within his mind, saying, ***"Son of the mighty Calabrael, how art thou searching for answers to questions that ye already know? Thy power derives from the laws of the most high; you are the principle that sustains all others. Your power is not to direct fire, water, Earth or air. Your power is greater than that. Mortals who have yet to ascend cannot see your ability so easily. It is sad to admit that you are missing the one thing that all of your brothers possessed before they passed through transition."***

Ethereael replied, saying, ***"What is it that I'm missing?"*** And the voice says, ***"You lack the belief that you're extraordinary in nature."*** Finally, the voice took form and Ethereael felt a presence nearby, and then, something touched and tapped his shoulder, Ethereael was startled as he turned around only to see an old man holding a staff of mixed metals shaped like the symbol for planet Mercury. The hairs upon his head and face were white. And his eyes appeared to be some sort of liquid metal, his robe was all black, and upon the chest area of the robe was the symbol for Mercury, which was burning in white flames of light.

He then introduced himself to Ethereael, and spoke in a loud voice, saying, ***"I am Hermes Mercurius Trismegistus, thrice great! I will show you the way to the paths of victory, and I will unveil the height of your cosmic abilities. More or less, I will also aid you in the comprehension of the universe within, and the universe without, and once I have, your powers will awaken, and you will have ascended enough to endure the battle against a great force who is making himself believe that he is the true creator of the universe; yet knowing that he is not. Because of the limitations of time, it is my duty to bless you with the secret teachings of all ages within the heavens and the Earth, so mote it be!"***

The old man grabbed Ethereael's hand, and Ethereael began to have a series of violent seizures as if he was being electrocuted. As his body violently shook like a great storm amidst a vast ocean, multiple visions of the secrets of mysticism took place within his mind, and Ethereael's hair was no longer jet black. His electromagnetic field began to glow like the sun that illuminates the Earth, and his hair became as white as a young dove's feathers.

The time had come, Ethereael had truly opened his eyes, and when he did, he had eyes like liquid mirrors. Those who would look into his eyes could only see themselves. No one would ever be able to look into the pupils of Ethereael's eyes ever again, for he had ascended, inherited and comprehended the secrets that his family had received for years. As Ethereael realized his ascension, he stayed in the secret room and read the contents of every book within the secret room. As he absorbed the contents of each book, he was excellently enlightened to a world that was only known to very few mortals. Strange diagrams of divinity and creation were present in every book. As Ethereael read each book, Hermes watched over him and made sure that he did not absorb too much knowledge.

And when Ethereael finished reading the thirty-third book, Hermes spoke aloud, saying, ***"It is done, the will of the cosmos is done, once again. Ethereael, grandson of Namsilat, son of Calabrael; your destiny is greater than can be imagined. Great responsibilities come to those who possess this power. You have attained mortal ascension. Consequently, the plan for mortal ascension is the very reason for demon rebellion against heaven and Earth, therefore, because God sought to give mortals a better comprehension of the life that they possess; man must prove that his plan is far from failure. Your siblings proved it; now, you must prove it, Ethereael.***

Before you go forth and attain the gift from your father, there is a gift that I have for you; this gift has only been given to mystics who have been found worthy in the eyes of the divine architect. Hermes turned his back and opened his palms to face the heavens. A bright and brilliant light shined all over the secret room, and Hermes was holding something in his hands. It was a robe, but not just any robe; it was a robe made of Mercury, a robe that was held together in one form. Hermes had somehow used the laws of cohesion, adhesion, attraction and repulsion to stabilize liquid Mercury as a robe of clothing.

The robe was heavy, but the heavy weight of the robe would naturally pose no problem for an ascended mortal, and wearing it was like wearing a mirror. Hermes had given Ethereael a robe that reflected all things. Ethereael's eyes were shocked as he began to put the robe on and wear it. And so, Hermes spoke to Ethereael, and said, ***"This is yours to keep, pass it down to your son, and your son's sons. Thou hast shown me that ye are worthy of this most sacred garment."*** Ethereael nearly looked like a walking, breathing mirror. After seven days of great meditation, Ethereael had attained greatness with the aid of Hermes Mercurius Trismegistus, thrice great.

The time had come to leave the secret room that had harbored so many years of mysticism. Again Hermes spoke, and said, "***Live wise and swift! So mote it be.***" And so, Ethereael had attained comprehension of what he is, and what he must do. Seven days have passed, and Ethereael finally emerges from the secret room as a new mortal man, one with the power to be triumphant and victorious over his enemy. And so, the bookshelf slid to the side of the left, and Ethereael emerged from it, and said to his self, "***What is the battle that awaits me?***"

He began to gradually move forward in his new mercury robe, and left the secret room that had been in his family for countless years. He then proceeded to the upper chambers of the mansion, and to the room where his father laid. He then walked toward his father's bed slowly, and his mother glanced at her son and was instantly startled and amazed by his appearance. Ethereael looked totally different within, and without. He then spoke to his father, and said, "***I have learned what and who I am, and before you say what you have to say to me, I want you to know that I wasn't angry at you for not being here, something in my heart told me that you had a good reason. If there was ever a man that is honorable among many things, that man is you. I remember the things you would say to me when I was just a child; you were always wise. Common sense let me know that a father as wise as you would never get up and leave his son astray.***"

After hearing this, Calabrael replied, saying, "***Ethereael, your brothers would have been very proud of you if they were here today. I cried for many years when I had realized that Lucifer had killed them. When you were born, you calmed the pain of having lost four sons that I loved dearly. By all means, they made me proud every day, and you make me proud as well. A mysterious spiritual power runs through our blood, and because it does, I never doubted whether you would catch on to the family***

secret at all. I knew you would, you were raised no differently than your brothers. All of you had a strong belief in the great architect of the universe. There was always a certain divine fire in your eyes, and on the day that each of you were born, I saw it. I have never been one to rush, but there isn't much time; the demon that did this to me is looking for the sword of Elohim at this very moment.

It is a weapon that I never thought would exist or be attainable to mortals because of the lack of peace in the world. However, I am proud to tell you that I have attained it because of the courage and faith that I displayed when I was trapped in that foul dungeon for so long. The gift that I give to you is a gift given to me by the great architect of the universe. Before I pass through transition and prepare for the greater works, I wish to pass this on to you, my son.

This sword is wanted by all demons, they either want to destroy it or use it for evil purposes. But today, I give this to you in hopes that you will know what to do with it." And so, Calabrael turned his head away from his son and looked at his wife Tri-dael. He then said, ***"O Tri-dael, O sweet wife of mine, I have loved you since the day I met you, and now, I must go. While I was gone, you took Ethereael and gave him the wisdom that I would have given him anyway. I suppose I never really left my family, you were always with me, and I was always with you.***

Without you, Ethereael may have never made it this far. To you, I will give my knowledge. And with this knowledge, you will guide our son, and our son's sons. Let it be known in the presence of the great architect. Tri-dael, you shall carry on my works, here on Earth." Finally, Calabrael closed his eyes and told Ethereael to hold his left hand while Tri-dael held his right hand. Tri-dael and Ethereael did exactly as they were told. As Calabrael's wife held her husband's hand, she began to shake her head left and right while she kept her eyes closed to witness and receive the mysterious knowledge of the man named Calabrael, she then fell to the ground and passed out.

The knowledge of Calabrael was so great that Tri-dael's body laid there illuminated with a light that only the heavens hath contained. As Tri-dael rested on the ground surrounded by heavenly illumination, Ethereael fell to his knees due to the holy force that the sword of Elohim carried in its blade. And finally, the sword was transferred to Ethereael, the son of Ether.

And after the universal knowledge was transferred to his wife and the sword of Elohim was transferred to his son, his hands dropped. Calabrael was no more; the man who was imbued with so much wisdom had finally passed through transition.

Thunder raced out of the sky, and heavy rains fell to grounds of the Earth. Another old mystic had moved on to the greater works of mortal men. Calabrael's body rested in his bed without life, he left his family behind to carry on his work, and to be fruitful and multiply so as to continue the Powers' family tradition. After losing his father and realizing that he had attained a great power that his father passed on to him, Ethereael picked his mother up and brought her to the living room.

Tri-dael was unconscious, but alive. Ethereael looked upon his bare hands and contemplated his destiny; however, he came to no conclusion and decided to go to the secret room below the house so that he could attain more equanimity. As he walked off, he thought he heard a quarter drop on the ground, and behold! The voice of his father spoke to him in his mind, and said, ***"My son, a great battle awaits you, one that is even***

greater than the battle that your brothers fought. Worry not, you have been well prepared to handle it, you are in possession of the greatest weapon given to mortal man, the tongue of God." Ethereael replied, ***"What am I suppose to do with it? How do I use it? What battle could be greater than the battle against the son of the morning?"***

There was no reply; the voice of his father had disappeared. And so, Ethereael proceeded to the secret room and sat down. He stayed there and hoped that he wouldn't have to fight a dangerous battle like his brothers before him. However, there was no way for Ethereael to avoid what was written in the stars. He stayed in the secret room for two hours, and then he realized that the only way he was going to truly attain peace was to fight the battle that destiny has given him. After two hours in the secret room, Ethereael stepped out of the room, and his mother stood in front of him. Ethereael was truly startled, he moved abruptly as his mother stood there and stared at him.

She spoke to him, and said, ***"Ethereael, I've been thinking since I woke up, and I don't want to bury your father on Earth. We should do something special. Ever since I woke up, I've been feeling something evil in the world of the living. I think that I understand these spiritual powers that your father had. I'm not used to them yet, but eventually, I'll get used to them. I want you to stay close to me, Ethereael. Something is wrong, I just can't put my finger on it yet, but I know it has something to do with that demon that kidnapped your father.***

Now that I have this newfound power, I should be able to become closer to the cosmos, and maybe kick that demons rear-end all on my own." Ethereael replied, saying, ***"If it was so easy to do, don't you think that dad would've done it already? Apparently something made dad powerless to stop him at the time."*** Tridael replied, ***"I was only joking, lighten up, I'm just trying to be***

positive. But I believe you may be right, however, all I can do is hope that you're prepared for whatever happens." And so, Tri-dael was a new woman, she possessed her husband's mystical and cosmic abilities.

However, Calabrael's body was still in the bedroom, for his body hadn't been moved since his death. His skin was beginning to change color. At this point, it almost broke Tri-dael's heart to go back to her bedroom because her husband's body was still there. Ethereael spoke to his mother, and said, ***"It's time to put him somewhere he'd be happy to be."*** Tri-dael replied, saying, ***"You have to hurry, but you have to do this on your own, I can't stand to watch him while he doesn't talk, I loved your father, and I knew him too well. There wasn't an instant where he wasn't saying something pertaining to wisdom."*** It was time for Ethereael to build a tomb for his father's body, somewhere that would honor his father's life and death.

The time had come for Ethereael to display his natural cosmic powers combined with the sword of Elohim. With the knowledge given to him by Hermes Mercurius Trismegistus, Ethereael had truly become a force to be reckoned with. Nearly an hour had passed, and Ethereael agreed with his mother, and decided that he did not want his father's body buried in the Earth as well.

So he decided to use his cosmic powers to create a great tomb dedicated to his father, Calabrael. Ethereael spoke to his mother, and said, ***"Mom, I have an idea, would you watch over dad while I do something?"*** She replied, and said, ***"What are you going to do?"*** Ethereael replied, ***"Something amazing."*** Ethereal walked outside of the house and flew high into the sky like a powerful missile.

He went higher and higher until he reached outer space, and then he stopped, floating amidst the presence of the universe at large. With the awesome power of ether and the sword of Elohim, Ethereael opened the palm of his left hand and made the rocks of the Earth come to him. And immediately, seven boulders flew from the Earth and stood amongst the great son of ether. The first boulder was flattened and became a large square that Ethereael could utilize to make a foundation for which he would finish and create an honorable tomb for his beloved father. Ethereael continued his creation by taking another boulder and making it stretch like a rubber band.

He then shaped four flat square walls to place upon the foundation. So far, it began to look like a small room without a roof to cover it. Therefore, Ethereael took another boulder and again he shaped it. Then he dived down into to the Earth and grabbed his father's body, pulling it with golden electricity. Calabrael's body began to lift itself off of the bed, from the bedroom, and out of the bedroom window.

Ethereael covered his father's body with a force field of ether as he gradually pulled his father's body to the outskirts of the planet Earth. Finally, Ethereael placed his body into the room that he created. As Ethereael became more acquainted with his newfound powers, his mind brought greater visions of his father's tomb. And as the visions presented themselves to Ethereael's mind, he built what his mind's eye desired.

And so, Ethereael built and built as if he was a great architect. A very small planet to harbor his father's body was created. With a square, a compass and the power of the great geometrician, Ethereael had finally finished. He stepped back and no longer did he have to float or fly upward or downward, Ethereael was standing on ground that he had created. The ground was covered with fine silver and gold. It became apparent that the sword of Elohim and Ethereael were a consummate combination.

The planet was a beautiful place; there were three large trees in three different places. At the middle of the three trees was a small mountain that was flat on its uppermost point. On the flat surface of the mountaintop was a room of stone where the body of his father laid at rest. And after fashioning a planet only to keep and honor his father's life and death, Ethereael returned to planet Earth so that he could speak with his mother about the situation at hand. At this point, it seemed that Ethereael's powers combined with the sword of Elohim were unmatched by any other mortal or demon known to man.

As Ethereael flew through space and back to Earth, he landed in front of his home and opened the front door; his mother stood still and wouldn't move, Ethereael looked at her, and said, ***"What's wrong?"*** His mother wouldn't reply. As Ethereael began to walk toward her, his cosmic senses helped him realize a strong evil presence in the house. Someone or something had dispelled the barrier that Calabrael had placed around the house to keep evil out of it. As Ethereael walked further toward his mother, he stopped and seen an eye peek at him.

Mephistopheles peeked at Ethereael from behind his mother's legs. There he was; a small sized demon with tremendous power. Mephistopheles could take many different forms; however, his favorite was that of a little green skinned creature that was two feet tall, and having a baldhead and the eyes of a cat. His attire was a dirty brown robe with a black rope round about it. His feet were webbed like a duck, but his hands were like human hands. Mephistopheles spoke out loud, and said, ***"Ah...Ethereael, I can smell the tongue of God all over your body, give it to me, and I'll spare your mother's life, and then you can serve and revere me all the days of thy life. Besides, your only human, don't think for one moment that you can defeat me in***

any way. At this point in time, I have the upper hand, and your powers need more time before you can use their perfect height.

Now, give me the sword of Elohim, or I'll separate every atom that she's made of, and help her return to the Earth from which she came." Ethereael was terrified and shocked; it was his first time seeing a demon. Though he heard the stories as a child, he had never really seen one in person. After building up a little courage, Ethereael replied, saying, ***"Let her go, now!"*** Mephistopheles replied, saying, ***"Foolish mortal child, you speak out of fear, and you know not what you possess, you're not worthy of having it!"***

As Ethereael raised his hand to use his powers, Mephistopheles laughed, and stopped time for a brief moment. He teleported in front of Ethereael, and pointed his index finger at Ethereael's head. A brilliant light floated out of Ethereael's heart, and Mephistopheles was eager with joy. When Mephistopheles let go of his cosmic hold on time, the sword of Elohim was gone, and Ethereael's mother was unconscious and stranded on the ground.

The sword of Elohim could only become a physical object if the possessor wanted to lessen its true power, and Mephistopheles was no fool, he took the sword in its most universal form. For the prince of demons was gone, he disappeared; there was no sign of him anywhere. He had been triumphant over the son of Ether. Ethereael felt like a fool, he had been tricked, Mephistopheles had already planned out what he would do, and there was no question as to why it was so easy for him to take it. After being tricked by Mephistopheles, Ethereael kneeled to the ground to help his mother get up, however, she wouldn't move, though she wasn't dead, she was unable to move or respond, she laid there like a zombie of some sort. Her eyes were filled with darkness, and Ethereael began to feel like the biggest fool that ever lived.

When Ethereael realized this, he picked her up and teleported himself and his mother to his father's bedroom and laid her down until he could figure out a way to dispel Mephistopheles' magic. However, Ethereael lost confidence in his self, and forgot about his mother's condition. Ethereael thought to himself, saying, ***"I'm a failure, I can't do anything right, I've dishonored my family, and I've failed my parents with ease. I'm no hero, how could I save anyone from anything when I basically froze when I saw a demon for my first time. Saving the universe and all this crazy stuff, this isn't for me, I'm not like my brothers; I just can't do this!"***

Being frustrated with himself, and angry that he failed his family, Ethereael took flight into outer space and disappeared, leaving his mother behind in an unknown state of mind. Using the power of the fifth principle known as ether, Ethereael transformed himself into pure energy, and placed himself into a meteor hopelessly floating through outer space.

After placing himself in the meteor, he never returned to planet Earth. He was too embarrassed to show his face ever again. Time passed, and Ethereael refused to take physical form and return. Two years passed, and the inhabitants of the Earth were fine, and everything in the universe seemed to be fine. Although Ethereael no longer cared to live, he could still hear the people of Earth speak and laugh. As time passed, Ethereael was filled with much sorrow, for he heard the laughs and cries of a planet that he believed didn't need his help with anything.

He began to think to himself, saying, ***"I've left the Earth astray, dishonored the Powers' family tradition, and now I hide like a coward permeating a meteor destined to travel across the***

universe with no desired destination, let the shadows of evil devour the Earth alive, I don't care. My father is dead, and I haven't the slightest idea of what Mephistopheles has done to my mother, I have nothing!" Ethereael was all alone, for he had not his father, mother, or brothers, and this weighted heavily on his heart. And so, the Earth was left astray, and the grand architect of the universe kept his word and did not interfere in the struggle between angels and humans.

Ethereael, the son of ether was unaware that everything he had done, and everything that took place is all a part of a grand design. As the son of ether, the time he spent in outer space was gradually forcing his natural cosmic abilities to grow immensely. The power of Ether that was naturally locked into Ethereael's bloodstream was being supercharged by the ether propagating throughout the whole universe, simply because he was closer to the direct source distributing ether throughout all of existence. Mephistopheles cursed Ethereael's name and called him a coward among cowards, and when Mephistopheles realized that Ethereael was hiding and wouldn't return, Mephistopheles went forth with his plans for evil manifestation without distraction or interference. And so, there is no defense for our planet, and the only thing that is certain is that the evil demon, Mephistopheles will have rule over the universe after the passing of many cycles. And now, we can only ***hope*** that the last son of Calabrael will return.

Chapter 8

Creating a Universe of Evil

Finally, Mephistopheles has attained what he was looking for. He is now in possession of the mighty sword of Elohim, the tongue of the creator of the universe. With the sword of Elohim by his side, his plan was complete. With it, he would manifest a new place for evil, a place he could call his own universe, composed of one solar system with his own planets, stars and millions of legions of demons that only he could command. And so, the powers families' worst nightmare was brought to fruition. With the sword of Elohim, the evil prince manifested six new planets surrounded by his own stars, and each having a diameter of 42,895,200 km (equatorial).

Mephistopheles took flight far off into the north of the solar system, and as he flew through the cosmos, he waved his hand and combined his mind with the sword of Elohim.

Each wave of his hand created a new mass of matter. After fashioning each planet with his newfound power, he would make a new race of demonic creatures, a race he called ***"Daemune-beings,"*** or the creatures connected to the evil within the hearts of human beings. As the small prince of demons flew across the galaxy, he thought to himself, saying, ***"By the same power that I defy shall I ascend. Foolish ramblings of the God who hurled us out of heaven like stars into the deepest of darkness' chaotic clutches. By the sword given to your precious shall I rule your heaven and earth? Under my foot will I trample the male and the female creature; I seek my rightful place amongst my own council. Today marks the beginning of the end of all creatures that have not been manifested by the fingers of my hands. No longer am I Lucifer's prince of hell, I am the great prince of the***

absences of good, I am my own ruler now.*"** And so, he waved his hand with all his might, and caused atoms to merge into a solid mass of matter that became a planet that he named ***"Artuseus." Artuseus is a purple planet having dangerous mortal eating demon plants that were given intelligence to move and live; plant-demon creatures that hungered to eat of the perfection of the soul and destroy the physical shell.

The creatures of Artuseus would simply eat the soul and destroy the body so as to leave it lifeless. After eating the soul, the demon plants would let the body decompose, and then they would absorb the physical body with their hands by using a dangerous acid within their blood to melt the flesh into a liquefied state. And when Mephistopheles saw the visualizations and images of their minds, he knew that the intentions of the creatures of Artuseus were a part of the fruits of his heart, he was pleased with their ways and methods of life. Mephistopheles was filled with an evil joy that not even Lucifer could comprehend. Being filled with such evil joy, the great demonic prince made the decision to name the creatures of Artuseus, he then thought to himself, saying, ***"Unto the manifestation of this day, I shall call them "Orchytuors," the soul eating plant-demons."*** The Orchytuors were green skinned creatures with living branches for arms and feet.

Their teeth were as sharp as the teeth of ravening wolves. They were bereft of a tongue, and were unable to talk. Their eyes were inane, and their heads were shaped like the head of a human. The Orchytuors were also covered in black leaves and had terrible countenances; they were created from pure evil, and had no care for any living creature other than their own kind, and above all things, their skin was as tough as the toughest tree trunks. Planet Artuseus was the first amongst its planetary brothers, for it was filled with defiled purple dirt that was plenty to tread upon. And so, Mephistopheles continued his manifestation, and moved further into the north of the galaxy and manifested another planet that he decided to name ***"Koythut,"*** a dark-yellow planet inhabited by powerful demons called ***"Archaukits."***

The planet Koythut was a land where fierce demon warriors lived by no honorable code, for they were the mighty rulers of anger and apathy. The Archaukits would fight against and amongst each other, and kill each other without remorse. They had no respect or love for themselves or others, Koythut was simply a brutal planet filled with murder and malevolence. The Archaukits were demons of black scaly skin, and inane eyes. They wore only loincloths and had pointy ears. They were very strong and barbaric creatures that made their weapons from the bones of those who they had brutally murdered for no apparent reason, and though their lifestyles were ignorant, they enjoyed killing more than anything, for killing was a sign of true Archaukit-hood. And so, Mephistopheles moved further into the north of the universe and waved his hand to manifest another planet to add to his new universe of evil. Mephistopheles raised his hands to the cosmos and from the palms of his hands emitted brilliant light that manifested and exerted billions of atoms to create a new planet. Mephistopheles looked upon the planet, and spoke to himself, saying, ***"Ah, but another masterpiece of greatness have I made of my own nimbleness of hand and mind. Unto this mass of material manifestation I shall also name it, and give it evil to be sustained. I hereby name this planet by the name "Nutoayt."*** The new planet was large and gray, and it was inhabited with demon insects that were called **"Malikutuhts."** They were evil eight-legged creatures that had acid instead of blood running through their veins. Their countenances were like the countenance of a filthy roach. Eight small legs sprung out of their black shells, and some had more or less than eight legs, however, their legs and razor sharp dangerous teeth made them quite formidable for any challenge.

They had an unnatural hate for humans, and loved to kill them by wrapping their legs around their bodies, and crushing their upper extremities while feasting on their heads. They more or less believed that the human encephalon was very, very tasty. And again, Mephistopheles had created another race of demons that he was definitely proud of. Witnessing the evil of his own creations and being proud therein, Mephistopheles flew away from the planet Nutoayt and scouted the north once again.

He then hovered in the midst of the north of the universe, and spoke to himself, saying, ***"I am the ruler of demons and demon-like life, I am the father and creator of darkness, there is none with knowledge or powers equipotent to my own, the divine architect will kneel before me, and when he does, I will laugh and imprison him just as he once imprisoned me!"*** Followed by a devious laugh, Mephistopheles lifted his hands high above his head, and immediately a dark-red energy appeared in front of the palms of his left and right hands.

He then spoke aloud, and said, ***"Dispose of all mortals; this is the will of all that have fallen from his heaven!"*** As Mephistopheles said this, a gigantic and mighty gray cloud arose from the palms of his hands. From the center of the cloud came wild and overactive electricity while meteors and stars began to be pulled-in by the electricity in the cloud. Great clashes and sounds of loud and destructive proportion marked the beginning of yet another planetary entity. As the cloud cleared, another planet began to take form. And after the planet's material form was solid and complete, Mephistopheles spoke aloud, and said, ***"It is evil, and it is mine to rule!"*** He then decided to name the new black and gray planet, he spoke in a loud voice, and said, ***"Planet Nuemonaeon, the planet of loyal evil doers; the destroyers of good!"***

The planet **Nuemonaeon** was a planet inhabited by a race

of demons called **"Arisyns."** The Arisyns were ravening creatures of deceit and anger towards mortals, if there were ever a large group of mortals who would not revere Mephistopheles, he would send them to the planet Nuemonaeon to be quickly disposed of. The inhabitants of the planet Nuemonaeon were handsome creatures; they were formed to favor the humans that Mephistopheles hated so much. They looked like humans, however, their skin was pale, and their eyes were inane. Their hair was long and gray, and they wore robes made of fine black silk.

They were created to become Mephistopheles' council of evil intelligence. The Arisyns were so intelligent that they developed a diabolical machine for the torture of the mortal soul. The Machine was constructed of fine silver and was easy to use. The machine was a tall silver square that had a hole to place mortals in, and once the mortal was placed therein, a sharp subtle spinning blade could be activated with a small button on its side. Once the button was pushed and the machine was activated, the subtle blade would spin quickly and tangle the soul around its blade. Once the soul was tangled, the mortal would scream in agonizing pain, and then they would lose all signs of life. And when Mephistopheles saw this, he smiled in grandeur joy, for the Arisyns had truly become evil intelligence, they were merciless and smart.

And so, Mephistopheles continued his journey throughout the north of the galaxy, he then decided that he would manifest two more planets. He looked around and spoke to himself, saying, ***"I am nearly ready to prepare my armies for war on heaven, but I still need one more legion of followers, I grow tired, but I must not stop at this point."*** After realizing that he couldn't stop creating until his goals were achieved, he opened the palms of his hands and two bursts of red energy was released from his hands.

He then directed the bursts of energy to halt, combine, and expand. The bursts of energy clashed and made a gigantic and frightening sound while expanding into a red cloud that began to take solid form. And when it was all said and done, the red cloud hardened and became a large mass of matter. Mephistopheles looked at it, and said to himself, ***"I will call this planet by the name of Strorthune."*** The planet **Strorthune** was brown, and consisted of nothing but rocks and mountains of spikes.

In the caves of the mountains of Strorthune emerged a race of demons that Mephistopheles held very close to his evil heart. For he admired them so much that he named them after himself; he named them **"Mephistophelons,"** creatures that were smart, deceitful and devious among all things. Each creature inhabiting the planet Strorthune was tall in height, each creature reaching eight feet in height. The Mephistophelons were creatures wearing demonic armor engraved with the name of their creator in the writing of the angels. Upon the chest area of their armor was written the words: ***Master Mephistopheles, King of darkness.***

Their countenances were hideous; they possessed red eyes and very little hair. Their facial features seemed as if they lacked facial skin, their faces revealed the structure of their skulls. Over their skulls was hanging dead skin which made the Mephistophelons horrible to look at. Those who looked directly into the red eyes of a Mephistophelonian would immediately lose their strength, whether it was physical or cosmic strength. Unto these creatures was the likeness unto a living skeleton. And so, the fifth planet was manifested and made from true evil. Mephistopheles looked upon planet Strorthune and knew that his power was awesome and could not be tested by any demon, for he was the only demon to rule over millions of his own followers, and he was the first to manifest his own worlds. And so, at this point, Mephistopheles was finally ready to create the planet that would be his home and throne.

Mephistopheles had it all planned out, the sixth and final planet would be named **"Oriah-nandah."** The prince of demons snapped his fingers, and meteors, space waste and stars that had burned out were combined to create the home planet for the evil demon prince. In due time, a humongous blue planet was manifested, and all demons would come to praise Mephistopheles on a daily basis. Mephistopheles made no castle or dwelling place for himself on Oriah-nandah, he simply fashioned a throne to rest upon. He was satisfied with his works, and in his satisfaction, he waved his left hand and brought forth a strong and great wind that continuously graced his home planet. He then realized how tired he was, and decided to close his eyes and manifest a guardian that would protect his home planet whilst he rested and ruled with his own laws. He whispered, and said, ***"Mukut-yoush-athath-omi,"*** and immediately two eyes of light appeared and a large figure was revealed, for Mephistopheles manifested his most powerful creation.

A creation he called Darknesseus, a gigantic demon that sat on top of the planet Oriah-nandah and wrapped its giant wings around it in order to protect its planet and its creator. Darknesseus was a creature with eyes of light, two great and gigantic black wings, the head of a bull, the body of a man covered in brown fur, and yet his lower extremities were like that of bull's. Mephistopheles was very intelligent and liked to plan ahead of time, he then thought to himself, saying, ***"If anyone or anything chooses to remove me from my throne whilst I rest or while I'm awake, they will have to defeat Darknesseus first. When and if someone or something would defeat Darknesseus, then and only then shall I find them worthy enough to see me face to face."*** And so, Mephistopheles was content with his creations of evil, and finally he rested and sat upon his throne and sent out a decree on his behalf. He spoke out loud, and his voice traveled to all of his manifestations.

He said, ***"All demons must report to my throne to revere me daily, and make me proud, so that I may bestow my blessings upon thee, so that ye may live a lengthy life of overwhelming evil."*** After Mephistopheles made his planetary decree on all of his manifestations, the inhabitants of all his planets reported to Oriah-nandah and followed his commands. He then stood up from his throne in front of the great multitude of demons, and spoke aloud, saying, ***"I have manifested true greatness, the time has come! Those of you who reside in the paradise universe of Mestophelue shall bring pain and suffering to the precious creatures of the God of the olden testament! For the rule of the newest testament is at hand! For we will rise up against the universe of the divine God who is supposedly almighty! We will overthrow the heavens and destroy their God! For now is the time, my sons! I want you to go forth to a multi-colored planet called Earth, and when you get there, I want you to slaughter the inhabitants, and show no mercy to their kind.***

Go forth, and destroy! Destroy half of them, and bring the rest of them back home so that we may enslave them and make them follow our commands. Let them build our kingdoms from scratch; let them slave for our sake. As far as I am concerned, they are not worthy enough to be our slaves, let them sweat and die completing our evil desires, let us torment them, let us break their spirits, and torment their souls! Go! Go now! Torment and destroy the planet of Earth!" And so, the multitude of demons followed his commands and quickly flew away from the planet Oriah-nandah as they headed straight for the planet called Earth. At this point in time, the son of ether was nowhere to be found, for Earth had no defense against the iron-fisted rule of prince Mephistopheles. The demons of the universe of

Mestophelue murdered thousands of mortals and showed no mercy or care for mortal life. Many were enslaved and killed, and in due time, the inhabitants of Earth began to gradually deplete.

Somewhere hidden in the universe was the only defense for the planet Earth. Though the son of ether heard the cries of men and women, he did not care, and the phoenix of strength and courage was caged-up in his heart. But little did Ethereael know he would no longer stay imbued in a meteor; something would open his heart to care again. Many have been murdered, mutilated and unmercifully killed, people are praying for a savior to come and change the situation that the whole planet has unfortunately endured.

Much time had passed, and Mephistopheles has truly defiled the planet Earth. When the inhabitants of Mephistopheles' universe were sent to the old universe of man, much of mankind was enslaved with ease. And so, Mephistopheles commanded the most powerful legion of demons he created, and made short work of planet Earth, for the cities of Earth were subdued to the power of the mighty Mephistopheles, and the inhabitants of Mestophelue.

Little did Mephistopheles know, the son of ether would return much more powerful than he was when they had first met each other. Mephistopheles was in for the shock of his life. The Ethereael that he knew was just a memory. The last son of Calabrael was still alive and well, and as long as he lives, there is a hope for all humanity, even though humanity doesn't realize or know it.

For five years, Ethereael remained in the floating meteor, unknowingly charging his cosmic powers to ultimate perfection. One day as Mephistopheles' legions forcefully snatched the humans from Earth in large numbers, Ethereael heard their cries for help. Ethereael listens and speaks to himself, saying, ***"I don't care anymore."*** And as Ethereael tells himself that he doesn't care, he begins to hear a female infant baby crying loudly, calling for help as if the small female infant knew something that could help was near.

As Ethereael heard the cries of an infant baby, something inside of him woke up and couldn't bear the pain of letting a small child die by the hands of a ruthless and evil demon tyrant. Ethereael began to control the meteor that he placed himself in. He then began to head toward Earth in a speed that not even he knew he possessed. As the meteor containing Ethereael moved faster and faster, it got closer and closer to the planet Earth. And as it got closer, it reached the Earth's atmosphere and quickly fell from the sky like a falling star, and finally, it crashed into a tall abandoned building that was destroyed upon impact.

Pieces of the abandoned building and the small meteor that was destroyed was scattered everywhere. A large pile of rubble was left on the ground, and Mephistopheles' legions noticed that something crashed into a nearby building, and whatever crashed into the building was starting to move. There was something in the rubble; it kept making a rumbling sound like the gigantic foot-steps of a great titan. Something powerful or gigantic was making its way to the battle-field.

And out of the large pile of rubble, something emerged and walked out of the disastrous smoke. It was Ethereael, the son of ether, he had returned, only to find the army of his bitter enemy. The son of ether raised his countenance to reveal his mercury eyes being graced with purple electricity. And when Ethereael realized his enemies didn't care for children or human beings in general, he spoke loudly in a confident and affirmative tone, and said, ***"Put the child down now!"*** The demon laughed, saying, ***"Make me, mortal!"*** Ethereael replied, saying, ***"Fine then, have it your way, demon."*** The demon gripped the female infant by her shirt as if he had no care for the infant at all, Ethereael saw the way that the demon held the child, and slowly walked toward the demon and disappeared, when he re-appeared, he stood directly behind the demon, and then he disappeared again, and finally, he re-appeared in front of him. As the demon stood face-to-face with him, the demon began to attack, and as soon as the demon moved, Ethereael moved like lightning as he took the infant and disappeared, and then he re-appeared from a distance while holding the female infant as if she was his own child. The infant gazed into the mercury eyes of the son of ether and began smiling and giggling at him.

The demon was surprised and in complete awe, for he only knew of one creature with power that was even close to Ethereael's powers, and when the demon saw this, he was scared of Ethereael's power. Ethereael stared at him with a look on his face that spoke for itself. The demon leader was afraid of the son of ether, and because of his fear of Ethereael, he then commanded a legion of ten-thousand demons to attack and destroy him immediately. The accompanying army of demons followed their chief's orders, and a swarm of demons attacked Ethereael while he rocked the female infant to sleep in his arms. As the army of demons got closer and closer, Ethereael didn't budge one bit, nor did he worry or stop trying to put the baby to sleep. He seemed to be a whole new warrior. He simply waited for the demons to get close enough to kill, and when that happened, he created a force field of ether around himself in order to protect the infant and himself from the attacks of the swarming demons.

To their surprise, they were unable to penetrate his ether force-field. And as the demons swarmed around him, they slammed their fists on his force-field and snared their hideous faces at him like the force field was made of glass. Ethereael never bothered to acknowledge them at all, he simply concentrated on putting the infant to sleep while the demons continued to swarm around him and make more than enough noise to wake the child anyway. Fortunately for Ethereael, there was no way for the swarm of demons to penetrate his ether force-field. And so, Ethereael finally looked at the swarming demons snaring their faces behind his ether force-field, and simply blinked his eyes. The power of the son of ether was so great that another force-field manifested outside of the force field protecting Ethereael and the infant, and without warning, it trapped the whole army of demons. And when the demons realized that they were trapped, they began to get scared while frantically trying to escape. Moaning and screaming indicated the fear placed in their minds. When Ethereael noticed that they were scared, he used his powers to combine both force-fields to make one big force-field bubble containing all of the demons. They were all trapped with no escape, and when Ethereael realized that there was no way out, he raised his hand and directed the force- field to rise into the sky. And when the force-field bubble rose into the sky, Ethereael balled his hand into a fist and the force-field got smaller in size, crushing each demon within the force-field like a bag of worthless toys, courtesy of the son of ether. After crushing a whole legion of demons by his self, and making short work of their attacks, their leader stood alone with no one to aid him against the unmatched power of the son of ether. He then looked at the demon, and said, ***"Tell your master, Mephistopheles, that I won't stand by and watch him takeover this galaxy without a fight, let him know that the last son of Calabrael has returned! And this time, his tricks won't save him!"***

The demon leader took flight into the sky so that he could return to his master's home planet to relay Ethereael's message.

If Etherεael had not hid within the meteor, it would've taken several decades to achieve his true powers. Though he was taught much by Hermes, he still had a small corner of doubt in himself. Fortunately, the day that Ethereael heard the cries of a small child, the phoenix deep inside of his heart broke out of its cage and took flight into the world of the living. Ethereael lifted himself into the air and began to search for the child's mother; he moved forward and saw no one. And as he moved further and further, he saw a woman screaming, and saying, ***"My daughter! Thank you! You saved my daughter!"*** When Ethereael heard this, he lowered himself to the ground and handed the infant child to her mother. The mother of the infant looked at Ethereael, and said, ***"How did your eyes get like that? Are you human?"*** Ethereael replied, and said, ***"I can't answer all of your questions, but what I can tell you is that you won't ever have to thank me, and yes, I am human."*** The woman replied, saying, ***"How can I become like you?"*** Ethereael flew off into the sky while saying, ***"Seek and you shall find!"***

After defeating thousands of demons with ease, Ethereael thought to his self, saying, ***"If they're capturing mortals from Earth, where are they taking them and what do they want them for? I know it can't be for anything good. But if it's happening here, then it must be happening all over the world. And if I'm right, which I probably am, then I have much more work to do."***

After taking care of the legions of demons in New York City, Ethereael began his journey around the world. Eventually, after saving various people, he found out that humans were being taken to a galaxy called **Mestophelue** and being tortured and enslaved by the commands of the prince of darkness, a demon known as Mephistopheles. And when Ethereael found out what was going on, his heart was filled with righteousness. He then attempted to stop Mephistopheles' rule by stopping as many legions as he possibly could. Though many human beings had perished due to torture and slavery, Ethereael had to take into account the people who could be saved. Thus, he did the best that he could, and in war, lives are likely to be lost, and sometimes, there is nothing any of us can do. Due to Ethereael's realization of the situation, he stopped legions of demons all over the world; the planet Earth had seen their greatest hero since the elemental children had battled the son of the morning. Blessings had once again shined upon the countenance of mankind. A true hero had taken destiny into his own hands and proved that he was no coward. In the galaxy of Mestophelue, its creator had become wroth. Legions residing on his planets and in his cities were reporting a fierce and nearly unstoppable mortal with unmatched supernal powers. When Mephistopheles heard this, he was so angry that he sent a meteor down from the sky to hit one of the planets that he created with his own evil hands.

Their own god killed some of his own followers; a small number of his own creatures that he deemed unworthy were destroyed upon impact of the meteor. Mephistopheles was a merciless and ruthless god of evil. Meanwhile, Ethereael continued his journey to release prisoners and prevent Mephistopheles' legions from kidnapping and enslaving human beings.

In New York City, California, England, Texas, Washington, Russia, Boston, and Alaska, the son of ether had released prisoners and prevented Mephistopheles' iron-fisted rule all over the world. Mephistopheles wanted more slaves to revere his creatures and build his monuments, but the son of ether stopped his plans with ease. In Washington D.C, an army of five thousand demons made it their business to kill the president and divide the order of the United States. Whilst the army of the United States and central intelligence agency used their primitive guns to stop the demons and protect the President, they realized that their weaponry was insignificant and useless against demons. In a small matter of time, Ethereael materialized directly in front of the President just as the forces of earth were backed into a corner near the president and forced to surrender or die. The son of ether closed his eyes and displayed the power of divine justice by lifting the whole white house off of the ground and encasing the President and his agents in a large ether force-field. Ethereael flew through the roof of the white house while causing the ceiling to collapse all over the attacking demons. Consequently, the large pieces of the white house ceiling weren't enough to destroy the attacking demons whilst Ethereael flew above the white house dragging the President and his associates by a stream of black electricity connected to one of his ether force-fields.

When Ethereael felt that he saved all of the people that he could, he released his hold on the white house, and the white house crashed into the ground and destroyed thirty-five hundred demons in one shot. Unfortunately, Ethereael's actions still weren't enough to complete the job; therefore, he had no choice but to fight the remaining demons while still carrying the weight of the ether force-field containing the President and his protecting agents. And so, Ethereael used his mind to shoot black electricity out of his eyes and disintegrate as many demons as possible. As expected by destiny, the son of ether was more than successful against the army, and made sure that the President of the United States was safe. And when Ethereael safely placed the President on the ground with all of his agents, Ethereael was just about to shoot off into the sky when the President said, ***"What are you?"*** Ethereael replied, saying, ***"The part of every man who believes in divine justice, the great geometrician, peace, and most of all, mortal ascension."*** The president stared at the son of ether, and said, ***"I owe you my life, young man."*** Ethereael shot off into the sky while saying, ***"No, you don't owe me anything."*** All over the world there were reports of a flying man with liquid-metal eyes and a reflective robe. The people of Earth were left in awe due to the spectacular abilities possessed by the son of ether. News reporters and people around the world are now calling him *"Reflectore,"* due to his mercury robe. Ethereael became the champion of holy light, he ascended and became the modern paradigm of what happens when mortal life and universal consciousness is consummately unionized.

After committing himself to helping every mortal he possibly could, Ethereael finally remembered that his mother was still under the influence of Mephistopheles' power, and after years of hiding in a meteor floating around the galaxy, Ethereael felt great, but realized that anger and sadness from one person could affect and cause great damage to not just himself, but to others around him. Because of his anger, he had totally forgotten about his own mother along with his home planet.

When the son of ether realized this, he took off at an unbelievable speed, and rushed home to undo what Mephistopheles had done. After speeding through the skies of Earth at the speed of light, Ethereael reached his home, the home where he grew up, and the home that held his greatest memories with his parents.

He stood outside of his home and spoke to himself, saying, ***"How could I have been so stupid, demons sometimes plague mortal creatures in the form of emotions that would cause them to do things that defy the commandments of the great architect, I gave into anger and I only worried about my feelings and how I felt. I totally forgot about my mother. But I was inexperienced at the time; it's been a few years now. I became a coward when Mephistopheles outsmarted me, then I became a warrior when I heard a baby crying.***

Something inside of me became alive, and I continued the destiny given to me by the cosmic. I know the principles necessary

to return my mother to normal now; it's time to bring her out of that demon's power." After thinking to himself about the mistakes that he made as a mystic warrior, he entered his home and teleported to his mother's bedroom where he had left her before he departed for outer space. His mother laid there silent and environed with cosmic light. Ethereael closed his eyes and put the palm of his right hand on her forehead, and immediately she was awakened.

His mother quickly sat up and opened her palms to use her powers and attack, but she soon realized that it was her son and quickly lowered her hands. She then proceeded to cry and give her son a hug, for you didn't have to have cosmic abilities to know that she truly missed her son. As she let go of him, she looked at him, and said, ***"Old mercury eyes, I see you still remember what you were taught in the secret room, I never got a chance to tell you that your mercury robe was a real fashion statement."***

She laughed; trying to make fun of her son's magical uniform. And when Ethereael heard what she said, he replied, saying, ***"I can see that nothing can break your sense of humor, mom. Anyways, I missed you too. You've been under Mephistopheles' spell for five years; you do know that, right?"*** Tri-dael replied, saying, ***"What!? Are you serious?!"*** Ethereael replied, saying, ***"Yea ma, I'm serious, I guess dad didn't have enough time to tell you what kind of strange situations you can get yourself into when you possess supernal abilities. Well, Bingo! Now you know!"***

After reuniting with his mother, Ethereael was truly happy. He then looked at his mother, and said, ***"Ma, there's one more thing that I have to do before we can actually say that the planet is safe, and just so you know, I'll take care of Mephistopheles myself, but before I leave, I must seek knowledge from someone***

in the realms of heaven, I'm going to need some help with the final fight. I'm going to the secret room to contact the help that I need.

And After I leave, I want you to place a force-field around the house to protect it from unwanted demonic presences. " Ethereael teleported to the secret room while his mother replied, saying, ***"Alright, I'll do it now."*** After Ethereael teleported, Tri-dael lifted her hands into the air with her palms open, and immediately the force-field that was placed by Calabrael was replaced and reinforced.

Tri-dael was becoming accustomed to her husband's powers after a few years had passed. And so, Ethereael finds himself in the secret room once again, environing himself with questions about his enemy. He sat quietly in the secret room that his father and his father's father had utilized for many divine purposes.

He sat there and contemplated the imminent battle that he would have to win in order to keep honor in his family bloodline, however, not only would he win to keep honor in his family bloodline, he would also win to keep and uphold the sacred laws of the divine architect of the universe. There was more than one reason why the son of ether had to win against Mephistopheles, some reasons he would rather keep to himself, for the sword of Elohim must be returned to its rightful owner at once.

Though Ethereael felt that he was strong enough to defeat Mephistopheles without the sword, he still wanted it back; it was a gift from his father before he passed through transition. And so, Ethereael meditated by himself for seven hours in the secret room, and when it was all said and done, he got up and prepared to leave for battle. As he began to leave the secret room, something appeared behind him, and said, ***"Wait, wait***

just one minute, son of ether. When Ethereael heard this, he turned around and saw Hermes Mercurius Trismegistus, the one who prepared him in the cosmic sciences of metaphysics. Hermes looked deep into Ethereael's eyes, and said, ***"Son of ether, I see you have found the light of life once again. It is getting close to the time for the great battle between the prince of demons and the last son of Calabrael.***

How will you engage in mystical combat with such a strong demonic force? Are you prepared? Time is of the essence, son of ether. I have returned to your family's holy secret room so that I can see you before you leave. And just so you know, all of heaven is waiting for you to succeed." When Ethereael heard this, he replied, saying, ***"Well, we'll see what I'm up against. If I have to fight until I can no longer fight, then so be it."*** Hermes whispered, and said, ***"Do well on your journey, son of ether, blessed be."***

The Great symbol upon Hermes' chest filled the secret room with brilliant light, and Hermes disappeared and departed to the heavens while Ethereael teleported to his mother's bedroom and said goodbye to her as if he wasn't sure whether he was coming back or not. His mother looked at him, and said, ***"You'll be back sooner than later, my son. Don't worry about whether you'll win or not, just do what must be done for all humanity."*** Ethereael heard what his mother said to him, and nodded his head, he then teleported to the front door of his house, and then, he thought to himself, saying, ***"This is it, I guess. I just don't understand how I'm supposed to fight the inhabitants of a whole galaxy by myself. I may be strong, but I'm not that strong.***

Aquari-on, Fireael, Airael, Earthael, I never had a chance to meet all of you because you died before I was born, I've only heard the stories of how brave the four of you were, I wish you were here now. I need you now, more than you could ever know."

After speaking to himself, Ethereael shot off into the air and broke through the Earth's atmosphere like a spaceship.

Finally, the son of ether hovers above the planet Earth and prepares to stop all demonic problems by destroying the very source of the current demonic activity so as to end the war between mankind and fallen angels by destroying the ruthless rule of the demon prince called Mephistopheles. How does one defeat many? The answer is unknown, but all is unveiled in due time.

Chapter 9

Demise of the Evil Universe

As Ethereael raced through outer space to reach the galaxy of evil, he spoke to himself, saying, ***"I refuse to fail. It is our family tradition to be mankind's defense against all evil forces in high places. I don't know what waits for me in his galaxy, but it doesn't matter what the danger may be, this is my mission, I must complete it."***

After a long and stressful travel throughout the universe, Ethereael finally reached Mestophelue. He arrived and witnessed the sword of Elohim's power to manifest on a large scale. He saw six planets of which he had never seen a day in his life, though he was amazed, he was also disgusted at the possibility of what kind of foul creatures may inhabit them. Nothing from the mind of Mephistopheles could make anything beautiful or pleasant.

And so, Ethereael gradually flew toward the planets manifested by the evil prince Mephistopheles. As Ethereael got closer to the planets, his cosmic senses overheard the voice of Mephistopheles himself. He was speaking to his guardian and his followers about overthrowing the heavens along with the grand architect. He spoke aloud, saying, ***"We are stronger than his armies, we outnumber them, and we can take his throne and rule the universe. Prepare for a large-scale attack on heaven. The time is come; I am the commander and prince of all demons. There is great power in great numbers of evil. We shall rule all things, and make homes that meet our truest evil desires. Are you with me!?"*** A large crowd of demons screamed and shouted to the top of their lungs, saying, ***"We are with you!"***

And then they began to loudly chant their master's name,

saying, ***"Mephi-stoph-eles, Mephi-stoph-eles, Mephi-stoph-eles!"*** As Ethereael heard this, he closed his eyes and used the ether propagating throughout the universe to carry his voice throughout Mephistopheles' creation so that everyone and everything, including Mephistopheles himself would hear him and know that he was in their midst, and that he was ready to settle the score.

Ethereael spoke aloud, saying, ***"You have yet to rid yourselves of the son of ether. I propose a battle between you, the inhabitants of all of your planets, and me. Think you're ready for it? Or are you scared of one mortal man?"*** When Mephistopheles heard this, he was wroth, and commanded all of the inhabitants of Mestophelue to destroy Ethereael so that they could proceed with their plans to overthrow heaven. The Legions of Mephistopheles left the planet of Oriah-nandah, and searched for Ethereael so that they could please their master and bring his head back to Oriah-nandah. All of the legions of Mephistopheles were five-hundred million in number, an army larger and greater than the legions of Lucifer, the king of evil. The entire inhabitants of Mestophelue searched endlessly for the presence of Ethereael, however, Ethereael had not left Mestophelue at all, and he simply used the hood of the mercury robe to cover his face. And because he did, he could only reflect what existed. After Ethereael realized that the demons scattered themselves while looking for him, he quickly revealed himself, saying, ***"Hey, I'm over here!"*** A demon nearby heard what he said and looked at him, saying, ***"He's over there!"*** When the army of demons heard this, they began to come to their fellow's aid.

Large groups of demons gradually flew toward the area where Ethereael was located. When Ethereael saw that the inhabitants of the five planets was larger than he expected, he spoke to himself, saying, ***"When I planned this out, it seemed***

like a really good idea, but now, why does it feel like that was a big, big mistake?! For some strange reason, I saw this going totally different in my mind." After witnessing the power of a large army, it was too late for Ethereael to escape. The large groups of demons began to surround him, while screaming in a loud voice, saying, ***"You're dead mortal! Hail Mephistopheles!"*** At this point, Ethereael shot off into the upper levels of outer space faster than a laser beam, and again they surrounded him, for there were too many of them. Ethereael looked to his left, and to his right, no matter what angle he looked at, he was completely surrounded.

Ethereael began to speak to himself, saying, ***"If I don't get rid of them, they'll kill me too easily, it must be millions of them. If I'm going to win this one, I can't hold back."*** As the demons of Mestophelue surrounded him, Ethereael saw a meteor that could help him clear out a few demons. He teleported to it, and grabbed it with his bare hands. He then began to push it so that it could gain speed, and as the meteor gained speed, Ethereael pushed it into a large crowd of demons.

Unfortunately, most of the demons dodged it with ease. When Ethereael saw that they quickly dodged it, he began to get very worried; he realized that he may have backed himself into a corner. And when Ethereael realized that the situation wasn't good, he closed his eyes and charged his powers to their greatest height by absorbing the ether propagating throughout the universe to give him immense divine strength. As he did this, he spoke to himself, saying, ***"God of Jacob, Isaac and Abraham, grant me the strength to destroy mine enemies!"*** As Ethereael opened his eyes, he raced off through the gigantic crowd of demons and headed straight for the space of his home planet.

And Just as Ethereael thought, the whole army followed

him. The battle began with a high-speed chase through the galaxy, and Ethereael was in the lead. They chased and followed him until he reached his home galaxy, and once again, the son of ether had disappeared. The army of Mephistopheles was unable to keep up with his amazing speed, and by the time they reached the solar system that Ethereael was heading toward, they had lost track of his whereabouts, but Ethereael was no fool, he used the robe of Hermes to disappear so that he could go through with his secret plan. All of a sudden, something unexpected happened. The moon began to move off of its axis, however, the army of Mephistopheles was totally clueless as to why the moon was being pushed off of its axis. Finally, the most amazing event took place; Ethereael had wrapped a large force-field of ether energy around the moon so that he wouldn't break it during battle. Then he attached a chain of ether energy to the force-field so that he could drag the moon back to Mestophelue.

When the demons saw him racing back to Mestophelue while carrying the moon behind him, certain demons in the army began to speak to themselves, saying, ***"What is this mortal fool doing, sending us on a wild demon chase!?"*** However, they paid no attention to him carrying the moon, simply because they were larger in number, and he was just one mortal, besides, what could he possibly do with the moon? And so, they followed and chased him again, without comprehending his plan to use the moon as an ally. As the son of ether raced back to Mestophelue pulling the moon behind him, he suddenly disappeared again.

The army began to search on, and around the moon that Ethereael carried to the new universe. And once again, they found nothing. When they couldn't find him, they decided to split-up so that they could find him and kill him as soon as possible. Ethereael was close to the moon, yet they never found him, and when he realized that they finally split-up, he revealed himself and began swinging the moon at them as if it were a mace. When the army of Mephistopheles saw this, they tried their best to dodge it, but they were unable to do so because of its size and mass. As the great son of ether swung the moon in a circular three-hundred and sixty degree angle, one hundred million demons were disintegrated and eliminated with ease. As the son of ether realized what he had done, he spoke to himself while laughing, and said, ***"Wow! I must've just broken a family record!"*** Though a large amount of Mephistopheles' army was defeated, there were still enough of them to defeat the son of ether.

Meanwhile, Mephistopheles watches the battle between the son of ether and his new creations. Mephistopheles laughs, knowing that the son of ether couldn't possibly defeat all of them by his self. But little did Mephistopheles know, for a group of familiar faces were on the way to help the son of ether attain victory for heaven and Earth.

And so, the son of ether stopped swinging the moon and decided to engage in hand-to-hand combat. He teleported his self from place-to-place eliminating demons with ether lightning and ether-force punches, but he soon realized that it was a bad decision. And once again, the armies of Mephistopheles cornered him. There wasn't much more that Ethereael could do, there were just too many of them. So he stood there and decided to stop planning things out. He realized that there was no way to plan a real attack on such a large number of demons, he also realized that he had been fighting to live, but living was no longer an option, so he finally decided to fight to the death in order to become triumphant.

He fought valiantly against the army with no help, and as he fought, he repetitiously thought of his brothers. He then spoke to himself, saying, ***"Fireael, prince of flames, Aquari-on, commander of the vast oceans, Airael, director of winds, Earthael, king of lands, I could use your help right about now."***

In the old galaxy, the sun changed its own color, and its flames turned purple. Then it gradually began to lose its flames as if it were extinguishing itself. The purple flames of the sun became smaller and smaller, and finally, the flames took the form of a fiery phoenix, the son of cosmic fire had re-appeared. The legendary Fireael had heard his brother's cry for help and resurrected himself. The blood that ran through his father's veins was present in another mortal that he had never met. Therefore, he realized that his father must have had a son or a daughter, and upon this realization, Fireael locked-on to the vital life energy pattern that followed his father's, and his own. He took off at the speed of light in the form of a fiery phoenix, and left the planet Earth without a sun. The Earth was dark, and the inhabitants were scared; they feared Lucifer had returned to destroy mankind once again. Preachers and pastors began to pray for long hours in order to attain a reason for the disappearance of the sun. The battle between good and evil has caused Earth much damage, for Earth truly relies on the rays of the sun to renew certain things, and make them grow healthy. Though the cosmic son of flames was gone, he would return soon enough.

As the prince of flames took off to aid his unknown relative, the oceans all over the planet Earth began to boil as if it were being heated with fire. An electromagnetic bubble of water raced out of the Pacific Ocean, and into the sky to reach outer space. And as it reached outer space, it began to take the form of a human being, but not just any human being, it was the legendary son of cosmic water who also heard the cries for help from his unknown relative. Aquari-on spoke to his self, saying, ***"I don't know who you are, but I can hear your heart***

wishing we were there, I'm on my way." Aquari-on, the commander of the vast ocean took flight at the speed of light while placing his self in a force-field of water.

As Aquari-on took off to help his brother Ethereael, a gnome crawled out of a crack in the Earth, and whispered Earthael's name seven times under his breath. Afterward, the Earth shook, and a large amount of the dirt from the Earth began to rotate like a twister; the particles of dirt merged into a human form and opened its eyes. The Legendary son of Earth was resurrected, he then looked into the firmament and spoke to himself, saying, ***"Wow, has it been that long, dad had another baby? We have a little brother or sister? I can sense our family's blood anywhere, sounds like my help is necessary."*** Earthael put his index finger over his brow, and a psychic center located at the middle of his head began to glow, and a great boulder arose from the ground beneath him, and as the boulder lifted him into the air, he locked-on to the vital life energy of his father's bloodline. Within seconds, he rode the boulder into outer space at an unbelievable speed that only a cosmic son could possess.

Finally, the winds of the Earth began to move swift and wildly, and a great tornado appeared over the Pacific Ocean as particles of cosmic energy merged together within it, and as the infinitesimal particles of cosmic energy merged, the whole tornado was concentrated into a human form; the son of cosmic air was also resurrected. Airael wasted no time; he only needed to hear the holder of his father's blood ask for his help one time. Airael raised his hands into the air, and a gigantic tornado appeared, picked him up and guided him to the location of his sibling who was born after his death.

As the four legendary elemental children went forth to aid their unknown sibling, the grand architect of the universe spoke to himself, saying, ***"Right on time, everything is going just as written, the four principles of my footstool have been resurrected by mutual indissoluble affinity, and the powerful love for one another. The fifth Principle will combine with the principles of my footstool, and Mephistopheles will comprehend that my throne is not only the place where all life begins, but the place where the path of victory begins, and love resurrects love."*** The divine architect laughs, and says, ***"This should be fun to watch."***

Fireael, Aquari-on, Airael and Earthael traveled far across the galaxy at a speed that only an awakened mortal eye could comprehend.

The undisputed champions of Fire, Air, Earth and Water reached their destination and stood there watching someone battle millions of demons alone without help. In due time, the four cosmic sons realized that their father had a son after they died. And so, Ethereael decided to fight to the death, he dodged and blocked various moves while eliminating tens of thousands of demons with ease. The son of ether teleported to a far distance and stood there as the demons looked to see where he went. Ethereael opened the palm of his right hand and spoke aloud, saying, ***"Let's finish this!"***

Out of the midst of Ethereael's palm was a dangerous flow of red and blue lightning that stretched out and electrocuted several demons. Though his powers were extraordinary, there were still too many demons to be defeated. The son of ether waved his hand, and separated the ether around five-thousand demons, and before they knew it, their bodies began to dissipate into particles. Ethereael fought valiantly against all odds, even so, he was still outnumbered, and logically he would not and could not succeed.

As Fireael, Earthael, Aquari-on and Airael watched their brother Ethereael; they were amazed at his powers and began talking to each other. Fireael spoke, and said, ***"Whoa! This kid must have a death wish."*** Aquari-on spoke, and said, ***"Fireael, send a warning shot; let them know that they have some more company."*** Fireael opened his palm and charged a large fireball that was the size of a boulder. He then threw it at the army of demons, and immediately five-thousand demons were disintegrated. When the army of demons saw this, they looked behind themselves and noticed four floating mortals having immense cosmic abilities.

Ethereael teleported amongst the four individuals, and said, ***"I thought all of you were dead, you were dead right?"*** Earthael replied, saying, ***"I guess we were, but we all heard the depth of your heart, and well, there's a strange love in our family, I guess. So, what's your name, little bro?"*** Ethereael replied, saying, ***"Dad named me Ethereael; right now I could really use a hand. Even though I can teleport and ride waves of ether, there are just too many of them, I kept hoping that you were here, and here you are. I've heard so much about you. But we can catch up on the family stuff later, unless you want to die talking."*** As the three-hundred and eighty million demons realized that the son of ether and the new group of mortals were together, they began an onslaught of attacks on all of them.

Meanwhile, Mephistopheles looked into his crystal ball and saw the ones who fought Lucifer, and when he saw this, he began to get scared, and spoke to himself, saying, ***"I thought they were dead, how much power has the grand architect given these mortals?! I don't believe this! Damned those plans for mortal ascension! Why won't these humans just die like everyone else?"*** At this point, it was time for the five elemental children to assume the position destiny had placed specifically for them alone. Aquari-on, the son of water stretched his arms out with his palms open, and a brilliant light appeared in front of both of his palms.

A swarm of demons headed toward Aquari-on as fast as they could, and as the demons were literally seconds from grabbing him, two giant glaciers and two giant icebergs flew past his arms and smashed into the crowd of five-thousand demons. The collision between the icebergs and glaciers slammed into the demons, and the icebergs shattered and destroyed countless demons.

And when Aquari-on saw the shattered iceberg, he then used his Hydrokinetic hold on the water element to direct the sharp pieces of the iceberg to stab them. Little-by-little, the army of Mephistopheles was getting smaller and smaller. After watching Aquari-on use glaciers and icebergs to defeat his enemies, it gave the legendary Earthael and idea. Earthael rode forth on the boulder of rock to execute his own move. He then forced his hands into two meteors and began to throw them with a powerful force.

The Meteors raced through the army of evil and instantly disintegrated them, killing them with ease. And so, the armies of Mephistopheles became smaller and smaller once again. Airael, son of cosmic air, looked at his opponents and felt no remorse for them. With the wave of a hand, Airael fashioned a gigantic cosmic tornado that spun wildly into the army of demons, trapping them and spinning so quickly that the demons that were caught within it were disintegrated immediately.

The armies of Mephistopheles had lost the power of numbers, the elemental children had lowered Mephistopheles' army to a smaller number, and only nine hundred, thirty-three thousand demons were left. Mephistopheles saw this and decided to end it all by sending his guardian, Darknesseus the gigantic fallen angel presiding over Oriah-nandah. The planet of Oriah-nandah shook violently as Darknesseus raised himself from it and began to head toward the elemental children. With many demons still alive, the elemental children decided to combine all of their powers so that they could eliminate the rest of the army of Mephistopheles with one move.

And so, Earthael summoned a boulder from Earth and asked Fireael to engulf it in flames, Fireael raised his right hand above his head, and revealed his palm, and immediately the boulder was surrounded in fire. Then Airael opened his palm and sent a gigantic cosmic tornado to stir the boulder of fire into a fire twister. Aquari-on summoned seven icebergs from Earth to circle the tornado of fire. Finally, Ethereael opened the palm of his right hand and used the power of ether to compress his brothers' powers into a golden orb the size of an egg.

Ethereael grabbed the orb and crushed it in his hand while rays of golden light raced out of his fist. Afterward, Ethereael's body began to dissipate into infinitesimal particles of energy, and as the son of ether, Ethereael propagated himself through the army in an energetic form and destroyed all of them in one shot. When they finally eliminated the whole army, a great and terrible creature with the wings of an angel arrived whilst roaring, moaning and groaning in an extremely loud tone.

It spoke, and said, ***"Die mortals!"*** When the five elemental children heard this, Ethereael said, ***"Will this ever end?"*** Fireael looked at Ethereael, and said, ***"In our experience, it doesn't stop until one or the other is vanquished."*** Earthael looked up at Darknesseus, and said, ***"No time for small talk, we have work to do, and evil doesn't defeat itself, let's go."*** As the gigantic Darknesseus stood over them, Ethereael said, ***"I don't believe this!"*** Darknesseus began to flap his wings and blow the elemental children away from him, and then he opened his mouth and spat out a deadly electrical flow of energy. The elemental children were surprised, and Earthael said, ***"It's time to turn it***

up a notch!" Earthael summoned all of the meteors floating in space along with the rocks of Earth immediately.

Countless amounts of rocks appeared and stood directly in front of the son of cosmic Earth; he then commanded them to merge into one large meteorite-boulder. As they combined, they formed a gigantic boulder that was large enough to crush Darknesseus with one hit. When Darknesseus saw the boulder, he opened his palm and prepared to blast it away with the energy of darkness. As Darknesseus charged his powers to destroy the boulder, Ethereael teleported in front of his hand, and placed an ether force-field around it, and then teleported back to his place amongst his brothers.

Darknesseus finally executed his move, and when he did, a large cloud of smoke rose up and blinded everyone. When the smoke cleared, Darknesseus had blown off his own arm. Ethereael laughed, and said, ***"I bet you he won't try that again."*** Earthael looked at Ethereael, and said, ***"Next time you plan on doing something like that, let me know."*** Afterward, Earthael sent the gigantic boulder at Darknesseus' chest.

The boulder crashed into the creature and made a large hole in his chest. Earthael laughed, and said, ***"When you have a big problem, try smashing it with a big boulder!"*** The four elemental children rejoiced, thinking that Darknesseus was finished. However, Darknesseus immediately revived himself, his skin began to expand and combine itself, and Darknesseus was in no way hurt. Ethereael screamed out loud, and said, ***"Your time is up, demon!"*** Ethereael looked at Darknesseus, and with the wave of his hand, Ethereael shot black lightning out of his eye, and directly at Darknesseus. And before the five warriors knew it, the body of the gigantic demon began to dissipate into ashes. Shortly thereafter, Darknesseus disappeared. Ethereael thought that he'd single-handedly destroyed Darknesseus by his self; consequently, he was wrong. A strange red orb of energy appeared, and began to expand itself, and before the five warriors knew it, Darknesseus was fully revived. At this point, the five champions of the cosmos looked at each other and realized that it was time to retreat and find a way to beat the gigantic demon of death by means of another method. The five warriors instantly flew off and began to speak to each other while dodging and evading giant energy bolts of darkness that Darknesseus wasted no time launching at them.

Ethereael looked at his brothers, and said, ***"If this thing can revive itself every time we impinge it, then how the heck are we suppose to defeat it?!"*** Fireael looked at Earthael, and said, ***"I remember an old trick that I learned when dad gave us the secret teachings of all ages, but I need a distraction to execute it."*** Airael looked at Fireael, and said, ***"If it's a distraction you need, a distraction you'll get."*** Airael turned around and put his arms in front of him while opening his palms, and immediately, seven giant tornadoes left his hands and headed toward Darknesseus.

The tornadoes began pushing him further away from the five warriors. At this point, Ethereael grabbed his brother Fireael and teleported him behind Darknesseus where he would be unable to see them, especially since the five cosmic warriors were about the size of soda pop cans compared to the size of Darknesseus. Fireael pointed his index finger at Darknesseus and used the fire of purification to trace and engrave a pentagram on his back. Then he spoke to Ethereael, and said, ***"Ethereael, get Earthael, Aquari-on and Airael as far away from here as possible, I'm about to do something that won't be pretty."***

Ethereael replied, saying, ***"No problem."*** Ethereael teleported away from Fireael and told Earthael, Aquari-on and

Airael that Fireael would take care of Darknesseus by himself. Earthael said, ***"What! Is Fireael out of his crazy mind?!"*** Ethereael looked at Earthael, and said, ***"Let's hope so."*** As the four warriors left Fireael behind, a great battle began between Darknesseus and Fireael. When Fireael realized that it was only Darknesseus and himself, he spoke, saying, ***"Let's see if the eternal flames of the son of cosmic fire can harm you, demon."*** Fireael landed on the demon's shoulder and ran down his arm while trying to quickly attack him; however, Darknesseus caught him with his hand and tried to crush him like a small ant. As Fireael began to feel extreme pain from being crushed, he engulfed himself in the purple flames of purification.

He then began to expand the flames around his body as far as he could. As he did this, Darknesseus began to roar and groan as if he was in terrible pain. Fireael's idea was beginning to work, Darknesseus began to disintegrate little-by-little, and when Fireael saw this, he expanded the flames further until Darknesseus' whole body was stuck in the flames of purification. As the flames covered Darknesseus' body, he began to gradually disintegrate, and finally, Darknesseus was destroyed, and Fireael was triumphant.

He knew that the pentagram combined with the flames of purification would instantly begin a purification process that would instantly destroy any demon. And so, Darknesseus was destroyed, and the son of cosmic fire was victorious by such means. Fireael used telepathy, and spoke to his brothers from a distance, saying, ***"Come back, I took care of our little problem."*** And immediately, Ethereael and the others flew back to Fireael and asked him what he did to beat Darknesseus.

Fireael replied, saying, ***"Why do you guys always have to ask so many questions? He no longer exists, that's all you need to know; now who's next on our hit list?"*** Ethereael replied, saying,

"Mephistopheles is next, but I'll take care of him, he's mine, don't interfere." Aquari-on looked at Ethereael, and said, ***"Ethereael, are you sure you want to fight him by yourself? He sounds like a real tough guy."*** Ethereael replied, saying, ***"Yeah, I'm sure, I have a score to settle with him, he stole something that dad gave to me, I want it back, and I want him sent back to where he came from."*** Aquari-on replied, saying, ***"Okay, then it's all on you little bro, but if he cheats one bit, we'll be right there to take him out."***

Ethereael nodded his head and the five elemental children sensed traces of evil leading to Mephistopheles, therefore, they headed straight for the planet of Oriah-nandah where traces of Mephistopheles' electromagnetic-field were scattered all over it. The five sons of the elements flew as fast as they could, and finally, they reached the planet of Oriah-nandah. Just as they decided to land on the planet, Mephistopheles appeared, and said, ***"I see you have defeated my whole army and my beloved Darknesseus. Not bad for a couple of mortals, but I tell you this, I personally won't be so easily defeated, and I always make sure I have a backup plan just in case. In other words, this is far from over, sons of Elion."***

When Ethereael heard what Mephistopheles said, he closed his eyes and Mephistopheles' body began to tremble, and then he began to hack and cough as if he was very sick or choking on something. Ethereael used the ether energy to force the sword of Elohim out of Mephistopheles' body.

A flash of light appeared, and the sword of Elohim shot out of Mephistopheles' body and back into Ethereael's soul. When Mephistopheles saw this, he was as angry as he could possibly be. He then spoke, and said, ***"You may have gotten your precious sword back and defeated my army, but it still won't help you defeat me, son of God. Today I'll leave, but when I return, I shall bring the thamiel back with me."*** And before the five warriors knew it, Mephistopheles teleported and disappeared, he was gone. Ethereael spoke aloud, saying, ***"You coward, this is far from over, when we next meet, I'll finish what you started!"***

And so, after a long and stressful battle, the five elemental children returned to their galaxy. When they returned, Fireael had just realized that the Earth was dark without his presence as the sun. He used his cosmic powers to fashion a sun that would be fit to illuminate the planet Earth once again. Ethereael returned the moon to its home near the Earth and, finally, the five warriors returned home and rested. Meanwhile, Mephistopheles headed for the realms of hell for assistance in the war against the sons of God.

Thamiel- *Adversaries of the holy living creatures, the demons of revolt and anarchy, the double headed-ones.*

Each order of angels in heaven has their specific adversaries. So as a man ascendeth further into the tree of life, there is a man who descendeth into the tree of death.

Fire, Water, Earth, Air and Ether have found each other, the pentagram is complete, and the sword of Elohim has been returned to its rightful owner. Now, the five warriors must find the keys to their existence as they represent five elements that unlock the secrets of creation. Ethereael, Fireael, Earthael, Airael and Aquari-on have embraced their destinies, and fought the greatest battles that mortal men can fight, for they are fit to battle the strongest demons alive.

What lies ahead? Only the grand architect knows, all is decided by one universal consciousness, the consciousness that made all things possible. Mortals are considered weak, and ignorant, only few have been considered worthy of mortal ascension, but the few that are worthy have the greatest responsibilities on their hands.

Now that Mephistopheles has escaped the hands of the five elemental children, he searches hell for a familiar ally of evil. A specific legion of demons called the *"Thamiel"* will rise to the occasion and attempt to defeat the chosen sons of the grand architect of the universe.

The Thamiel are extremely powerful. All mortals who have attempted to defeat them have failed terribly. The five warriors elected by God must somehow find the secrets of creation in order to stop the rise of the Thamiel, the Thamiel are well informed and imbued with the secrets of creation, for they were present at the high councils in heaven before they fell from grace.

The Thamiel have plagued mankind for hundreds of thousands of years, they are formidable adversaries. However, they constantly war with each other. The leaders of the Thamiel are Satan and Moloch, two powerful demonic forces with a lengthy history of deceiving and fooling men into revering them. Very little is known of Satan's history against man. However, Moloch has appeared various times throughout the history of man.

Primitive men and women would build a gold statue to Moloch so that they could sacrifice their infants to him. They would then heat the idol up with fire until it glowed like the sun, and then they would place an infant in the arms of the idol of Moloch, then they would watch their infants suffer excruciating pain as they were burned to death; a horrible scene. However, sacrifices were not limited to infants; children ranging from infancy to the age of six years old were sacrificed to the idol of Moloch.

Thousands of burned bodies, all sacrificed to the demon named Moloch, a demonic creature of evil. Many say that this is not true, due to archeological evidence. Some say that etymological research shows that *"Moloch"* simply means sacrifice;

however, only few know the truth of this matter; the grand architect and Moloch himself.

If primitive men and woman have done this, then we truly have changed as modern men and woman. However, that does not mean that it is not still practiced elsewhere in the mundane world, and with this being said; the truth will eventually show itself. After battling millions of demons in outer space, five warriors shall prepare themselves for a most ancient evil that has existed numerous centuries and decades before their birth.

Fireael, Airael, Earthael, Aquari-on and Ethereael have returned home, they've missed the presence of their father, the great mystic named Calabrael. The return home was long awaited. Fireael, Airael, Aquari-on and Earthael had been gone for so long, when they heard Ethereael's inner cries for help while he was in battle, they came to his aid immediately, however, they had no idea that their father was dead.

When the four elemental children sat down with Tri-dael and heard how their father died, they all wanted a piece of Mephistopheles. It was a trap set by Mephistopheles that caused the death of such a great mystic. The four elemental children shed great tears after hearing what their mother told them. When they realized that their father was gone, they all left the house and went their separate ways. As they left, their mother screamed out loud, and said, ***"Don't leave, it's not your fault!"***

Not one of the four sons replied to what their mother said, they continued to walk away with their countenances down. Ethereael stayed home and never bothered to stop his brothers from leaving the house, he knew exactly how they felt. He knew that they just needed to blow off some steam before they would come back. Ethereael knew it was only a matter of time before they would make the decision to return home, no matter how wise you are; the death of someone you truly love can always hurt the strongest of men.

Though they were all very strong, Calabrael was the very reason that they became so wise, Calabrael wasn't just a good father; he was the fire that helped comprehend the father divine. The death of their father broke their hearts. They felt lost without him. Eventually, the four elemental children would return, but returning wasn't the problem; Co-existing with the fact that Mephistopheles was the true cause of why their father died was the real problem.

Now, the four elemental children must follow the principles of their father by themselves. He always told them to stay calm and to try their best to not give in to the devilish dangers of anger. And so, mortal ascension: an esoteric story is far from over. If Mephistopheles returns with the order of the thamiel, then *who'll stop him?* The five sons of the elements are separated, and the pentagram has dispersed. Over the span of time, the final journey of the five warriors would prove to have an unbelievable purpose, for a much, much greater journey awaits the cosmic sons of God....

Chapter 10

Rise of the Thamiel

At this point in time, the five sons have split apart, due to the realization of their father's murder. Fireael flew off into the cosmos above and began to contemplate the current events of his life. He thought to himself, saying, ***"I know my father, he would've been more than able to stop Mephistopheles on his own, but he didn't. Maybe Mephistopheles used the golden shackles of divinity to prevent him from using his powers, or maybe he did something else, either way, it doesn't matter now. I will not succumb to anger, but I will not let that demon get away with having killed my father either."***

Meanwhile, a familiar commander of water hovers above the Pacific Ocean in a meditative form. He then speaks to himself, saying, ***"Mephistopheles, you will not get away with this, I will honor my father's death with your defeat."*** As Aquari-on spoke to himself, another voice intervened, and said, ***"It is I, Hermes Mercurius Trismegistus, thrice great!"*** When Aquari-on heard this, he quickly opened his eyes and looked behind his self. Hermes Mercurius Trismegistus hovered in the midst of the air and began to speak, saying, ***"I have seen many things, however, the five of you have proved to be one of the most amazing things I have ever seen, you have valiantly fought the son of the morning, you have also ruined the plans of the most notorious prince of demons, and now, you all seek to find and defeat him face-to-face. Consequently, your current powers are no match for him at this point in time. Lucifer was no easier to fight than Mephistopheles. But at this point in time, if you wish to defeat Mephistopheles, you must now destroy the universe of evil that was left behind in your last battle.***

Mephistopheles is currently drawing his strength from the six planets of evil that he has created. He has escaped and returned to hell to obtain assistance in the assurance of your demise. He has now obtained a true partnership with Satan and Moloch. The order of which they command in hell is called the "Thamiel." Mephistopheles, Satan, and Moloch are an evil trinity that ascended mortals will most definitely have a difficult time defeating. By all means, the five of you are not enough to take on the three of them in a battle to the death. If you want to defeat them for good, and rid the universe of their presence, then summon your brothers and meet me at the secret room of your home, and when you've done this, I will further explain the rest of your journey."

And so, Aquari-on closed his eyes, and said, ***"Fireael, Earthael, Ethereael, Airael; meet me over the Pacific Ocean immediately."*** In less than a minute, the four brothers raced off into the sky and headed to the Pacific Ocean. Within twenty seconds, they were all present amongst their brother Aquari-on. Fireael looked at Aquari-on, and said, ***"I hope you called us here for a good reason."*** Aquari-on replied, saying, ***"I spoke with a cosmic being named Hermes Mercurius Trismegistus, he told me that we wouldn't be able to fight Mephistopheles on our own. He said that we should meet him at the secret room. He apparently has a plan of some sort, I say we meet him, and find out how we can defeat Mephistopheles. He told me some stuff you might all want to hear. I want you to know what he told me, so if anyone disagrees with this meeting, speak now or forever hold your peace."*** Ethereael spoke, and said, ***"I know Hermes, and if he says something, believe me, he knows what he's talking about, and I say we all go."***

Everyone nodded their heads and agreed to meet at the secret room. The five sons left the skies over the Pacific Ocean, and reached the place that they all called home. As they hovered over their home, a cloud of black smoke and the smell of sulfur revealed a powerful demon. He wore a black silk robe, and had curved horns upon his brow, and also, another curved horn sticking out of his chin. Upon his head and face was facial hair that burned like fire. When the elemental sons saw him from above, they looked at each other and knew that they all felt an enormous presence of evil. Having fought Lucifer one on one, they knew that the man standing near their home was a force to be reckoned with.

The sons of God gradually landed upon the grounds of the Earth, and as they landed, Fireael said, ***"I don't know who you are, but what I do know is that you should make things easier on yourself, and leave this world now."*** When the demon heard this, he began to teleport from place-to-place in order to strike fear into the hearts of the five warriors. The demon replied, saying, ***"I am the deceiver, the accuser, and the voice of ill will. The tempter and the one who offered to give all of the cities of Jerusalem to the first son of the universal and vital living consciousness permeating all of existence. I am a grand part of the evil that has been the cause and effect of the current events of mischief."***

When the five sons of God heard this, they were greatly filled with fear. Ethereael looked at Airael, and said, ***"Are you serious! This cannot be happening!"*** The demon spoke again, and said, ***"You don't think that people normally murder and kill each other for fun, do you? No, they don't, I give them a helping word, all human beings need is a little convincing to realize that they have an unspeakable desire to do evil, however, I don't make anyone do anything, I simply speak a few words, and their simplistic and idle minds do the rest for me. And now, I am very surprised, you five have yet to experience the relentless and vast power of evil intent.***

No matter, in due time, I will surely have your mortal caucuses hanging in my fiery throne room like souvenirs. You may all call me Satan, and in due time, you shall all succumb to my will. And don't think that your little meeting with Hermes will change anything; I know of Hermes' plans, go and meet with him if that's what you want to do, it will do you no good. Unlike Lucifer, I will not fall so easily to mortals; we shall meet again, sons of Eloah." Immediately, a flash of darkness appeared, and the demon named Satan had disappeared, there was no sign of him. After meeting one of the greatest forces of evil in the world of men, the five sons were sad and unsure of their destinies. Satan was stronger than they had anticipated; his aura was in a class all by itself. Though they were unsure of how they would defeat something so powerful, they decided to meet Hermes Mercurius Trismegistus in the secret room anyway, hoping that they could find a way to defeat the enemies of God, and the murderer of their beloved father.

The five sons walked into the house and stared deep into their mother's eyes, when they did that, Tri-dael said, ***"I understand more than you know, my sons. I know that you want this to all disappear; but it won't disappear unless you make it disappear, and even after you do that, there will always be another evil force rising to destroy our kind. In order for others to live tomorrow, we must make a sacrifice today. I have foreseen a great journey that all of you may have to take in order to end all of this madness. I wish you the best, my sons."***

After hearing a few wise words from their mother, they made no response, and proceeded to the depths of the secret room. After finally reaching the secret room, the five sons of God sat down amongst each other in the form of a circle, and then they closed their eyes and attempted to summon Hermes Mercurius Trismegistus by cosmic telepathy. And when the five sons of God opened their eyes, Hermes stood within the midst of their meditative circle. Hermes looked at the five sons, and said, *"You all look as if you have no faith, however, I know you better than you all know yourselves. And most of all, I know that the flame within a microcosm shall never cease to exist. Therefore, all of you still have plenty of faith left. A great journey awaits you; it is time for all of you to attain the omega secrets of your cosmic gifts. Fireael, you shall become a master of light, Aquari-on, you shall become as strong as the waves of the seven seas, Earthael, you'll become as strong and beautiful as a diamond, and you Airael, you shall no longer move the winds, you shall become the winds. Ethereael, you are the holder of the sword of Elohim, when the time comes, you will one day comprehend what the sword's true power is. And when this happens, all of your cosmic abilities will be merged with the tongue of Yahuah.*

When your cosmic abilities are merged with the tongue of Yahuah, the son of Yahuah will place all of you in the east, and then he will appear in the midst of battle. The sword of Elohim contains the strength of the first Son of God. Yahuahshua will rise and supply the power necessary for all of you to succeed. But before you can all experience these things, you must first travel across the spiritual lands of undines, gnomes, Salamanders, and sylphs. First, you will enter the land of Flam-Ura, and then portals of grace shall be opened unto you.

The land of Undenuendia will be revealed, then one of you shall go on to the land of Estheera, and after you leave the land of Estheera, one of you will travel on to the land of Artriol. Only one of your journeys shall be different. Ethereael, you shall travel to the universe of Mestophelue, and destroy the six planets that now give strength and power to the demon called Mephistopheles. And when your journey is done, I will appear immediately, and then, and only then will I give you further instruction. Before I open the portal to the land of spirits, all of

you must first give a visit to Daggarael, the angel of forge. If you thought that this journey would be easy, you're wrong, when you go to see Daggarael, he shall forge shackles of divinity, which will prevent you from using some of your cosmic abilities in your physical body. Therefore, all of you will be strictly relying on the cosmic abilities deep inside of your soul, psychic body, interior strength, and any magic you may have learned from your father. Is that understood?"

Aquari-on replied, saying, ***"How are we going to win without our powers?"*** Hermes responded in a wise voice, saying, ***"You will not be without your powers, however, you will not be able to use some of them in your physical body. Therefore, faith is imperative in your overall survival on these journeys."*** When Aquari-on heard this, he immediately thought to himself, saying, ***"I guess it's time to prove that we don't need our physical bodies to be triumphant, either way, I hope we're doing the right thing."*** When Aquari-on spoke to himself, Hermes heard him loud and clear, afterward, Hermes said, ***"Aquari-on, do not question your mission, trust your heart."***

Aquari-on was startled, and said, ***"How did you hear my thoughts?"*** Hermes replied, and said, ***"At this point, that is irrelevant, worry not about the powers of others; learn yours."*** Afterward, Hermes raised his hand, and out of his palm came green electricity that immediately ripped a hole into reality. A portal of pure brilliant white light surrounded by electricity appeared, and the sons of God walked through the portal of light and prepared to visit Daggarael, the mighty angel of forge.

Daggarael was once ordered by God to create chains and shackles designed to prevent the use of cosmic abilities in the Nephilim, angels and demons. Centuries ago, when angels took it upon themselves to engage in sexual intercourse with human females, God sent his word out on high, and ordered Daggarael, the angel of forge to do great works. These are the shackles that were mysteriously placed on Goliath's forearms before David slew him.

With the shackles of divinity on, one's powers would be rendered useless. The shackles of divinity were first designed to prevent the Nephilim from destroying the inhabitants of Earth with evil intent. And so, the same shackles will be used on the cosmic sons so that they can earn all of their powers with honesty and faith in God. A great portal opens and the cosmic sons of God arrive at the chambers of forge where Daggarael, the angel of forge resides. The chamber of forge was like the chamber of a roman king and a blacksmith combined, for it had weapons and armor hung upon its walls. Its walls were made of pure silver, and the ground was made of symmetrically sustained light. Also, there was a window where one could see all of the planets in our solar system.

A great surprise is given, Daggarael realizes that five mortals have entered his throne room; he then speaks loudly, saying, ***"Who Dears to enter the chamber and humble abode of the forge? Verily, I say unto you, there shall be great consequences to any mortals amongst this holy place."*** Daggarael stood ten-feet tall with the head of a bull, eyes of fire, horns of fire, and four wings. His body was like that of a man's, and there was also a giant throne made of gold, and next to his throne was a humongous axe engraved with a name of God almighty.

Fireael looks up at the powerful angel, and says, ***"My name is Fireael, the son of cosmic flames, my brothers and I have come to ask you to make the golden shackles of divinity, so that we can attend our most important journey, will you help us?"*** Daggarael replies, and says, ***"If you can defeat me and prove your strength, I will not only forge that in which you ask of me, I will also forge***

weapons for thy journey. Do we have a deal?*"** Fireael looks at his brothers, and says, ***"Let's take him, he's huge, the bigger they are, the harder they hit the ground."

Whilst the five brothers were speaking amongst each other, Daggarael took up his mighty axe and began to swing it with all of his angelic strength, and when the five sons realized what he had done, they quickly retreated and split-up to strategize. Fireael engulfed himself in destructive flames, and immediately began a deadly assault on the mighty angel of forge. Fireael opened his palms and began to throw flames at Daggarael's feet. When Daggarael saw this, he simply swung his axe and knocked Fireael out cold with a precise hit. Fireael seemed to be no challenge for the angel of forge; his powers were insignificant compared to Daggarael's cosmic power. When Aquari-on saw this, he immediately closed his eyes and opened his hands; two streams of water drenched the angel of forge immediately. Daggarael was surprised that such puny mortals had such great powers. While Aquari-on drenched Daggarael with water, he used his powers to trap him in a force field of water, and when Airael saw this, he waved his hand and shot cold wind from the palms of his left and right hands. Before Daggarael knew it, he was frozen and trapped in a boulder of ice. Just when Ethereael, Earthael, Aquari-on and Airael thought that they had won the battle, Daggarael broke out of the ice and shattered it like glass.

And again, Daggarael swung his axe and hit the ground, nearly killing Ethereael with ease. When Ethereael realized that he had almost met his demise, he levitated into the air and absorbed the ether permeating heaven to give him great strength. He then charged toward Daggarael and impinged him with dangerous blows to his face with his fists. Daggarael staggered back and opened his eyes to the strength of the son of ether. Ethereael had raw cosmic strength derived directly from the ether. When Daggarael realized Ethereael's strength, his attention was focused on getting rid of him first.

And so, Ethereael went one on one with the angel of forge, and in the heat of battle, Daggarael swung his mighty axe and made a direct hit on Ethereael. Ethereael wildly crashed into the walls of the chamber of forge. Ethereael got up, and began to throw bolts of yellow lightning at him; however, it was of no use, for Daggarael was too powerful. The two forces of power knocked each other down over and over, impinging each other with hit after hit. Meanwhile, Earthael sprung into action, and sent a tremor under Daggarael's feet, the power of the tremor was strong enough to send Daggarael crashing into the ground below his feet.

And again, Daggarael quickly recovered and attacked. It would seem that Daggarael couldn't be defeated, however, anything is possible. Daggarael swung his axe once again, and knocked Earthael out cold. After realizing that the five mortal warriors were no match for his axe, he swung his axe with more force, and finally caught Ethereael and Aquari-on with a clean hit, knocking Ethereael and Aquari-on unconscious. Airael saw how easily the angel of forge had bested his brothers, and backed his self into a corner with fear in his mind. Just as Airael stood in a corner scared that the angel of forge would kill him; a furious flaming-eyed Fireael awoke and levitated into the air engulfed in wildly vivifying flames. Daggarael turned around, looked at Fireael, and laughed, saying, ***"Foolish mortal of fire, feel the power of my axe!"***

As Daggarael swung his axe at Fireael with all of his strength, Fireael stood still and didn't move not one inch, and when the axe was just about to cut Fireael's head clean off, he opened his palm and stopped the axe with his bare hands. Daggarael was amazed as he applied more of his angelic strength to his axe, and realized that he could not budge his axe not one bit. Fireael bent Daggarael's axe into the form of an arch, and then he made a fist with his right hand, and fueled the never ceasing flame of God within his self.

As the interior flame within his body grew, Fireael punched Daggarael in the stomach with all of his strength, and Daggarael fell to his knees, saying, ***"Spare me! You and your brothers have won; I'll make the shackles of divinity once again. I shall keep my word."*** Fireael replied, saying, ***"Good! You should've done that in the first place!"*** Daggarael stood up, and said, ***"You have already defeated me, but before I can make the shackles, I must have permission from an angel called Zadkiel."*** Fireael said, ***"Where can I find him?"*** Daggarael says, ***"You must use your spiritual eye to see him, he sits upon the planet called Jupiter, find him and return here immediately."*** Daggarael opened his palm and created a portal to the outskirts of the planet Jupiter, he then said, ***"Take this portal and return with it, I will be waiting to forge your weapons and your shackles if you are allowed by authority."*** Airael ran out of the corner of the chamber and into the portal without saying a word. Ethereael, Earthael, and Aquari-on woke up preparing to fight, however, Fireael had already taken care of Daggarael, he stood next to the portal, and said, ***"Hurry up! Get up! We have another mission to complete."*** Ethereael, Earthael, and Aquari-on quickly stood up and ran into the portal without asking any questions, and immediately they found themselves hovering at the outskirts of the planet Jupiter.

Fireael looked at Airael, and said, ***"Airael, you froze on us back there; we've faced worst than that, stay focused next time."*** Airael nodded his head, and said, ***"I didn't think I could help the situation, I was shocked, we've fought fallen angels before, but we've never fought an angel of God, besides, that angel was out of his eternal freakin' mind! I won't freeze on you next time."***

Fireael said, ***"Good, now let's finish this mission so we can be home in time for dinner."*** Ethereael looks at Fireael, and says, ***"Fireael, why exactly are we here?"*** Fireael replies, saying, ***"after I was about to beat the crap out of Daggarael, he gave up and told me that we would have to ask an angel named Zadkiel for permission to make the shackles for us, so now we have to find Zadkiel and return to Daggarael so we can finish this crazy mission, and stop Mephistopheles and whoever else wants a piece of us."***

Ethereael replies, and says, ***"Okay, let's do this!"*** Aquari-on says, ***"Whoa! I know that's planet Jupiter, but what the heck is that on top of it!? Its wings are huge! I hope we don't have to fight that thing, he's way bigger than Darknesseus was."*** As the five cosmic sons flew through the cosmos, they encountered an angel sitting upon the planet Jupiter, an angel named *"Zadkiel."* Zadkiel had eight wings, the head of an eagle, the body of a lion, and eyes of flames. When the five cosmic sons reached the planet Jupiter, Fireael spoke aloud, saying, ***"We humbly ask that you grant us the permission to have the golden shackles of divinity forged by Daggarael, the angel of forge."*** Zadkiel says, ***"One must prove that he is worthy to ask for such a thing, therefore, there are five of you, elect the one amongst you who'll fight me."*** The five brothers decided to huddle so that they could choose who would fight Zadkiel.

Fireael looked at his brothers and whispered, saying, ***"I beat Daggarael, so I'll choose who fights this one, and I choose Airael."*** Airael heard what Fireael said and shook his head while saying, ***"Are you serious! I froze when we fought Daggarael, how exactly do you think I'm going to beat this thing, he's thirty-times the size Daggarael was. I don't think that's a good choice, let Ethereael take him."*** Fireael said, ***"No! I know you can do it, one on one, you and him, I know you can do it, I know you won't***

freeze on us when we need you the most Airael, don't hold back, give it all you got."

Fireael looked at Zadkiel, and said, ***"We choose Airael, master of cosmic air."*** Zadkiel raises himself off of the planet Jupiter, and raises his paw, and out of his paw came a flash of brilliant light. Before Airael knew it, Ethereael, Aquari-on, Fireael, and Earthael were trapped inside of a force field that would only allow them to watch the battle between Zadkiel and Airael. The voice of Hermes traveled throughout the universe, and said, ***"Let the battle begin!"*** Airael took flight into the height of the cosmos like a speeding torpedo; Zadkiel had lost him, for Airael had disappeared. And when he re-appeared, he stood still and made no movement. Zadkiel blinked his eyes, and immediately Airael exploded. Zadkiel roared a great roar, and said, ***"Your warrior has failed, the battle is over, I have defeated him with ease, permission to have the shackles forged is denied."*** Fireael, Ethereael, Earthael and Aquari-on dropped their countenances and became filled with sorrow while believing that Airael had easily failed. After Zadkiel spoke, Airael appeared again, and before Zadkiel knew it, there were seventy-five duplicates of Airael. Airael had not failed, he was still alive, and Zadkiel was greatly surprised at this.

Fireael felt that his brother was still alive, so he picked up his countenance, and saw his brother using his father's mystical duplication technique. When Fireael saw this, he screamed out loud, saying, ***"Take him down Airael, you can do it!"*** With his brothers cheering him on from a far, Airael knew he could win. Altogether, there were seventy-six duplicates of Airael. Zadkiel saw this and began to flap his gigantic wings so that he could eliminate all of the duplicates with one move, when Airael saw this, he commanded his duplicates to put their hands in front of themselves, and follow after him. Seventy-six category seven tornadoes raced out of a hundred and fifty-two palms.

And when the tornadoes fought against the might of Zadkiel's wings, they overpowered him and proved to him that the five sons were worthy of their request. And so, Zadkiel returned to his seat upon the planet Jupiter.

Ethereael, Fireael, Earthael and Aquari-on were freed, and Zadkiel spoke, saying, ***"Permission is granted, now leave and do what thou wilt."*** The five warriors returned to the portal that Daggarael set for them, and once again they were present in the chamber of forge. Fireael stood amongst Daggarael, and said, ***"Zadkiel has granted us permission, now give us what we need in order to do what we have to do."*** When Daggarael heard this, he grabbed his axe, and it morphed into a great hammer to forge weaponry with. Daggarael left his chamber, entered another room, and slammed the door behind him so that he could do the will of God in a secret place.

As the five sons remained in the outer chamber, they heard Daggarael making loud noises, and banging on something, whilst saying, ***"By the God of Jacob! Isaac! Abraham! Enoch! And John the Baptist! I, Daggarael, angel of forge; command that these weapons and shackles be blessed by the Alpha et Omega! Aleph and Tau! By the hidden name of the order of Chaioth ha-Qadesch! And he whose name hath been placed in the height, the depth, the east, the west, the north, and the south! Behold! The will of the divine architect hath been accomplished! Selah!"***

Daggarael raised his right hand with his hammer gripped tightly in his palm, and then he struck something that sounded like metal one last time. And when the door opened, the smell of cherries and ivory imbued the chamber as Daggarael walked forth whilst holding ten shackles of divinity and five pentacles. Daggarael spoke, and said, ***"Earthael, I give thee the seventh and last pentacle of Saturn. The power of the orders of angels maketh the universe tremble. To Airael, I give thee the first***

pentacle of Mars. Madimiel shall slay your enemies with a sword of cosmic lights. Aquari-on, to thee I give the fourth pentacle of mars. Without doubt, thou shalt be triumphant and victorious in battle. Fireael, to thee I grant the sixth pentacle of mars. Your enemies' sword shall enter into their own heart, and their bow shall be broken. And last, but not least, Ethereael, I grant thee the sixth pentacle of the sun. Let their eyes be darkened that they see not; and make their loins continually to shake, they have eyes and see not."

When Fireael, Ethereael, Earthael, Aquari-on, and Airael saw the final products of the angel of forge, they were greatly astounded. Their battles were not fought in vain, their courage had truly paid-off, and the time to take their journey was near; the adventure had just begun. A portal of light opened, and the five warriors took the shackles and pentacles, and entered through the portal. When they all reached the other side of the portal, they found themselves back in the secret room of their home. When Fireael realized that he was back home, he said, ***"We've come this far, we can't stop now, we have to go all the way. We've gone the distance, and there's no turning back now."***

Aquari-on replied, saying, ***"Since when did you become the president of the united states? You have a speech for everything don't you? I can remember when you first realized you were on fire, you fainted like a little girl, now all of a sudden your Mr. brave-a-lot. Wow! You really are something aren't you?"*** Fireael looked at his brother Aquari-on, and said, ***"Sounds like somebody is a little cranky from a lack of rest."*** Ethereael looked at his brothers, and said, ***"Okay, can we try to get some rest now; all of this yapping is making my ears bleed. Just please go to sleep!"***

And after a long battle, the sons of God were extremely fatigue, therefore, they all decided to rest in the secret room for a few hours before preparing for their final journey to the spirit lands. After sleeping for seven hours, the five warriors woke up, and Hermes stood before them, and said, ***"This is your final journey, after traveling through the land of elementals, you will go forward and reach the gates of Sheol, however, I must warn you, Sheol is a gruesome place where living mortals, such as yourself, must be on your guard at all times, you'll literally be fighting your way through hell, also, there is no telling whether you will return after this battle.***

For the thamiel are formidable demon warriors. Satan and Moloch are strong enemies that will not be easily defeated. I give you great blessings on this journey; you are the last defense the universe has against spiritual wickedness in high places. As you may or may not know, the God of the universe has left these battles to your kind, his sons. He knows that you will succeed, therefore, do yourselves a favor and know the same. When you reach the end of your journey, I will appear at the gates of Sheol one more time so that I can speak with you before you go to war with the demon creatures, and also, I will take your shackles off so that you can complete the will of the grand architect."

Hermes waved his hand, the shackles of divinity wrapped themselves around their wrists, and another portal opened, the five warriors went through it without saying a word. When they reached the other side of the portal, there was a land of red dirt graced with tiny crystals and filled with burning bushes. The flowers of the land were on fire, the trees were on fire and rather large, and they covered the land greatly, for there were many. The roses that sprung from its grounds were fashioned from fire, while mountains of stone vivified with wild flames of beauty. When Fireael saw this land, for some strange reason he felt as if he was at home. However, little did Fireael know, the land of Flam-ura was the land of Salamanders, the spirit creatures of fiery flames. And so, Fireael gave all of his brothers a hug, and said, ***"Well, it's time for all of us to split-up and go our***

separate ways, I guess I'll meet up with you at the gates of Sheol. Be on guard, this is the final test for all of us." And so, the four warriors walked two miles each, and at the end of their two miles, four individual portals appeared, Ethereael, Aqauri-on, Airael, and Earthael took their respected portals so that they could finish their journey and complete the will of the great architect. Afterward, Fireael went forth and walked toward a large tower that looked identical to the empire state building. The tower was tall and red with millions of red ants crawling all over it.

While Fireael walked seven miles to his destination, he finally reached the tower and began to get tired. Before Fireael knew it, he passed out, and fell to the grounds of the red lands of Flam-ura. Deep within his slumber, a voice called out to him, and said, ***"Your journey is of great importance, the time for mortal ascension has come forth. You have all made me proud. A true father loves his sons with all of his heart; seek not to destroy Mephistopheles because he imprisoned me. Do not seek revenge; seek to make the world of the living a better place. The three-fold form of one supreme intelligence is your power source; therefore, your abilities are unlimited. Worry not, for I am completing the great works in the kingdom of God. As we speak, the divine architect is directing legions of angels for the Great War. The archangels of heaven are focusing their strengths in you and your brothers. I am truly blessed to have had all of you as sons. The heavens stand behind you in every movement. Go forth and attain that which will increase your strength."*** Fireael said, ***"Dad! Where are you?! We need you now more than ever."*** As Fireael's body lies upon the grounds of Flam-ura, an abundance of tears rushed out of his eyes whilst they were closed.

The tears touched the ground, and flames began to surround his body. The son of cosmic flames had experienced a great righteousness within his heart, and before he knew it, a flash of light occurred within his mind. His psychic centers were illuminated, and his physical body was once again strengthened with the might of Elion almighty. Something mysterious happened; his soul was enlightened with the amazement of life, mortal ascension was at an all time high.

Chapter 11

The Journey of Divine Bestowal

After two hours, Fireael woke up and spoke to himself, saying, ***"I can't fail."*** He picked himself up from the ground and began to walk further toward the tower. Whilst walking, he heard a voice speak out to him, saying, ***"Fireael, the rise of the thamiel is near."*** Fireael replied, saying ***"Who are you?"*** The voice responded, saying, ***"I am the lord and king of salamanders, the creatures of fire; thou hast fought many battles and succeeded where others would've failed, and now, ye are worthy of the omega secrets of cosmic fire."*** Particles of red dust began to gather into one place, and a dragon engulfed in flames was formed from the gathering of the dust. When Fireael saw this, he stood still, and said, ***"What is it that you can teach me that I've yet to learn?"*** The fiery dragon disappeared and a portal of flaming light opened, and out of the portal, the voice of the fiery dragon spoke again, saying, ***"Enter the portal to our world if you are truly a warrior of fire."*** And so, Fireael noticed the portal and spoke to his self, saying, ***"I need all of the knowledge I can get."*** He then entered the portal and immediately he was knocked unconscious. When he finally woke up, he looked around and saw a large crowd of salamanders, and as he looked in front of himself, he saw a bizarre sight for mortal eyes. The land was inherited by thousands of salamanders that resembled snakes that were two feet long, but each salamander had two small arms and legs that were like an alligator's limbs, whilst their scales and eyes were flames of fire.

Fireael looked forward, and saw a throne of gold that stood before him and in the seat of the throne was a small flame vivifying by itself. When Fireael witnessed the flame upon the golden throne, he became speechless immediately. The throne was all gold and its armrests were carved to resemble two snakes. After Fireael began to stare at the vivifying flame, a voice began to vibrate from it. And it said, ***"The essence of the soul vivifies like a flame of fire, but if the flame is imbued with the secrets of eternal life, the flame can naturally stabilize itself and light the way to the paths of victory occult in the cosmos within and without. If you comprehend the wisdom of the flames, your heart shall become a sword of flames capable of burning under cold waters."*** When Fireael heard the words of the small flame, he replied, saying, ***"Teach me what you must, but make no mistake, I am the undisputed champion of cosmic flames."***

After the flame upon the golden throne heard this, it replied, and said, ***"So mote it be."*** Before Fireael could speak another word, the flame upon the golden throne began to grow larger until it engulfed the whole throne. Finally, the flames revealed a creature having two angelic wings of fire. His eyes were inane and his skin was made of lizard-like scales that were dark brown. He then revealed his name to Fireael, and said, ***"I am Flareus, king and lord of the flames of fire."*** Fireael heard him clearly, and said, ***"Where am I? And what is this place?"*** Flareus Replied, saying, ***"This is the southern quadrant of fire where salamanders reside at most times. At the current moment, we are in a cave, which we mostly call home. Here is where your final training begins and ends, Fireael. Now, if you're ready, it is time to begin."*** Fireael replied, saying, ***"What exactly is it that you're going to teach me?"*** Flareus answered, saying, ***"The cosmic technique of primary flames, after you learn this technique, the flames that emit from your body will combine into one form of fire. At this point in time, you have two forms of fire, a destructive flame, and a purifying flame, if these two were combined, you would attain immense cosmic abilities linked directly to all spirits of fire, and all fire of spirit. The flames that engulf your body will become flames of light, then, and only then will you truly be prepared to vanquish and prevent the rise of the***

thamiel. And now, the final question stands alone, are you ready, Fireael?"

Fireael answers, and says, ***"Teach me the way, and I will be triumphant."*** Flareus replied, saying, ***"Fireael, there is a great dragon of holy fire that guards the omega secret of cosmic fire. If you can pass one test of strength and determination, then, and only then will you attain the omega secret of fire. Across the mountains of Firea and upon the lands of Flam-ura, there are evil and malevolent creatures called "Urolai." They are true masters of fire, and they also possess great potential to possibly attain the omega secret. If the Urolai are not defeated, the omega secret of cosmic fire will be lost for all eternity. The Urolai are always on point, and if they see someone or something that seems to be a threat to them, they'll waste no time eliminating their target. I have warned you, son of cosmic flames, do not cross the mountains of Firea, for if you do; you are as good as dead. Be cautious, the Urolai are worthy adversaries. They have trained day and night to destroy the holy dragon so that they can dominate the land of Salamanders, and wreak havoc upon our sacred lands.***

Today, you will not only fight against the Urolai, you will also attain the power that will aid you in the great battle against the mighty thamiel. Today, you will astral travel through our homeland, and it won't be easy for you, and once you have completed your mission, a portal will open, and you will arrive directly at the gates of Sheol. Now, walk with me to the training circle of salamander warriors. The journey begins now." And so, Fireael followed Flareus to the circle of salamander warriors. The circle of salamander warriors was a slab of stone engraved with the writing of the angels, and the words within and around the circle said: ***"The worthy shall project their physical counterpart instantly when amidst the center herein."*** The son of cosmic flames stood within the circle, and the battle to attain the holy fire had begun. Fireael placed his index finger over his heart, and immediately his psychic body was lifted from his physical body, and the eyes of his psychic body were dominated with fire whilst his whole psychic body was engulfed in the flames of destruction. Fireael levitated his psychic body into the air while having a serious look upon his countenance.

Fireael took destiny into his own hands and decided to fly over the mountains of Firea in the land Flam-ura just as he was warned not to. As he flew over the mountains of Firea, he spotted a dragon surrounded by strange creatures that seemed to be attempting to destroy it. While Fireael flew over the mountains of Firea, a Servant of Flareus spoke, saying, ***"Master Flareus, what exactly is he doing? Did you not warn him about flying over the mountains of Firea? Did you not tell him that he would be eliminated with ease if the Urolai spotted him? I don't understand, Master Flareus."***

Flareus replied, and said, ***"Yes, I did warn him of these things of which you speak of, however, if this mortal man hath true faith in the Grand architect of the universe, then the tables would surely turn, and the Urolai will be eliminated with ease, and Fireael will be triumphant. I felt the courage in his soul, I believe that he will succeed, however, nothing is ever easy, and no journey is too hard, for we would not receive more of a journey than we can handle. Let's see the outcome of this great battle of mortal creatures and spirit creatures."*** Fireael flew over the mountains of Firea and saw creatures that resembled lions, and had flames for fur, whilst their eyes were made of green flames. Eventually, as Fireael moved through the skies, the Urolai spotted him and began an onslaught of attacks that would seem to be good enough to destroy Fireael immediately. Out of the mouths of the Urolai came hundreds of flaming balls of black electricity. Fireael dodged all of their attacks, though he had a hard time doing so. As he dodged the greatest attacks that the Urolai had ever used, he began to repeat what Daggarael told him when he had given him the sixth pentacle of mars. Fireael spoke to himself, saying, ***"My enemies' sword shall enter into their own heart, and their bow shall be broken."*** After Fireael said this, the attacks of the Urolai reversed themselves, and killed the Urolai immediately, and when Fireael saw this, he spoke to himself, saying, ***"Whoa! Now that's what I'm talking about baby!"*** No longer were the Urolai able to shoot bursts of energy at him through their mouths, for the sixth pentacle of mars had shown the contents of its power.

After the swift elimination of the Urolai, Fireael spotted the great dragon that would bring forth a change in his abilities, and as he saw this dragon, he flew down to the lands of Flam-ura, and stood still in front of the great dragon. When the great dragon saw Fireael standing in front of him, he spoke, saying, ***"Who dares to face the serpent of lights? Thou hath a death wish that I refuse to fulfill. Be gone from my presence mortal, for thou art far from prepared to attain what you seek, be gone!"***

Fireael heard the words of the great dragon, and said, ***"You are mistaken, serpent of lights, choose your test, if you dare."*** When the serpent of lights heard this, he replied, saying, ***"Very well then, maybe I have underestimated you, mortal man, I shall give you a test that will prove your worthiness. If you fail, you shall die, and if you prevail, you shall attain the abilities in which you seek diligently."*** After the serpent of lights spoke, he roared a great roar that shook the land of Flam-ura like an earthquake, before Fireael knew it, a great portal opened, and the serpent of lights spoke again, saying, ***"This portal leads to the land of Manhattan in the place called New York City. When you walk through this portal, you will immediately be standing at the uppermost point of a building called empire state.***

When you arrive, there will be a fallen angel by the name of Marideael, he will be in possession of a thirty-three year old

virgin woman who's blood is connected to all of humanity, thus, if Marideael kills her, all mortals shall be slain in one moment, your duty is to save her, and reach the bottom of the empire state building before Marideael murders her in cold blood, and destroys all of humanity in an instant. If you accept this challenge, all human creatures could perish, and the weight of the planet earth shall rest upon your shoulders. Do you accept this challenge?" Fireael looks deep into the dragon's eyes, and says, ***"I accept your challenge, serpent of lights!"*** And so, Fireal walked through the portal, and he stood at the very top of the empire state building, tip-toed on his left leg baring the purple flames of purification, and having his arms outstretched as if he were a living symbol of the cross.

Marideael stood eight feet tall with long silver hair and great black wings that were covered with the smell of sulfur and decomposing flesh. His eyes were fearfully inane, and he held a katana sword that seemed to be sharp enough to cut cleanly through the thickest concrete. And beside him was a beautiful virgin woman wearing golden handcuffs that seemed to be forged by Daggarael. And so, Fireael jumped off of the top of the building, and landed directly in front of Marideael, and said, ***"Marideael I presume? The name's Fireael, I'm here for the girl!"*** When Marideael heard this, he immediately began using unknown sword-styles in a speed that even the most awakened spiritual eye would deem invisible or difficult to see. Fireael dodged every move to the best of his ability; however, he was slightly cut on the right arm, for the sword of Marideael was as sharp as an electric saw when he swung it with all of his might. When Fireael realized that he had been cut, he turned it up a notch.

Before Marideael knew it, Fireael no longer dodged his demon katana-yoki sword; amazingly, the son of flames began blocking Marideael's sword with his bare hands and forearms.

And when Marideael saw this, he stepped back and realized that Fireael was no ordinary mortal man, for there were only twelve angels in heaven that could block his mighty sword. As Marideael stood speechless, Fireael grabbed the virgin woman and threw her on his back, and before Marideael knew it, Fireael had gracefully jumped off of the ledge of the empire state building whilst heading to his destination to complete his test.

However, Marideael was far from slow; he followed Fireael and began an all out attack with his demon katana-yoki sword. The son of cosmic flames adjusted his power's vibratory frequency so that he could use his cosmic flames without disintegrating the virgin woman when he used the depth of his abilities, he then stopped in mid-air while attaching his feet to the exterior structure of the building, and amazingly, the son of flames began to run swiftly down the side of the empire state building while carrying the virgin woman on his back, and being chased by an angry fallen angel who began attacking him with an extremely sharp sword. Marideael was driven by the intentions to exterminate all mankind, whereas Fireael was driven by faith.

Fireael blocked, and dodged swing after swing while running quickly down the side of the building, and finally, the son of flames blocked the sword with all of his strength, and shattered Marideael's demon katana-yoki sword into particles of metal. When Marideael realized his beloved sword was destroyed, he was uncontrollably angry. And as soon as Fireael realized Marideael's pause in movement due to anger, he impinged dangerous blows to Marideael's stomach and face, and before Marideael knew it, he was knocked out cold. The son of flames was triumphant. Faster and faster he ran down the side of the empire state building, and when he was halfway to his destination, he engulfed himself in the flames of destruction so that he could send a message to those who had eyes to see.

A message that said, ***"Anything is possible through the creator of all existence."*** And so, he held the virgin woman upon his back while moving at luminous velocity. The people were shocked, and the citizens of New York who saw the empire state building from a distance began pointing at it, and saying, "***Someone's office is on fire!***" People began to panic until they realized that the flame was moving down the side of the building, but not burning it, and while Fireael ran faster and faster, Marideael's body falls to the ground floor right beside him. Finally, he reached the ground floor, and before Fireael knew it, he was back in the land of Flam-ura standing directly in front of the serpent of lights. No one in the city of New York could understand what had just happened, for they were all confused. The serpent of lights looked at Fireael, and said, ***"I definitely underestimated you, mortal man. This day, you have proven yourself worthy of the merciful and severe flames of God, to you, great power is given, and my purpose is fulfilled in the grand design of divine architecture."*** After the serpent of lights spoke his final words, his body lit-up the land of Flam-ura like a flame of light in a darkened room, and within seconds, his body was bereft of a physical form, it'd taken on more subtle form. And finally, the serpent of lights roared loudly, and took flight into the depths of Fireael's heart. The son of flames closed his eyes, and when he opened them, his psychic body was engulfed in the flames of light, Fireael Powers, the grandson of Namsilat, and the son of Calabrael Powers had become the new paradigm of what the combination of mercy in God-guided judgment and mercy of good mortal heart would manifest in the nature of humanity.

His newfound flames of light vivified wildly like an uncontrollable fire that refused to be put out with the largest amounts of water. After receiving the flames of light, Fireael took flight into the skies and flew across the land of Flam-ura with the mighty speed of thought. A flash of blinding light covered the skies, and Fireael mysteriously appeared directly in front of Flareus, the lord of salamanders. The light of the son of flames was so blinding that not one salamander witnessed the arrival of his psychic body, for the king of salamanders and his followers opened their eyes, and there he stood, the new keeper of the primary flames. He returned to his fleshy envelope, and felt like divine royalty.

Flareus was astounded that he had succeeded and attained such a great power. Flareus looked at Fireael, and said, ***"Your powers are seven-fold what they were before; you have our blessings, son of flames, go forth, and trample the thamiel under thy feet. The gates of Sheol await, do what must be done."*** A large portal in the sky opened, and Fireael shot off into the sky while saying, ***"We'll meet again, Flareus!"*** A flash of light occurred over the land of Flam-ura, and the son of cosmic flames had disappeared for good. And so, Fireael's journey ended as he entered the portal to the gates of Sheol where he would impatiently wait for his four brothers.

Meanwhile, Aquari-on visited the land of undines called **"Undenuendia."** As Aquari-on stepped foot on the other side of the portal, he looked around, and saw an unusually large castle, and a vast land of water inherited by creatures that resembled mortal men and women, however, the only difference between humans and undines was that the undines' skin was blue and pale, and the length of their hair was so long that it reached their knees. Also, they had a symbol upon their brows, a symbol of three ridged lines. When Aquari-on saw this, he was greatly astounded, and then, he looked down with amazement, and realized that he was standing on water, for all undines could naturally walk on water.

Just as Aquari-on realized that he was standing on water, an undine appeared before him, and said, ***"Ah, Aquari-on, our master has long awaited your arrival, are you prepared to attain the final secret of cosmic waters?"*** Aquari-on looked around in amazement, and said, ***"I don't think I have much of a choice, and who's your master?"*** The undine answered, and said, ***"His name is Undurah, he is the king of undines, he is also the one who ordered that the great sword of light called "Excalibur" be given to the legendary king Arthur who founded and formed the Knights of the Round Table. We have a little bit of history dealing with mortal men; so don't feel lonely here on your journey in Undenuendia. Now that we have established a small conversation together, it is time for me to take you to our master's throne room where you'll begin your test, and hopefully leave here with great understanding of your element. We've heard so much about you, the whole kingdom is waiting to see how you will do on your test of strength with the three-headed serpent."*** Aquari-on replied, saying, ***"The three-headed what!? Damn, I never get to fight anyone my size."*** And so, Aquari-on walked across the waters of Undenuendia until he reached the kingdom where Undurah, the master of undines resided. The great and large castle was fashioned from sparkling water that would amaze anyone who saw it. And after a long walk, Aquari-on reached the door of sparkling water that led to Undurah's throne room; he then opened it, and was greatly amazed at the appearance of the master of undines.

Undurah was seven feet in height, and unlike other undines, he did not bear three ridged lines upon his brow, instead, he had five ridged lines upon his brow, and the five-ridged lines represented ultimate comprehension, courage, wisdom, faith, and soul. Unlike other undines, Undurah's hair was made of strands and rays of light; therefore, Undurah would have to cover his hair with a black silk scarf before anyone could see him. All who came to see him would have to cover their eyes while talking to him if he did not cover his hair.

Aquari-on covered his face, saying, ***"My cosmic senses tell me about something called the orb of torrents? Will you help me attain it?"*** Undurah replied, saying, ***"No, son of cosmic waters, I cannot help you attain it, but I can guide you to its whereabouts. My name is Undurah, master of undines. I've long awaited your arrival, Aquari-on, you and your brothers have been elected by God to defeat Satan and Moloch, the leaders of the thamiel. Yes, I know exactly who you are, however, there is no time for much talk, east of this kingdom is a three-headed dragon that holds the final secret of cosmic waters. If you fly east, and go straight, there will be a three-headed dragon that is thirty-three feet in height, and believe me, if you follow my instructions, you will not miss him. Go to the dragon, and speak with him, and from there, you shall complete your journey and return here. Do you comprehend?"***

Aquari-on says, ***"I'll have to psychic project in order to fly, do you have a magical circle that I can use? Without it, I can't really use my powers; a part of this journey requires us to use our mortal given virtues."*** Undurah answered, saying, ***"Yes, follow me, Aquari-on."*** Undurah walked behind his throne and Aquari-on followed. Behind the throne of the great Undurah was a magical circle which contained an occult name of God in the middle, and round about the circle were pentagrams and hexagrams exteriorly lined and contained with another circle.

When Aquari-on saw this, he wasted no time; he immediately stepped into the circle, and sat down in a meditative form that would allow him to immediately utilize his psychic body. Once taking his meditative form, his psychic body arose from his physical envelope, and Aquari-on looked around, and spoke through telepathy, saying, ***"Which way is east, Undurah?"***

Undurah pointed his index finger to the east, and said, ***"That way, go straight, and keep your eyes open so that you do not miss what you are looking for."*** Aquari-on heard Undurah clearly, and began flying toward the east of Undenuendia where the three-headed dragon would change Aquari-on's life forever. After miles of flying with his psychic body, Aquari-on bumped into something and fell out of the sky, and onto the waters of the land of Undenuendia. He then got up, and said, ***"What just happened?!"*** And as Aquari-on asked himself that question, he looked up, and saw the three-headed dragon of Undenuendia. When Aquari-on saw the dragon face-to-face, he got scared, and said, ***"My name is Aquari-on, and I've come to attain the orb of torrents. Do you have it?"*** The three-headed dragon replied, saying, ***"Yes, however, you must earn such a mystery, son of cosmic waters."*** Aquari-on said, ***"How'd you know that I was a cosmic son?"*** The three-headed dragon replied, and said, ***"Everyone knows who you and your brothers are, you didn't think that you could fight the son of the morning and not gain some sort of reputation; did you?"***

Aquari-on replied, saying, ***"Ah, I guess so. Hmm, so that's how you know me. Well, I guess that's a good thing. In any event, now we have to fight the prince of darkness, so I need the orb as soon as possible. May I have it?"*** The three-headed dragon answered, saying, ***"Yes, but first you must pass a test that will prove you are worthy of its powers. No mortal man may attain the orb without being tested, I will summon a portal, and on the other side of the portal will be a great demon who's skill is unimaginable, if you can defeat him, unto thee I grant the orb of torrents, do you accept such a test?"*** Aquari-on answered, saying, ***"Yes, I do."*** The great three-headed dragon roared, and a large portal appeared.

Aquari-on looked up at the dragon, and said, ***"Only time will tell how strong I am when the odds are against me, no matter***

what the danger, he that dwelleth in the secret place of the most high shall abide under the shadow of the almighty, I will not fail." The dragon replied, saying, ***"We shall see, Aquari-on; we shall see."*** And so, the son of cosmic water walked through the portal, and on the other side of the portal was a desolate land with a nearby ocean, and a demon that stood still while surrounded by a force field of water. When Aquari-on saw this, he immediately placed himself in a force field identical to that of the demon's force field, he then said, ***"And what exactly is your name, demon?"*** The demon replied, saying, ***"Axericon, demon of perilous waters, and I think you should do yourself a favor, and surrender now."*** Aquari-on looked deep into the demon's eyes, and said, ***"Uh, no. I think you're the one that should surrender, but then again, you could retreat too, either way, I really don't care, the only one leaving this place alive is me."***

When Axericon heard Aquari-on telling him that he should quit, he flew off into the air like a torpedo, while saying, ***"We'll see who'll be triumphant, prepare to die, mortal."*** Aquari-on waved his hand, and large orbs of water began to rise out of the palms of his hands. Altogether, twelve orbs of water began to raise high into the skies, and as the orbs of water lifted into the skies, they began to chase Axericon all over the desolate lands. Eventually, Axericon disappeared and there was no sign of him.

When Aquari-on realized that his orbs of water were unable to seek and destroy him, he waved his hand and ordered them to return. He then thought to himself, saying, ***"I know this trick too well, if this demon is thinking about a sneak attack, he's got another thing coming."*** Aquari-on was no fool, he was well prepared for Axericon's sneak attack by using his hydrokinetic hold on water to create and surround himself in a square of water that was six-feet high, and twelve feet wide. And of course, Axericon appeared, and attacked Aquari-on with a fearsome blow; however, the thickness of the water surrounding Aquari-on was too thick to punch through without hurting oneself. When Axericon punched through the water surrounding Aquari-on's square water force field, Aquari-on commanded the water to entrap him. The water around Aquari-on began crawling over Axericon's arm until it covered him completely.

Axericon was trapped in a humongous orb of water controlled by yours truly. Aquari-on lifted the orb of water above his head, and said, ***"The rule of your kind is over, beginning now!"*** Axericon was greatly surprised, but the battle was far from over. Axericon disappeared, and before Aquari-on knew it, the demon was standing directly behind him, he then grabbed Aquari-on's arm, and shot off into the sky like a bullet while dragging Aquari-on through the sky like a balloon attached to an airplane.

Axericon just knew that he had Aquari-on exactly where he wanted him, and before Axericon knew it, Aquari-on was gone. Axericon looked to his left and saw nothing; he then looked to his right, and saw Aquari-on flying right next to him. Aquari-on smiled, and waved his hand while saying, ***"If you're looking for me, I'm right here."*** He then plunged forty-feet into the waters of a nearby ocean. And when Axericon saw this, he was wroth, and began to speak to himself, saying, ***"Damned mortal, when I get my hands on you, I'll break every bone in your worthless body!"*** Axericon tried his best, but couldn't sense where Aquari-on had gone, and because he couldn't figure out what Aquari-on was trying to do, he decided to land while speaking to himself, saying, ***"Where is he?! And why does he play games with me, instead of fighting me?"***

Before Axericon could say another word, two hands made of water reached out of the ocean, and snatched him, and pulled him under the ocean. Amazingly, Aquari-on was much more formidable when using his psychic body during battle. Axericon was scared to death, he thought that Aquari-on was a simple mortal, but of course, Aquari-on proved him wrong in every way. Finally, Aquari-on shot out of the water while having a hydrokinetic hold on an orb of water surrounding Axericon once again, but this time, Aquari-on let him go and disappeared. Axericon fell back into the ocean, and gradually levitated out of the ocean while trying to lock-on to Aquari-on's location; however, Aquari-on had quickly disappeared without a trace.

As Axericon stood there, clueless as to what Aquari-on would do next, the water of the nearby ocean began to rise one hundred feet into the air, and before Axericon could realize what was happening, the water began to chase him, and fell on top of him with a force and speed that obliterated him. Aquari-on re-appeared, and spoke loudly, saying, ***"The demon is defeated, I've passed your test!"*** The three-headed dragon spoke, saying, ***"Yes, you've won, I am quite surprised at your abilities, I have found you more than worthy, Aquari-on. However, Axericon was a lesser demon, the demons that you face in the future shall be much, much harder to defeat."*** After the three-headed dragon spoke his final words, a portal opened and Aquari-on flew through it, and returned to the land of Undenuendia.

Aquari-on stood in front of the three-headed dragon, and said, ***"I think that you have something that I've earned."*** The three-headed dragon replied, saying, ***"It is yours to have, I present you with the orb of torrents."*** As the three-headed dragon spoke, all of his heads became one. He then roared, and the orb of torrents shot out of its mouth, and into Aquari-on's psychic body. Of course, Aquari-on knew nothing of its powers after he attained it. After completing his mission, he returned to his physical body and began to feel very strange. Undurah looked at Aquari-on, and began to back away from him, Aquari-on's eyes began to leak, and then water began to pour out of his eyes as if his insides were made of water. Aquari-on placed his hands over his eyes, and began to shout out loud, saying, ***"I can't see! My eyes! It won't stop, Undurah, help me!"***

At first he panicked, but soon enough, he saw visions of his father, and then he stopped, and before he knew it, he was able to see again, and within the time that he could not see, his whole body was morphed into water. No longer was his body made of flesh and bones, Aquari-on had become living water with the ability to return to his human form at any time. Undurah was dumfounded, Aquari-on had attained the orb of torrents, and when Undurah realized Aquari-on's true potential, he bended on one knee, and said, ***"There was no mistake made when you were elected as the first son of cosmic water, you've shocked us all, blessed be."***

Undurah waved his hand, and a portal to the gates of Sheol was opened. Aquari-on transformed into an aggregation of liquid, and floated through the portal while saying, ***"Next time I come back, Undurah, I want you to take me out and show me around."*** Undurah replied, saying, ***"Not a problem, the realm of Undenuendia shall always welcome your presence, Aquari-on."*** The son of cosmic water left the land of Undenuendia, and met up with his brother Fireael at the gates of Sheol. When Fireael looked at his brother Aquari-on, he said, ***"What the heck happened to you?"*** Aquari-on replied, saying, ***"The orb of torrents, that's what happened to me. Why do you always have to ask so many questions?"***

Fireael began laughing, and answered, saying, ***"Well, I was kind of wondering if you would let me borrow your arm so I could make a big pot of tea."*** Aquari-on looked at Fireael, and said, ***"I***

guess you think that was funny, but it wasn't, and where's everybody else?"Fireael answered, saying, ***"We have to wait till they all finish their journey, for now, all we can do is wait."*** Afterward, Aquari-on looked in front of his self and saw that the gates of hell were made of human bones and fleshy remains, he then looked at Fireael, and said, ***"Whoa! Whoa! Whoa! Is this for real? They actually took their time out to make the gates with human flesh and bones? I hope Ethereael, Earthael, and Airael hurry up, I don't like this one bit."*** Fireael said, ***"Well, at least their crafty."***

Meanwhile, Airael entered the land of **Artriol** and witnesses a land between the heavens and the Earth. In Artriol there was no ground, simply red cloud and space, for it was merely the space between the heavens and the earth wherein all sylphs resided. The land of Artriol was also called the land of sylphs. As the son of cosmic air flies freely through the land of Artriol, a sylph appeared, and said, ***"Hey, you're kind of cute mortal, what's your name?"*** Airael replied, saying, ***"My name is Airael, grandson of Namsilat, and son of Calabrael."*** The sylphs were seven inches tall with four wings, their faces were made of light, a small flame covered their loins, and they had arms, feet, hands and legs like that of a human.

The sylph replied, saying, ***"Are you serious?! Calabrael Powers? I heard that God had given him the sword of Elohim, wow! You're his son? Cool! But your still not suppose to be here, I don't think that I have to remind you that you're human, our master may not like it."*** When Airael heard this, he said, ***"Take me to your master, and I'll leave thereafter."*** The young sylph said, ***"Okay, but I won't be responsible for anything that happens to you if she doesn't like you, let's go!"*** And so, Airael and the young sylph flew through the land of Artriol until they reached a red orb hovering in front of them. The red orb began to speak, saying, ***"It is your turn to find reflection in the cosmic, Airael. I am Tritomia, the queen and master of sylphs.***

I have been assigned instruction from Araboth; someone in heaven is really waiting to see how you and your brothers will face off against the thamiel." Whilst Tritomia spoke to Airael, the young sylph who brought him to her was confused. She spoke, and said, ***"Master Tritomia, you know this man, how?"*** Tritomia answered, and said, ***"My dear sister, this is one of the mortal warriors who fought Lucifer, his powers have been ordained by God, he's the one referred to as the cosmic son of air. He causes the winds to move with his will; yet, he is but a mortal man."*** The young sylph said, ***"Oh! Your one of the warriors that fought Lucifer on Earth, I must apologize for my ignorance, Airael, I didn't know who you were, please forgive me."*** Airael said, ***"Don't worry about it, not everyone wants to remember that day, I don't think that I need to mention that we died that day. In any event, all of that stuff is irrelevant at this moment, I've been resurrected, and I'm here now. Let's focus on getting rid of the thamiel, my brothers and I have a score to settle with a demon called Mephistopheles before we can take on Satan and Moloch. Tritomia, I feel a great power in this place, where is it coming from?"***

Tritomia answered, and said, ***"The power that you feel is called the wind horse of Artriol; it is the powerful and uncontrollable embodiment of air. The shackles of divinity also chain it so that its powers can be kept somnolent. However, the wind horse of Artriol is guarded by an evil sylph named Atentael; she is destructive and ill mannered. I banished her to the north of Artriol centuries ago, for trying to destroy our race. She deceived us, and gave her life to the thamiel when they were under the control of Lucifer. She has been trying to take the wind horse of Artriol for herself; but the horse would not accept her because of the evil that she has filled her heart with.***

The wind horse is a creature of calm, and it would never submit to being an ally of evil, nor will it submit to one who has

evil intentions deep within their heart. By all means, a wolf in sheep's clothing does not easily trick the wind horse. I believe that if you can attain the wind horse, Satan and Moloch will tremble before you. The power held by the wind horse is unbelievable. If you want the wind horse, you have to let your heart guide your battles. Now, when you pass into the north, your physical body will be left behind, and you'll have to fight with your psychic body." Airael says, ***"Okay, I'll head north, find Atentael, and return here."*** Tritomia says, ***"Beware! Atentael is extremely powerful, unlike those who have been granted power by Satan and Moloch; Atentael's powers have been granted to her by Lucifer, the son of the morning.***

Her powers are nearly unmatched; it took all of my strength and wisdom to banish her to the north of Artriol. Even though I won the battle, and imprisoned her in the north, her powers are still quite active. After I sent her to the north, I manifested a barrier strong enough to keep her away from my people. If your faith in God is not strong, she will kill you. If you choose to head to the North, and go through that barrier, you must be more than prepared to fight, for she is a minister of trickery." Airael says, ***"No offense, Tritomia, but I really don't have a choice. If I don't, the thamiel will rise and destroy everything that they can, and I can't let that happen. Therefore, pray that I win."*** Tritomia was astounded by the bravery and courage that Airael displayed. Then she said, ***"Go! Go forth, and trample your enemies. So mote it be."***

And so, Airael traveled to the north by flying through the free land of Artriol, the land of sylphs. And as Airael traveled through the land, he stopped and heard a voice speak, saying, ***"I know who you are, grandson of Namsilat, and the son of Calabrael. I know your works, and I also know that you and your brothers are the reason that master Lucifer has been banished for 7777 years. Had you not died, the divine architect would've***

never appeared on the mundane plane to cast him away. I blame the four of you for the imprisonment of my master.

Be warned, if you pass this point, I will slaughter you, and paint the north of Artriol with all of your blood. Turn away, and return to your realm, mortal!*"** Airael said, "I came here to get the wind horse of Artriol, I don't have time for your empty threats, either you move out of my way, or I'll move you myself!***" Before Airael knew it, a beautiful woman with four black wings, and black hair as dark as night appeared behind him. Airael turned around, and said, "***You have two choices, get out of my way, or die.***" Atentael blinked her eyes, and in an instant, she held Airael by his throat, and said, "***Foolish mortal man, do you really think that I would be defeated by you, human?!***" Airael began to lose his breath due to the strength and power of Atentael's grip.

Though Atentael's powers were immense, Airael broke her grip, and said, "***Great architect of the universe; strengthen these hands!***" Airael flew pass the point of no return, and entered the realm of imprisonment that Tritomia had trapped Atentael in for years. As Airael spoke his faith, Atentael disappeared and grabbed Airael by his throat once again, she then shot off into the sky while still holding Airael by his throat, and when she reached the height of the land of Artriol, she opened a portal to Egypt below herself. When the portal opened, she dived into it while still holding Airael by his throat, and as she went through the portal, she continued diving until she slammed Airael into the mighty sands of Egypt with all of her strength. Atentael smiled, and said, "***I warned you, man creature!***"

There was no sign of Airael at all; it would seem that Atentael had killed him. Atentael was pleased with herself, for she killed one of God's beloved chosen ones. As Atentael realized that she had killed Airael, she decided to wreak havoc upon Egypt, and destroy it. She began destroying pyramids, and murdering as many humans as she could. After seven minutes of havoc in Egypt, a mighty twister formed, and Airael was far from finished. A great sand storm covered the land of Egypt as its people were in panic and struck with pure fear. The sand storm made it hard to see anything, but Airael had no choice, he had to do what he could. After several seconds passed, the extreme force of Airael's deepest power caused his flesh and bones to gradually dissipate, and finally, out of the portal created by Atentael, a great horse emerged.

The horse was black with six white wings and inane eyes. The wind horse of Artriol felt the presence of great courage, and when that happened, the wind horse of Artriol chose its keeper. Airael was far from dead, he had become one with the wind horse of Artriol. Airael was no more; the wind warrior of Artriol was a new worry for Atentael. The powers of the wind horse could grant its keeper with the power to become the wind, and ascend all abilities to their climax. Having been equipped with the awesome power of the wind horse of Artriol, Airael was able to transform into hurricanes and twisters at will. No longer did he have to eject wind from his hands and so forth, for Airael was able to synchronize and separate from the wind horse, he could become one with it, ride upon it, or absorb it into his body and operate it at any time. By all means, the wind horse of Artriol was a creature of energy that could transform into energy or horse form at will. The ability to be triumphant over evil was one hundred percent possible. Airael showed up while riding on the wind horse of Artriol, and said, ***"There is no way that you will ever kill me."***

Atentael hovered above the pyramid of Giza preparing to destroy it, and said, ***"I sense the powers of the wind horse of Artriol within you, and I don't know how you attained it, but now I believe that I should kill you. Had you not come, I would've***

eventually attained its power. Let's make this the last time we see each other, man creature!" After speaking, she placed her hands down with her palms open, and out of her palms came two black colored beams of energy surrounded by electricity. Airael said, ***"The wind horse would've never surrendered to you.***

The courage that I displayed showed it that I was the host for its abilities, and now; this is where you pass through transition, and beg for mercy." Atentael's beams bounced off of Airael, and Airael smiled, and said, ***"Your wasting your time, you can't win, demon."*** Atentael ignored Airael's words, and raised her right hand toward the heavens while it began to rain with fire and brimstone for approximately ten seconds. Egypt was scorched and nearly destroyed for good. In the midst of the fire and brimstone, Airael looked up into the sky and said to his self, ***"No demon shall prosper!"***And when Airael said this to himself, he lost all fear of being harmed by the fire and brimstone created by Atentael. Atentael had much pride in herself, and because she had such a great pride in herself, she deeply felt that no one other than Lucifer was more powerful than she was.

However, little did she know, Airael's powers had overpowered the power bestowed upon her by Lucifer, the son of the morning. Airael closed his eyes and spoke to Atentael using telepathy, saying, ***"Faith, faith in God is essential for victory, and because you don't have faith in our father anymore, you'll always fail."*** When Atentael heard this, she was wroth, and sought to kill Airael by using all of her speed and quickness. She disappeared, and when she re-appeared, she stood directly in front of Airael. Airael made a choice to have faith in God; therefore, he stood still, and looked directly into Atentael's eyes without blinking or moving one bit.

Atentael looked at Airael, and said, ***"Oh, so you think you're***

brave now, well, I'll just have to scare you again." Atentael grabbed Airael's wrist, and said, ***"This is the part of the day where you die!"*** As Atentael held Airael's wrist as tight as she could, Airael began to transform into the wind warrior of Artriol again. He and the wind horse dissipated into particles of purple energy while beginning to rotate into a great twister. And before Atentael could do anything about it, she was trapped within the power and strength of a mighty rotating twister of death. Atentael was unable to move due to the strength and rotation of the twister, her powers were no longer a threat to the son of cosmic air anymore.

As Atentael endlessly rotated at the very middle of the twister, her eyes could only see one thing, and that one thing was Airael, the son of cosmic air. While Atentael rotated, Airael said, ***"Trapped like a fly on a spider's web, I was killed by Lucifer and his abilities once before, and I won't be killed by his powers again, today marks the evolution of mankind, demon. I refuse to be defeated by any demon ever again. This is where it all ends for the wicked."*** Within seconds, the speed of the twister would rotate so quickly that Atentael's body began to transform into smoke, and when it did, the twister absorbed it, and Atentael was no more. Seven small aggregations of light energy appeared at the middle of the twister, and the rotating twister was absorbed into the seven aggregations of light energy. The twister no longer existed, and the seven aggregations of light energy combined, and after they combined, they took on the shape and size of a human body.

A great flash of light covered the land of Egypt, and Airael appeared with his eyes closed, and said, ***"It's time to try these new abilities on the thamiel now."*** Airael finally completed his mission, and then he flew through the portal leading to Artriol, and returned to Tritomia, the queen and master of sylphs. When Airael returned to Artriol, Tritomia spoke in a loud voice, and said, ***"Airael, your bravery was so strong that the wind horse of Artriol could no longer be held by the shackles of divinity. Your courage and your heart have surpassed the power of evil with ease. And now, you must go to the gates of Sheol where your final battle awaits. The time is now, wind warrior of Artriol, go forth, and destroy evil. You have the blessings of Artriol, Airael."*** And Tritomia spoke once again, and said, ***"Ocinun-synkratius!"***

Two magical words called a large portal leading to the gates of Sheol. Airael took flight through the portal while riding upon the wind horse of Artriol, and when he reached the other side of the portal, the wind from the six wings of Airael's horse pushed his brothers away from him immediately. Fireael said, ***"What in the world is that?! Oh, come on man; can this get any crazier than it already is? How come I didn't get a horse!? Well, you look like you're ready to make some noise bro. I hope that horse is strong enough to take on the thamiel, we're going to need all of the help we can get."*** Aquari-on said, ***"Six wings, hunh? What's its name, Airael?"*** Airael replied, saying, ***"In the land of sylphs, they called it the wind horse of Artriol, but I think I'll call him wind-storm, he keeps me company."***

As the three brothers continued to talk to each other, the horse began to talk to them using telepathy, saying, ***"Wind-storm, not a bad name, although I prefer quick-storm."*** The three brothers heard the words of the horse, and their eyes lit up like light bulbs. Fireael said, ***"Whoa, why didn't you tell us that it could talk, Airael!?"*** Aquari-on said, ***"It can talk!?"***

Airael looked at his horse, and said, ***"You're telling me that the whole time I was fighting that crazed sylph, you could talk?! Keeping secrets from me already, hunh!?"*** The wind horse replied, saying, ***"Well, I didn't think that it was a big surprise that I could talk, besides, it's been a while since I've spoken to anyone at all. And if you don't mind, it's been a few centuries and***

decades, and my back is killing me, do you mind getting off of me for a while, so I can rest a little?"

Airael replied, saying, ***"Oh, no problem. Out of all of the horses in the world, I get the one that's probably going to complain all day."*** Airael got off of his horse, and said, ***"Well, if you like Quick-storm better, then I'll respect your wishes, and call you by that name."*** The wind horse replied, saying, ***"Thank you, I appreciate it."*** Airael looked at his two brothers, and said, ***"Well, I guess we'll have to wait a while for Earthael and Ethereael."*** And so, the son of cosmic air had attained a friend for great power, and now, Airael and his brothers would wait until Earthael and Ethereael returned from their missions.

Meanwhile, Earthael stood alone in the land of gnomes within the Earth, the land called ***"Estheera."*** He walked for two miles until he witnessed a great palace having two guards at its front gates. The palace was made of stones bigger than those that consist of a pyramid of Egypt. Its front gate consisted of carved stones that were as hard as gold. The guards had long gray beards, which rested upon their basketball-sized stomachs. Their eyes were filled with a green energy that represented the pureness of Earth.

They also wore navy blue robes, which had a green rope tied round about their waistlines. The gnomes were small creatures who stood only twenty-six inches tall. As Earthael began to get closer, both of the guards spoke approximately at the same time, and said, ***"Halt! We know who you are. You are Earthael, the son of cosmic Earth, and the son of the divine architect of the universe. You are scheduled to meet with our master. Beware, we are in the middle of a small war with a race of gnomes who have chosen to side with the Thamiel. It is imperative that you meet with Landizsar, our master."***

The guards stomped on the ground five-times, and the

carved stone gates to the palace were opened immediately. And so, Earthael walked through the gates and spoke to himself, saying, ***"Time is running out, I can feel my brothers waiting for me, I have to complete this mission, and find whatever it is that I was sent here to find. I can't believe I'm actually in a land where gnomes live freely. I've only known these creatures to be summoned for aid in battle; I had no idea that they had their own lives, well, not like this at least."*** Earthael looked up at the high palace of gnomes in awe as its height was near the sky.

As Earthael entered and walked through the halls of the palace, a gnome walked up to him, and said, ***"Earthael, we've heard so much about you. I was one of the gnomes who came out of the Earth to help you fight off a legion of demons when you and your brothers fought against Lucifer. Do you remember me?"*** Earthael replied, and said, ***"I'm sorry, but I don't remember you, I was in the heat of battle, but I can always get to know you."***

The gnome replied, and said, ***"Well, don't worry about it; we have a bigger problem anyway. Our kingdom has been divided, half of our race has decided to side with the thamiel. Many have chosen their own destiny; therefore, those of us who serve God must fight against those who have decided to serve the thamiel. Oh, and I'm sorry about what happened to your father, though he may have passed through transition, he was the first mortal to attain the sword of Elohim. My brother was assigned a special mission to bring him bread and red wine when Mephistopheles held him captive. My brother told me that he could see why the five of you are so powerful.***

He also said that your father survived the fifteen years of imprisonment, and ate mostly of the word of God to survive. Earthael, your father was a great man, he stood his ground, and didn't let Mephistopheles break his spirit one bit." When Earthael heard this, he began to cry, due to the memory of his father. Earthael's heart was filled with righteousness, for he had finally realized that his father died peacefully serving the divine architect of the universe. After the gnome spoke to Earthael, he bowed down on one knee, and said, ***"I truly hope that you and your brothers can defeat the thamiel, for they are truly causing problems in our realm, and yours. Earthael, have faith in God; Satan and Moloch are extremely strong, you and your brothers are our newest, and greatest defense against the wicked devils of Sheol."*** After speaking, the gnome asked Earthael to follow him up the stairs to meet Landizsar, master of gnomes. In front of Earthael were four flights of stairs that twisted and turned into different areas of the castle. The gnomes of Estheera were banging and making loud noises as they rushed to make weapons to fight against their adversaries in order to return peace to their land. Earthael walked four flights up the stairs until he reached a giant door. Unbelievably, the door opened by itself, and a fireplace burned bright in a dark room where Landizsar sat quietly upon his throne as the king of gnomes.

Earthael walked through the door slowly while looking to his left, and to his right. As he became closer to the throne, a voice spoke out, and said, ***"Ah, Earthael, the son of cosmic Earth, your destiny is one that is quite esoteric. More or less, the current situation is completely esoteric overall; however, it is a pleasure to see a true warrior face to face. You and your brothers are a most definite depiction of inwardly strengthened warriors of God. As much as I would love to show you our realm, and have a talk with you, we currently need your assistance. The thamiel have given certain gnomes the power of evil. Satan and Moloch have issued evil power to idle minds. We don't have much time; therefore, my throne rests upon a magical circle that will allow you to immediately utilize your psychic body with ease.***

Your test and mission is simple, amongst the gnomes who

have sided with the thamiel is a gnome named Azazelael. Satan and Moloch have charged him with leading an army of evil gnomes to destroy all of those gnomes who simply serve God whole-heartedly. They plan to destroy our land so as to extend the power of the thamiel. But you, the son of cosmic Earth shall stop Azazelael and return to me. When you return, I will give you what you need to extend your powers, for I know why you have come, Son of God.

If you fail, your physical body will set itself on fire, and turn your bones into ashes. And if you succeed, I will give you the crush-diamond, which gives its holder a great and holy power to destroy evil. Right now, the thamiel are winning against us, I fear the worst, but now that you're here, I know God has bestowed his blessings upon us, for he has sent his elect to aid us in battle." A magical circle was engraved under Landizsar's throne, so all Earthael had to do was sit in Landizsar's throne in order to start his mission. Landizsar got up, and left his throne so that Earthael could complete the will of the grand architect of the universe. Earthael sat down in his throne, and immediately his psychic body was released from its physical envelope, he then flew into the air, and used his heart to locate the battle where he would find Azazelael, the leader of the evil gnomes commanded by the thamiel.

And before Earthael knew it, he was hovering directly above a gruesome battle in the east of the land of Estheera, and the followers of the thamiel were brutally killing the gnomes who kept their faith and belief in God, for they were the good gnomes.

The battlefield was stained with the glowing green blood of the gnomes who continued to fight in the name of Elion almighty. It seemed that the good gnomes were losing, and when Earthael saw this, his heart was automatically filled with courage and compassion for the good gnomes of Estheera. He then opened his right hand, and charged an aggregation of Earth energy. A bright green light flashed, and blinded all who were on the battlefield. The gnomes who sided with the thamiel and the gnomes who served God were wiping and rubbing their eyes so that they could see again, and as they opened their eyes, the cosmic son of Earth stood in front of them. He then spoke, and said, ***"Enough! Your quarrel is no longer with the gnomes who serve God; your quarrel is with me now, let them go, or perish!"***

Azazelael heard this, and said, ***"Foolish son of God, you dare mettle in the affairs of the divine evil?! After I kill you, I'll destroy all of the followers of God, and serve the thamiel for eternity. You pose no threat you fool! Do you not know that the princes of darkness chose me? You stand no chance, retreat while you can."*** Azazelael was twenty-six inches in height, and wore a black robe with a brown rope round about his waist. His beard was as white as snow, his eyes were filled with red energy, and his countenance was hideous as it hadd scars and cuts from the current battles against the good gnomes. His teeth were rotten, and his tongue was six inches long, accompanied by a pair of long pointy ears. Earthael looked at his opponent, and said, ***"If you're so confident in the bestowal of the evil power that the thamiel have granted you, then fight me one on one.***

A fight to the death, if I win, you release these gnomes from their trance, and return them to their palace where they belong. Do we have a deal?!" Azazelael answered, saying, ***"It's a deal."*** When the good gnomes and the evil gnomes heard this, they retreated and left Earthael and Azazelael to fight so that they could battle each other without any interference. Earthael raised his left hand into the air, and before Azazelael realized it, the ground beneath him began to crumble. A great chasm opened, and Azazelael fell into it immediately.

Earthael thought that Azazelael had fallen into the chasm and perished. In order to make sure that Azazelael was dead, Earthael began to slowly walk near the chasm, and before Earthael knew it, Azazelael slowly levitated out of the chasm while bearing an angry countenance. Azazelael waved his left hand, and out of his palm came green electricity that surprisingly shocked Earthael, and knocked him to the ground. Time was running out, and the Thamiel were getting well prepared for their assault on earth. Earthael picked himself up from the ground, and said, ***"I will die a billion deaths before I let you or the thamiel destroy Estheera or earth!"***

Earthael kneeled, and knocked on the ground of Estheera three times. The ground began to rumble violently, and the great Earth titan that his father Calabrael had once used was summoned to the land of Estheera. The great earth titan fell from the sky of Estheera and slammed into the ground while waiting for Earthael to command its movements. The titan picked Earthael up, and placed him upon his left shoulder.

Earthael whispered in the titan's ear, and the titan transformed into a humongous boulder that was nearly indestructible. As the son of cosmic Earth stood on top of the large boulder, he summoned the depth of his cosmic abilities, and raised the boulder as high into the sky as he possibly could. He then left it there, he had a plan, and hopefully, it would work. Azazelael spoke, and said, ***"You fool, what is it that you think you're doing? That boulder cannot save you from death.***

I am through playing games with you, mortal! It is time for you to die!" Earthael stood still, and made no movement. Azazelael shot off at Earthael like a bullet so as to deliver the final blow. Earthael thought to himself, saying, ***"That's right, come to daddy."*** As Azazelael got closer and closer to Earthael, Earthael disappeared. Azazelael stood still, and hadn't a clue as to what Earthael was trying to do. Azazelael looked around to his left, and to his right, however, he saw nothing. And finally, he looked up, and before he could do anything about it, Earthael's fist was less than an inch away from breaking the large boulder that he himself sent into the sky.

The impact from Earthael's strength broke the boulder into a million pieces. Azazelael laughed, and said, ***"Pitiful mortal!"*** As thousands of rocks and pebbles fell, Earthael stared at Azazelael with a determined look in his eyes, and before Azazelael knew it, the rocks and pebbles began to home-in on him as if they were heat-seeking missiles seeking to destroy a specific target. Using his cosmic abilities, the large count of rocks and pebbles began to smash into Azazelael's face and body.

Azazelael began to stagger as the rocks and pebbles began to make him bleed. Azazelael was still standing, however, Earthael was far from done. The son of cosmic Earth balled his hands into fists, and all of the pebbles combined into several basketball-sized stones. And again, they continued hitting Azazelael with dangerous blows to the head and body. The evil follower of the thamiel was gradually losing his life. Earthael continued his attack, and before he knew it, Azazelael had fallen to the ground while bleeding to death, for Azazelael laid dead on the grounds of Estheera, and not a breath or movement came from his body. Earthael spoke to himself, saying, ***"I need to return to the palace of Estheera, this battle is over."***

Earthael flew into the skies of Estheera, and headed to the palace where Landizsar would be awaiting his return. As Earthael arrived over the palace of Estheera, a great crowd of gnomes were screaming and yelling, while saying, ***"Blessed is Earthael, you have won!"*** they chanted loudly, saying, ***"Earth-a-el! Earth-a-el! Earth-a-el! Earth-a-el!"*** Earthael heard this, and he immediately landed at the front gates of the palace. Waiting for him at the front gates of the palace was Landizsar, the king of the gnomes patiently waiting to give Earthael his divine prize.

Earthael looked at Landizsar, and said, ***"Landizsar, Azazelael has perished, I'm eager to join my brothers at the gates of Sheol so that we can finish this war once and for all."*** Landizsar replied, saying, ***"Worry not, for you have proven yourself beyond the shadow of a doubt, to thee I grant the crush-diamond."*** Earthael opened his right hand, and received a mysterious diamond cherished by the gnomes. Before Earthael knew it, the diamond began to glow like a full moon on the darkest of nights.

Earthael fell unconscious due to the power of the crush-diamond, and the gnomes carried his psychic body back to his physical body, and seven minutes later, he awoke. No longer was his arms made of flesh and bones, they were now made of pure diamonds. Earthael was amazed, his arms were made of diamonds, but they were easier to move, he was faster, and strong enough to punch a planet and knock it off of its axis with one hit, but only if that was his will to do so.

Landizsar spoke, saying, ***"Now that you have the power of the crush-diamond, we want to give you our strength for aiding us in a time of peril."*** Landizsar extended his arm, and touched Earthael's arm. Another gnome touched Landizsar, and another gnome touched another gnome, and as each gnome began to touch each other upon the shoulder, the whole race of gnomes combined their strength with Earthael's new power.

Earthael's body began to shake violently, and finally, his new arms were given an extra advantage. His arms were equipped with the powers of the magnetic field surrounding the planet Earth. Earthael looked at himself, and said, ***"Thanks, but there***

is much more to accomplish. Landizsar replied, saying, ***"The power of the universe is in your hands, Earthael."*** Landizsar waved his hand, and a portal opened, he then spoke, and said, ***"Here is the portal to Sheol or hell, whatever you choose to call it. Your brothers wait for your return Earthael, don't fail us."***

Earthael walked up to the portal and turned around, and then he said, ***"I'll be back one day."*** And so, the great Earth warrior walked through the portal, and when he reached the other side of the portal, he met up with Aquari-on, Airael and Fireael. Fireal looked at Earthael, and said, ***"What happened to your arms?"*** Earthael answered, saying, ***"Nothing, nothing at all. I only know one thing, I'm itching to find Mephistopheles, and break every demonic bone in his body, when I'm done with him, I guarantee that he'll kneel before me, and apologize."***

Aquari-on looked at Earthael, and said, ***"Those are some pretty high expectations you have, I can only hope your right though."*** Fireael said, ***"I have no idea what happened to your arms, and I have no idea what their made of, but what I do know is that we're going to have more money than Donald trump."*** Aquari-on said, ***"What do you mean by that, how are we going to be richer than we are now?"***

Fireael laughed while saying, ***"After all of this is over, we're going to pawn Earthael's arms, and get wealthier!"*** Earthael heard what Fireael said, and replied, saying, ***"Hey, Fireael, can you do me a favor?"*** Fireael said, ***"What?"*** Earthael answered, and said, ***"Shut-up!"*** And so, Ethereael was the only one who hadn't reported to the gates of Sheol, however, in due time, the war would end, but the question is, who would win? For now, four warriors must wait until the son of ether has completed his greatest test, a test that would give him the small practice that he needs in order to utilize the tongue of God in a skillful manner.

Meanwhile, Ethereael took a portal to the universe of Mestophelue, where six planets that were once inherited by gruesome demons of evil became the power source for a notorious evil force named Mephistopheles. As Ethereael arrived at the desired destination, he once again witnessed the evil manifestations of his most disliked enemy. Ethereael slowly flew through the universe of Mestophelue, and as he slowly flew through it, he stopped and closed his eyes. Whilst his eyes were closed, he concentrated on his powers with the ether propagating throughout the universe, and in due time, the planets of Mestophelue began to tremble as if they were all experiencing detrimental Earthquakes. The Planets of Mestophelue were being subdued by the awesome power of the son of ether. Each planet began to crack and crumble into small pebbles of matter.

One-by-one, planet by planet, the extraordinary strength of the sword of Elohim combined with the ether force was amazing. Ethereael's task was far from hard, for his powers combined with the sword of Elohim would act as an extreme force of holy proportion. Frightening and extremely loud noises of pure destruction indicated the great force of the tongue of Elion. As each planet crumbled and cracked, Ethereael began praying in his mind, saying, ***"Hear my cry, O God; attend unto my prayer. From the end of the earth will I cry unto thee, when my heart is overwhelmed: lead me to the rock that is higher than I, for thou hast been a shelter for me, and a strong tower from the enemy. I will abide in thy tabernacle for ever: I will trust in the covert of thy wings. Selah. For thou, O God hast heard my vows: thou hast given me the heritage of those who fear thy name. Thou wilt prolong the king's life: and his years as many generations. He shall abide before God for ever: O prepare mercy and truth, which may preserve him. So will I sing praise unto thy name for ever, that I may daily perform my vows."*** As Ethereael said the 61st psalm to himself, his powers were heightened once again, and the small pebbles of matter began to disintegrate one by one. Ethereael opened his eyes, and the universe of Mestophelue was no more. Ethereael had completed his mission in a matter of moments. A great portal of light opened, and Ethereael made his way to the path of the final task.

He arrived at the other side of the portal, and saw his brothers waiting to do the unthinkable. The final assault on Sheol was at hand, the first assault on hell, and the journey to peace all over the world.

Chapter 12

The Final Assault on Sheol

After a long journey, Earthael, Ethereael, Fireael, Aquari-on, and Airael must take on Satan and Moloch, the angels of darkness. Finally, the five warriors have the chance to fight face to face with the enemies of God and the murderer of their father. As the five warriors wait at the gates of Sheol for the final assault, Hermes appears, and says, ***"So, you have all succeeded in passing your tests, I am well pleased, there is someone who would like to talk with you, therefore, I present to you, the most divine king of all existence, the grand architect of the universe."*** As Hermes spoke, three orbs of light forming a triangle appeared and began speaking through their minds, saying, ***"In you five, I am well pleased. My will hath been done, consequently, the hearts of some men are wicked with trickeries, lies and great deceits, but you five have allowed my son Yahuahshua to reign supreme in thy heart, and for that, ye have attained greatness.***

No man commeth unto me without my son. He hath given his life so that men may live and learn to master life, it is good that the five of you have followed in the footsteps of mine son, and because you have, my mercy upon thee is beyond great grandeur. Earthael, your courage maketh the lands to tremble. Fireael, your faith moveth the stars. Airael, your mind ascends into the heavens I so patiently manifested. Aquari-on, your wisdom sways the seas with the intent to carry those who need you. And last, but not least, Ethereael, your strength hath lifted greatness to heaven, and allowed you to withstand the mighty force of the sword of Elohim. The five of you have represented your kind with all of your being. It is with great love that I appear unto you this day. Know that wherever you go, there I am, in your hearts eternally therein!"

And so, the lord of the universe disappeared and prepared to view the final assault on Sheol from his throne room in Araboth. When the cosmic sons received a chance to hear the thoughts of the divine architect concerning their actions, they were filled with a confidence and respect that was altogether inexpressible. The journey begins as the five warriors stand before the mighty gates of Sheol, the land of impure and defiled creatures and their unfortunate victims. The gates of Sheol were made from the bones of human arms and legs, and there was also a round golden seal baring an upside down pentagram representing the mundane world ruling over the spiritual world.

The five warriors who represent the manifestation of the spiritual governing the mundane world were about to enter, and the Great War was about to begin. Hermes spoke once more, saying, ***"Afurmarmra!"*** And immediately, the pentacles and shackles levitated off of their bodies and flew off into the firmament, for they had disappeared and returned to Daggarael, the mighty angel of forge. And again Hermes spoke, saying, ***"This is your final journey, may your lights burn bright, and your minds be in consummate attunement with the lord of the universe, so mote it be!"***

And before the five warriors knew it, Hermes Mercurius Trismegistus had disappeared. Earthael looked at his brothers, and said, ***"Last time we went up against great evil, we all died, and I remember it like it was yesterday. This time, there are five of us, and there are always too many of them. If I hadn't gone through so much to get here, I think I'd walk away, but then again, I'm too brave for that."*** Etherеael heard what Earthael said, and turned his back while looking toward the heavens, and said, ***"Well, I've fought millions of demons by myself, and I may have been killed if you guys didn't get to me in time.***

When I was fighting by myself, and before you guys came, I had no idea how I was going to beat nearly a billion demons by myself, but what I do know is that something deep inside told me to fight with every ounce of my heart. I wasn't born when you guys fought Lucifer. But the stories that they tell about you guys is awesome, they said that Fireael once destroyed a whole legion of demons without even touching them. People said that the four of you were our last chance to restore the mundane world to peace. And when I heard all of the stories, I wanted to be just like you guys, I used to say it to myself all the time.

And then, one day I got the chance to, but when I got the chance, I was tricked by Mephistopheles, and when he tricked me, I lost my faith, my confidence, and I almost lost my love. Of course, I came to my senses, but now, when I fight, I hear innocent children crying, and begging for help, and when I hear that, something inside of me gives me the wacky idea that I should protect them with all of my heart. Finally, I have a chance to fight with the undisputed champions of fire, air, water, and Earth. If we all die today, I want all of you to know that I have waited for this for a long time, and it is an honor to fight amongst the greatest mortal warriors that ever lived."

Fireael looked at Ethereael, and said, *"Whoa! People said that about me?! Wow, I would've never thought that. I don't want to cut this conversation short, but is everyone ready to find Mephistopheles and his friends, and show him who's the boss or what?"* Aquari-on looked at Fireael, and said, *"Yeah, let's take it to the next level. Let's show them what mortal ascension is all about."* Shortly afterward, Airael said, *"Demons have been living here for centuries; I wonder how they pay rent here. Then again, who cares, let's get this over with!"*

And so, the five warriors pulled the gate of bones open, and walked into the land of Sheol where demonic evil reigns wildly. The five sons of God shot off into the dark red skies of Sheol, and prepared to take on the princes of darkness.

***The Hell called** "Rhythium."*

As they flew together side-by-side, they began to speak to each other. Fireael looked at his brother Ethereael, and said, ***"There are ten hells in an unknowing microcosm: Hate (Rhythium), Anger (Uorium), Jealousy (Hitisum), envy (Hythurah), apathy (Nuvuyol), unforgiveness (Rhavulor), self-exalting pride (Yangyinoum), lust (Lufthremn), Deceit (Decetum) and Unreason (Auhutukulm). At this very moment, we are flying through the land of Rhythium; the demons that hate all that are good. If you close your eyes, you can feel the hate emanating from the vibrations of the devils that reside here. We should be very careful in this place, for it is without a doubt that the demons that inhabit this place will feel the presents of good in their midst, and rise against us with all of their strength. Make no mistake; we will have the greatest battle that we have ever had on this very day. I highly doubt that we will easily make it to where we need to go, well...not without nearly losing our lives in just about every battle at least."***

Ethereael looked at his brother Fireael, and said, ***"I don't care how much hate they have, today is the day that the sword of Elohim and I display the grand power the grand architect."*** The land of Rhythium was a land of dark skies and miles of concrete. There were no trees, flowers or anything for that matter, Rhythium was simply an empty place for which anger could constantly build up and manifest a great evil that would eventually become detrimental to the health and mortal ascension of human beings. As the five brothers continued their flight through the dark skies of Rhythium, the realm of Rhythium became as dark as a bottomless pit. The five brothers stopped and realized that they could no longer see anything. Therefore, the five cosmic warriors charged their electromagnetic fields and looked around to see what could have caused the sudden darkness. Airael looked at his brother Aquari-on, and said, ***"Be on guard, something feels really wrong."***

A voice spoke out to the five brothers, and said, ***"Sons of Elion, what business do you have here in my realm?! Have you not embarrassed us enough in the name of God? Leave this place and go no further!"*** Earthael replied to the voice, and said, ***"We're going to the tenth hell, and I dear you to try and stop us! We have a mission to complete, and we don't have time for small talk, demon!"*** The demon replied, saying, ***"Very well then, it is your life that shall be lost in the darkness!"*** The realm of Rhythium was lit with a great red light, and the five cosmic sons realized that they were no longer alone; behold! A legion of one million demons had arrived for battle whilst the darkness shielded their arrival.

The son of Ether placed his hand over his heart, and the sword of Elohim's strength and might was immediately operated. Ethereael's body was covered in some sort of gold electricity that signified the power of the philosopher's stone in conscious manifestation. The golden lightning spewed out of the sword and into his physical body in an instant. Aquari-on, Airael, Fireael and Earthael looked at their brother Ethereael, and didn't know what to say to him; they were speechless. With the wave of a hand, Ethereael was no longer amongst his brothers in the skies of Rhythium. Before Ethereael's brothers knew it, demons began popping-up into the air like popcorn kernels being heated in a microwave. The son of Ether began terminating thousands of demons with pure ease.

A gigantic surge of golden electricity began to expand and terminate demons that were simply heading toward or standing around him. Fireael looked at his brother Airael, and said, ***"Let's do ourselves a favor and at least look like we want to fight, come on; let's go!"*** Earthael dives into the ground of Rhythium with his fist in front of him, and smashes into it in order to display the power of cosmic earth to all that is evil. One-hundred thousand demons crashed into the ground and disintegrated as the power of the son of cosmic earth made the reality of the plane of Rhythium shake and ripple. The son of cosmic fire saw what his brother Earthael could do, and said, ***"Whoa! I didn't know he could that."***

Afterward, Fireael closed his eyes, and with the wave of his hand, the son of cosmic fire was transformed into a giant orb of light that shot off into the skies of Rhythium and stood there like a small sun. Aquari-on and Airael looked into the sky and couldn't understand how Fireael's actions were going to help defeat the legion of demons. And before anyone could realize what he was doing, Fireael's voice vibrated through hell, saying, ***"The light of love is beyond the strength of hate."*** And with the blink of an eye, the sun-like orb of light that Fireael was encased in began to emit tiny rays of light that started to seek out and disintegrate as many demons as possible, for the power of light was brilliant and awesome in all of its being.

After Ethereael, Earthael and Fireael displayed their cosmic might; Airael was astounded, and said, ***"Okay, now it's time for me to show them something new."***The son of cosmic air raised his hand into the air while riding on his wind horse and disappeared immediately. A powerful and formidable breeze windswept the remaining demons and began to repetitiously toss them into the ground as Aquari-on sprung into action in order to aid his brothers in eliminating the rest of the demons. The son of cosmic water raised his right hand into the air and caused the skies of Rhythium to rain heavily. As soon as there was enough rain to go around, Aquari-on used his cosmic ability to shape millions of rain drops into sharp spikes that began to impale all of the remaining demons that were still alive. The power and skill of the five warriors proved to be most challenging to their adversaries in Sheol.

After finishing off the inhabitants of Rhythium, the five warriors thought that they were done, but they soon realized that a portal to the next realm had not opened. Ethereael looked at his brothers, and said, ***"If a portal didn't open, that means that there is someone or something that we didn't defeat."*** A giant demon fell out of the sky and landed on the ground. The realm of Rhythium shook, and the five brothers turned around, and said, ***"Oh, that can't be good!"*** The giant demon was so large in size that the five cosmic sons of God simply looked like roaches in his eyes. The great demon noticed them and tried to step on them immediately, and as soon as the five sons saw it coming, they flew off into the firmament of Rhythium so that they could re-group and fight the demon the best way that they could. The demon was a great giant with eyes of green energy, six horns upon his brow, and four black wings that sprung out of his back. His face was like that of a dragon with indigo scales. His body was like that of a human that was covered in the hairs of a lion, and his hands and feet were identical to the claws of an eagle. To the cosmic sons of God, size was nothing, for they had battled many that were bigger than they are. And so, Fireael looked at his brothers, and said, ***"I'll take care of this one, it'll be easy; trust me."*** Fireael flew behind the demon as fast as he could while his brothers played the decoy roll and flew away from the demon as if they were scared of it. And of course, the demon played right into their hands. Fireael flew into its ear and started emitting all of the light that he could possibly emit. The demon stopped running after his brothers and realized that something was wrong. The demon's body was engulfed in light and exploded shortly thereafter. Fireael was triumphant over his enemy with ease once again. The demon was no more, and a fiery portal appeared so that the five warriors could enter the next level of Sheol. Fireael shouted to his brothers, saying, ***"See! I told you it would be easy. And if the rest of the demons in Sheol are as dumb as that one, then they're definitely in for a real shock!"*** And so, the potential hate that existed in humanity was destroyed so that human beings would never hate again. The first emotional hell within the mystery of the microcosm was no more. The five warriors entered the portal and found themselves in another place of Sheol; a place called Uorium.

The Second Hell called "Uorium."

Uorium is the place called anger in the land of Sheol. The sky was as green as earthly grass, and its grounds consisted of millions of flaming skulls that endlessly spoke in a calm voice, saying, ***"Why?"*** And so, the five warriors stepped foot into Uorium with caution, as they have no idea what is about to happen to them next. They walked through the flaming skulls of Uorium with no expectations due to their experience with fighting demons. The flaming skulls of Uorium continued their endless questioning as the five warriors walked through them, and eventually, Fireael said, ***"Uh...I don't know about you guys, but these skulls are seriously freaking me out. Let's get the heck out of here, and let's do it quick; this is crazy."*** After Fireael told his brothers that he couldn't deal with the land of Uorium, Small demons that were the size of tarantulas began to crawl out of the flaming skulls and grow to the size of human beings. Aquari-on looked at Fireael, and said, ***"Do you ever shut up?! Every time you say something, we get attacked!"*** Fireael replied, saying, ***"O stop complaining and fight, water boy!"***

Aquari-on looked at his brother Airael, and said, ***"This just keeps getting weirder and weirder doesn't it?"*** Airael replied, saying, ***"What do you expect; a trip to Hawaii?"*** Earthael looked at his enemies, and said, ***"Well…I guess this is our purpose, let's not sit here and talk about it; let's do something about it!"*** Earthael kneeled to the ground and whispered to it, saying, ***"I am that I am; swallow mine enemies."*** The ground cracked open, and swallowed the demons in an instant. Enormous portions of the flaming skulls were gone, and the five sons continued their journey without knowing what would become of them as they traveled the place of Sheol, called Uorium. As the five warriors continued their journey, a portal opened and a giant demon walked out of it while holding a strange staff that was engraved with the name of God written backwards in the Hebrew language. The demon's body was like the body of a strong man covered in fur, inane eyes, and six horns upon his brow, one wing, the head of a crocodile, and the hands and feet of a crocodile.

The demon looked at the five sons of God, and said, ***"To what do I owe this visit from the sons of my creator? I understand you are trying to reach Auhutukulm where our masters reside. You are making quite the noise down here, but it stops right now."*** Earthael replies, saying, ***"We don't have time to play around, demon. Either you move out of our way, or we'll make you move!"*** The demon replied, saying, ***"You Dare talk to me in such a manner, mortal!?"*** Ethereael looked at the demon, and said, ***"What is your name, demon?"*** The demon replied, saying, ***"I am Oktahrael, the king, prince, duke and chief of the anger in all human beings, for it was I that caused men to kill and murder each other by simply using anger against them. I made a choice, and now, I am cursed by inhabiting this place that I no longer care for. At the time of the rebellion against our divine creator, I was a beautiful angel who stood beside Lucifer in war, for I know a Galactic prince is truly the cause of all of this pain and suffering that you see now. Lucifer listened to the Galactic prince, and in his greed to rule what was not his to rule, I joined***

him and we were cast down from heaven by the hands of God. I only wish I could return to my true home, but now, this is my home, therefore, my duty as of this very moment is to kill the five of you. Make no mistake; this is the moment that you all shall die, for your journey ends here."

The five sons of God looked at each other and paid the demon no mind because they've defeated many demons, and they felt that he was no different. Fireael steps up, and says, ***"So, if we get rid of you, we'll get rid of all of the anger in mankind, that sounds pretty fair for a reward."*** And so, the divine sons of God rose up from the ground and prepared to battle the cause of all anger within humanity. Aquari-on looked at his brothers, and said, ***"I'll take him by myself, I haven't had a good one-on-one in a long time, I think it's time to test my new powers to their limit, that is, if there is a limit."*** Aquari-on's brothers' nodded their heads, and Aquari-on stepped up to the plate to take on the embodiment and personification of all anger by his self.

The demon waved his hand and his electromagnetic field glowed with a strange blackness that indicated that his powers were extended and magnified for battle. The vibrations of the aura of anger surrounding the demon was so strong that Aquari-on was knocked out of the air and violently crashed into the grounds of Uorium. Though the demon of anger was strong and Aquari-on was knocked to the ground, he got up and levitated into the air as if he had no worries. He then spoke to the demon, saying, ***"Your anger will cause your death, Oktahrael. The Sons of God shall take you out of your misery, worry not, demon."*** Oktahrael made no comment, and charged toward Aquari-on as he swung his giant staff in hopes to terminate the son of cosmic water for good. Aquari-on lifted his right hand into the air, and the sky of Sheol became dark and gloomy with thunder and lightning. He then raised his left hand, and manifested a giant orb of water that he simply used to ride on.

And so, the two warriors charged into each other and slammed fist-to-fist. A loud and frightening sound signified the ultimate clash between good and evil. The small human fist of the Son of God against the giant hand of the demon of anger who was ten-times Aquari-on's size. The demon jumped ten miles away from Aquari-on and began to run as fast as he could toward him. The demon got closer and closer, and when the demon felt that he was close enough, he swung his staff and knocked Aquari-on off of his water orb. Aquari-on flew off of the water orb and violently landed into a pile of flaming skulls that began to fly everywhere when he landed. The demon was sure that Aquari-on was finished, so he slowly walked toward the area where he landed, and said, ***"Foolish Son of God, what has our creator said to you to make you believe that you could defeat the very forces of Sheol?"*** Little did the demon know; Aquari-on was nowhere near done.

Aquari-on quietly levitated out of the flaming skulls and hovered behind the demon as he looked around to see if he could find Aquari-on's body. Aquari-on slammed his fist into the demon's back, and the demon went flying thirty miles from where he stood. Aquari-on shouted out, saying, ***"I would never be defeated so easily, Oktahrael, you're going to have to do much better than that if you're going kill a Son of God!"*** Oktahrael lied on the ground terribly hurt and Aquari-on loved every moment of it. Oktahrael struggled but raised his self from the ground while laughing, and said, ***"Ah…I have forgotten how it feels to face a formidable opponent. It seems I have underestimated you, mortal. Even so, you shall not win today, fate is against you."*** The demon slammed the edge of his staff into the ground and the ground cracked in half. Thousands of flaming skulls fell into the chasm never to return.

To Aquari-on's surprise, the demon had much strength. Oktahrael jumped into the air and started spinning his staff so quickly that it looked like a helicopter propeller. Aquari-on stood still as the demon started his next attack, however, what Aquari-on didn't know was what would happen after the demon spun his staff. Out of the demon's staff came giant bolts of electricity that chased Aquari-on until he could no longer evade its speed and power. The violent lightning of the demon's staff shocked Aquari-on and sent him spinning into the open chasm created by the demon's staff. And when the demon saw that Aquari-on was lost in the chasm, he slammed the tip of his staff into the ground once again, and before Aquari-on could recover and escape the chasm, it closed. Oktahrael laughed, and said, ***"Such powerful mortals, they would have made great fallen ones."*** Oktahrael walked forward and pointed his finger at the four remaining Sons of God, and said, ***"Your brother is dead! Now which of you that lives now values your life?!"***

The four brothers looked at the demon with pure disgust in their eyes and said nothing to the demon. A small hole in the ground began to sprout a large amount of water, and out of the small puddle formed from it, the cosmic son of water emerged. Aquari-on's body gradually utilized the existing water to take form once again. Aquari-on had not perished; he simply took his time returning to battle. The demon quickly turned his head, and said, ***"This cannot be, how much power has the great architect given these mortal men? No matter, I shall take care of this pest sooner than later."*** Aquari-on closed his eyes and used telepathy to speak to his brothers, and said, ***"If you know what is good for you, I suggest that the four of you fly as high as you can, I'm going to wipe this whole plane out of existence."***

The four brothers wasted no time listening to their brother. And as soon as his brothers could fly as high as they could, Aquari-on started his attack right away. Aquari-on shot off into the sky so fast that he shook reality. The demon watched his every move, and couldn't understand what his next move would be. Oktahrael looked into the sky, and said, ***"Son of God, you know not what you do! Your death is inevitable."*** Cracking thunder and thousands of bolts of lightning shook the place of Uorium, and out of the skies Aquari-on spoke throughout the whole plane, saying, ***"Oktee-O-Sunthra-Luiquitum-divinorum!"*** The demon was lifted from the ground and rotated in a three-hundred and sixty degree circle, and Aquari-on's wrath was just beginning. Oktahrael began to worry, and said, ***"What manner of power is this?! Release me at once!"*** As the demon continued to worry, he began to spin faster and faster.

And before Oktahrael knew it, he was falling out of the sky and landing face first into a giant pile of flaming skulls. The demon stood up from the ground and looked into the sky while three giant drops of water fell from the sky and landed right next to him. The demon looked into the sky again, and said, ***"You have missed, you fool! What foolishness will you do now?!"*** Just as the demon spoke his last words, he failed to realize that the giant drops of water were transforming into duplicates of his enemy. Altogether, the giant drops of water formed one hundred duplicates of Aquari-on. Oktahrael looked to his left and realized that he was surely doomed. The duplicates of Aquari-on began an onslaught of physical attacks that would gradually obliterate the demon at once. Oktahrael shouted and yelled to the top of his lungs while the force and pressure of the blows were like the obliterating strength of a tsunami. As the duplicates of Aquari-on pounded away at the demon's face and chest, the demon's body began to dissipate into particles of black energy, and finally, the demon of anger was completely destroyed.

And so, as the battle between the cosmic sons of God and the devils of Sheol continued, mankind was gradually reaching the universal goal of worldly peace and harmony, for the places of hate and anger that plagued mankind was no more. The Sons of God were completing the ultimate mission. Aquari-on returned to the ground of Uorium, and called out to his brothers, saying, ***"Hey! It's over, let's go! We have a long journey ahead of us."*** Fireael looked at Aquari-on, and said, ***"Wow, I guess we've all ascended to great levels. Hey bro, your powers are awesome, I would've never thought that we would all ascend so quickly."*** Earthael said, ***"We are the Sons of God and the new paradigms of mortal ascension, I had an idea that we would ascend to great heights, but not like this."*** Ethereael said, ***"If I was that demon, I would've been shaking in my boots. How did you do that, bro?"*** Aquari-on replied, saying, ***"I don't know; something inside of me just went into overdrive or something, for a moment there I felt like living energy."*** Airael looked at his brother Aquari-on, and said, ***"If we all fight with our hearts and not our powers, I think we'll win this one for everyone; let's move on."*** A portal of light opened up, and the five warriors passed through it in order to enter the third place of Sheol called ***"Hitisum."***

The Third Hell called "Hitisum."

The Sons of God found themselves in another strange and devilish place of evil where they would have to battle against the devilish forces of Jealousy in mankind. Hitisum of Sheol resembled a great, mighty and vast junkyard filled with scrap metal and the bones and remains of all creatures of flesh. The sky was dark brown, and its clouds released the smell of burning flesh and death whilst also casting persistent green lightning that struck the ground repetitiously. The cosmic sons found themselves flying through a place where an old angel that looked like an old lady was calling them from the ground below, saying, ***"Sons of God; come by here! I have something to***

whisper to your ears!" The five sons went to him and realized that the old man looked like a witch. His skin was nearly falling off of his bones, his wings were old and ragged, his eyelids were sewed closed, and his druidic-like robe had many holes and rips all over them. He slowly walked over to the Sons of God, and said, ***"The five of you are making much noise on the spiritual plane. The word is going around Sheol that Satan and Moloch are offering the throne of Lucifer to whoever can bring them your heads and limbs so that they can present them to God and prove your unworthiness. You five must be awfully strong to have made it thus far. I can smell a very small fraction of the universal architect's power in each and every one of you. You have truly been elected for greatness. It is only by the grace of God that such a mission be placed upon five young mortal males. In due time, mortals will actually attain peace because of your persistence to do the will of God. The demons of Sheol are hunting for your lives, most mortals would be scared, but the five of you continue the journey as if you are natural born madmen. No mortal or angel has ever decided to execute a full-scale assault on Sheol. This is the home of all of the most notorious demons that ever lived. It is without a doubt that the courage you display is ejected from the depths of your hearts' true intent."***

Fireael looks at his brothers, and says, ***"I keep telling you, this just keeps getting weirder and weirder. Who knew that the heavens and hells were talking about this fight?"*** Ethereael looks at the old man, and says, ***"Who are you, old man?"*** The old man replies, saying, ***"I am Juraha, a fallen watcher from heaven. I was once the chief of the watchers that were sometimes called Grigori. I came here after the lord of all existence caught me having sexual intercourse with mortal females. I was cast down for my curiosity of the feeling and emotion I constantly saw mortals express mid-coitus. I wanted to comprehend the lives of mortals and their reproductive activities. I believed that it was much better for me to experience mortals' sexual intercourse in order*** *for me to better comprehend it. However, I simply defied the laws of God when I did such a thing. In due time, one of the women of the village of Gath begot a male child that she named Goliath, and eventually his angelic power gave him a leading place in the army of the philistines.*

Without mistake, the divine father knew that it was my son that the woman of Gath was having, and eventually I would be punished for my transgressions. A race of giants sprung out into the earth, and the men of earth referred to them as Nephilim, or the sons of Juraha. The word got out in heaven that I was the main cause for the race of half men and half angelic monsters that walked the earth. After time took its regular course, my son, Goliath began to lead village raids where he murdered numerous men and took all that they had. Eventually, Goliath's angelic half forced him to realize that he was superior to men; therefore, the God of all existence sent one of his chosen warriors to slay my son. A man named David, the son of a man named Jesse. David was a man of God who was instructed by God to slay my son. My son's height was six cubits and a span, his weapons and armor was made from heavy metals that no regular man could wear or carry; he was strong and powerful, and because of his angelic strength, he was deemed the champion of the philistines until David prevailed with a sling and with a stone, and smote my son, and slew him with his own sword. Though my son was strong, his strength and size wasn't completely human, for his angelic half was unfair to those who fought valiantly with all human strength, therefore, the divine architect ordered the angel of forge to create shackles that would make cosmic abilities subside. Eventually, the shackles fell from heaven and wrapped themselves around his wrists. Because of those shackles, David was able to slay him with ease.

Yes, it is true that the mightiest power of God can be found in the smallest grain of sand, for he is truly powerful among all

that is. Of course, the death of my son was a modicum hurtful, yet it would have only been pure stupidity to go against the throne of God, for many have met their end by simply thinking of it, therefore; I knew where I stood. I had to take my punishment and deal with it. And so, here I am, standing before you at this very moment." Ethereael looked at the old Grigori, and said, ***"I have no remorse for you, fallen Grigori. Which way do we go to get to Hythurah of Sheol?"*** The old Grigori replied, saying, ***"Go sixty six miles forward and when you reach the end of the sixty six miles, you will see a giant upside down flaming pentagram that I am more than sure you will not miss.***

At its center is a chasm filled with darkness. Go there and fly into the chasm to enter the next hell." Fireael looked at the old Grigori, and said, ***"I don't trust you, demon Grigori. Those directions better be right, and if they're not, we'll be back for your head."*** The old Grigori walked away while saying, ***"If I were the five of you, I wouldn't be worried about my head at all, until next time, Sons of God."*** The five warriors flew the sixty-six miles and dived into the center of the chasm of the up side down flaming pentagram. And as they got deeper into the chasm, it got so dark that they could no longer see themselves. As the five warriors went deeper into the chasm of the flaming pentagram, a great and loud roar occurred, and the five warriors decided to stop where they stood. Aquari-on said, ***"Hey Fireael! Maybe you can light things up a bit."*** With the wave of a hand, Fireael's power of light lit the whole chasm and revealed that the five warriors were hovering face-to-face with a gigantic two-headed lion with a dragon's scaly tail. The two-headed lion's eyes were like red energy, and upon its two heads was an upside down pentagram and a set of black horns for each head. Its teeth were like sharp knives of death, and its tail was like that of a dragon's; yet, its scales were all black with spikes on it.

The five warriors looked at each other and flew out of the chasm while the two-headed demon lion chased after them immediately. And so, the five warriors had to slay the two-headed lion in order to reach Hythurah of Sheol. The Lion was the personification and embodiment of Jealousy as well as the guardian of the portal to Hythurah; therefore, it was imperative that the demon lion be killed. The son of Ether pointed at the two-headed lion demon and out of his finger came a surge of purple lightning that shocked it. The two-headed lion demon shook it off and looked at the son of ether as if he was as weak as a newborn child. The two-headed lion demon roared, and then he spoke, saying, ***"Sons of God, you have no business here in Hitisum of Sheol. Be gone or face my wrath!"***

Airael looked at the two-headed lion demon, and said, ***"What is your name, demon?"*** The demon replied, saying, ***"I am called Jusariel, angel of jealousy. I will not warn you again, mortals; be gone!"*** Earthael looked at the demon, and said, ***"I don't know who you are or why you're here, but I don't think you know who you're talking to!"*** And when Jusariel heard what Earthael had said, he teleported right next to him and swiftly struck him with a swing of his fiery paw. Earthael was knocked out of the air and went violently crashing into the ground of Hitisum. A great and large chasm that caused a gigantic earthquake was created from the impact of Earthael's body slamming into the ground. Jusariel laughed as hard as he could, and said, ***"Now, the rest of you shall meet the same doom as your brother."*** And when Ethereael heard this, he teleported next to Jusariel, and punched him so hard that he roared loudly with pain as he slammed into the ground and roared in anger right before he went unconscious. Jusariel seemed to be totally out of commission; meanwhile, Ethereael joined his brothers in a search for their brother, Earthael. Fireael shouted to the top of his lungs, and said, ***"Earthael! Where are you, bro?!"***

There was no response, Ethereael's mercury eyes began to release tears, and the son of ether spoke with the pain of loss in his voice, saying, ***"Fireael, I can't feel his vital life energy anymore; he's gone."*** The four warriors dropped their countenances, and had no words to speak, for they had all thought that they had lost their brother. Meanwhile, as the four warriors began to lose their will to continue their journey, Jusariel quietly rose up without their knowing, and struck them with all of his demonic might. At last, the five cosmic warriors had been down and out. Jusariel laughed and shouted out to the firmament of Sheol, saying, ***"Can you see now, Satan? Can you see what your nephew can do?! The Sons of God have been slain once and for all!"*** Jusariel was filled the power of evil, and said, ***"Now, I shall rule in Lucifer's place for the remainder of his imprisonment! For it is I that should lead Sheol against the heavens! It is I who is worthy of all praise, for there is no demon that had the strength to smite the sons of the God of Jacob, Isaac and Abraham; yet I, Jusariel, nephew to Satan has become triumphant over the power of God."***

Just as Jusariel spoke his last words, something extraordinary occurred. The ground of Hitisum trembled all of Sheol, and the chasm that was thought to be Earthael's final resting place was perfectly lit with green light. The son of cosmic earth gradually levitated out of the chasm surrounded by millions of small pebbles that began to combine and take the form of giant spikes. Earthael looked at Jusariel with eyes of green fire, and said, ***"There is no demon that can destroy me or my brothers; you are mistaken if you thought that I was dead."*** Jusariel's countenance was overwhelmed with fear, and then, Earthael began his deadly assault. With the wave of a hand and the blink of an eye, the giant spikes created from the small pebbles of Sheol were launched into Jusariel's body with the speed of a lightning bolt. Jusariel's body oozed with black blood as the rock spikes of the son of cosmic earth pierced his limbs, heads and tail. The son of cosmic earth was powerful and victorious in the final battles that marked the beginning of a new lifestyle for all of humanity.

Jealousy no longer existed in mankind; however, the journey was far from over. After defeating jealousy, all of the human beings on earth fell into a deep sleep, and Earthael lifted the ground that his brothers were laying on in order to carry them with him into the next place of Sheol. The portal to the next realm was opened, and Earthael flew off into the portal while telekinetically dragging his brothers behind him on a slab of the ground of Hitisum. And so, the five warriors made it to the next hell with the help of their brother that was thought to be dead.

The Fourth Hell called "Hythurah."

Earthael reached his destination and slowly lies down the slab of Sheol in the place called Hythurah, the place of Envy. The four warriors were knocked out cold, and they have no idea that their brother is alive, or that they have actually made it to the fourth place of Sheol. Earthael placed his left hand over his brothers' bodies, and raised his right hand into the air, and a jolt of green electricity sprung from the darkness of outer space and rushed into Earthael's right hand. Earthael's left hand began to glow with a strange green light, and then, green electricity wildly sprung out of his left hand and began to spread all over the bodies of his brothers who were unconscious. The four brothers opened their eyes and noticed that their brother, Earthael was still alive.

Ethereael picked his self up from the ground, and said, ***"We all thought you were dead. When we thought that you were gone for good, we kind of gave up the mission and left ourselves***

vulnerable enough to be killed." Fireael picked his self up and gave his brother a big hug while saying; ***"We thought that we'd lost you for good, bro."*** Earthael replied to his brothers' comments, and said, ***"I don't care how dead you thought I was, never give up just because one of us is dead; continue the mission, and keep going, this mission is more important than any one of our lives! We are here to do the will of God whole-heartedly; never forget that! Now, let's get to work, we have a mission to accomplish."*** Earthael shot off into the sky and flew straight ahead as he followed the directions given to him by his heart's intent. His four brothers followed behind him, and looked at each other with a smile on their faces. Only the elected champions of God could have made it thus far.

It is only by the grace of the three-fold form of one supreme intelligence that the cosmic sons were able to prevail over their toughest adversaries. The place of Sheol called Hythurah was a strange and unknown place, for its skies were brown and looked as if it was overly polluted with evil vibrations, and its ground was made like that of a vastly flattened mountain. As the five warriors flew through the skies of Hythurah, they saw a large army of demons that saw them flying through the skies and decided to retreat to the tenth hell so that the Sons of God would not smite them. They ran like cowards as fast as they could so that their masters, Satan and Moloch could protect them. A swift retreat to the tenth hell would save their lives from the divine wrath of God. For the Sons of God had placed the fear of God in the hearts of the remaining demons inhabiting the final places of Sheol. Their courage, strength, and will to be victorious had surely destroyed the faith of evil that lies in the hearts of all demons. As the five warriors continued their flight across Hythurah of Sheol, they stopped in mid-air, and Aquari-on says, ***"Wait! Do you guys feel that, it's Hermes Mercurius Trismegistus, can you feel it?"*** A voice sprung out in their minds, and said, ***"Yes, you are correct, Aquari-on. I see***

that the five of you have proved yourselves beyond the shadow of a doubt; the great architect is most impressed by your love for one another. You have shown yourselves to be the perfect warriors of goodness, I am most proud of you. However, I have come to give you a small tip about your next few battles. Without a doubt, you have seen that the inhabitants of Hythurah have retreated like the cowards that they are, but there is one problem that you must solve. The demons of the other places of Sheol are beginning to use their combined powers to stop all of you, for they now see that you are all too powerful to be easily killed. A portal will appear in this loathsome place, and the five of you will be transferred to the next hell, and unfortunately, one of your greatest tests will begin. In the Fifth hell, you will face the titan of apathy, unforgiveness and self-exalting pride. These three titans are the purest forms of the evil places. I noticed that all of you had problems fighting Jusariel, and now, you shall face the physical form of three hells in one place. Be on guard, and fight with every ounce of your being, for the true tests begin now." The voice of Hermes in their minds had disappeared, and a portal of mercury ripped into reality in order for the great battle to occur. The five warriors flew through the portal and ended up in a place called Nuvuyol of Sheol.

The Fifth Hell called "Nuvuyol."

The place of apathy was a place of endless stones and thundering dark skies that resembled a full night on earth, however, everyday in Nuvuyol was a dark night. As the sons of God stood still in the fifth hell, a great and terrifying noise began to rise from the north, south and west of the area. The galactic prince named Hermes warned the sons of God that a great battle would occur. As the frightening and terribly loud noises got closer, the sons of God opened their eyes to the might of three hells embodied as enormous titans of evil. The titan of apathy arrived, and said, ***"The five of you are formidable champions of God, but you are still mortal men. Turn away and leave this place if you know what is good for you."***

The five warriors looked up at the titans as if they were looking up at the top of the empire state building from the ground, and Ethereael said, ***"I've got a really bad feeling about this. We can do one of two things; we can fight them, or we can be cowards and leave. So, does anyone have a plan for this fight; I'm fresh out of ideas right about now."*** The second titan arrived, and said, ***"Thou shalt surely die if you fight us, what is your choice? Let the heavens, hell and the earth know now, for the time to die hath come, Sons of God."*** The third titan arrived, and said, ***"Surrender now, mortals, we cannot allow you to go any further; resistance is futile!"*** The titan of apathy had eyes of flames and a body of stone. The titan of unforgiveness had inane eyes and a body made of red cement, and the titan of self-exalting pride had eyes of light and a body made from the dark red mountains of Auhutukulm. The five cosmic sons stared in awe as the three titans' size was unlike that of any giant they had ever seen. After looking at the great height of the titans of Sheol, the five warriors levitated to the height of the titans' eyes and charged their powers up for battle. With the wave of a hand, *Ethereael* was surrounded in black ether lightning and ready for battle. *Earthael* raised his hand into the sky, and the universe trembled and shook at the might of the son of cosmic earth, the stars moved and exploded, the planets shook and stopped spinning for a brief moment.

Airael placed his hand over his heart and strong and intense winds began to blow and slightly push the titans backward. *Aquari-on* raised his left hand into the sky, and a stream of water left the palm of his hand and took the shape of a pentagram in order to let the titans of Sheol know that they are the five elements in their purest forms of existence. Fireael looked at all of his brothers, and said, ***"This is it! Either we fight like warriors or run away like cowards!"*** Fireael pointed at the titan of apathy, and said, ***"Airael! Aquari-on! The titan of apathy is all yours!"*** Airael and Aquari-on flew onto the titan's head and began using their fists to pound away at its head. The titan's head shook left and right as the son of cosmic air and water caused the titan to stumble back and fall to the grounds of Nuvuyol. Fireael saw his brothers take the first titan down, and said, ***"Earthael! Ethereael! The titan of unforgiveness is all yours!"*** The son of ether grabbed his brother Earthael and teleported near its left foot in order to trip him and send him crashing into the ground.

Fireael spoke to his self, and said, ***"Self-exalting pride, after today, the earth will no longer have your presence, and I'll make sure of it!"*** Fireael flew into the titan's left hand, jumped on to its wrist and started speed running up its left arm while the titan used its right arm to slap his left arm and crush Fireael like an insect. There he was, the son of cosmic flames; a tiny flame of light running along the titan's left arm. Fireael continued running until he reached the titan's neck, and without warning, he began to slam bolts of light energy into the titan's neck so that he could decapitate it. Each bolt of light caused the titan extreme damage that chipped away at its stone neck but never decapitated it. As soon as Fireael realized that the titan was stumbling due to the force of his light bolts, he quickly levitated to the level of the titan's eye, and tossed a bolt of light into it so that the titan would be transiently blinded and Fireael could distribute more damage to its body as soon as possible.

While the titan stumbled and struggled to get its sight back, Fireael landed onto the titan's shoulder and ran down his collar bone to execute what Fireael thought would be the last move he would have to inflict on the titan in order to end his battle and help his brothers finish the job. The titan regained his sight, and when he did, Fireael placed his fist above his own head and flew full speed into the titan's chin. A flying uppercut straight to the titan's chin caused the titan's face to crack, and the titan's face began to fall apart within multiple seconds. The titan's enormous body began to slowly fall to the ground of Nuvuyol while Fireael hovered and watched. Fireael looked at the titan, and said to himself, ***"He's not getting up any time soon."*** He then sought to aid his brothers' take on the other two titans. He looked to his left and right, and saw Airael, Aquari-on, Ethereael and Earthael struggling against the remaining titans of Sheol.

Fireael shouted out to his brothers, saying, ***"Airael! Earthael! Aquari-on! Ethereael! We have to re-group!"*** The four brothers left the titans alone and flew side-by-side while trying to come up with a plan to put the titans out of commission. Ethereael looked at Fireael, and said, ***"These titans are freakishly powerful, I might have to step it up a notch, but either way, you can always depend on me."*** Fireael said, ***"It's going to take everything we've got to take these guys out of the battle. I want everyone to take it to the next level; let's not play games this time, this is our chance to bring peace to earth, for good. We'll never have another chance like this again, let's do it right or not do it at all."*** The five warriors turned around and prepared to pull off full-scale attacks on the titans of Sheol and finish them off for good. The five warriors stopped in mid-air, and Fireael said, ***"Wait! I thought that titan was finished for! Oh no! This can't be! They can regenerate…"*** While the five heroes were re-grouping, the titan of self-exalting pride had completely regenerated all of the damage that Fireael caused to its body.

Fireael was surprised, for the titan of self-exalting pride was standing tall without a blemish, for he was far from harmed after Fireael's multiple attacks. The titans of Sheol were strong beyond imagination. Fireael looked at his brothers, and said, ***"Okay, they can regenerate themselves; we're going to have to totally obliterate them with every ounce of power and force that we have. This time, we're going to tag team. On my command, I want everyone to do their best."*** Fireael pointed the index finger of his right hand at the titans, and said, ***"Aquari-on! Go now!"*** Aquari-on flew off at full speed and filled his right hand with the force and power of a great tsunami as he slammed his fist into the enormous jaw of the titan of apathy. The titan stumbled and Aquari-on landed on its nose. He then jumped off of the titan's nose and flew into the titan of self-exalting pride and stunned it with an extreme blow to the chest. Once again, another titan stumbled away from Aquari-on's hit.

And when Aquari-on knew the first two titans were still stumbling or stunned, he charged a powerful orb combined with water and cosmic energy and sent it crashing into the third titan. The third titan's chest attained a hole in it after Aquari-on's bolt of water and cosmic energy went straight through him. When Aquari-on saw this, he shouted at Fireael, and said, ***"All done!"*** Fireael looked at his brother Airael, and said, ***"Airael! Try and knock them down so I can send Earthael in to help Ethereael and I finish the Job!"*** Airael flew off into battle and prepared to do his very best to knock the titans of Sheol out cold. Airael hovered directly in front of the chest of the titan of unforgiveness and placed the palm of his right hand about seven inches away from its chest while a gigantic twister burst out of his palm and lifted the titan into the air. The great power of the son of air was displayed without doubt as he stretched his left arm out, and another twister ejected from the palm of his left hand and raised the titan of self-exalting pride into the air. Airael floated a midst the air using the height of his power to raise the titans as high as he possibly could.

The third titan spotted Airael and swung his hand at him

all too late, for Airael looked at the titan and two great twisters sprung out of his eyes and power lifted the titan of apathy into the air so as to make him vulnerable for any attack. Airael displayed the strength of good while being the size of an ant or a small glowing dot to the titans of Sheol. Airael shouted to the top of his lungs, and said, ***"This is for heaven and earth!"*** Airael lifted the titans higher into the sky of Nuvuyol and tossed them ten miles away from him when they least expected him to. He then flew into the height of the sky and shouted out to Fireael, saying, ***"Fireael! I did it, we have to keep up the momentum, let's finish this!"*** Fireael looked at Earthael, and said, ***"You're up next, Earthael. Use your powers to somehow keep them on the ground."*** Earthael nodded his head, and flew to the bodies of the three titans laid on the ground, for Earthael was ready to prepare the titans of Sheol for total annihilation.

Earthael pointed his index finger at the ground below him, and the ground cracked and created a gigantic chasm that was seemingly useless, however, with the wave of his hand, the contents of the chasm revealed its purpose without a doubt. Three gigantic spikes made from the very ground of Nuvuyol levitated out of the chasm and placed themselves over the faces of the three titans. And when Earthael saw that the titans were beginning to regenerate and pick themselves up from the ground, he directed the three gigantic spikes to quickly plunge themselves into the faces of the titans of Sheol. The titans' faces were nearly destroyed and gallons of their blood leaked out of their solid faces and drenched Nuvuyol with their own blood. Earthael's part in battle was the easiest to execute with little time. Earthael shouted at Ethereael, and said, ***"Ethereael! Do your magic, bro!"*** Ethereael received the signal from his older brother, and said, ***"No problem!"*** Ethereael teleported over the area where the titans bled to death, and with the wave of his hand, gold electricity covered his entire body within two seconds time. He then placed the palm of his hand over the three titans, and golden electricity environed the three titans and prevented them from moving or regenerating themselves once again. Ethereael shouted out to Fireael, and said, ***"Fireael! This is it; let's finish this, once and for all!"*** Fireael replied in a loud voice, saying, ***"Ethereael, use your ether-shield; this is it!"*** Fireael flew over to his brother Ethereael and landed on the titan of unforgiveness to deliver a bombardment of light bolts to its body.

He then super jumped off of the titan of unforgiveness and on to the thigh of the titan of self-exalting pride while running up its thigh and launching multiple light bolts of energy at it. Afterward, Fireael super jumped onto the titan of apathy, and ejected a powerful stream of light out of his right index finger. He then used the stream of light like a sword as he began to wave his finger to slice and dice the surface of the titan of apathy's skin. Then he reversed his movements and super jumped back to the titan of unforgiveness and swiftly chopped its arms from its body while running across its shoulder to make his final jump. Fireael jumped off of the titan of unforgiveness' shoulder, and onto the titan of self-exalting pride's waistline. Fireael got on his knees and placed his palms on the titan's skin surface and used the force of his light bolts to lift him into the air while dealing major damage to the titan's waistline. Blood sprouted out of the titan at the approximate time that Fireael was lifted into the air.

As the son of cosmic flames lifted into the sky, he environed his self with a brilliant and blinding light that emitted one powerful and thick ray of light on each titan. Fireael intensified his powers by concentrating on his purpose as the rays of light began to annihilate the titans' atom-by-atom. The five cosmic sons took deep breaths knowing that they were victorious. The five warriors landed upon the ground of Nuvuyol and sat down because they were exhausted. Fireael looked at

Ethereael, and said, ***"Man, I hope we never have to do that ever again; I'm beat."*** Aquari-on looked at Fireael, and said, ***"Nice moves, I would've never thought you could do something like that, bro."*** Airael looked at Fireael, and said, ***"Yeah, everything worked out the way you figured it out, but who died and left you in charge, Mr. Know-it-all?"***

Earthael looked at Airael, and said, ***"Hey! Air monkey! Did you have a better plan at the spur of the moment?"*** Airael replied, saying, ***"Uh…no?"*** Earthael said, ***"Well, it doesn't matter who planned it, all that matters is that we beat them, and that we finish this journey. Besides, give light head a little credit, we kicked those titans butts didn't we?"*** Airael replied, saying, ***"Yeah, of course we did, I don't want to say it, but it worked, Fireael; good plan, bro."*** Ethereael looks at Earthael, Airael and Aquari-on, and says, ***"Hey! Look at Fireael."*** Earthael looks at Fireael, and says, ***"I don't believe this! He's sleep, and snoring at that, I never could stand his snoring."*** Ethereael slaps Fireael in the face and he wakes up, saying, ***"Is it time to go already?! Oh well, I guess we still have a long ways to go."*** Fireael gets up, and levitates into the air, saying, ***"Come on! Let's go, you bunch of snails!"*** Earthael looks up at Fireael, and says, ***"Oh okay, I see somebody's happy to be alive."*** And so, a portal of light opened to the sixth hell, and the five warriors proceeded to the place of Sheol called Rhavulor, or the home of unforgiveness.

The Sixth Hell called "Rhavulor."

The land of Rhavulor was the only land of Sheol that simply consisted of black sand and a sky that looked as if it held heavy rain in its clouds. At the very center of Rhavulor was a gigantic golden statue of the titan of unforgiveness; the statue stood sixty-thousand feet high. Of course, the statue resembled the titan that the five warriors had already defeated. As the five warriors flew through the land of Rhavulor, the statue crumbled because the five warriors had conquered it, the statue shattered into a billion pieces of gold, and the five sons of God paid it no mind as they had battled long and hard to attain safe and easy passage through the sixth and seventh evil places of Sheol. A fiery portal opened, and the five warriors flew through it one-by-one and ended up in another place of Sheol.

The Seventh Hell called "Yangyinoum."

The devilish place called Yangyinoum was a place of dedication to the son of the morning. The ground was made of thick flat stones that had his name engraved all over it in the writing of the angels. The engravings read, ***"Hail Lucifer, ruler of Sheol."*** The sky of Yangyinoum was like night without day ever existing, however, there were no stars or anything scintillating in it. It smelled like rotting human flesh and burning bones. The five sons realized the crafty evil of Yangyinoum, and knew that they had done a good thing when they defeated the three titans of Sheol. It was truly a blessing that the five warriors were able to fly through Yangyinoum and not have to touch the ground that was polluted with the words of their enemy. And so, another fiery portal opened, and the five sons of God had safely made it through the sixth and seventh places of Sheol without being harmed or having any problems whatsoever. Then they entered the loathsome place called Lufthremn, also called, the lustful place of Sheol.

The Eighth Hell called "Lufthremn."

The eighth place of Sheol called Lufthremn was simply strange, weird and seriously vast amongst all other places of Sheol. The sky was dark red, and there was a wide and long path of black hexagon shaped stones, and if you listened closely, you could hear some sort of gigantic beast roaring loudly in the background as if it was close, yet still far away. The five warriors were tired of flying and decided to land on the path of what seemed to be black hexagon shaped stones while the rest of the land was simply grey stones. When the five warriors landed on the black hexagon shaped stones, Aquari-on looked at his brothers, and said, ***"Hey look! Let's follow the black stone road, maybe it'll get us where we need to go, so we can get this mission over with."*** A loud and frightening roar of a beast of some sort occurred, and Ethereael looks over his left and right shoulders, and says, ***"Did you hear that?"*** Airael looks at Ethereael, and says, ***"Hear what? I don't hear anything."***

Fireael looks at Ethereael, and says, ***"I heard it, but I'd pay it no mind, I mean, we are in hell, right? Anything could be down here, but I don't think it's anything to worry about."*** Earthael replied, saying, ***"I heard it, too. What could it possibly be? Okay, let's follow this weird path so we can try and get out of here as soon as possible. I know something is really wrong about this place, but I just can't put my foot on it."*** The five warriors walked as far as they could until they all decided to sit down for a little while. And just when they had placed themselves on the ground, the path of black hexagon shaped stones began to rumble and shake wildly. The five warriors couldn't understand what was happening until they all watched it happen. The black hexagon shaped stones weren't stones at all; the five warriors had been walking along the back of the gigantic dragon that is called Leviathan. The path moved and moved until the great dragon showed its face. Earthael looked at his brothers, and said, ***"Why? Why does this always happen to us; cant we just go through one of these places without some gigantic creature trying to eat us, or kill us?"***

The five warriors levitated into the sky and stood face-to-face with the mighty Leviathan who raised itself into the height of the sky of Lufthremn, however, Leviathan was so enormous in size that he could hardlyly see anything smaller than he was. Leviathan was six-thousand feet wide, and sixty-six thousand feet long. Leviathan roared, and the ground of *Lufthremn* cracked and trembled at the might of its tongue. The five warriors were speechless and didn't know what to say at first, but eventually, Fireael said, ***"Well, I guess that explains the roaring that we heard, and it kind of explains why the path seemed so damn long. Whoa! That thing is seriously huge. And I'm going to be real honest with you guys; I have no idea how we're going to hurt that thing!"*** Airael said, ***"We can't just stand here and talk about what we can't do; we have to do something, or this whole mission was for nothing. Let's go!"*** Airael speeds off into battle and gets ready to use the height of his power with all hopes that he can inflict the slightest damage on the legendary Leviathan. The son of cosmic air moves at full speed and lands on Leviathan's tail in order to impinge it with as many powerful blows as possible. Airael rides on Leviathan's tail and tries his best to run up to its head while it twists and turns with all of its might.

Airael begins to punch Leviathan with the power of a hurricane in his right hand, and the power of a twister in his left hand. Airael's punches had no effect, and eventually Airael realized that it was hopeless to try, as he continued to punch the surface of Leviathan's nearly invincible skin. Airael knew that his strength wasn't enough to inflict any damage on Leviathan, so he closed his eyes, and said, ***"Quick-storm! I need you now, old friend!"*** Airael's body dissipated into energy and began to twist and ascend in order to use all of his power against Leviathan. Airael became a gigantic cosmic twister that ascended and descended at the height and depth of Lufthremn. The power and force of his powers was so extreme that it burrowed a hole into the ground and sky immediately. Airael's attempts to inflict damage to Leviathan were unsuccessful. Meanwhile, Airael's brothers were trying the same thing with their powers. The four brothers unleashed multiple attacks to Leviathan's body; however, they were also unsuccessful in inflicting any damage to the enormous dragon, it would seem that the dragon was totally indestructible to their cosmic gifts. As the five warriors came to the complete realization that they were unable to damage Leviathan, they all flew off together and tried to plan something out.

Fireael said, ***"Airael, I admire your courage, bro. But this time it seems like the end, we're lucky he's so big he can't really see us. But above everything, I didn't come this far to lose to some overgrown lizard! There has to be something we can do."*** Earthael looked at Ethereael, and said, ***"We have no other choice; it's time for us to send in our secret weapon."*** Ethereael kept flying and glanced at Earthael, saying, ***"Secret weapon? What secret weapon?"*** Earthael replied, saying, ***"The son of ether; you, Ethereael."*** Ethereael looked at Earthael with a confused countenance, and said, ***"Are you crazy?!"*** Earthael said, ***"No. I'm far from crazy, bro. You should have more faith in yourself. Ever since we met you, I felt the extreme force of ether and the sword of Elohim flaming through your heart. It's time for you to use it so that we can save earth and finish this journey, little bro."*** Ethereael replied, saying, ***"What if I fail?"*** Earthael replied, saying, ***"You won't; just do it before I beat you up! And I don't care how powerful you are, just remember; I'm your big brother."*** Ethereael said, ***"Okay, here goes nothing."***

As Ethereael Flies off to fight Leviathan by himself, Aquari-on shouted out loud, saying, ***"You can do it, little bro!"*** Airael says, ***"Show em' what you can do, little bro!"*** Fireael says, ***"Give em' a few hits for me, you can do it!"*** Earthael says, ***"Make him fear you!"*** Ethereael lands on Leviathan's tail, and begins to absorb large portions of the ether propagating throughout the universe. And when he felt like he was strong enough, he said, ***"Sword of Elohim, I, the son of ether, calls on your power at the time of the earth's greatest need."*** Ethereael's body was immediately surrounded with a force field of ether that was vibrant with gold and purple electricity. Ethereael Shouted, and said, ***"Let's see what you've got, dragon!"*** After shouting out loud, Ethereael took up his right fist and smashed it into Leviathan's tail. Leviathan roared, and surprisingly spoke, saying, ***"That accursed sword of Elohim! I can smell it! Whoever possesses that accursed gift from Eloah shall perish!"*** It had been done, Ethereael not only hurt it a bit; he made it speak!

Leviathan spoke again, and said, ***"Die! Die, Servants of Yah! You have no business here!"*** Ethereael teleported right in front of Leviathan's eyes and threw a powerful bolt of lightning into its left eye, and destroyed it. Leviathan roared with immense pain, as the fact was known that no one hath ever inflicted damage upon it. No demon, angel or mortal hath ever beaten it. Leviathan was angered an hundred fold, and opened his mouth to deliver a shower of red electricity that stunned Ethereael and sent him crashing into the ground of Lufthremn where he was transiently buried under pounds of stone. It seemed that the awesome force of Leviathan had knocked Ethereael out of commission for good. Meanwhile, Leviathan notices that there were four mortals watching him. The gigantic dragon headed in their direction and began to pursue them immediately. Earthael said, ***"Now I'm worried! He's spotted us!"*** Fireael looked at Leviathan, and said, ***"Ethereael's down, we can't run. We'll have to fight, especially since we don't run! Let's go!"*** Airael said, ***"If we die, we die knowing that we did our best."*** Aquari-on says, ***"Ethereael, I hope you're still alive, and if you are, I want you to obliterate this beast."***

The four brothers charge their electromagnetic fields, and battled Leviathan in hopes that Ethereael would return and finish the mission on his own. Fireael flew onto the dragon's head and began pounding away at it with all of his cosmic strength. He even bombarded it with his famed light bolts and only succeeded in making it angrier. Earthael did the same and only made Leviathan's wrath worst. Airael raced into it with his fist carrying the force of a thousand hurricanes, and once again, it only angered Leviathan. Aquari-on took up his right fist and placed the power of a thousand tsunamis in it as he too pounded away at Leviathan's head. Leviathan was wroth, and the great horns on his head began to glow with a strange red energy that telekinetically pulled the brothers off of him and stunned them. The four warriors shouted to the top of their lungs with immense pain. Leviathan said, ***"I know who you are, sons of Yah. You have committed suicide by coming here. It is without a doubt that you are the sons of Yah, only the sons of Yah would attempt such braveries with faith repetitiously driving their souls to defy and defile the land of Sheol with their accursed loyalty to goodness. Today marks the end of your lives, accept it and relinquish the foolish notion that you will prevail over all devils, for you shall not prevail over me, you are only mortals having part in a futile attempt to be triumphant over one who is much more powerful than thee."***

Leviathan opened his gigantic mouth and used the power of his devilish mind to telekinetically guide the four warriors into it while he swallowed them and they became less than a small appetizer to him. The four warriors who had fought so long and so hard to get so far were eaten by the dragon called Leviathan, the ruler of lust in Lufthremn of Sheol. After swallowing the four warriors, Ethereael regained consciousness and levitated out of the stony debris that could've become his grave. He looked into the firmament, and spoke to himself, saying, ***"I know I can beat this thing, but how?"*** When Ethereael asked his self that question, the divine architect spoke through his mind, and said, ***"It is only by my will that the five of you have come***

this far. I help those who help themselves, my son. Leviathan is no more than a coward among cowards, but you, Ethereael, you are mine son. Calm your mind and intensify your relation to the cosmos. The gifts that I have given you is sufficient to crush all devils; use it!"

Ethereael powered his electromagnetic field and flew off into the sky to find Leviathan and destroy him for good. Shortly thereafter, He spotted Leviathan, and shouted out loud, saying, ***"Leviathan! I still live!"*** Leviathan heard the words of the son of ether, and said, ***"Ah...I know who you are, mortal, and I too have ears to hear. The rumors of Sheol speak of you and your brothers bringing peace to your kind. I see that look in your mercury filled eyes, and I assure you that I will crush you and guide your soul to the very teeth of the jaws of torment! I have made the death of your brothers quick and easy, but you, Ethereael, I shall make you pay for taking my left eye!"*** Ethereael replies, saying, ***"It is you that will die!"*** Ethereael teleports in front of Leviathan's face once again, and showers his right eye with ether lightning. Leviathan roars loudly with pain, and says, ***"You shall pay for that, servant of Yah!"*** Leviathan opens his mouth and releases multiple destructive orbs of red energy that Ethereael dodged quickly with swift teleportation. The orbs that missed went crashing into the ground of Lufthremn.

Lufthremn was ruined beyond imagination, the son of ether and Leviathan battled, and the whole realm of Sheol was shaken and trembled with the clashing force of good and evil. Leviathan could no longer see, for Ethereael had destroyed both of his eyes. Leviathan wildly twisted and turned in the firmament of Lufthremn, for he could no longer see his powerful opponent. Ethereael was well aware of what he was doing, and finally, he decided to attack Leviathan with all of his might. However, just before Ethereael could teleport near his enemy and destroy him, Leviathan used the power of his devilish horns to telekinetically toss Ethereael back into the ground of Lufthremn. Ethereael crashed back into the stone ground, and instantly flew out of it. By the time Ethereael returned, Leviathan's eyes were completely regenerated, and the great lust beast could see his opponent once again.

The Belly of the Lust Beast

Meanwhile, the four warriors were far from dead; however, their adventure had gotten harder and harder every time. The four warriors were knocked unconscious, but eventually they would wake up and realize that Leviathan had swallowed them. The sounds of loud thumping sounds and loud roars signified that something that was powerful was pounding away at Leviathan's body. The four warriors woke up and had no idea where they were until they noticed the wet bodily tissue of the gruesome Leviathan, where a small stream of blood and millions of bones and skulls had been passing around in its body for who knows how long. Fireael regained consciousness, opened his eyes, looked around, and said; ***"Well, we could be dead."*** Earthael picked himself up, and said, ***"We're standing in blood and a whole bunch of bones and what not; where the heck are we?"*** Airael looked around, and said, ***"We're inside of Leviathan's body, and this just keeps getting weirder and weirder every time."***

Aquari-on said, ***"Wait! I have an idea! If we're inside of it, I can drown it from in here. The only problem is that, if I do it, we would still need a way out. If we couldn't penetrate his skin from the outside, then I'm pretty sure that we can't do it from the inside."*** Fireael said, ***"Hey, Airael, see if you can speak to Ethereael so he can get us out of here."*** Airael said, ***"No problem."*** Airael closed his eyes and visualized Ethereael's face while saying, ***"Ethereael, we're alive, and we've got a plan."*** Ethereael heard Airael's voice in his mind, and said, ***"I'm a little tied up right now, give me a second, and hold on."*** Ethereael stopped attacking Leviathan, teleported to the ground of Lufthremn, and telepathically responded to Airael, and said, ***"I don't have much time, Leviathan's on his way down here now. What's the plan, Airael?"*** Airael says, ***"Aquari-on's going to flood Leviathan from the inside so you can get the upper hand on him. But we need you to hit him hard enough to put a hole in him.***

After you do that, we'll just take the water ride out of here." Ethereael said, ***"Great, get ready, I'm about to do it now."*** Aquari-on said, ***"Okay, I'm going to do it now."*** Fireael said, ***"Wait! Wait! Did you hear that?"*** Airael said, ***"Hear what? I don't hear anything."*** Fireael said, ***"It sounds like bones knocking against each other."*** Fireael turned around, and realized that the bones inside of Leviathan had put themselves together in order to kill them. Fireael threw his light bolts at them, and said, ***"Earthael, give me a hand while Aquari-on washes this place up."*** Fireael, Airael, and Earthael threw various energy bolts at the living skeletons and destroyed each one that came their way. Aquari-on placed two-inch thick water shields around his brothers while he began to manifest large orbs of water that filled Leviathan's body with enough water to have filled an ocean. With little time, Aquari-on was done. The living skeletons were eventually washed up and stuck floating around inside of Leviathan's body after Aquari-on was done. Leviathan began to hack and cough up large amounts of water that showered the ground of Lufthremn.

Meanwhile, on the outside, Ethereael continued to pound away at Leviathan's outer skin surface until he raised his right hand into the air, and environed it with black electricity. The son of ether plunged his fist into the great dragon, and moved his fist upward in order to rip a hole in the great dragon's body. The water rushed out of the hole like a faucet, and the four warriors rode the water flow to the way out. And after several minutes, the four cosmic sons came leaking out with the rest of the water. Finally, the four warriors were free, and Fireael saw Ethereael on the way out, and said, ***"We'll wait on the ground, finish him off, little bro!"*** The four warriors retreated to the ground to wait for their brother while he battled Leviathan to the death. Ethereael used the water distraction to his advantage, and teleported under Leviathan's neck while using gold ether lightning to chop Leviathan's head off.

The golden lightning showered out of Ethereael's palm, and cut through Leviathan's head like a katana sword cutting swiftly through linen. Leviathan's head plummeted toward the ground of Lufthremn, and the rest of his body gradually dissipated into nothingness. The mighty son of ether had won, and the journey continued, for the five warriors had deserved every ounce of victory that they worked for. When it was all said and done, Ethereael teleported to his brothers so quickly, that the head of Leviathan was still plummeting toward Lufthremn. The five brothers watched from a distance while the head of Leviathan slammed into the ground, and created a crater that was the size and depth of the Grand Canyon. The five warriors began to hack and cough from the rising smoke that covered a wide area of Lufthremn. Fireael continued coughing, and said, ***"Hey, Airael, can you try to clear out the smoke?"*** Airael coughed, and said, ***"Yeah, hold on a sec."*** Airael lifted his right hand above his head, and a great wind blew from the east of Lufthremn to remove all of the smoke, which revealed a giant hole created by the impact of Leviathan's head crashing into the ground.

After Airael cleared the air, the five warriors slowly walked over to the gigantic hole, and looked into it to see if the battle was over. Fireael said, ***"Man, that is one humongous head, and look at this hole, it's the size of the Grand Canyon!"*** Earthael said, ***"Let's get out of here, now. I want to get this over with."*** Airael said, ***"Ethereael, you kicked his tail, little bro. nice work."*** Aquari-on said, ***"Something still doesn't feel right about all of this; ah...whatever."*** The five warriors walked away from the gigantic hole created by Leviathan's head and started looking for the next portal to the next hell. And as the five warriors walked away, the head of Leviathan levitated out of the gigantic hole, and said, ***"Sons of Yah! You will pay for this!"*** The five warriors turned around and couldn't believe that Leviathan wasn't completely dead. Fireael said, ***"Okay, we're not done, let's get done!"*** The five warriors raced off into the sky and surrounded the head of Leviathan in order to team up on it and bring it down. The five warriors made their first movements to hit Leviathan's head with their fists, and before they could, Leviathan's horns lit up with red energy, signifying the use of his demonic telekinetic powers. The five warriors' fists were one inch away from impinging Leviathan's skin when the great dragon tossed them away from him with the power of his superior telekinesis.

Leviathan laughed, and said, ***"You all are no match for the relentless powers of evil."*** The five warriors heard the words of the great dragon as their five bodies slammed into the stone ground in pure pain. Out of the five brothers who crashed into the stone ground, Ethereael recovered the quickest and began showering Leviathan with black ether lightning. The ether lightning began to fry Leviathan's head like an egg. Leviathan roared loudly as the son of ether continued to eject the ether lightning at him until he was totally dead. However, the dragon became angered with Ethereael, and used his powerful horns to toss Ethereael away from him again. Meanwhile, the four cosmic warriors lifted themselves out of the ground and headed back into the sky while Ethereael came plummeting down. Fireael saw his little brother gradually preparing to crash into the ground and flew to him immediately. As Ethereael continued plummeting, Fireael grabbed his arm while spinning him in a circle and flung him back into the sky, while saying, ***"Don't give up! The whole world is depending on you; we're all depending on you. Go Ethereael, go!"*** Ethereael charged his ether lightning to its climax, and showered Leviathan with it once again.

The great head of the great dragon exploded, and the battle was finally over. Ethereael stopped in mid-air, and teleported back to the ground of Lufthremn, and said, ***"Finally, it's over."*** Another Fiery portal appeared, and Earthael said, ***"It's about time; I thought we'd never leave this place!"*** Airael shouted out to Fireael, saying, ***"Hey, Fireael, it's over, Ethereael did it!"*** Fireael landed on the ground, and said, ***"Good work, Ethereael, I knew you could do it, little bro. We all knew that you could do it. Let's get out of here."*** The five warriors flew off into the fiery portal, and prepared their minds for whatever evil forces the ninth hell could possibly offer.

The Ninth Hell called "Decetum."

The ninth land of Sheol called Decetum is a place with a beautiful firmament like that of earth, however, millions of rusted old chains of divinity hung from it, and at the end of each chain was a decomposed human body; some of which had been there for so long that if you simply touched one of them, it would crumble into a pile of dust. The chains were filled with evil magic, and due to that fact, it was without a doubt that they could easily be used without having to touch them. The grounds of Decetum were hot coals that moaned and groaned like zombies, simply because they had inherited the souls of those who had died there. The pain and suffering of the past was displayed in their cries of deceit.

Men and women that deceived all that loved them and allowed their pride to disable their ability to apologize, for they felt no remorse for their repetitious deceptions of evil throughout their lives. Finally, the five cosmic sons have entered the land of Decetum, a dangerous journey to which much must be done in order to destroy Satan, Moloch and Mephistopheles. The five cosmic warriors have become fatigue from their journey through Sheol; however, they have fought the most experienced and powerful demons existent, and they have succeeded in fulfilling the will of the great architect of the universe.

In the land of Decetum awaits bigger surprises and more imminent danger and death. The five warriors look around and come to the realization that they are gradually becoming closer to the end of their journey as the powerful defenders of earth. As the five cosmic sons of God fly through the land of Decetum, six chains of divinity attacked the son of cosmic fire. His powers were no longer active, and his ability to wield the light of God was rendered useless. He wiggled, moved and tried to use his powers to free his self, however, he was unsuccessful, and realized that the chains that had bounded his arms and legs were not regular chains. And so, he screamed out to his brothers, saying, ***"Stay back! The chains are the same ones made by the angel of forge! I can't use my powers! Leave me behind! Leave now!"*** Aquari-on, Earthael and Airael heard their brother's voice and decided to leave him behind for the good of the mission, for the mission was much more important than their brother's life. However, the son of Ether was not about to leave his brother behind to die, so he stopped, and said, ***"Aquari-on! Earthael! Airael! I'll stay back with Fireael to see if I can get him out of here, we'll meet up with you later!"***

The three brothers headed to the next realm through a portal of fire that took them to the final realm of Sheol. Ethereael teleported to Fireael's location, and hovered beside him, saying,

"I could never leave you to die here, we've been through too much together for me to let you die like this, I'll get you out of here, just give me a second, bro." Ethereael closed his eyes and began to charge the power of ether to destroy the chains of divinity that held his brother captive. As Ethereael began to use his ether lightning to release his brother, a loud roar occurred, and the demons of deceit came sliding down the chains of divinity to eat their victim, the son of cosmic fire. One demon slid down from a chain of divinity and grabbed Ethereael before he could make a move, and the two of them crashed into the hot coals of Decetum. Ethereael was pinned down, and the demon's strength was unbelievably unimaginable. Another demon slid down one of the chains of divinity that captured Fireael, and began using its hideous twelve-inch tongue to lick his face and roar at him so as to frighten him. And so, out of the one-million chains of divinity that reached out of the beautiful skies of Decetum, six-hundred sixty-six thousand six-hundred sixty-six demons of deceit slid down with their twelve-inch tongues looking to feast on the divine blood of the cosmic sons of God.

The two brothers seemed to be getting close to fighting their final battle, for Fireael was helpless to do anything, and Ethereael wiggled and couldn't understand why he couldn't move. Fireael screamed as loud as he could, and said, ***"Ethereael! Help me!"*** Ethereael charged his power over the ether and his body began to generate the dangerous ether lighting that had caused the demise of so many demons in the past. However, the demon that had him pinned down wasn't affected by his powers at all.

And at this point, the voice of God spoke in Ethereael's heart, and said, ***"My son, there is no fallen angel stronger than thee. Speak my word, for you have my tongue which is sharper than any double-edged sword!"*** Ethereael calmed his mind and body, and said a psalm called Tau. ***"Let my cry come near before thee, O lord: give me understanding according to thy word. Let my supplication come before thee: deliver me according to thy word. My lips shall utter praise, when thou hast taught me thy statutes. My tongue shall speak of thy word: for all thy commandments are righteousness. Let thine hand help me, for I have chosen thy precepts. I have longed for thy salvation, O lord; and thy law is my delight. Let my soul live, and it shall praise thee; and let thy judgments help me. I have gone astray like a lost sheep; seek thy servant; for I do not forget thy commandments."*** said Ethereael.

The land of Decetum began to rumble, and the chains of divinity hanging from its firmament began to swing side to side as if a great force was traveling through all of Sheol. The chains began to tangle and knot themselves continuously, and the power of deceit was shaken away with the power of absolute truth. The demon that had Ethereael pinned was violently tossed away from him in the blink of an eye. Ethereael was free, and the time to use the power of the sword of Elohim had come once again. Ethereael quickly teleported to his brother and with the wave of a hand, the power of the sword of Elohim broke the chains immediately. Fireael was free, and the two brothers hovered back-to-back as they prepared to take on a legion of powerful demons that wouldn't dare go easy on the servants of God.

Fireael placed his hands in front of his self and began shooting bolts of light out of the palms of his hands with extreme force. The son of ether placed the index fingers of his left and right hands on his forehead, and black lightning began to wildly shoot out of his eyes. The black lightning of the son of ether began to shoot through the demons of deceit like a thousand rounds of speeding bullets. Though the two brothers were eliminating many demons at one time, there were just too many of them. And so, Ethereael grabbed his brother's hand and charged the power and force of ether into it.

Fireael's ability to generate light was heightened, and no longer was he able to simply generate light; he was able to generate strange purple bursts of energy that were able to guide themselves to their enemies, and destroy them. Before the demons of deceit could understand what had been done, they were all being chased by bursts of purple energy that were moving so fast that the demons of deceit simply started disintegrating in amounts of seven. Every second that passed, seven demons would disintegrate and moan in pain as the awesome power of the two cosmic sons proved more than worthy when combined. And so, the legion was defeated, and the two warriors took an open portal to the next and final level of hell. Upon reaching the final level of hell, Ethereael grabbed Fireael's hand and teleported to their brothers' location by locking on to their vital life energy. Ethereael and Fireael appeared out of thin air, and hovered amongst their brothers. The five brothers were reunited, and the mission continued to the final battle that would change the lives of all mankind. Aquari-on looked at Fireael, and said, ***"I see you're free now, what happened back there?" "There is much more to our little brother than we can imagine,"*** said Fireael. Airael said, ***"Well…what happened?"*** Fireael replied, saying, ***"It's a long story that we don't have time for, let's get the rest of this show on the road."***

The Tenth Hell called "Auhutukulm."

And so, the five cosmic sons flew under the evil lands of hell on a mission that only they could complete in due time. The home to Satan and Moloch was called Auhutukulm, the dwelling place of the princes and kings of darkness, the right and left hands of the mighty Lucifer. Lucifer manifested the land of unreason in order to hide his face and the faces of his brethren from God after the war in heaven, for their faces had changed and turned hideous when they defied the laws of God. No longer were their faces beautiful like their fellow angels in the seven heavens. Because of their actions, they lead the totality of all unreason.

And so, the land of sheol called Auhutukulm was a land of limitless mountains, red concrete, red dirt, and volcanoes filled with green lava. Its firmament consisted of smoke and red clouds that could rain fire and brimstone at any given moment. And all of the mountains of sheol were thirty-thousand feet in height, and they were also half-covered with sulfur in a yellow crystalline solid form.

In the midst of their final travel through the skies of Auhutukulm, they encountered a large legion of demons that witnessed five rays of light flying through the skies of Sheol. When the legion of demons saw this, they began shooting off into the air to attack the five cosmic warriors immediately.

At the speed that the five warriors were traveling at, it was sometimes hard to see everything. However, Aquari-on was the first to realize that there was a legion that was beginning to attack; therefore, he took it upon himself to stop flying and get rid of the legion while his unknowing brothers continued to fly while not knowing that he was no longer with them. Aqauri-on outstretched his arms, and a burst of light appeared in front of his chest, and water poured out of his chest like a waterfall. All of the demons that attacked were immediately drenched and knocked down by the force of tons of pouring water. The four warriors had been traveling through the skies of Sheol so quickly that they didn't notice that Aquari-on wasn't with them.

The four cosmic sons continued flying until Fireael stopped

and noticed that Aquari-on was gone, so he turned around and felt the forces of the legions of the thamiel fighting against Aquari-on alone. Fireael looked at his brothers, and said, ***"Ethereael, I think we left Aquari-on a few miles back, I have a bad feeling that he's outnumbered back there, you think you can get us over there fast enough to help him out?"*** Ethereael opened his left hand, and said, ***"No problem."*** His left hand began to acquire strange black electricity around it, and before his brothers knew it, they were standing directly in the midst of the battle between Aquari-on and fifty thousand demons.

Fireael said, ***"Let's do this!"*** Ethereael raised his hands above his head, and his whole body was surrounded with black electricity. And after charging his body with ether energy, he was immediately surrounded and attacked by thirteen demons. However, his powers combined with the sword of Elohim allowed him to fight all thirteen demons at once. Eventually, they got the best of him, and sent him crashing into the grounds of Sheol. A gigantic crater filled with smoke was made by the impact of Ethereael's body crashing into the ground. However, the son of ether quickly recovered, and flew out of the smoke while throwing ether lightning, a black colored electricity having the power to immediately disintegrated anyone who would get shocked with it.

Meanwhile, Earthael was surrounded by one-hundred demons, he fought valiantly, however, the demons got the best of him, Earthael called out to his brothers, but they were all too busy to help or hear him in the heat of battle. The legion of the thamiel got the best of Earthael, and knocked him unconscious. After defeating Earthael, they telekinetically lifted his body into the air, and used all of their strength to throw him into a nearby mountain in the land of Sheol. Earthael crashed into the mountain and never returned to the battlefield; however, Ethereael seemed to be able to take care of himself with ease. Airael and Quick-storm were having difficulty fighting their adversaries, for the legions of the thamiel were much more powerful than the standard demon warrior or anything they had battled in the previous places of Sheol.

However, the son of cosmic air would never accept early defeat. He combined himself with his new ally, and once again transformed into the wind warrior of Artriol. He then touched the back of his knee, and his leg was turned into a small twister that took off into a crowd of ten-thousand demons, and terminated each one with ease. When Fireael saw what his brother Airael could do, he came up with an idea. Then he said, ***"Airael! Come here! I have an idea!"*** Ethereael overheard what Fireael said during the battle and teleported Aquari-on to his location, and said, ***"What's the idea this time?"*** Fireael said, ***"I know how we can get rid of all of them at once."***

At this point, the demons began to attack them while they were talking. Ethereael waved his right hand, and surrounded his brothers and his self with a force field made of ether so that they could save time to plan things out. Fireael said, ***"Airael, can you surround me with a twister without killing me?"*** Airael said, ***"Yeah, but I'd have to adjust the vibratory frequency of my powers."*** Fireael said, ***"Ethereael, get us out of this force-field, out of the air, and back to the ground."*** Ethereael stopped generating his force field, and teleported his brothers and himself to the ground two seconds before the legion of the thamiel were about to terminate all of them. Then Fireael said, ***"Airael! I'm ready, let's rock!"***

Airael's body began to dissipate into infinitesimal particles, and as soon as it did, Airael had become a great and disastrous twister of death surrounding his brother, Fireael. Ethereael, and Aquari-on stood behind them surrounded in a force field of ether so that they wouldn't be destroyed when Fireael and Airael used the fullness of their abilities. The two brothers watched as the twister containing their brothers began to expand and move toward the remaining demons. And as the twister expanded and moved forward, Fireael filled the twister with a brilliant bright light that was so strong it began to forcefully fight its way out of the twister.

Finally, the great twister began to emit rays of light that disintegrated all of the remaining demons, and made short work of the army of the thamiel. After eliminating a large legion of the thamiel, Fireael said, ***"Where's Earthael!?"*** He then shouted to the top if his lungs, saying, ***"Earthael! Earthael! Where are you?"*** The four warriors had their hands so tied up with so many demons that they hadn't realized that Earthael had been killed in the midst of battle.

Ethereael, Aquari-on, Fireael, and Airael began to cry, and many tears ran down their faces. After realizing that their beloved brother was gone, the four warriors shot off into the sky, and headed to their destination to avenge their brother Earthael immediately. Though the four warriors had won the fight against the legion of demons, they had lost their brother, and they were running out of time. The leaders of the thamiel were preparing for their assault on Earth. And so, the four warriors shot off into the skies of Sheol again, and continued to finish the mission that they struggled so hard to complete.

The four warriors traveled for many miles, and finally, they reached the end of their six hundred and sixty-sixth mile, they stopped and saw a large army of demons standing before one of the princes of darkness. It was Moloch, the powerful demon who ruled Sheol with Satan after the imprisonment of their leader, Lucifer. Moloch had a head like that of a lion having two black horns springing forth from his brow. His body was like that of a man's body, yet the skin was scaled like a crocodile.

His eyes were like a bottomless pit, and six black wings stood out of his back. He stood twelve-feet tall, and the nails of his hands were as sharp and long as well forged knives, a monstrous creature that would terrify any mortal who looked at him. Moloch began preaching to his legions, saying, ***"The time to rule this universe is now! For many millenniums our creator has ruled, and his rule has been unfair to those of us who are now considered fallen, or outcasts. Today we take that which is ours, we shall march to the earth, and destroy all that exists within it, and if we must, we shall also take on the throne. Our angelic brethren in heaven have betrayed us and left us astray. Today, it shall be fallen angels against God and his so-called human beings. No one shall stop us, not even the elect of God. And now, I will let a familiar angelic brethren speak, and explain to you what we are truly fighting for."***

After speaking, Mephistopheles appeared, saying, ***"You all know who I am, I am the torturer of souls. I was once close with our recent ruler. However, Lucifer failed where we shall succeed. I once ruled my own worlds, and my own planets inhabited by my own creatures. However, in due time, five mortals sent by God destroyed my work, and ruined my plans to make my galaxy a better home for evil. But we shall not accept defeat, our duty is to plague this universe with evil, and annihilate all mortals. God has given them strength and he has also given them favor. Centuries and millenniums ago, God created a plan for mortal ascension, and afterward, he commanded our ruler to bow down to mortals, and asked us to do that which we felt is unruly of angelic beings.***

Our ruler took liberty into his own hands, and refused to bow before mortal men and mortal women. And because of his choice, and our choices, we were cast down from heaven. He gave them a woman to romance, and he gave the woman a man to romance. Yet we stood there, and for years we served his throne, and what

did we receive?! We received nothing; therefore, we shall give no mercy unto mortals. And because of his love for humanity, he has cast us aside, and his pet Michael never leaves his side. Our rule is now come!

He calls himself a judge, yet he rules unfairly. Men are allowed to sin, and are forgiven because of Yahuahsua, but where is our freedom?! Where is our gift to sin and be forgiven? He sent his son to save all of mankind, yet he left us here in Sheol to rot like old fruits begotten by broken branches. The time is come, our day is today, let us reign supreme, the time is now! Destroy earth! And cast down the followers of God!"

Meanwhile, the son of cosmic Earth was far from dead. He opened his eyes, and shot out of the mountains like a bullet and landed near a cluster of mountains, and said, ***"If I would've had some spare time to learn these new abilities, I would've never been beaten so easily."*** Earthael's cosmic senses went off, and he felt that his brothers were in trouble. He turned around, looked at the mountains of Sheol, and pointed at them with the index finger of his right hand while saying, ***"It is said that faith in Yah that is as small as mustard seed can move mountains."*** Earthael punched his hands into the ground, and began lifting the mountains of Sheol off of the ground. And when it was all said and done, the mountains popped into the air, and then they began to fall, but before they could fall, Earthael shot off into the sky, and caught it with his index finger. The son of Cosmic Earth had lifted the mountains of Sheol off of the ground as if it was as heavy as a feather. He then flew around it, and landed on top of it. The awesome faith and strength of the son of cosmic Earth was unbelievable; he'd lifted mountains from the ground, and rode it to his brothers' location immediately.

The four warriors stood still in the midst of the dark skies of hell, and stared at the army of demons as Moloch and

Mephistopheles gave their speech. Ethereael said, ***"I suppose this is it, I know we don't have a game plan, but I think we'd do better if we just started beating everyone up."*** Fireael spoke out loud, and said, ***"This is it, everyone here dies now; we're here to end the battle between fallen angels and mankind for good!"*** Moloch heard this, looked up, and said, ***"You come here thinking you will succeed at destroying us, you must be fools, for our reign shall never end, foolish mortals."***

When Fireael heard this, he opened his palm, and charged a small ball of vivifying light, and said, ***"One way or another, we will no longer stand for your evil in our world."*** Afterward, he threw the aggregation of light into Moloch's face, and the land of hell shook violently as Fireael's new power caused Moloch to stagger backward. The great fight had begun, and after being hit by Fireael, Moloch was as angry as an uncomfortable bull. He Roared like a lion, and said, ***"I know that our legions are no match for your powers, therefore, you shall not have to worry about them."*** Moloch roared again, and the legion of demons that stood amongst him began to explode, and their blood was scattered all over Sheol. Moloch laughed, and said, ***"I don't need my legions to kill mortals; I'll rip your heads off, and crush them like grapes under mine feet!"*** Moloch levitated into the air, and said, ***"Now is when you all die!"***

Moloch waved his hands, and the four warriors were immediately encased in a force field of darkness surrounded by red electricity. The four warriors were unable to move or do anything to stop Moloch. Moloch's power was pure demonic evil. After realizing that his enemies were weak compared to him, he began to telekinetically make the force field smaller so that he could crush all of his enemies at one time. As the force field gradually shrunk, the grounds of Sheol began to tremble and crack as if a great and mighty earthquake had occurred.

Something extremely powerful was heading toward the battlefield, however, no one knew who or what it was that was heading toward the battlefield. The ground trembled again, and Moloch fell to the ground and lost his hold on the four cosmic warriors. Moloch lifted himself off of the ground, and looked up, and to his surprise, it was Earthael, the cosmic son of Earth hovering in the sky while standing at the uppermost point of three floating mountains directed by his will.

Earthael looked at Moloch, and said, ***"It's going to take more than a few ten-thousand demons to get rid of me. And if I were you, I'd start running right about now!"*** Earthael utilized the height of his powers, flew off and under the mountains, and grabbed the bottom of the mountains with his telekinetic powers just before he hurled the three whole mountains at Moloch. Moloch teleported and escaped the likely destruction of the impact between the mountains and the ground. Mephistopheles however, was not so fortunate, for he was unable to escape the impact of the mountains; he was wiped out of existence by the force of the speed and impact. After the death of Mephistopheles, Satan appeared, looked around, pointed his finger at Earthael, and said, ***"You'll pay for this, monkey!"***

And so, Earthael went one-on-one with Satan, the prince of darkness. Meanwhile, Aquari-on, Airael, Fireael, and Ethereael prepared to take on Moloch. Satan and Earthael clashed like two forces to be reckoned with. The fight was ongoing, and the powers of the mortals were unbelievably formidable. Earthael used his new diamond arms to punch Satan as hard as he could. However, Satan's powers were unimaginable, and Earthael was forced to do his best in order to win. Earthael hit him and he hit Earthael. Satan grew tired of Earthael and with the wave of his hand; Earthael was immediately knocked to the ground. Satan had gotten the best of him, and Earthael was forced to regroup with his brothers. Satan laughed, and said, ***"You shall never defeat us!"***

Meanwhile, Aquari-on, Airael, Fireael, and Ethereael Fought their best to get rid of Moloch, however, Moloch was too strong. Moloch blinked, and the four warriors were immediately thrown to the grounds of Sheol. The four warriors laid there helpless, for they had been fighting and journeying for such a long time that they were low on energy. Satan and Moloch realized that they had beaten their opponents senseless, and decided to open a portal to the east universe in order to escape. Satan and Moloch flew off into a portal leading to outer space, and prepared to make their assault on the cosmic sons in a wider area. They were confident that they could kill the five warriors, but knew that they would have a hard time doing so. Fireael stood up out of his crater, and spoke through telepathy to his brothers, saying, ***"This is not over, we've gone through too much to be defeated now; Earthael get up! Aquari-on get up! Ethereael get up! Airael get up! We have work to do! Get up!"***

And sure enough, the four brothers heard their brother's voice, got up, and looked at Fireael as if he was crazy. Ethereael says, ***"I'm with you bro, it's not over yet, either we win or we die losing."*** Aquari-on said, ***"We can do this!"*** Earthael says, ***"The great architect told us that he was proud of us, we shouldn't let him down."*** Airael said, ***"Where did they go?!"*** Fireael said, ***"They went through that portal up there, they're trying to escape. We cannot let them get away, what would dad say? Let's go!"*** The five warriors remembered their mission and flew through the portal like speeding missiles whilst looking around to see if they were too late, however, they weren't. Ethereael spotted Satan and Moloch heading to the east, and said, ***"There they go, come on!"***

And so, the battle was taken into outer space in order to prevent Satan and Moloch from escaping. Fireael waved his hand, and a flash of light covered the universe and blinded Satan and Moloch immediately. Whilst Satan was blinded, Fireael asked Ethereael to teleport him directly in front of the two leaders of the thamiel of Auhutukulm, and when Ethereael teleported and took him where he wanted to go, he surrounded his fists with the fires of light.

And when Satan and Moloch opened their eyes, Fireael began punching both of them in their faces with all of his strength, he then grabbed both of them, and wasted no time tackling them, and taking off at full speed toward the planet Jupiter. As Fireael held Satan and Moloch as tight as he could, he quickly reached the planet Jupiter, and slammed Satan, Moloch, and himself into it. A loud and frightening crash impact occurred, Satan, Moloch, and Fireael fought all while tunneling a hole through planet Jupiter. They went into one side of the planet fighting, and exited another side of the planet while still fighting.

After they exited the other side of the planet, it exploded while they were still fighting. Satan, Moloch, and Fireael fought within the fires of the explosion of the planet Jupiter as if they had a serious vendetta against each other, however, that was not the case, the will of God drove Fireael to fight when he was tired, and even when he was weak. Aquari-on, Airael, Earthael, and Ethereael watched closely so that Fireael wouldn't get killed in battle, and if Satan and Moloch would have become too much for him to handle, Ethereael was more than ready to jump in, and take over for his brother, Fireael.

Finally, as the battle between Fireael and the princes of darkness continued, Satan and Moloch got the best of him, and before Fireael knew it, Satan had grabbed his arm, spun him around, and threw him so hard that he quickly crashed into planet Venus and was buried under its surface. Ethereael realized that his brother had been hurt, and as soon as he realized it, he immediately teleported directly to Satan's location. Satan wasted no time; he immediately disappeared. Ethereael looked to his left, and to his right, yet, he was unsuccessful in finding Satan at all.

Ethereael looked up, and by the time he looked down, Satan had grabbed his leg and began spinning him in circles. When the timing was just right, Satan used all of his might, and threw Ethereael into planet Mars so that he could face the same death his brother Fireael would face. Ethereael crashed into the planet Mars, and wasted no time preparing his next move. He rose up from the ground of Mars, and said, ***"I hope he doesn't think it's over, it's going to take much more than that to get rid of me, this is far from over."***

Little did Satan know it would take much more than that to stop the five warriors. Satan believed so heavily on his evil intentions that he quickly assumed that Ethereael and Fireael were dead once again. Due to his belief that he had gotten the two warriors out of his way, he laughed while gradually achieving a secure escape. And as the two princes of darkness got closer and closer to escaping, Ethereael appeared directly in front of him. Satan was startled, and said, ***"What!? It can't be! You're dead!"*** Ethereael said, ***"No, that's your problem, you underestimate us, and now, and today, my brothers and I are going to make you respect human beings."*** Satan replied, and said, ***"I'll never respect or kneel to you, human! Die mortal, die!"*** Ethereael grabbed Satan's horns and used all of his strength to throw Satan into a nearby meteor.

Satan crashed into the meteor that cracked and broke into a thousand pieces. Satan was wroth, and his eyes were filled with the fires of hate. Satan was a great decoy because Moloch was almost about escape for good. Meanwhile, a familiar face raised his self out of a crater created by the impact of his body crashing into the surface of planet Venus. Fireael spoke to himself, saying, ***"If we fail now, we fail the divine architect, and our dad. I refuse to let these demons continue their attempts to rule the universe."*** He then shot off into the sky and back into outer space where it became obvious that Ethereael had been backing him up since Satan threw him into Venus. Satan bested Ethereael, and when it was all said and done, Ethereael backed away from Satan, and let him fly off. However, Ethereael was no fool; he only backed off because Fireael was on his way. Just as Satan thought that the warriors had given up, Fireael blasted out of nowhere, and tackled Satan Immediately. They struggled like two wrestlers of identical strength. Satan began to grow tired of the two brothers, and before Fireael knew it, Satan had tossed him into his brother Ethereael. The battle was nearly never-ending.

As Ethereael and Fireael battled their hearts out with the princes of darkness, Earthael, Aquari-on, and Airael sprung into action, and began attacking with all of their strength. Airael spoke to Quick-storm, and said, ***"That's our cue, Quick-storm, let's go!"*** Airael's body transformed into a yellow energy, and went into Quick-storm's nostrils. Quick-storm disappeared, and the wind warrior of Artriol appeared. Then he morphed into a cosmic twister, and headed straight for Satan while completely forgetting that Moloch was free, and without an opponent. Airael caught Satan in his twister, and began spinning him so quickly that he was immediately tossed into planet Pluto like a rock being thrown into a lake. The impact of Satan's body crashing into Pluto destroyed it immediately.

Satan rushed out of the explosion and back into Airael's twister as if it never harmed him. He then began to chant some strange words, saying, ***"Amee-shuntos-circlos windthor!"*** Upon saying these words, Airael was returned to normal, and as he returned to his normal form, Satan waited, and hit him so hard that he began hurling into the depths of the universe and was unable to regain his momentum. Quick-storm rushed off and caught him before he vanished into the depths of space without a trace. Ethereael and Fireael watched as they hoped one of them would match the strengths of evil and win, but they were truly unsuccessful.

Aquari-on flew off, and attempted to tackle Satan, but his effort to do so was stopped immediately. Satan waved his hand, and trapped him within a force field of darkness; Aquari-on was unable to move. Eventually, he freed himself, and stood there as if there was nothing he could do. And so, Earthael pointed at Satan, and before anyone could realize what was happening, the sounds of speeding space shuttles occurred. Earthael began to direct various meteors to crash into his enemies. In due time, Satan simply punched each meteor with his fist, and broke each one that attacked him, it seemed that the five warriors could do nothing to defeat the great prince of darkness.

A voice spoke to the minds of the five warriors, and said, ***"Let the symbol of five become one with the tongue of God, that which is sharper than any double edged sword, five warriors, four sacrifices; one destiny!"*** When the five warriors heard this, they gathered together, and closed their eyes. Ethereael said, ***"Place your hands over my heart, I think I understand how to use the sword of Elohim now."*** Fireael, Aquari-on, Earthael, and Airael stood in front of Ethereael, and placed their right hands on his heart. A heavenly trumpet sounded off seven times, and then, a horn sounded off five times. Moloch and Satan nearly escaped, but before they could completely escape, they heard something. They heard the sounds of horns and trumpets, and when they did, they stopped what they were doing, and knew that serious trouble was coming. The horns and trumpets of the son of Yahuah had been blown. Moloch said, ***"This cannot be! How could they summon him?"***

The echo of the horns and trumpets traveled throughout the whole universe, and when it was all said and done, the five warriors were immediately encased in an aggregation of light energy surrounded by gold electricity. Satan and Moloch were completely aware of what the cosmic sons had done. The leaders of the thamiel were at a standstill, for they were well aware that Yahuahshua was present after the horns and trumpets were blown. But one thing was for sure; Satan and Moloch would soon find out with their own eyes what had been done. The aggregation of energy surrounding the five warriors shot off into the east of the universe and disappeared. All of a sudden, all of the existing planets in the universe began to move aside, and stop rotating.

Satan and Moloch found themselves in great fear whilst they had no understanding as to what would be done to them. The whole universe began to tremble, and at the east of the universe two gigantic eyes of golden electricity appeared, and afterward, a whole countenance appeared. The Son of God had unveiled his self to the universe, the one who refused to be tempted by Satan in the past. The one called ***"Jesus Christ,"*** ***"Son of Yahuah,"*** ***"Yahuahshua,"*** ***"The good shepherd,"*** and the ***"Savior."*** The ancient shepherd son was so great in size that he held our whole universe in the palm of his hand, and brought it close to his eyes so that he could be seen closely. Upon the brow of the Son of God was a triangle baring a Hebrew letter at its center, the letter called ***"Yod,"*** or the tiny flame that will never cease to exist within a microcosm.

When the thamiel saw this, they were terrified at the sight

of Yahuahshua, the first Son of God. The thamiel retreated to the north of the universe in an attempt to escape the judgment of Yahuahshua, the Son of God almighty, for there is no escape from the lord thy God. As the Thamiel made their attempt to escape, Yahuahshua witnessed what was going on with his own eyes, and opened his mouth. And as he opened his mouth, his tongue resembled a sword crafted with light, his tongue stretched across the universe, and the two princes of darkness were disintegrated immediately. The thamiel had perished, for the tongue of God had cut them into particles and terminated them. The planets aligned themselves in their proper places, and the Son of God disappeared.

And so, after Yahuahshua had terminated the leaders of the Thamiel, the five warriors of the light were instantly teleported to Araboth as if nothing had ever happened. They stood in front of God, and the light of his existence in pure form was so brilliant that the five warriors were forced to close their eyes and simply listen closely. The great architect spoke, and said, ***"Tests of valor have been given to each and every one of you. Each test represented the strength and potential of every mortal man that liveth at this very moment. Mortal men whom I have created in my own image, your triumphant will to be victorious is amazingly outstanding. And because of your love for one another, it is now that you shall fulfill your final journey. What is it that the five of your hearts truly desires as mortal men?"***

Fireael said, ***"We know that you already know, therefore, what I say will go for all of us because I know my brothers, and they are my keepers. I want for my brothers what they want for me."*** Ethereael, Aquari-on, Earthael, and Airael nodded their heads, and God said, ***"It is done, and there are many things that can be done, but it is up to your kind to utilize their liberty in a positive manner. No man is truly urged to do so, but it is joy and love that I seek to view in all of my creatures.***

Four of you have passed through transition, and resurrected yourselves with the strongest force in your solar system. Love endures much pain before it is perfected to greatness; the five of you have followed mine precepts, and honored mine laws. At this moment, you all leave here with the greatest reward that a mortal man can receive. And that reward is the pureness of mind, body and soul." And so, the five warriors blinked, and before they knew it, they were all floating above the state of New York, and all that was destroyed in battle was renewed.

After returning to planet Earth, the five warriors used their powers to enter hospitals around the world without being seen, for they had become invisible, and with their invisibility, they healed all who were sick with disease. Those having cancers and other uncured diseases were cured as the five warriors worked together for decades traveling to each state of the United States of America. And when they had finished their healing in the United States, they went on to the United Kingdom and healed more people with the blessings of God; even Africa became bereft of all diseases. Eventually, the government began to lose significant and considerable amounts of currency, due to the existence of the five warriors. Pharmaceuticals and doctors became poor, and police forces, guns and so forth became very unnecessary, for the defeat of the Thamiel caused a grandeur peace to cover the world.

The existence of all demons was greatly lessened, and because of the decrease in demonic activity, the race of humanity had changed, for violence, murder, and death by disease was at an all time low, and the need for hospitals became a modicum unnecessary. After a considerable amount of time, the government sent out their most trained assassins to eliminate the five warriors and attain the height of their wealth once again.

A time came to pass where Ethereael was present in the

U.K while healing a woman having a disease deemed incurable, and as Ethereael placed his palm facing downward over her body, an assassin sent by the government pulled the trigger of a sniper aiming for Ethereael's head, and attempted to eliminate him as he was ordered by his superiors. The bullet shot out of its barrel and speedily headed for the head of the son of ether. However, the son of ether was no fool, he knew what was coming.

He raised his hand, and stopped the bullet in mid-air, then he made a fist with the same hand, and before the assassin knew it, the bullet had been dispersed into particles. Ethereael looked into the scope of his sniper and waved his index finger left and right while saying, ***"Unh unh unh, tell your superiors that the time for world peace is now, also, tell them that we will continue to show this world the things that truly makes life worth living."***

As Ethereael said this, the sniper in the hands of the assassin began to fall apart and melt into liquid. The destiny of the five cosmic sons was fulfilled, and the planet called Earth was no longer the land of blood spill and kill, it became a place to live long and satisfied, a place to cherish, it became the true land of milk and honey. And in due time, Lucifer, the son of the morning floated endlessly in his prison of the depths of space, saying, ***"I shall return in due time, and when I do, the bloodline of Namsilat powers will pay for this, for I shall trample their very hearts under mine feet and pick my teeth with their very bones, for I will hunt their generations and smite their children and their children's children! They have done naught but postpone their deaths, for I am imminent in all creatures!"***

Chapter 13

Return of the Magus

Many decades have passed since the great battle between the cosmic sons of God and the fallen angels of evil. It is thought that all of the demons that existed within the world of mankind were banished or vanquished due to the heroic actions of the cosmic sons of God. Lucifer and his most notorious followers have been locked away for 7777 years. Mephistopheles, Satan and Moloch have been vanquished, and the planet earth has been imbued with love and peace for a considerable amount of time. Fireael, Ethereael, Earthael, Aquari-on, and Airael have become wise masters of mysticism; for they have grown long beards and have become old men.

Since the world is in peace at the present time, the five cosmic warriors saw no need to continue their journey of healing and so forth, for the world had changed after many decades. The cosmic sons have become ripe in age, yet they are still in good shape. They combined their powers, and fashioned temples similar to the pyramids of Egypt. The temple of Ethereael was made of stones of mirror. The temple of Fireael was made with large red stones, and at its doorway was a flaming door that only the purified could enter through. Aquari-on fashioned a temple of large blue stones, and an open doorway that led to his presence. Airael formed a temple made with purple stones, and at its doorway was a large stone door that only he or a well-ascended mortal could open. Earthael fashioned a temple located seven feet within the earth, and at the stairway leading down into his temple there were three large statues of gnomes.

Fireael and Aquari-on's temples are located in New York

City, Ethereael's temple is located in Egypt, Airael's temple is located in Rome, and Earthael's temple is located in the beautiful lands of Ireland. Many mortals from all over the world came to their temples to learn the secrets of life, and to comprehend the existence of the primary being referred to as ***"God."*** On the Sabbath day, the five cosmic warriors would leave their temples and teach all of the people who lived near their temple, and whoever would want to come and learn about God. On the weekdays, everyone would have to come to their temples of their own free accord if they wanted to seek deeper into the mysteries of the universe. After bringing peace to the world of mortals, the five cosmic sons had children of their own, and opened individual schools dedicated to the study of the universal consciousness permeating all of existence. Ethereael married a woman named *Athenis*, and together they had a son named **Amistael.** Amistael is five years old and gradually learning the secrets of the universe from his father, Ethereael.

There are no signs of cosmic abilities yet; however, his power derives from the universal soul and allows him to merge with the smallest units of matter. By all means, Amistael will soon find out that he is the most dangerous descendant of the Powers' family bloodline. His ability will allow him to destroy his opponent from the inside out, for he is ***the cosmic merger***, and only he can transfer himself into the atoms composing anything. Though Amistael is only five years old, a grand future stands behind him. Tri-dael, the mother of the five cosmic warriors has become very old, and has also chosen to live with her son Ethereael in his pyramid. She sits in a rocking chair and often speaks with her grandchildren about their grandfather, Calabrael. However, in due time, Tri-dael will soon see her husband once again.

Fireael, the son of cosmic flames has also had a son by a woman named Mistika, and in due time, Fireael and Mistika decided to name their son **Magister.** Magister Powers is also five years old and gradually learning the mysteries of the universe at large. Mistika often wonders if her son will attain cosmic abilities like her husband. However, little does Mistika know, Magister's cosmic ability is universal alchemy. In due time, Magister will become a master initiate of transmutation.

His ability to transmute all material substances will prove useful in the protection of mankind in the days of tomorrow. Earthael, the son of cosmic earth has married a woman named Celestia, and together they had a female child that they named **Ovalael.** Ovalael is five years old and has already shown signs of cosmic ability. Ovalael's ability enables her to raise the dead, manipulate light vibrations and transform into light vibrations as well. The awesome power that she possesses can cause her opponent's objective consciousness to perceive a whole new world that doesn't exist. Her ability can be dangerous if she isn't guided correctly as she runs around her home tricking her parents and getting into plenty of trouble using her powers.

But in due time, Earthael will guide her to the paths of victory within her interior self, and in the years to come, her ability will prove most worthy of God. Aquari-on has aged well and married a woman named Xiowa. Aquari-on and Xiowa had a son named **Crimson-sky.** Crimson-sky has yet to show any cosmic talents, however, in the mind of the divine architect, the talents of Crimson-sky are gifts of great cosmic proportion. Crimson-sky will soon realize that his cosmic ability is to manipulate all five elements. He will be able to manifest and manipulate fire, air, water, earth and ether. The talents of the five prior warriors are concentrated within one child. Last but not least, the cosmic son of air named Airael has married a woman named Satada. Airael and Satada have been blessed with a beautiful baby boy that they've named **Astralai.** Astraelai's cosmic talent remains hidden, but in due time, his ability will prove most useful to mankind. Astralai's cosmic ability enables him to resurrect, and regenerate his self anytime he feels that it is necessary. However, his power does not stop there; Astralai also possesses great cosmic strength. And next to his great strength is the cosmic ability to manifest electricity that he can direct wherever he chooses.

As the five cosmic sons lived in peace and continued to teach the world about the unknown principles that caused them to ascend, a galactic prince endeavors the olden state of evil that the earth endured before the cosmic sons of God were born. Meanwhile, deep within the grand realms of the macrocosm, the divine architect calls on his council of six angels to meet him at his throne room in Araboth. And so, Metatron, Sandalphon, Michael, Raphael, Uriel and Gabriel teleported to his throne room as the primary creator commanded them. As they arrived, rays of brilliant light sprung from his mighty throne, and out of the rays of light, he speaks, and says, ***"Though time does not apply to our realm, earth has passed many cycles. The brave effort of my sons has proved worthy beyond the shadow of a doubt. The inhabitants of my footstool have done well, for the earth is at peace. And now, after the passing of so many cycles, another one of my creations has taken the liberty of solely believing upon his self. He is one of my galactic princes, and it is he who collaborated with Lucifer, and began to aid him in his revolt against my throne. And in him is great power, power even greater than that of Lucifer's.***

He has lost his patients with demons, and is now deciding what he will do with my footstool of which I have appointed him prince. His heart is filled with the ignorance of all devils, yet he is as wise and intelligent as you, Metatron. He has completely succumbed to the sophistry of spurious personal liberty, and he will cause much havoc upon the peace of the earth. I want the six of you to investigate any further intentions, go now." The six archangels asked no questions and teleported to the chambers of prince Caligastia, the true ***"devil"*** of evil.

As the council of God materialized at the chamber of Caligastia, a creature of great power sat quietly upon a small throne in a room made of gold. His chambers had old swords on its walls, and a glowing red carpet leading from his throne to a window of the cosmos, where one would be able to see stars and meteors up-close and personal. He sat upon a throne of half silver and half gold. Prince Caligastia, the cosmic being with immense cosmic power sits upon his throne, and ponders the death of mankind. His skin was made with ice, his nails were made with fire, his eyes were made with mercury, the hair upon his head, and his facial hair was made of flames. His armor was like that of a roman king's.

As the six angels stood in front of him, he spoke by means of telepathy, and said, ***"Ah, to what do I owe this transient visit from my superior officers? Is it possible that the primary living energy has sent all of you? Or do you come here to mock my efforts against the so-called primary creator? I think that you are here to find out what I am planning to do, and if you are, do not waste your time giving me a nescient questionnaire, I'll just tell you what you want to know right now. I've sat back and planned an attack on earth, and that has failed. Lucifer has failed me, Satan and Moloch have failed me, and now, I believe that it is time to do the job myself. I'll walk the lands of earth, and manifest the olden days of evil upon it once again. Watching that planet live in complete peace is making me sick to the divinity that forms my stomach. After ages of hard work getting those mortals to go against the word of God, the primary creator has somehow caused me to be viewed as a failure once again. No matter, I'll restore the earth to its evil energy just as it belongs. I and I alone will do it. There is no need for my pawns anymore, for they have proved to be more than failures, not even Lucifer was as smart***

as I thought he was, and if he had any cosmic intelligence within him at all, he would have never killed those four mortals. I thought he was smarter than that. Therefore, I'll finish where that fool has left off, for the time is now brethren; join me! Let angelic intelligence rule the universe!" Metatron replies, saying, ***"For you have seen what happens to those who take on the throne, and yet you still continue this relentless grudge against the great master initiator? Why have you taken such a destructive path of evil, Caligastia?! You exalt yourself above he that is not created as you and I was; you are mistaken just as your lieutenants. I can assume that you are the direct source of all this angelic madness that has been taking place for quite some time now. You are the mastermind of evil that has collaborated with the sophistry of the past attacks on earth. Verily, I say unto you, judgment upon your actions rests solely with the creator of manifested existence. And in due time, your eyes shall also come to view the universal father that knows all."***

Metatron and the rest of the council has heard the plans of the galactic prince, the council of God disappeared, and returned to the throne room of God to relay the message. Metatron stands before God, and says, ***"My lord, O my lord, Caligastia is surely exalting his self. He has plans to return earth to its old state of evil without the help of Lucifer and his minions. I have a plan though, my lord."*** The divine architect replies, saying, ***"Well, what exactly do you propose shall be done, Metatron?"*** Metatron replies, saying, ***"I am well aware that the powers given to your last sons on earth will not be enough for a galactic prince that is in a higher jurisdiction than Lucifer was. At this point, my lord, I propose that we send the magi to deal with him immediately. Caligastia has become foolish quickly. He is unaware that we know the reason he hadn't joined Lucifer is due to the existence of Calabrael Powers and the other Magi. If we return Mike Melville, Yahti and Asu, then I believe that they will give Caligastia the fight of his life. Ascended mortals have***

***defended their earth for this long, why stop now? Let us resurrect the magi.*"** The divine architect replied, saying, **"*Splendid, I'll deliver their souls to their physical envelopes in due time.*"**

Though all of the demons have been vanquished, and the world has seen peace after many years of sorrow, there is but one more evil that must be destroyed. Consequently, his powers are beyond belief. However, Caligastia is not only a planetary prince; he is also a Galactic prince having seven planetary princes under him. There is a planetary prince for each planet in our universe. Presiding over ***earth*** and all other planets is **Caligastia**, presiding over planet ***Jupiter*** is **Naemestai**, presiding over planet ***Venus*** is **Faustislogheus Istemijus**, over ***mars*** is **Maestrumyrit**. Over ***Pluto*** is **Durtunimitia**. Over ***Saturn*** is **Telahspeiut**. Over ***Uranus*** is **Venyulylus**. Over ***Mercury***, the ***moon***, and the ***sun*** is **Hermes Mercurius Trismegistus** who is also a galactic prince having authority over a different universe. The liability of the planetary or galactic prince of each planet or galaxy is that the thoughts of their personality may eventually give into the exaltation of self, and therefore, cause them to believe that they are more powerful than the primary creator. Of course, the divine architect was aware of such events due to his original possession of the divine scheme of the universe and all of its creatures overall. All other planetary and galactic princes truly pledge allegiance to their creator, however one of them has his own plan and belief. Caligastia speaks to his self, and says, ***"It is time to crush these mortals like roaches, today is a most glorious day for the destruction of his beloved creatures."*** And then, he leaves his chambers and teleports to earth in order to place himself in the minds of men so that they would forget the teachings of the cosmic sons, and return to their nescient ways. He walks around the lands of earth and begins placing himself within the minds of mortals who would easily accept his notion of divine destruction.

In due time, half of the earth had returned to their ignorant states. Another war began, and mortals began killing and hurting each other for no apparent reason. The peace of the earth had finally been broken, and Caligastia loved every bit of it. Caligastia chose to make no man his follower; he simply came to earth and caused much mayhem without second-guessing his self. The five cosmic warriors sensed a great disturbance in the peace of the world, and before they knew it, mortals from all over the world began stealing, killing, and going mad everywhere. The cosmic sons opened their eyes to a potential evil that their powers were insignificant to. The powers of the cosmic sons were like the buzzing of small flies to prince Caligastia. And after two days, the mortal creatures of earth had returned to their old ways.

Aquari-on quickly realized what was happening, and called his brothers by telepathy, and said, ***"Fellow brothers of the cosmic, meet with me at the height of the skies over the pacific ocean. Something is very wrong; it seems that our effort to bring peace to the world has been disturbed by a force beyond that of Lucifer's power. Time is of the essence, we must council immediately, for it is imperative that we do."*** The four brothers heard Aquari-on's message immediately, and prepared to teleport to the rendezvous as soon as possible. The four brothers set cosmic barriers over their temples to protect their wives and children from the madness, and left their homes for cosmic duty. After teleporting to the desired destination, the five brothers hovered amidst the skies over the Pacific Ocean, and began to talk about the possibility of getting rid of the cause of the current events. Fireael looked at his brothers, and said, ***"It seems that something else has decided to plague mankind with its recent state no matter what we do to change it. However, that is apparent, the question is: what can we do to stop it?"*** Earthael looked at Ethereael, and said, ***"Ethereael, you have the power to transiently council with the heavens, can you do it now?"***

Ethereael says, ***"Yes, but what information do we need?"*** Airael says, ***"We need you to speak with the primary creator so that we can play our roles in the design of this new situation."*** Fireael says, ***"If anything out of our cosmic jurisdiction has happened, you should be able to find out by contacting Archangel Metatron."*** Ethereael closes his mercury eyes and sends his psychic body into the occult realms of the macrocosm. As he arrives, Archangel Metatron greets him, and says, ***"Ah, I see you have realized the change in peace on earth, Ethereael. A galactic prince named Caligastia has gotten fed up with his lieutenant's failure, and has decided to return earth to its original state of ignorance."*** Ethereael says, ***"Who is Caligastia?"*** Metatron replies, saying, ***"He is the one true leader of the Lucifer rebellion, it is he who gave Lucifer the idea of rebelling against the throne. It is he, and only he that is the one that mortals call the devil. All of the angelic madness that you have seen in your time is due to the plans of Caligastia who was appointed planetary prince of earth and galactic prince of your galaxy one hundred thousand years ago in mortal time. I will not lie to you, Son of God; you and your brothers are no match for him. His powers are beyond imagination, and his intelligence is superior to yours in every way, the only earthly creature that can defeat a galactic prince is a magus, for the magus has the knowledge to defeat such evil. Indeed, the power of the star hopper technique would indubitably prove most useful against Caligastia.***

Lucifer was no problem; however Caligastia is a whole new subject, a subject that must now be dealt with immediately. For now, there is nothing that the five of you can do; however I am sure that the primary creator has a plan that will surely take care of Caligastia. Therefore, I suggest that the five of you stay quiet, and hide yourselves whilst Caligastia submits the earth to evil once more." Ethereael replies, saying, ***"I believe it is best for us to take your advice Metatron, when I return to my physical envelope, I'll brief my brothers on the situation and take it from there.***

We appreciate the information given. Hopefully, we'll hear some good news later on. Call us if you need us to do anything, we'll be on standby."

After finding out what the cause is for the strange behavior on earth, Ethereael returns to his brothers and spreads the word to them. He then says, ***"I spoke with Metatron; he says that we cannot win against the force that walks the earth at this point. So we must somehow retreat and leave the people to fight their own battles. The most we can do is watch, and pray."*** Fireael looks at Ethereael, and says, ***"Well, I don't care how powerful it is, if it tries to kill our people, I'm fighting it, no matter what the cost. Besides, I've passed through transition once before, it's not all that bad."*** Ethereael replies, saying, ***"Fireael, you won't win, none of us can succeed against a galactic prince."*** Fireael says, ***"Galactic prince!? We've never attained any knowledge concerning the existence of any galactic princes. I thought that knowledge was said to be well hidden."*** Ethereael says, ***"That's right, this isn't just some demon from Sheol, this is a galactic prince. The power of a galactic prince is way beyond our jurisdiction.***

You cannot interfere; only the divine architect can deal with this matter. It's true that we are powerful ascended mortals, but not just any ascended mortal can fight against a galactic prince. The only type of ascended mortal that can match up against a galactic prince is a magus, also called a celestial intelligencer. The only magus that we've ever known was our father. When Mephistopheles kidnapped our father, dad could've stopped him if he wanted to, but he knew that the powers of the magus were not to be used for such a simplistic matter, besides, if he would've, I would've never received the sword of Elohim, and basically, things just wouldn't have happened the way they did. Our father knew that a simple demon was no reason to use the power of the magus, and that's why he allowed so much to take place. Though he may have passed on certain powers to our mother, our father

was no fool. He gave our mother a certain level of his abilities and kept the power of the magus to himself. Such a power cannot be passed on to someone who isn't ready for it. And unless there is another magus in this world, then I can't see anyone other than the divine architect stopping this galactic prince gone evil. I hate to say it, but this time, we won't be saving anyone. We'll have to simply stay out of this one. I suggest we find a place to dwell away from the destruction until the divine architect solves this one." And so, the five warriors disappeared and left the earth to the wrath of the galactic prince, Caligastia. Meanwhile, the grand architect of the universe takes on a mortal form and teleports to the canyon of souls located in a realm called ***"Tetra-axim."***

At the top of the canyon was a giant angel who sat on a throne of silver while watching the canyon of souls and keeping order in its place. The angel was fifteen feet tall and usually kept the form of a mortal man wearing the attire of a great Pharaoh of Egypt. His eyes were made of light, and on his arm was a fiery phoenix resting upon his wrist. And upon his face was facial hair that was made of fire. For the Tetra-axim is a place where the souls of human beings walk and meet their judgment before finding out the truth about the life that they lived whilst incarnate. Billions of souls floated side by side until they reached the very end of the canyon. At the end of the canyon, an Angel named Ipotael served as the junior judge who passed judgment on the souls before they would reach the universal judge of Araboth. Much work was to be done; therefore, God had to be present everywhere. After Ipotael had done his part, God would complete fair and final judgment, which would determine what would happen to a soul's future.

Therefore, if your life wasn't lived according to divine law, you were automatically blessed to be reincarnated, simply because *God loved, and to have hate in his heart would defy him as he is.* And so, there was no punishment or being sentenced to a hell or any form of purgatory. The only way that a mortal man could end up in Sheol is by knowing their wrongs and continuously living it, thus, they could only sentence themselves to hell by being enslaved by their emotions, and those emotions being so strong that they would simply end up in a place where they should not be after passing through transition. God had sent his son, and his blood has washed away their transgressions, and given them life eternal. But the angels who fall from grace have not a man to wash away their transgressions. Angels could not suffer and sacrifice themselves as a man could. The grand architect materializes and stands face-to-face with an angel named Logael, the watcher of the canyon of souls. The divine architect looks at Logael, and says, ***"Logael, give me the soul of Calabrael powers, Mike Melville, and the magi brothers, Yahti and Asu Bailey. They have one more errand to complete before they join my holy council."*** Logael replies, saying, ***"May I ask what has happened that you want the souls of the mighty magi, my lord?!"***

God replies, saying, ***"Caligastia, for he has lost all patients, and has now decided to return my footstool to shambles, yet I have a surprise for him and his plans. The return of the magi will most definitely change his mind. I am well aware that Caligastia would've never attacked earth if Calabrael and the rest of the magi were still incarnate; he knows that the first duty of the magi is to terminate galactic and planetary princes who exalt themselves and shun my throne, which is why Caligastia sent Lucifer and his legions to do his work for him. Caligastia knew that he would have to put up a fight if Calabrael and the magi were still incarnate. Of course, Caligastia's heart has become evil, but he has also become a coward. And now, I shall return the magi to their fleshy envelopes, and watch Caligastia's failure once again."*** Logael says, ***"Ah, I see, please say no more, my lord."*** Logael points into the canyon of souls, and the golden souls of the magi transformed into a ball of light and came to the palm of his hand. The divine architect revealed his palm, and the souls of the magi were pulled away from Logael's hand, and absorbed into the eyes of the divine architect so that he could deliver them personally. The divine architect leaves the canyon of souls and teleports to the graves of three unknown warriors from Namsilat's childhood and resurrects them, and shortly thereafter, he teleports to the tomb of Calabrael, the mighty magus.

God stands near the lifeless fleshy envelope of Calabrael, and says, ***"Calabrael, you have followed my laws and pledged allegiance to my word. You have made me very proud and exceeding with joy. When the world of men needed assistance against the devils, I gave them your sons. And now, the world needs again, and now I shall send you. Of all mortals, you have shown great strength in mind, soul, and character. You slept yesterday, and today you shall live once again."*** The divine architect kissed Calabrael's forehead, and Calabrael was no longer dead, for he was alive and well. He sat up, and said, ***"O my lord, I am alive, but why hast thou returned me to the mundane plane of existence, my lord?"*** God replies, saying, ***"I have returned you to this plane of existence to represent your kind once again. The power of the magus is necessary against an evil galactic prince. Your sons have aged well, thanks to you, they have brought peace to the earth, however, a galactic prince named Caligastia has decided to wreak havoc upon the earth in order to break the peace that your sons have worked so hard to bring to mine footstool. It is now your turn to represent mankind and battle for their sake. But first, there is one task that you must complete so that you can prepare to battle Caligastia. There will be a great meteor shower that Caligastia will manifest in order to ruin the surface of the earth, and defile it. You must stop it, Calabrael, you're the Celestial intelligencer, and your sons cannot stop the shower, it is written that only the magi can. Amongst yourself you will be completing this mission with three other mortals who have***

reached the level of the magus, and together, the four of you shall complete my will on earth. It is time for you to take your place amongst the inhabitants of my kingdom. Complete this task, and return to me as soon as possible."

Calabrael stood up, and said, ***"Divine father, I have never been one to fail much, but what if I fail?"*** The divine architect replies, saying, ***"Do not doubt yourself, Calabrael, you have never failed me, and you never will."*** The divine architect blinked, and an orb of gold electricity hovered in front of Calabrael's chest, and before Calabrael knew it, the divine architect had disappeared. Calabrael wasn't surprised, for he'd seen many great and amazing things throughout his life. He looked around, and spoke to his self, saying, ***"Wow, this place is amazing, but how did it get here?!"*** Calabrael walked out of the stone room, and looked upon the ground and realized that it was covered with the finest of silver and gold. And then he looked around again, and saw three large trees in three different places. And then he thought to his self, saying, ***"The three trees form a triangle around my tomb."*** Calabrael was amazed at the celestial brilliance that fashioned his tomb and eventually it made him curious as to who created it. And so, he took his index finger and touched the ground of his tomb while closing his eyes. And then he saw mental images of his son, Ethereael creating the much-flattened mountaintop that he stood on. And then he spoke to his self, saying, ***"And my son, Ethereael created this tomb for me? This is brilliant; I can't believe my own eyes. I've seen many things in my time, but this is truly amazing."***

Just after speaking to his self, a voice spoke out of the golden orb of electricity left by the divine architect, and said, ***"Calabrael, I am the powerful uniform that has been passed down from magus to magus. Take me and place me within your heart so that you can wear the uniform that so many great ones before you have worn, namely, the magi that came from the east***

of Jerusalem to give gifts to Yahuahshua when he attained the physical vehicle utilized by mortals who live, move and have their being. " Calabrael closed his eyes, and used the subtle energy of his heart to pull the golden orb into his heart. His heart absorbed the orb, and brilliant light surrounded the planet made as his tomb.

And when the light disappeared, the hair upon Calabrael's face and head was transformed into vivifying flames of light. And no longer was Calabrael wearing the ragged cloths that he died in, he was wearing the uniform of the magus, a silk black robe with white stitching of the writing of the magi all over it. Round about his waist was an apron with strange symbolism on it. Upon the apron was a skull, and within the eyes and mouth of the skull were pentagrams. Calabrael's bones were transformed into diamond, and his body was surrounded by black electricity. Calabrael was ready to do battle in the name of the three-fold form of one supreme intelligence, the king of kings, God of gods, and the creator of all existence.

And so, Calabrael shot off into the sky and left the planet made to be his tomb and resting place. Upon entering outer space, a voice spoke out, saying, ***"You're still a feather weight, Calabrael!"*** Calabrael replies, saying, ***"Who are you?"*** The voice said, ***"An old friend of your father's?"*** Mike Melville revealed himself and Calabrael opened his arms to give him a big brotherly hug as if he knew him. Mike looked at Calabrael, and said, ***"You're not the only magus you know, I've been on the path of the ancients for quite some time now. I became a magus soon after I lost touch with your father. I passed through transition a while back, and all of a sudden, I wake up out of my grave, and the divine architect tells me that a galactic prince is attempting to destroy the planet. One day, long ago, I found the secret to the philosopher's stone, I lived long, but eventually I had to pass through transition like everyone else. I was present when your***

sons fought the son of the morning though, I must say, you raised them quite well, son of Namsilat. I knew your father when he was just a boy. We even studied together. And just so you know, there are two other people who became magi too. They are also long time friends of your father, Namsilat." Calabrael looks at Mike, and says, ***"Who else could've become a magus?"***

Out of the darkness of space, two faces revealed themselves, Yahti and Asu Bailey, the mystical brothers who had aided Calabrael's father on his quest for perfection decades ago. The two brothers had become powerful mystic magi. Asu and Yahti were twins, both having flaming dreadlocks of light which had grown long and surpassed their knees, and they both had flames of light for eyes. There were thirty-six names of God written in flames upon Yahti's brow, and another thirty-six names of God written in flames on Asu's brow. Together, Yahti and Asu formed seventy-two names of the universal almighty initiator. Years ago, during the time that Calabrael's father was alive and well, *Yahti had single handedly vanquished a demon named **Baphomet**, and Asu had single handedly vanquished a she-demon named **Lilith**. After vanquishing these demons, the demons of Sheol and the angels of heaven referred to them as **"The Magi Brothers."** Master Magus Mike Melville* was also wearing the uniform of the magus, yet his eyes were inane and vibrant with white electricity, and his hair was also made of flames of light. After years of studying the universal knowledge, it was Mike Melville who fought and vanquished a demon named ***"Samael the terrible."*** After finding out that Samael was planning to wipe out the human race by pushing a star into the earth, he stopped the star and confronted the gigantic demon. During battle, Mike was nearly killed trying to save his planet. And just Before Samael could strike Mike with the final blow; a ball of light came from the far east of the universe and consumed him. It was at this moment that he became Master Magus and vanquished the gigantic demon, Samael the terrible.

When Calabrael saw them, he was amazed and exceeding with joy. And then he said, ***"Why is it that the three of you are appearing now? I'm here on a mission from the creator."*** Asu replied, saying, ***"The divine architect visited us personally in order to make sure that Caligastia was defeated for good, not to mention that the divine architect thought it would be acceptable for all of us to be together on this journey."*** Calabrael looks at Yahti, and says, ***"Yahti, it's good to see a friend of my father's. The divine architect must know the outcome of these events, I believe we should go forth, and terminate this galactic prince immediately."*** Yahti replies, saying, ***"It's good to see that the son of an old friend has reached such a level of ascension. Now, let's do what we were resurrected to do, let's not waste time, the fate of our planet weights in the balance once again."*** The four elect warriors of the divine architect wasted no time flying to the earth anymore, they teleported there immediately. When they arrived, they used their abilities to turn invisible so as to view the events of what was happening without being seen by mortal eyes.

As they stood there and watched the inhabitants of the earth slaughter and kill each other, something within the hearts of the magi filled their electromagnetic fields with perfect righteousness. Meanwhile, the galactic prince Caligastia felt the presence of the only ascended mortals that had the slightest chance of terminating him. Caligastia speaks to himself, saying, ***"Ah, can it be that the divine father has sent the magi to battle? When I eliminate these foolish mortals, the divine architect will finally agree that cosmic beings are much worthier than those filthy mortal creatures. This is truly a day to present the ill happiness of my mind to the whole universe. It is almost time for me to display one hundred percent of my cosmic nature. Unlike Lucifer, I shall not waste my time going easy on these mortals; I'll make sure that they all die a terrible death not even the divine architect can imagine within his universal mind."***

In due time, the galactic prince spoke to all of the inhabitants of the earth through telepathy, and said, ***"O how I love mischief and evil, and of course, those who can stop me are already too late. Hear me, O creatures of the earth! Your God created this universe in seven days; I will destroy it in three! I ask you now, where are your five heroes? Where are the five warriors who have saved your worthless lives so many times? Why have they become cowards?! Ethereael, possessor of the sword of Elohim; come embrace your fate so that I may embarrass you in front of your world. And be warned, your brothers are no match for me. The truth is that you don't stand a chance either, however, if you know how to utilize the sword of Elohim, you may stand a chance. Let us make this interesting, if you come and fight me now, I shall not send down a meteor shower to wipe the inhabitants of this planet out of existence."***

Ethereael replies through telepathy, saying, ***"Your threats are empty Caligastia, and you truly are a coward! You only want to fight me because you know that I will not succeed against you. Even so, I shall fight you."***

Ethereael looks at his brothers, and says, ***"Well, I suppose this is the last time we see each other, I don't need to say that I love you, you already know it. And whatever you do, don't interfere! Our father chose to give me the sword of Elohim, and with it I have great responsibilities as its possessor. Pray for me, that's all I ask of you."*** After speaking with his brothers, Ethereael closes his eyes and teleports to London, England where Caligastia has been driving the world of men into madness. After materializing, Ethereael shouts out loud, saying, ***"Where are you, Caligastia, I'm here, show yourself, you coward."*** Caligastia materializes right in front of him, and says, ***"O Ethereael, I have waited a long time to be face-to-face with the possessor of the sword of Elohim. This is truly a glorious day. Now, fight me with all of your knowledge and soul!"*** Ethereael looks at Caligastia, and says, ***"I don't want to fight you, but you continue to threaten the inhabitants of this world. My brothers and I once saved this planet from cosmic tyrants like you, and you are no exception! Unlike you, I don't fight for my own pleasures or display of my abilities, I fight for every creature that has life, and praises God by doing his will whole-heartedly. Therefore, do not think that you will defeat me with ease, I may or may not win, but even so, my brothers and I will always be more powerful than you are, because our abilities rest solely upon his commandments. And before we fight, just so you know, I would've easily wiped the floor with you in my younger days! If I pass through transition today, I would've died for a grand reason, let us begin!"***

Caligastia laughs while saying, ***"You are very ambitious, son of God, but it won't save your life today!"*** Caligastia disappears, and says, ***"Today is the last day that you protect your people, mortal!"*** Ethereael revealed the palm of his hand, and black electricity surrounded his body. And then he shot off into the sky until he reached outer space, and said, ***"Caligastia, let's get this over with, I'm tired of your small talk."*** And before Ethereael knew it, Caligastia appeared directly in front of him, and hit him so hard that his body moved at a speed that exceeded the speed of light and transported him far away from the earth. Ethereael looked around and realized that the earth was so far away from him that it looked like a tiny marble. And when Ethereael realized how far he was, he began to get scared, for his opponent's powers were awesome. Ethereael spoke to himself, saying, ***"I will have to use all of my power to even put a scratch on him."*** Caligastia teleported behind Ethereael, grabbed him by his face, and slammed him into a star. The star exploded, but Ethereael transformed into ether energy and hid himself just in time to escape the explosion. Caligastia looked around, and said, ***"Son of ether, I am surprised, why are you hiding like a coward in the heavens?"*** The son of ether used his energetic form to surround Caligastia in a force field of ether so as to trap him, and of course it worked. Caligastia screamed to the top of his lungs, and said, ***"You fool! Do you not comprehend that I've already won!"***

Ethereael made no response, and began to use his telekinetic abilities to impinge him with dangerous blows to his stomach and face. He thought that he had Caligastia trapped, but in due time, he realized that Caligastia was too strong. Caligastia raised his right hand and absorbed Ethereael into his palm in the form of a black orb of electricity. And then he tried to crush it with both of his hands as if he was crushing a soft grape under his foot. Ethereael dissipated and distributed himself into twenty different meteors floating throughout the universe. And before Caligastia could figure out what he'd done, twenty meteors were speeding toward him and crashed into him immediately. Ethereael materialized, and said, ***"Is this all that you have to offer, galactic prince?!"*** Caligastia materialized in front of Ethereael, and said, ***"Not at all, son of God!"*** Before the son of ether could physically respond, Caligastia telekinetically grabbed Ethereael and threw him into planet mars as if he was no challenge at all. Ethereael laid in a crater on mars, and spoke to himself, saying, ***"If I don't get up, he'll destroy everything."*** Ethereael tried his best to move, but he couldn't. And so, he chose to lie there and accept death and defeat for what is was. Caligastia appeared and hovered above him, and said, ***"Poor son of ether, what's the matter, you don't seem as if you can continue to fight anymore. Shall I take you out of your misery now? Or would you like to continue defeat?"*** Ethereael made no response, and before Caligastia knew it, an aggregation of light came out of nowhere and slammed into his face while knocking him off of planet mars immediately. Fireael quickly landed near his brother, and said, ***"You didn't actually think that we would listen to you, did you? Don't worry about Caligastia, just rest for a while, and let's see how well he does against the son of cosmic flames."*** Fireael shot off into the outskirts of mars, and said, ***"Caligastia, your fight is no longer with my little brother; your fight is with me now!"*** Caligastia replied, saying, ***"Ah, the son of cosmic flames, I'm surprised you came, I thought you'd hide like a coward while I tortured your brother to death. Well, since you're here, I suppose you can die as well."*** Fireael looked to his left and to his right to see if he could spot Caligastia, and just as he looked to his left again, Caligastia materialized on his right side and grabbed his arm immediately. Fireael tried his best to shake him off of his arm; however he was unsuccessful in doing so.

And when Caligastia saw that Fireael couldn't break his grip, he began to swing his body into a full circle, and tossed him back into the earth. Fireael knew the consequences of his landing on earth, therefore, he used is powers to slow his self a bit. He was well aware that if he landed too hard, it could be catastrophic. Fireael landed in the Pacific Ocean, and caused a gigantic tidal wave accompanied by a frightening sound that scared the whole inhabitants of the planet earth immediately. And as soon as he regained full momentum, he shot out of the Pacific Ocean and headed towards mars once again. He then spoke out loud, saying, ***"This is far from over, Caligastia!"*** Fireael revealed the palms of his left and right hands, and ten stars headed toward Caligastia and stopped directly in front of him. Caligastia laughed while not understanding what Fireael had planned. Before Caligastia knew it, Salamanders ***(spirits of fire)*** began jumping out of the stars and on to Caligastia. The Salamanders began hitting and biting on him as if he was a piece of food. Caligastia dissipated into small particles and disappeared as if the Salamanders did him no harm. And when Caligastia re-appeared, he grabbed Fireael by his robe, and tossed him into mars with his brother, Ethereael. Fireael called his brother Ethereael by telepathy before crashing into mars, and said, ***"I did what I could, Ethereael, if we die, we shall die together."***

Caligastia laughed, and said, ***"Foolish sons of God, did you seriously think that your powers could possibly compare to mine?!"*** As Caligastia continued gloating, the son of cosmic earth showed up riding upon a meteor, and said, ***"You still have three more of us to deal with before you can claim victory, don't get too happy yet!"*** Earthael jumped off of his meteor, waved his hand, and the ground of Mars began to break into spiked stones that threw themselves at Caligastia in an attempt to stab him with every blow. Caligastia stood there and let each spike break into pebbles while crashing into his chest and face. Caligastia looked at Earthael, and said, ***"You cannot be serious; you didn't think that would harm me, did you?"*** Caligastia snapped his fingers, and Earthael was immediately sent crashing into mars and pinned to the ground, helpless to do anything else. Caligastia looked at the last two brothers, and said, ***"Um-rum-ra-thah-are,"*** and Aquari-on and Airael appeared in front of him immediately. Caligastia laughed, and snapped his fingers again. And before Aquari-on and Airael knew it, they were both sent to mars to lie next to their brothers, as they too were pinned to the ground, and unable to move. The galactic prince was so powerful that he bested the champions of earth with pure ease. The great warriors who had banished and vanquished so many demons were helpless and unable to save their world for the first time in their entire lives.

And so, it would seem that all was lost, but little did Caligastia know, the real challenge was just around the corner. Caligastia looked at the five brothers, and said, ***"Before I kill all of you, I'll allow you to watch your beloved planet lose all life existent. Now, watch closely, mortals, you could learn a thing or two watching a true master."*** Caligastia raised his left hand to the heavens, and three thousand meteors directed themselves toward the earth in order to destroy it, and kill all that live on it. Caligastia laughed, and said, ***"Today, the earth dies, and all that exists with it."***

Meanwhile, the magi strategically hovered above the earth waiting for the meteors to strike. The inhabitants of earth looked into the sky and began to run wildly all over the planet while screaming ***"God, please God! Save us all! Please!"*** The magi heard the words of the inhabitants of earth, and made no comment. The meteors came toward earth just as Caligastia had commanded, and when it was all said and done, the powerful magi raised their right hands toward the heavens and disintegrated all three thousand meteors with ease. And then, they locked on to the galactic prince's location and teleported to him immediately. And when the magi materialized, Caligastia acted as if he didn't care he was about to meet his demise. Mike Melville spoke up, and said, ***"You've lost all sense of things heavenly and good-willed. You knew we were coming, and yet you still attempted to destroy our planet, the divine architect has sent us to deal with you personally."*** Asu looked at the five warriors, and said, ***"It looks like you were picking on the cosmic sons. You truly are a coward, Caligastia. You knew they were no match for you. Why would you do such a thing?"*** Yahti looked at Caligastia, and said, ***"The ignorance that you've displayed proves that you're not worthy to be a galactic prince. You abuse your powers and exalt yourself, your rambunctious abuse of your authority and cosmic ability ends here, Caligastia."*** Calabrael walked over to his sons, and said, ***"You've done well, my sons, now it is time for the magi to deal with him. Open your eyes and see that your father still lives."*** Ethereael opened his eyes, and said, ***"Father? Is that you?"*** Calabrael responded, and said, ***"Yes, I live once again."*** Calabrael waved his right hand, and all of his sons were healed and able to stand up. The five warriors of the olden days looked at their father standing amongst other mystic warriors and couldn't believe it. Fireael, Ethereael, Aquari-on, Airael, and Earthael's eyes began to drip with tears, for they truly missed their father for a long, long time.

Calabrael looked at his sons, and said, ***"You all have aged*** *well in my absence. Fireael, Earthael, Aquari-on, and Airael; long time no see. It appears that the four of you were resurrected after I passed through transition. When I last saw you, you left the house to fight the son of the morning, yet you never returned. It took me years to get over your deaths. It is never easy for a father to lose his sons, no matter what the cost. Together, all of you brought peace to the world, and upheld the laws of God whole-heartedly, a father couldn't ask for more from his own sons. I want the five of you to watch this battle closely so that you can learn as much as possible from the teachings of the magi. I am very proud of you, and one day soon, you'll all become magi."* Ethereael looked at his father, and said, *"I missed you, when you died; I thought I was a failure. It took years for me to understand that there are things more important than myself, I had the power, but not the understanding."* Fireael said, *"Father, I knew you would come, everything that you taught me is still in my mind, I'll never forget."* Airael looked at his father, and said, *"We know now who we truly are, and because we do, we know that the universe is simply a reflection of ourselves."*

Aquari-on looked at his father, and said, *"I know that it hurt to know that we all died, but I realized something before Lucifer killed us. Our purpose was much more important than our fight."* Airael looked at his father, and said, *"After years of fighting demons, I learned a lesson as well. I learned to pray for everyone, whether they are good or misguided."* Calabrael looks at his sons, and says, *"It may have taken a considerable amount of time, but I see now that all of you have truly learned yourselves. You have learned the ways of the magi. Now stand back and watch the skill of the magi. This is how we used to do it in the old days."* Mike Melville steps up, and says, *"Calabrael, he chose to hurt your sons, you should fight first. May the essence of the divine architect guide your hands to victory."*

Calabrael looked at Caligastia, and said, *"Choose your place*

of battle, corrupted one!" Caligastia replies, and says, ***"Planet Jupiter, Mr. Powers."*** Caligastia and Calabrael disappeared and materialized on planet Jupiter to begin the great battle between the galactic prince and the magus. Caligastia looks at Calabrael, and says, ***"So, I stand face to face with the legendary Calabrael powers, I must tell you, it truly is an honor. I understand you were quite the psychic combatant in the olden days. Many years have passed and you have become a legend, but after today, you will become history, mortal. I must say though, I think you would have given Lucifer the fight of his life. Though you may be a magus, you'll need much more than power to defeat me, Calabrael. I feel bad for your sons."*** Calabrael replied, saying, ***"Why?"***

Caligastia said, ***"Because I'll kill all five of them after I'm through with you."*** After threatening to kill Calabrael's sons, Caligastia disappeared, and said, ***"Today, you die, Calabrael!"*** Calabrael shot off into the heavens, and commanded a nearby star to come to him immediately by using the great power of the magus. The fiery star arrived and stood still whilst Calabrael teleported and stood upon it, for all magi knows the ***star hopper technique*** *(The ability to travel across the galaxy by hopping from star-to-star)*. The flames of the star vivified wildly as the magus stood on its very surface without catching fire or disintegrating immediately. Calabrael rode the star through the galaxy while saying, ***"Show yourself Caligastia, and cease this repetitious hiding before you get hurt."*** Caligastia re-appeared and raised his right hand to reveal an aggregation of light that he threw into the heavens above. Calabrael looked at him and knew that he had done something extreme. The aggregation of light ripped a whole into reality and summoned a green aggregation of energy that contained the souls of foul angelic warriors who swore to kill all that is good. The aggregation of green energy popped, and the souls were released. The souls flew around wildly and surrounded Calabrael immediately.

Calabrael disappeared, and said, ***"If you want to have a contest in summoning subtle angelic forces, then you have already lost, Caligastia!"*** Calabrael re-appeared, and out of his eyes came a giant orb of light that lit up the universe and disappeared.

And before Caligastia knew it, certain nearby meteors began to combine and form a great titan with magnificent strength. Just as Caligastia thought Calabrael was done, a star crashed into the great titan and set it on fire that changed color and turned purple. Caligastia began to get scared, and began speaking to his self, saying, ***"Why has the architect given these mortals such great power?"*** Just as Caligastia began to move, the meteor titan grabbed him and shot off toward planet Jupiter and slammed him into it. The planet Jupiter cracked and exploded immediately. Calabrael and Caligastia raced out of the explosion during hand-to-hand combat at the speed of light. Dodging, punching and blocking as if they were well skilled cosmic martial artists. The two warriors battled nearly endlessly. They fought so much that they ended up near planet Venus and circled it seven times within fifteen seconds while still fighting.

Eventually, Caligastia got the best of Calabrael and made a direct hit to his face; Calabrael was knocked into the planet Venus and caused it to explode immediately. Caligastia could've sworn that Calabrael was finished, but before Caligastia knew it, Calabrael was shooting out of the explosion like a rocket with his fist in front of him. A loud clapping sound signified a perfect and direct hit that stunned Caligastia and sent him racing into a nearby star that exploded upon impact. Caligastia recovered from Calabrael's punch, and by that time, Calabrael teleported to mars, and said, ***"Brother Mike, Asu, Yahti; he's all yours. I see now that Caligastia is truly no challenge for me."*** Yahti charged up his electromagnetic field with light, and said, ***"Brother, I thought you'd never ask."*** Asu, Yahti and Mike shot off into the heavens, transformed into pure energy and locked on to Caligastia's energy immediately. And as soon as Caligastia looked behind himself, Yahti, Asu and mike materialized in front of him.

Mike looks at Caligastia, and says, ***"It ends here!"*** Asu closed his eyes and transformed into energy that permeated a five hundred mile radius of the universe. Yahti waved his hand, transformed into pure light and surrounded Mike in a force field of mercury engraved with seven names of the grand architect divine. The two magi disintegrated and became one with the whole universe. Caligastia knew the outcome of battling the magi and accepted the amount of damage that would be dealt upon him. Three sets of eyes appeared within the darkness of space, and before Caligastia could comprehend what the magi had done, stars from all over the universe began to crash into each other and explode. A celestial catastrophe occurred while Caligastia teleported and dodged as many as he could, but the power of the magi was too great for him. Eventually, several stars and meteors that seemed to have gone out of control had impinged Caligastia several times. Caligastia had finally opened his eyes to the true power of God somnolent within all mortal creatures, for the magi returned to their human forms and bended all of reality existent on the mundane plane within a thousand mile radius.

The power of the three magi combined made it possible to direct all of the contents of the universe for a transient moment of time. Caligastia showed strength in cosmic character by still standing ready to battle. He looked at the magi, and said; ***"It is far from over, magi!"*** Caligastia closed his eyes and manifested a pentacle made of gold having a pentagram with a hidden name of God written at its center and threw it into the earth's sun. The earth's sun moved off of its axis immediately while moving across the galaxy in the blink of an eye. And as the earth's sun arrived in the presence of Caligastia, the great galactic prince took the form of pure energy and permeated the sun. The galactic prince permeates the sun while laughing, and says, ***"Come here magi, if you're enlightened so, then you can surely fight the flames of your planet's personal star."***

The magi flew onto the sun and stood within the very heart of its flames as if the flames never existed. And before they could understand the evil intentions of the galactic prince, the flames of the sun began to transform into arms and hands that leaped and lashed out at the magi. The magi fought the hands of flames the best that they could, but before they could go any further in battle, the rest of the flames transformed into fiery duplicates of Caligastia. The galactic prince had utilized the energy of the sun and directed its flames to take his form and character, which made him stronger and stronger. The overall look of the sun had changed, it was no longer a sun; it was an entity combined with the life force of the great galactic prince. The magi stood on the sun subjecting themselves to hand-to-hand combat with fiery entities manifested by Caligastia. However, the flame entities were extremely strong, and the magi were immediately beaten. Mike, Asu and Yahti flew off of the sun and stood amidst the universe trying to figure out how they could stop the galactic prince from fighting at all.

Though the magi were formidable challenges, the galactic prince's powers were awesome among many things. Asu looked at his brother Yahti, and said, ***"Call Calabrael, it's going to take all of us to deal with this."*** Yahti closed his eyes, and used telepathy to reach Calabrael, and said, ***"Calabrael, your aid is necessary at this point, we need to combine our strengths."*** Calabrael disappeared and materialized directly in front of his brethren, and said, ***"His powers are beyond great, and it is almost impossible to terminate him. He isn't eternal though, so there must be a way."*** Asu looks at Calabrael, and says, ***"I have an idea, one that***

the galactic prince hasn't thought of." Asu waved his left hand and manifested the chains of divinity, and shortly thereafter, he telekinetically sent the chains into the sun. The sun's fiery contents calmed, and the galactic prince hovered out of the sun while chained and bound with the shackles of divinity.

The galactic prince shouted to the top of his lungs, saying, ***"Of all of the things that can stop me, well; this is not one of them!"*** Caligastia broke out of the chains and laughed as loud as he could, and said, ***"You did not think that an old galactic prince such as I would be easily defeated, did you? If you think that you've won; then you're far from mistaken, you're outright wrong!"*** Calabrael looked at his fellow magi, and said, ***"I'll take care of him alone, just get my sons out of here now, I'm going to take him out by myself. Don't just stand there, go!"*** The magi retreated to planet Mars and wasted no time getting there.

Asu, Yahti and Mike landed on mars and looked at the cosmic sons as if something big was about to happen. Mike looked at Ethereael, and said, ***"We have to get out of here as soon as possible!"*** Fireael looked at Asu, and said, ***"What's wrong? Where's our father?!"*** Yahti looked at Fireael, and said, ***"Your father has decided to battle Caligastia by his self. If we don't get out of here soon, we'll be feeling the same pain Caligastia's about to feel."*** Airael looked at his brothers, and said, ***"Well, what are we waiting for?! Let's get the heck out of here! I'm getting too old for this stuff!"*** The elemental sons and the magi flew off of planet mars and headed straight to earth while a gigantic explosion took place behind them. Calabrael and Caligastia battled for hours, and nearly eliminated each other several times.

The powers of the magus and the powers of the galactic prince were so great that anything near them would simply explode due to the mighty clash between good and evil. Calabrael waved his right hand, and duplicated his self twice.

Caligastia looked at Calabrael, and said, ***"Ah, mystic duplication, that is an old trick, but it won't save you, Calabrael! I'll fight all three of you and prove it to you, mortal."*** Caligastia disappeared and re-appeared so quickly that the force of his movement made Calabrael's duplicates disintegrate immediately. Calabrael looked at Caligastia, and said, ***"How long will you keep up this endless fight, Caligastia!? Look around; our fighting has caused much destruction. So be it, I'll end your life today, Caligastia!"*** Caligastia disappeared, and said, ***"Armit-potent-thasis."***

And before Calabrael knew it, they were no longer a midst the universe, they were floating over the earth. Calabrael looked at Caligastia, and said, ***"I know what you're trying to do; your ruthless attitude will give you no mercy in the days of judgment. Whatever you're thinking, Caligastia, don't do it!"*** Caligastia looked at the earth and revealed the palm of his left hand to manifest a black orb of energy that was the size of a golf ball. And before Calabrael could say anything else, Caligastia sent the black orb of energy into the earth's atmosphere. The black orb entered the earth's atmosphere, and began to gradually slow down, and without anyone knowing what happened, the black orb began to suck up all of the oxygen on the earth. Plant-life disintegrated and billions of people began to suffocate immediately.

Calabrael waved his right hand and disintegrated the black orb immediately. And when Calabrael realized that the orb was gone, he waved his left hand and the Galactic prince was teleported to Pluto immediately. Calabrael looked at the earth and teleported his self to Pluto as well. Caligastia looked at Calabrael, and said, ***"How long do you think you can protect your precious earth from my wrath, old man?! Can you not see that I have already won?"*** Calabrael looked at Caligastia, and said, ***"Victory is not achieved until the war is over; cease***

claiming what is yet to be yours. " Calabrael waved his left hand, and Caligastia was encased in light. Caligastia broke out of the force field of light, and said, ***"You shall never become triumphant with those old tricks, old man!"*** Caligastia disappeared and re-appeared in front of Calabrael to stand face-to-face with him. Calabrael did not make a move, and said, ***"Stop talking, and just fight!"*** Calabrael threw a punch, and Caligastia dodged it immediately.

The magus and the galactic prince engaged in hand-to-hand cosmic combat again, while jumping from one star to another star. The amazing power possessed by the two entities was so awesome that the deceased began to wake out of their graves and stare at the sky. The living humans of earth were in shock, for two powerful forces refused to lose. The battle continued, and the two warriors clashed fist-to-fist while fighting, and a shockwave of force and energy destroyed planet Pluto and everything around it within a seven mile radius. The magi and the cosmic sons witnessed the people of earth during the time they almost suffocated, and knew that the reason they hadn't all suffocated was due to their father holding Caligastia off as long as he could.

The son of ether felt the presence of two great forces fighting to the death, and said, ***"Wait! We can't just leave him to fight a galactic prince by his self!"*** Fireael looked at Ethereael, and said, ***"Ethereael, there's nothing we can do now! We have to let him do what he has to, this is not our mission, and we've already done enough as it is!"*** Ethereael said, ***"No, you're wrong, Fireael! I still have the sword of Elohim, if I give it to him now, he'll eat Caligastia alive!"*** Ethereael closed his eyes, and said, ***"To thee, O Calabrael Powers, I grant the tongue of the eternal father almighty."*** Ethereael's voice echoed throughout the earth, and an orb of light shot out of his heart and raced off to Calabrael and placed itself within his heart during battle.

Calabrael's body was filled with the tongue of God, and a force field of light surrounded him completely. Caligastia began to notice an aroma that smelled like ivory and cherries of heaven. Caligastia thought to himself, saying, ***"The sword of Elohim has been returned to its rightful owner. Now I suppose this mortal has a chance. Let's see what he can do."*** Calabrael's speed was enhanced so much that Caligastia could no longer see him make any movements whatsoever.

The Magus was no fool however, he knew Caligastia could no longer see him, and as soon as he realized that, he began an onslaught of attacks that Caligastia would have nightmares about for the rest of his worthless existence. Flashes of light disappeared and re-appeared and Caligastia suffered several fatal blows to the face and body every time Calabrael moved. Caligastia's eyes were amazed; he couldn't believe it. A magus combined with the sword of Elohim was equal to that of seven galactic princes. Caligastia spoke to his self in a panic, saying, ***"This cannot be, only a powerful galactic prince can become one with the unknowable light. This is ridiculously absurd! It cannot be! Impossible!"*** Caligastia stood still amidst the universe and hadn't an inkling of what to do or how to defend his self.

Calabrael continued his attacks over and over, and Caligastia was helpless to do anything. A grand flash of light occurred, and the Galactic prince's body began to transform into a black hole that sucked itself in, for Caligastia was no more, and Calabrael was triumphant in battle. A large amount of energetic light particles combined, and began to take human form, and the mighty magus materialized once again as the reality of the whole universe bended. Calabrael took a deep breath, and said, ***"The more they continue to hate us, and the more we succeed. I am living proof of what the divine plan for all mortal men decrees, farewell Caligastia!"***

And so, Calabrael returned to his planet and reunited with Yahti, Asu, Mike and his beloved sons. The nine warriors hovered at the height of their world, and began to speak to each other. Mike looked at Calabrael, and said, ***"Well, son of Namsilat, I would've never known that you would've become so powerful. Namsilat has taught you well. You traveled deep into the universal mysteries, and you've gone very far by studying the knowledge of God. I'm very proud of you, Calabrael. And if I know your father, I am sure he would be very proud of you too. So, I guess you're not a feather-weight."*** Yahti looked at Calabrael, and said, ***"Your sons have grown wisely in their age. I suppose that is your doing as well. Who would have ever known that the son of Namsilat would become a powerful magus? You've shocked us all, Calabrael."*** Asu looks at Calabrael, and says, ***"Well, your father always knew that you would become a force to be reckoned with, Calabrael. Today, you have truly proven the strengths of mortal ascension. If there was ever a man to ascend utilizing the knowledge of God, it is you, Calabrael. It is true that we have also ascended, but you have done well, son of Namsilat."***

Mike, Yahti and Asu waved their hands at Calabrael and said goodbye. Mike looked at Calabrael, and said, ***"Farewell, son of Namsilat. May the divine fire vivify wildly in your soul forevermore."*** The three magi transformed into pure energy, and returned to the divine architect so as to take their place among the macrocosm with him. And so, the five cosmic sons, and their father were able to have a private moment together after so many years. Fireael looked at his father, and said, ***"Father, why don't you come to earth with us so that we can show you what it's like now?"*** Calabrael replied, saying, ***"I don't see why I can't, I am here for a limited time, I might as well make the best of it."*** The six spiritual warriors flew through the earth's atmosphere, and landed in Egypt where Ethereael's pyramid temple resides. The six warriors entered the pyramid of ether, and sat around a pool of mercury that Ethereael utilized to view certain areas of the earth.

As the six warriors sat amongst the pool of mercury, Ethereael looked at his father, and said, ***"Father, much time has passed since you were last here, I believe that there are things that you are not aware of. Since the battle against the son of the morning, I joined with my brothers and confronted and vanquished the demon that held you captive before your death. You may even wonder as to why Fireael, Aquari-on, Airael and Earthael are resurrected. Well, to be quite frank, in the heat of a great battle, I was confronted by nearly a billion demons of which were all manifested by Mephistopheles. In due time, I fought against them, however, it was much too many of them for me to succeed. In due time, I hoped that my brothers could fight with me, and before I knew it, they were all amongst me and ready for battle, I could never forget that day. After defeating a large amount of demons, the five of us sought to bring peace to the mundane world by vanquishing as many demons as possible.***

However, in due time, some of us would have to attain new power to take on higher authorities in hell. As time passed, we had to go directly to the hells of the microcosm, and defeat envy, lust, jealousy and other imperfect vices within mankind, and when we did, we fought; we won, and stopped the madness within our realm. After the battle, we returned to the mundane plane, and peace was brought upon the world, for there was no longer a reason to fight. Once we all found peace, we not only grew ripe in age, we have all elected wives, and have also had offspring. Your grandchildren continue to carry the awesome power of our bloodline." Calabrael looks at Ethereael, and says, ***"If this is so, my son, then where is your wife and son or daughter?"*** Ethereael looks at his father and disappears. And when he re-appeared, he was standing with his wife, and his son, Amistael.

Ethereael looks at his father, and says, ***"Father, this is my son, Amistael, and my wife, Athenis."*** Calabrael stands up, and says, ***"I take it that you love my son with all of your heart, young woman?"*** Athenis gives Calabrael a hug, and says, ***"Mr. Powers, it's a pleasure to meet you, I've heard so much about you. And yes, I do love your son with all of my heart, for he has taught me much about the universe, I have loved him since the day I laid eyes on him."*** Calabrael looks at Amistael, and says, ***"So, young man, how hast the universe been fashioned to sustain life?"*** Amistael replies, saying, ***"The divine architect has placed his name at the eternity of the height, depth, east, west, north and south."*** Calabrael looks at Ethereael, and says, ***"You have taught him well, my son. I am well pleased, a grandfather couldn't ask for more, however, what cosmic abilities has Amistael developed since birth? Have you seen anything yet?"***

Ethereael replies, saying, ***"I haven't seen anything yet, but I'm sure there is something extraordinary about him."*** Calabrael replies, saying, ***"Well, which of you is currently dealing with a son or daughter that has shown signs of cosmic abilities?"*** Earthael speaks up, and says, ***"Ah, that would be me, father."*** Calabrael says, ***"How so, my son?"*** Earthael disappears for seven seconds and re-appears while standing with his wife and his daughter. Earthael looks at his father, and says, ***"Father, this is my wife Celestia, and my out-of-control daughter, Ovalael. Her cosmic ability is to transform into light vibrations, and manipulate them as well."*** Calabrael looks at Ovalael, and says, ***"How art thou?"*** Ovalael utilizes her powers with the wave of a hand, and before Calabrael knew it, Ovalael and Calabrael stood alone in a place that seemed like a jungle. Calabrael looked at his granddaughter, and said, ***"There is much for you to learn, Ovalael."*** Calabrael waved his hand, and he and his granddaughter were amongst family once again. Ovalael's eyes opened wide, and she said, ***"You must be my grand poppa, Calabrael. Dad always talks about you, and says that you were a magus, the highest***

level of mortal ascension that a human can reach!" Calabrael replies, saying, ***"Yes, that is correct, my dear."*** Calabrael looks at Earthael, and says, ***"My, it seems that all of you will be going through the same thing I went through when I raised you with your mother, ironic isn't it?"***

Airael, Aquari-on and Fireael disappeared and also returned with their sons and wives. Calabrael looked around his self, and said, ***"O my, this is a rather large family you have here. Can it all be real that my sons have had children of their own? Wow, I never imagined this day!"*** Calabrael greeted all of his grandchildren, and said, ***"It truly is a grand day to see all of you, but I must go now. My father would be well pleased with our progress. Let the Powers' family tradition continue, for I will be watching all the days I exist. As much as it hurts to leave at this point, I must go; it is time for me to join the divine architect amongst his throne room where I will receive the finality of my fate."*** Fireael speaks up, and said, ***"Wait a minute, father. There is someone else who wants to speak with you."*** Calabrael replied, saying, ***"Who?"*** A strange purple energy began to gather and take form, and before Calabrael knew it, Tri-dael appeared while rocking in her rocking chair. Calabrael's countenance changed, and he realized that he was in shock for a transient moment. Tri-dael looked at her husband, and said, ***"It's been a long time, honey. I'm old now, and I can hardly leave this chair these days. It hurts to have you see me like this."*** Tri-dael's eyes started to tear, and finally, she began to cry. Calabrael walked over to his wife, and said, ***"My dear wife, I had almost forgotten about you, and of all the things I missed, I missed you the most. I'm sorry, but my stay here on earth will not be long, I only wish that I could stay here with you, but there are cosmic duties to which I am obligated. You know that God comes first in my life better than anyone."*** Tri-dael replies, saying, ***"I do know better than anyone. I just wanted to see you again; I couldn't stand being without you when you gave me some of your powers and passed away. I felt lonely;***

a man like you only comes once every hundred years." Calabrael dropped his countenance, and said, ***"Tri-dael, when you look into my eyes, you can see everything that you want to see, but now, you'll have to look to the heavens. My obligation to God is above all things. I gave him my life, and he sufficed for everything."*** Calabrael took his wife's hand, and said, ***"You know I love you, but I must go once again."*** Calabrael cried as he closed his eyes and dispersed into particles of purple energy, while saying, ***"I love you all, and may the divine architect bless your lives, and keep you, goodbye."***

And so, Calabrael returned to the divine architect, and his sons lived their lives and loved their families as much as they possibly could. In due time, Tri-dael could no longer live without her husband, thus, she passed through transition and left her children to take care of their own families. Her sons and grandchildren missed her, and had no regrets.

And in due time, earth returned to peace and mortal ascension proved to be a most worthy divine scheme, however, somewhere on earth, during a time of peace and happiness, a child is born with the eyes of a slithering snake. This particular child also has a great destiny behind him, yet he holds the eyes of the serpent. Another battle shall arise in the future, a battle between the eyes of the serpent and the all-seeing eye of God. Although much has transpired, this does not mark the end of our great journey, for the war is far from over. Our five heroes are old and ripe in age, therefore, the sons of descent must rise, for the battle for the safety of the universe hasn't ended; it has just begun.

These are the generations of the Powers' family tradition:

Edward Powers lived and begat Namsilat and Eddie Powers. Eddie powers passed through transition whilst Namsilat lived and begat Calabrael Powers. The mighty Calabrael Powers lived and begat Fireael, Earthael, Airael, Ethereael and Aquari-on Powers. Fireael lived many years and begat a son named Magister Powers. Ethereael lived wise in the ways of God and begat a son named Amistael Powers. Earthael lived many years meditating upon life and begat a daughter named Ovalael Powers. Aquari-on lived wisely for many years and begat a son named Crimson-sky Powers, and Airael lived for many years and begat a son named Astralai Powers.

*M*ortal *A*scension:

*A*n *E*soteric Story

Glossary

Consciousness- The state of being conscious; Awareness. All of one's thoughts, feelings, and impressions.

Divine/Great/Grand Architect-

Consummate- Complete or perfect

Nescient- Ignorant.

Adept- Highly skilled; expert.

Magi- The wise men from the east who brought gifts to the infant Jesus: **Matt. 2:1-13**

Macrocosm- The universe.

Microcosm- A little world; miniature universe.

Heaven- Any place of great beauty

Cosmic- Vast; enormous.

Salamander- A reptile in myths that was said to live in fire

Slyph- A subtle being/ creature of the air.

Gnome- A dwarf that dwells in earth and guard its treasures

Undine- Spirit/subtle creature of water

Universal soul- The primary animating principle within all life and matter.

God- In monotheistic religions, the creator and ruler of the universe thought of as being all-powerful, all-knowing, and perfectly good.

Universal- Present or occurring everywhere.

Divine- Supremely great, good, etc.

Three-fold- Having three parts.

Form- The shape, outline, or configuration of anything; structure.

Grand- Complete; Overall, Most important; main

Sheol- A place deep in the earth where the dead are believed to go

Astral- of, from, or like the stars

Altar- A table, stand, etc. used for sacred purposes in a place of worship

Meph- A devil in medieval legend

Moloch- (Molech) An ancient god of the Phoenicians, etc., to whom children were sacrificed by burning. Anything demanding terrible sacrifice.

Satan- The chief evil spirit; the devil

Mystic- Mysterious, secret, occult, etc.

Vanquish- To conquer or defeat in battle

Ascend- To go up; move upward; arise

Seraphim- The highest choir of angels.

Cherubim- The choir of angels described by the biblical prophet Ezekiel as creatures having four faces.

Ether- An intangible energy deriving from the original source and center of all creation.

Psychic body- A Subtle vehicle/natural component of the divine human composition. The subtle counterpart of the physical body.